BORN A QUEEN

Book Three of the Queens

NIKITA SLATER

*xoxo,
N. Slater*

Copyright © 2020 Nikita Slater Writing Services Ltd.

This book is a work of fiction. The names, characters, places and incidents are products of the writer's imagination or have been used fictitiously and are not to be construed as real. Any resemblance to persons, living or dead, actual events, locales or organizations is entirely coincidental.

All rights reserved. No part of this book may be reproduced, scanned, or distributed in any manner whatsoever without written permission from the author except in the case of brief quotation embodied in critical articles and reviews.

"They're dying to kill
And living to die
Snub nose, headshots
If you touch anything that's mine."

Amore, Pitbull & Leona Lewis

PROLOGUE

Mateo lit a cigar and leaned forward in his chair, placing his elbows on his knees and allowing fatigue to settle over him like a cloak. He was tired, but it was a good kind of tired. It'd been a long two years. Mateo acted as second-in-command, enforcer, and diplomat to the Butcher, Isaac Sotza; flying around the world, using the might of the Venezuelan cartel to convince both friends and competitors that they needed to work with the Butcher instead of against him.

Mateo had also taken on a special project, one that was personal to Sotza. Something that he only entrusted Mateo to complete. Hunting the Mexican cartel boss, Nicolás Garza. Mateo looked down at the bloody heap that used to be Nico Garza. After several long seconds, the mess of bones and gore that used to be his chest lifted and dropped. Garza was still alive.

Good. Mateo wasn't quite done with him yet. He had strict orders from Sotza to prolong the suffering. This man had shot the Butcher's wife. Though it was only her arm, and she'd recovered in a matter of days, it didn't matter. In this world, the underworld, such insults couldn't be allowed to pass unchallenged.

Mateo was impressed with Garza. Impressed with his ability to run and hide. It had taken twenty-three months for Mateo to finally hunt him to ground. And disappointingly, Garza's second-in-command and lover, Desiree, wasn't with him. Maybe Garza knew Mateo was closing in and hid her somewhere, drawing Mateo's focus onto himself to protect her. It was a noble attempt, but ultimately useless. Mateo would find her too and finish the woman who helped try to bring down the Venezuelan cartel. Despite his dislike of killing women, Mateo would do his job.

Nico let out a moan. Or maybe it was more of a gurgle since he didn't have any teeth or a tongue.

"Are you waking up?" Mateo asked in surprise.

Garza had more stamina than Mateo had given him credit for. Not that Mateo minded, he liked playing before the kill. It was something he had in common with his boss. It helped ease the ever-lurking darkness staining his soul. Death and suffering grounded him in a way nothing else could.

Nothing else except a pair of sharp blue eyes attached to the only woman that he'd ever looked at twice. She consumed his thoughts. She was his perfection, though she was far from perfect. Her quick wit, her barbed tongue, her fiery temper. It all belonged to him. Raina would be his prize for completing this mission. Sotza had promised and the Butcher didn't break his promises. He agreed to give Mateo two things if Mateo took out Sotza's enemy; his stepdaughter and the American east coast.

Now, Mateo was ready to collect.

He bent over and pressed his lit cigar into Garza's now empty eye socket, putting it out. God forbid he start a fire and be forced to leave before his job was completely done. He pulled out his phone and tapped the screen into camera mode. He pointed it at the dying man, "Smile, Garza." He took several shots and sent them to his boss. He'd get rid of the phone with the evidence once he was finished.

He stood, stretched his back and cracked his knuckles before reaching into his pocket for the gloves he wore when he worked. He stared down, not a flicker of emotion over what he was doing except for a sense of satisfaction over a job well done. He'd managed to keep Garza alive for five days of torture. If he was at home, at the compound, in the 'shed' as they called the building where they detained prisoners, he'd be able to keep Garza alive for weeks.

As it was, Mateo would have to finish up soon. He was hearing some concerning gossip coming out of Italy, Raina's current country of residence. He needed to get to her, extract her from whatever the hell she'd managed to get herself into and then take her home. Not to Venezuela, but to Miami. Their new home.

"Okay, Garza," Mateo announced. "Let's finish this."

Since Garza was close to the end, Mateo decided it was time for his signature. He picked up a pair of garden shears he'd set aside on the table and bent to his prey. Gently he picked up Garza's mangled hand and worked the shears between his fingers. He sniped Garza's trigger finger off and tossed it onto the table. The other man didn't say anything, but his gurgled screams spoke eloquently.

CHAPTER ONE

It was Raina's twenty-first birthday. She wanted to go out and party, dance all night, make friends, flirt, maybe take a guy home if she really felt like it. She'd never done that. Never taken a guy home before. In fact, she'd never even had sex. It wasn't that she didn't want to. She really, really did. But life had thrown a major curveball at her two years ago and she'd been running ever since. This time, it appeared she was running into a dead end.

Raina didn't think she was going to get to party for her birthday. No, she was pretty sure she was going to die. She peered out into the dark night from the window of her rented room. She was on the fourth floor of a very old building. One that was sinking. But then, all the buildings in Venice were sinking.

Italy was her ninth country in two years. When she left Venezuela, leaving the mother she just met behind, she went on the run. She had to assume there were people after her, or at least watching. Sometimes she would come home from an evening out and she would have that eerie feeling that someone had been in her apartment. She suspected dear old stepdad, Isaac Sotza, the Venezuelan mob boss, had people keeping an eye on her. He probably knew where to find her from the moment she left his estate.

But did his second-in-command? Her mind flashed back to her time in Venezuela. The brief month before her mother ushered her out of the country in a daring escape. Mateo Gutierrez. Cartel to the marrow of his bones. Sotza's right hand man and her constant shadow while she was in Sotza's care.

Mateo was everything she hated in a man, arrogant, dangerous, rude. But he was also indecently attractive. And for some reason he'd wanted her. She wondered if the two years since she last saw him had dimmed his regard. Somehow, she doubted it. Even in her brief time observing the mafia, she noticed the guys didn't let things go. They held onto their grudges, their obsessions. She suspected those qualities were what made the men so hard and so successful.

Raina flitted around her apartment, shoving her possessions into a small suitcase. She didn't have much. She travelled light because she never knew when she'd have to pick up and run. She had done it before, but never in this much of a hurry. That was because she'd done something stupid. She crossed the wrong people and it was only a matter of time before they found out and came after her. She suspected sooner rather than later.

And she was right. Seconds after that thought entered her head, as she was reaching for her purse, preparing to leave her tiny apartment for good, the door crashed open. The only thing that saved her from being shot in the heart as she stood gaping at the man who kicked the door in was the fact that he kicked it so hard it rebounded off the wall and slammed shut again. The bullet meant for her thudded into the heavy wooden door.

Raina dropped her purse and ran for the only place in her

apartment with a door that would close and lock. Her bathroom. As she ran, reaching for the frame, her front door was flung open again and the room sprayed in bullets. She felt a tearing, hot pain hit her in the back. The force of the bullet flung her into the bathroom. She landed hard on her knees. She didn't have time to assess herself. She rolled onto her back and kicked the door shut, reaching up to lock it. Thank god these old Italian buildings had thick doors. Bullets thunked into the wood as she crawled toward the bathtub and dragged herself inside.

"Fuck!" she snarled, reaching behind her to touch the spot on her back. Her hand came away covered in blood. She really hoped the bullet hadn't taken out her only good kidney. Even if it didn't, the blood loss for someone like her could be catastrophic.

She had to get out before the man who shot her got inside the bathroom. She'd picked this place because it had a window in the washroom with a fire escape. She was going to have to get out of the bathtub though, since the window was over the toilet. She took a deep breath, eyed the bathroom door, which was still in one piece and flung herself out of the tub. As she was kneeling on the toilet reaching for the latch, she realized there was no more sounds hitting the door. Had they given up on coming after her?

That didn't make sense. The front door was thicker than the bathroom door and they'd had no problem breaking through that one. She stopped, her hands hovering against the window, and listened. At first there was nothing, and then she heard muffled thumping sounds. A man shouted, but it was cut off. What were they doing out there, killing each other?

Raina wasn't going to wait around to find out. Whatever was happening it couldn't be good. And she needed medical attention right away.

She turned back to the window. A scream leapt from her and she fell off the toilet as bullets crashed through the window. A man had come up the fire escape to cover the window and she'd come face to face with him. She huddled on the floor as small as she could get and covered her arms with her head.

She knew she was a dead woman when she finally heard the sound she'd been expecting. The bathroom door crashed open, smashing against the bathtub. She tensed, waiting for that awful hot tearing sensation to rip through her again as she was shot full of holes. Instead, she heard two muffled shots and a shout from the balcony.

When the seconds ticked by and she was still alive she chanced a peek through her arms. Mateo Gutierrez was standing over top of her; tall, scowling, eyes and gun trained on the window.

"Mateo!" she gasped.

"Raina," he acknowledged grimly and looked down at her. He reached for her, dragging her off the floor.

She groaned in pain but was forced to follow as he pulled her out of the bathroom and into the main room. She gaped at the two dead men decorating her place. They hadn't stood a chance. Probably thought they were going to kill a helpless woman. They would have no idea that she had an entire cartel at her back and, apparently, at her disposal.

"Jacket, shoes, purse. Hurry up," he barked at her.

Raina didn't pause. Her only chance of survival was with this man. She dragged a leather coat on, flinching in pain as it stuck to her back. She bent over to tie up her running shoes, but as she straightened, dizziness engulfed her. Mateo caught her before she hit the floor, grabbing the part of her back that had been shot. She cried out, clutching his arm to shove him away.

"What's wrong?" he demanded.

"Shot," she muttered.

He turned her around and lifted her jacket and shirt. He muttered something she suspected was a nasty swear word in Spanish.

"Is it bad?" she asked, peeking at him over her shoulder.

"No," he growled, and then picked her up in his arms.

This was the second time he'd done this. The first time he'd been kidnapping her from her university campus. This time? She didn't know. He was definitely saving her life, but she suspected there was more to him being here. The timing was too convenient.

"Mateo?" she whispered as he glanced into the hallway before striding out her door.

"Si, Raina?" He took the stairs two at a time, careful to hold her tight against his chest so he wouldn't jar her wound.

"Thanks for coming for me." She had to say the words in case she didn't get another chance.

He paused for a moment on the second-floor landing and looked down at her, his dark eyes hot with anger, possession and longing. "I will follow you into hell, chica."

"Let's hope not," she sighed right before passing out.

CHAPTER TWO

"Fucking stupid," Mateo muttered darkly.

Raina gritted her teeth and sat as still as she could while he worked to patch her up. She'd woken up in a room she didn't recognize. It was filled with empty cages and smelled like antiseptic. Mateo explained to her that he brought her to an animal hospital that was closed for the night. He couldn't risk taking her to a regular hospital, not with the Italian Cosa Nostra hot on their heels.

"My people are looking for ways to get us out of the country. Airspace is being carefully monitored, as are trains and buses. The family you chose to cross have their fingers in everything." His voice was devoid of emotion, but she could feel the accusation and anger swirling around him.

"I didn't choose to cross anyone." She flinched as he pressed an alcohol-soaked gauze pad to the wound on her back. She was sitting on a metal exam table, leaning forward with her back to Mateo. He'd pushed her shirt up. "I was ordered to work on documents for Antonio Savino. Not my fault the asshole didn't want any loose ends."

His hand dropped to squeeze her hip. "Watch your fucking language, Raina."

She twisted around to look at him with a laugh. "You watch yours, gangster."

Mateo's sharp gaze softened. He reached up and pushed Raina's pink glasses up her nose. "I forgot to say happy birthday," he said softly.

Raina's smile faded as her heart fluttered at his unexpected touch. "I was sort of passed out. It's not a big deal."

"Yes, it is," he said seriously, then got back to work.

It felt good to be near Mateo again. It was as though the years faded and they were back in Sotza's garden together in Venezuela, Raina trying to read a book while Mateo stalked and bullied her. Tried to get her to go back inside where he deemed it was safer.

Two years ago, Sotza had ordered Mateo to kidnap Raina and bring her to Venezuela to meet her birth mother, Elvira. As much as Raina had resented being taken against her will, she didn't actually hate her time there. In fact, she loved a lot of it. Venezuela was beautiful. Sotza's mansion was high up in the mountains; practically a natural fortress. She definitely wanted to go back someday.

But not today. Not tomorrow, and not anytime soon. She was enjoying life too much. As nice as it was to see Mateo again, she wasn't ready to go back to that life permanently.

Raina suspected that Mateo wanted permanent. He was older than her, he was looking to settle. He was far more serious. And when he looked at her... he stole her breath. He made her heart pound. He terrified her. The things that he wanted from her were not things that she was willing to give him yet. She didn't want a home, a family and babies. She didn't want the mafia.

Maybe one day, but not today.

Yes, Italy might have been a mistake. It would have been a fatal mistake if Mateo hadn't stepped in. But that didn't mean the rest of her time on the run had been a mistake; she'd had so many new experiences and made wonderful memories. She'd visited the Louvre and the Eiffel Tower, gone dancing in Edinburgh, met a hacker in Jakarta and learned some awesome new digital printing techniques that would keep her up to date with her forging business. She wasn't willing to give that up. Not yet.

"You been taking your medications properly?" The question was so unexpected, spoken in a gruff tone of voice, that she almost asked him what he meant. Then she realized he was talking about her immunosuppressants; her antirejection drugs from the kidney transplant she'd had when she was twelve.

She pulled her purse closer and nodded. "Yes, I never forget them."

He gave her a piercing look. "Be sure that you don't."

Her temper flared. "Don't treat me like a child, Mateo. I'm well aware of the sacrifice made to me by my mother. I wouldn't be alive if she hadn't donated her kidney."

"Wasn't talking about your mother. I care that you survive, and you need that kidney to survive. You only have one functioning kidney left, you need to be more careful. Stop being so reckless with your health. The bullet could've easily taken out the kidney, killed you."

She twisted on the table to glare down at him where he'd pulled a chair up to the table to work on her. "Thanks for the reminder, I nearly forgot."

He tilted his head until his eyes met hers. They were a beautiful velvet brown, but serious. "You won't be given the opportunity to endanger yourself again."

Raina didn't respond. Mateo was convinced she didn't take her health seriously. She wouldn't convince him otherwise until he saw her taking care of herself, taking her pills regularly, eating healthy foods, exercising. But that wasn't in the cards, at least not right now.

"How do you plan on getting us out of here?" she asked.

Not that she actually intended to go with him, but talking to him, having him talk to her, distracted her from the pain.

When she had woken up, he told her that he managed to pull the bullet out while she was passed out. Thank the fucking gods, because the patch job on her bullet wound hurt so bad, she couldn't imagine anyone digging around inside while she was awake.

Raina was used to pain. She had gone through some of the most painful treatments of her life as a child. Pretty much anything else, including a gunshot wound was child's play compared to a kidney transplant.

"We'll probably drive out," he said. "Then take an airplane from a neighboring country. It's the only way I can think of to get you out safely without the Italians coming after us."

She smiled to herself, looking down at the table that she was sitting on. She tapped her fingernail against the stainless steel. "Yes, my safety. It's the most important thing, isn't it," she said drily.

They all wanted to treat her like a precious pampered princess. In reality, she was raised a farm girl, became a college drop-out thanks to Mateo and Sotza, and was now a career criminal, making some of the world's best forged documents. It was almost laughable that these tough guys wanted to lock her up in a tower and surround her with guards and bubble wrap.

He grunted. "You haven't seen what your stepdaddy is capable of. Yes, little girl, your safety is the most important thing here."

That comment sobered her. As much as she loved her family, she couldn't forget for a single minute that they were involved in organized crime. And that some of them, Mateo and Sotza most of all, were determined to push her into the life too.

Her mother was equally as determined to keep her out. Raina was on her mother's side. She couldn't imagine spending her life that way. She had too much to live for, too much she hadn't seen or done yet. The mafia felt like a cage, she just couldn't do it.

"So we drive out," she echoed his words. "Sounds good."

She tried to sound listless and pathetic as she thought of ways to escape. She didn't think Mateo would be overly vigilant with her right now. He'd come to her rescue; he wouldn't expect her to run away. Not in her current shape.

It took another half hour before Mateo finished with her. He cleaned the wound, stitched it shut, taped gauze over it, then wrapped more gauze around her middle, holding everything in place. She sucked in a breath as his knuckles brushed the bare skin of her belly, burning a path of sensation where he touched. Mateo didn't seem to notice. He was quick, calm and professional.

He helped her put her shirt back on, rolling it over her head and then one at a time pushing her arms through the arm holes. Raina wrinkled her nose at the dried blood all over the shirt, but she didn't have an alternative.

Mateo gently slid her closer and helped her stand, taking her hand in his and easing her off the table. He didn't back away immediately, just held her loosely in his arms. Raina leaned in closer, enjoying the human contact. It felt good being held by him, feeling his strength against her body. She felt safe.

For a brief moment she considered staying with him. Allowing him to take her home. She'd come to know him well enough, from their time in Venezuela and some of the things her mother had told her about him, to understand that he was a man with integrity. Though he was a mob enforcer, he held himself to a standard of ethics. It was a twisted kind of ethics, where murder was okay, but lying was wrong.

If he took her home, if she allowed the seemingly inevitable progression of their relationship to continue, she knew he would take good care of her. Forever. It was a thought that was almost irresistible.

But so was the lure of the whole wide world at her feet. And she wasn't willing to give it all up to become a young bride. Not yet.

Taking advantage of the moment and the fact that Raina wasn't pushing him away, Mateo touched her lightly, running his fingers from her waist up her arms. Tingles ran up and down her sides even though he was touching her through her shirt. She ignored the blatant chemistry, stepping to the side and breaking his hold. She didn't have time for that right now.

Mateo picked up her leather coat and held it open for her. She turned around giving him her back and put her arms out while he carefully slid the sleeves on and tugged it over her shoulders. She groaned as she twisted and her back twinged.

He put a hand on her shoulder and said in her ear, "I'm sorry, it's going to hurt for a while."

"You know what it feels like to get shot?" At first the question was said with sarcasm, but then she realized given his profession he might actually know what it felt like.

Mateo confirmed her suspicion. "Si, I do."

Raina forgot her dilemma for a moment. "When were you shot? Where were you shot?"

He gave her a long look. "Now you're interested in me?"

If only he knew. Raina was always interested in him. Not a day had gone by in the past two years that she hadn't thought of him. Especially when she was alone in her bedroom, late at night, remembering each and every encounter with him. The way he'd looked, smelled, sounded. Those memories had kept her close company.

She shrugged. "I guess we finally have something in common."

He pinched her chin between his fingers and tilted her face up to his. He towered over her. She wished she wasn't so short. She hated looking up to virtually everyone she spoke to. "We got plenty in common, little girl. And once we're back home you're going to have all the time in the world to get to know me better."

That last comment jarred her back to reality. No, she wasn't, because she was getting the hell out of there.

She scooped up her purse and pretended to walk with him to the door, but before they reached it, she grabbed his arm and stopped him. "I have to go to the bathroom."

He glanced around the room and then shook his head. "You can wait until we get to the hotel."

"I have to pee right now, Mateo. I've had to go for a while, but, well, the hole in my back sort of took precedence."

His face hardened but he glanced around the room again then opened the clinic door and growled to one of his men, "We'll be right out, get the car started."

Taking her arm in a firm grip he walked through the clinic, mindful not to jostle her too much. He found the bathroom door, pushed it open and looked inside.

"You expecting to find shooters in the toilet?" she asked sarcastically.

"I haven't stayed alive this long by getting lazy." He opened the door wider for her to go in and then closed the door behind her.

Raina turned the water on so he wouldn't be able to hear through the door. She surreptitiously locked the door, careful to slide the bolt as slowly as possible so it wouldn't click and alert him to what she was doing. She breathed a sigh of relief.

There was a decent sized window in the bathroom, most likely because no one expected a person to crawl through it in an animal clinic. She was about to test that theory.

But first, she really did have to pee. She did her business quickly, washed her hands in the running water and grabbed her purse. She slid the window open as delicately and quietly as possible while still trying to be speedy.

It was a bitch crawling through that window with a gunshot wound. She tried to do it without pulling any stitches, but a sharp pain went through her ribcage when she was forced to drop a few feet from the window to the ground. She hit hard and almost lost her balance but managed to catch hold of the side of the building. She gasped in pain and reached around to touch her back. She brought her fingers up in front of her face, but it was too dark to see if there was any fresh blood. Hopefully she hadn't torn the stitches.

She glanced around and didn't see anyone nearby. All of Mateo's men were at the front of the building waiting for them. No one expected her to try to escape.

She melted into the shadows, running as quickly as possible while trying to be invisible to anyone who looked. As she left the scene, her quick brain came up with a few possibilities of what she could do next. Staying in Italy wasn't an option. But leaving Italy was going to be really difficult on her own with the Italian mafia after her.

One very stupid plan kept popping into her head as she mulled over the possibilities. Perhaps it was time to finally use her stepfather's name, show the Italians why it was a colossal mistake to fuck with a Sotza.

CHAPTER THREE

"This is a bad idea," Raina muttered to herself. "This is such a bad idea and I'm definitely going to get myself shot... again."

She didn't have a choice though; she was going to have to dig deep, find her guts and find a way into this nightclub.

The nightclub, Banditos, was an exclusive invitation-only social establishment. And Raina did not have an invitation. However, she did need to speak to the man who owned the club along with half the city. The father of the man who tried to have her killed.

Raina forced her shoulders back and stood straighter. Pain shot through her back and abdomen and she nearly bent over in agony. She reached out blindly, using the wall of the alley next to the nightclub to steady herself. She took long deep breaths, in through her nose and out through her mouth, until the waves of dizziness passed. She had no choice, she had to go inside. She straightened her jacket and ran her fingers through her hair, combing it first and then fluffing it, trying to give herself a sexier appearance.

Though she felt like a corpse warmed up, she figured she

could still pull off sexy. She was young, she was confident, and she was determined.

She approached the doorman. "I need to meet with Signore Savino please."

The bouncer eyed her up with interest, but his cold dark gaze was shuttered. His massive body blocked the doorway, making it impossible for her to dart around him.

"Better get out of here," the bouncer said with a wave of his hand. "The boss likes blondes and you're too delicate for what he'd have in mind."

Raina was insulted that the bouncer assumed she couldn't take care of herself. She might look delicate but in reality, she was hell on wheels. Just ask her parents. Any of them.

"Tell him Raina..." she hesitated. She'd never invoked this name before. She loved her adopted parents and she was more than happy to have the last name Duncan. But Duncan wasn't going to get her into an establishment like this. "Tell him Raina Sotza is here."

"You don't hear real well, do you – " The bouncer started to speak and then stopped himself, thinking for a few seconds. "The Butcher? That Sotza?"

"My stepfather," she said truthfully. The fact was it didn't matter if Sotza was her birth father or her stepfather, any relation of Sotza's had automatic protection.

The bouncer's eyes bulged as he took her in, connecting enough dots to realize exactly who she was. Sotza's relationship with Vee Montana had rocked the underworld. Two titans, first colliding, then falling in love and rising up to rule the Venezuelan cartel had caused waves the world over.

"Please follow me," the bouncer said formally.

He led her through the entrance and down a hall, his big body blocking her view. They reached a door on the other end, which was blocked by another very large man. Her bouncer said a few words to the other one, jerking his thumb back towards the entrance door, indicating the man should go take over. Then he led her through the nightclub itself. A beautiful and gaudy piece of art that must've cost a fortune to build and decorate. Although, if the crowd was anything to go by, the nightclub likely brought in plenty of revenue. Maybe it doubled as a front for Savino's other operations.

As Raina was looking around with curiosity, her eyes caught on someone she feared she would see there. Antonio Savino. The moment her eyes landed on him, he looked up and caught sight of her. His face reflected shock for a few seconds, then anger. Raina took a step closer to the uncertain protection of the bouncer as Antonio hurtled toward them.

"You!" he snarled, trying to shove past the bouncer to get at her.

"Surprised to see me?" she asked tauntingly.

She tried not to look as pale as she felt. If he didn't know she'd been injured in the attack, she didn't want him to find out.

"I'm going to fucking – " he started to threaten her, but the bouncer stepped between them.

"I'm taking her to meet with your father."

The look on Antonio's face was almost worth the gunshot wound in her back. Part terror and part impotent rage.

Antonio turned to the bouncer and growled in a low voice, "Give her to me. She's an ex-girlfriend. I'll take care of her and make sure she doesn't come back to cause more trouble."

The bouncer wasn't fazed at all. Maybe he was used to dealing with Antonio. "I'm taking her to see your father. If you want her, you can negotiate with him." He took Raina's arm and walked away, dismissing Antonio. Raina decided that this moment was one of the most satisfying in her life.

As they approached the chained off VIP area, her personal bouncer said, "Stay here," and pointed at a spot on the floor, then strode away. Raina glanced at the spot, amused. Did he actually expect her to stand exactly where he put her? Raina trailed after him, though she gave him a wide berth. After all he was a very large man and she had plenty to lose.

Raina stopped when the bouncer stopped. She stood waiting about fifteen feet away as he bent over to speak into a man's ear. The man appeared to be in his 50's and was decently good-looking. Cassie, Raina's best friend, would call him a silver fox. He wore a tailored suit, dark grey with a blood red tie and handkerchief in his pocket. His dark grey hair was slicked back and he wore rings on several of his fingers. He had that look about him; the one she was beginning to recognize from all the mobsters she had dealt with. A hard, cold, dead look. It sent a chill straight through her.

She lifted her chin. It didn't matter. She'd lived a lifetime in only twenty-one years. She was a fighter. She wasn't about to let one scary ass man stop her from forging ahead and taking care of herself, the way she'd always done.

The Italian's head jerked up once the bouncer was finished speaking. He stared at her, at first in shock, and then with something closer to speculation. He was sizing her up, trying to figure out why she was there, in his town, alone. Without them saying a word to each other he would know that she was vulnerable. She was voluntarily walking into his lair knowing that he could easily have her killed. She was banking on her stepfather's name to keep Signore Savino from doing that.

Raina walked forward, adding some swagger to her step, trying to project an air of both confidence and femininity. She sensed he would respect both, and in this moment, she needed the man on her side.

"Signore Savino, thank you for seeing me."

He tilted his head toward her, acknowledging her words.

Though they both knew that he had not agreed to see her, that she had pushed her way into his nightclub using the only weapon she had; her connection to Sotza.

"I have information about your son."

Raina slid into the booth. The Italian raised an eyebrow at her and then lifted his drink, some kind of amber liquid in a crystal glass, and took a long sip.

Instead of asking her about his son, he said, "What do you drink?"

Raina's head was swimming from the pain in her back, from lack of food and from anxiety. She was not about to add alcohol to that mix. "Nothing for me, thank you."

He stiffened noticeably and flicked a finger at her. "In my bar, you drink. If you drink with me, I will listen. Otherwise you leave." He glanced to the side where his son was pacing outside the VIP area like an angry tiger.

Raina's heart pounded. If she left without the promise of his protection, Antonio would pick her up and finish her off. And if she somehow managed to slip past Antonio, she would have Mateo to contend with. She needed Savino on her side.

She licked her lips and thought for second. What should she order? Because of her kidney, she rarely drank. She really didn't even like alcohol. She thought about ordering a glass of red wine, which was slightly more tolerable than the hard stuff, but she suspected that Giovanni would respect her more if she had a real drink with him.

She nodded her head. "Vodka, straight up, with ice please."

There, now she sounded like a gangster. The Italian looked amused, as though he knew that she didn't drink. He beckoned a nearby waitress over, a tall thin woman with sky-high heels and a skintight black dress. He gave her Raina's order and then waved her away, turning his full focus on Raina.

"Now, you tell me what mio figlio has been up to." All of the amusement drained from his expression, leaving behind an utterly terrifying man.

Raina felt more than compelled to tell him the truth, she felt real bone deep fear. For the first time since entering the nightclub it occurred to her that she may not survive this conversation. Perhaps brazen wasn't the way to go with a man like this. He was the Italian Godfather for a reason.

"Your son hired me to create documents for him," she said honestly. There was no point beating around the bush. "A fake passport and driver's license."

"I have a forger in my employ; I would know if my son were looking for documents. You must have mistaken him for someone else," Savino said dismissively.

"Your son is Antonio Savino, though the false name he chose was Antony Ricci." Savino's eyes narrowed when she mentioned his son's alias, as though he'd heard it before. Raina proceeded to give Savino every detail of her encounter with his son, up to and including the shooting.

Antonio had insisted on knowing who would be doing the forgery, he insisted on telling her why he needed the forgery and he'd used his reputation to try to intimidate her. Of course, given who her parents were, intimidation was the last thing she felt. Annoyance, disgust and amusement had been her top emotions. She didn't like being bullied into work. Antonio's arrogance had left a bad taste in her mouth, but his threat to make her life in Italy difficult, and the tidy stack of bills he placed in front of her, had convinced her to do the job despite her bad first impression.

When Raina stopped speaking, Savino looked convinced that it actually had been his son that'd asked for her services. He demanded to know everything Antonio had said to her.

"He thinks your policy on the Malta underground is weak.

He believes you're wrong not to pursue more territory and he's decided that he'll go in and do it himself."

Savino's fist came down so hard that the table jumped, knocking over his drink. Raina sort of wished her drink had arrived first, but it arrived shortly after. The waitress set it down in front of her and, sensing the tension in the air, scurried away as fast as she could on five-inch heels.

"Why the fuck would my son defy me in such a way? He knows my plan for Malta. I will have him skinned alive." When Savino turned to scan the club, Antonio was conspicuously absent.

A shiver went through Raina and she wondered if Savino was serious. Would he kill his own son over such an infraction? And more important, would he kill the messenger?

"If it helps, I believe he was doing it, in part, to please you. As though he wanted to lay a lucrative win at your feet," she hurried to tell him. "I think he thought if he took on such a feat and was successful, you might be willing to give him more responsibility. More power."

She wasn't lying to the older man to pacify him. His son had spoken to her a lot. She didn't know if he'd been driven by arrogance, or the need to unload something off his chest to a person that didn't know his family. Whatever it was though, he'd given her the ammunition she needed to speak to his father. And she didn't have a single qualm about throwing Antonio under the bus like this. When he had her shot, he declared war with the youngest Sotza.

"And why are you telling me all this?" Annoyance coloured his voice. He clearly didn't like having anything out of his control and Raina was placing a cluster fuck at his feet.

"I think your son realized that he said too much to me, gave me something I could use against him. If he knew my background, he probably would've realized I would never do that. I have too much to lose too. He sent three men after me, tried to have me killed."

"And yet you're not dead," the Italian remarked coldly.

He didn't sound as sorry as she rather thought he should, considering his asshole of a son tried to murder her. "I was shot in the back earlier today," she snapped. "A friend of mine came to my rescue and shot your son's men."

Savino frowned. "And your friend is?"

She hesitated, unsure if she should tell Savino about the threat that lurked in his city, taking the element of surprise from Mateo if Savino decided to take exception to his presence. Raina decided it was best to be honest. She had too much to lose. "Mateo Gutierrez."

Savino couldn't hide the surprise on his face. "Sotza's second."

She could see the moment he realized how much trouble Raina was bringing to his door. "So, Mateo Gutierrez is spending time in my city, attempting to collect the Sotza princess. And you chose not to stay with him? A man more than capable of protecting you?"

Now that was a hard question to answer. She sensed that she was at a critical moment in her negotiations with the Italian Godfather. She straightened in her chair, picked up her glass of vodka and knocked it back. It took herculean effort not to gag, but she managed. She set the glass on the table and gave Savino a hard look.

"No, I don't wish to go with him. I was doing fine on my own, building my forging business, before your son came along and fucked it up." She narrowed her eyes. "I'm asking for your help, to keep me safe from your son and hidden from Mateo until I figure out what to do. I'm asking as a Sotza; as a potential ally."

The Italian boss eyed her with a new kind of appreciation. She may be bringing a barn full of shit to his doorstep, but she was also handing him an opportunity on a silver platter. She was valuable now as not only Sotza's stepdaughter, but as the woman Mateo, one of the most fierce and feared men in the mob, was looking for.

"I will place you under my protection," he said decisively, his eyes gleaming. He waved the bouncer over. "Have Roberto take her to the house."

The bouncer "helped" Raina from the booth, his giant fist wrapped around her arm. Raina's heart sank right into her stomach. What exactly had she gotten herself into?

CHAPTER FOUR

When Mateo realized that Raina was gone, a rush of emotions swept through him, anger and worry topmost. He wasn't used to having emotions like these and he wasn't entirely sure how to deal with them. He was a cold-blooded bastard, a fact that no one who knew him would dispute. Yet from the moment he met Raina in person, from that first moment he touched her, smelled her, he was lost. There was no denying how he felt about her.

Despite knowing that she was it for him, he wasn't entirely sorry when she disappeared from his life two years ago. Though he'd been furious, enough to almost make an enemy of Raina's mother, he had recognized that she was too young to claim at the time. Only nineteen. Old enough in some cultures, legal for marriage, but Raina had been raised in America with the ideal of freedom foremost in her upbringing. The past two years proved exactly how much freedom meant to her. Coming back to her family would be clipping her wings. Yet he had to do it.

It was time for Raina to claim her crown and it was time for him to claim his queen and rise up to take his rightful place in the underworld. He had mentored under the Gentleman Butcher for two decades with the promise of a future in the organization. Sotza's word was as good as gold.

It didn't hurt that a marriage between Mateo and Raina would solidify Mateo's position. He might want the girl more than he wanted his next breath, but he was still willing to use her to gain position.

Mateo touched a smear of blood on the outside of the clinic window where she had clearly pushed herself through and then either dangled or fallen to the ground. Another bolt of anger rushed through him. She was too reckless, couldn't take care of herself. It was well past time for her to come home. Where she would no longer be allowed to put herself in such danger.

Without turning, Mateo said to his people, "Find her."

He didn't need to say more. Though his men were not familiar with the city, they knew enough about the underground workings of Italy to find their way around. To find the people that mattered. To find her.

Mateo walked away from the clinic, his shoulders tense as he thought of all the things he wanted to do to her when he got his hands on her. Of course, she was injured, so any punishment would have to wait. He needed to teach his woman her new place in life.

CHAPTER FIVE

This was a bad idea and she was probably going to die.

Raina was sitting in the back seat of a vehicle driven by one of Savino's henchmen and sitting next to another. Savino's men retrieved the car at the parking lot near the Venice train station and were driving through Mestre, a borough of Venice. They were making sure that she wasn't going anywhere. She was starting to realize that by going to Savino she had leapt out of the frying pan and right into the fire. At least with Mateo she could be 99% positive that he wasn't going to kill her on sight.

She eyed the massive mansion as it came into view when the car rounded the long, winding, curved driveway. She heard the buzz of the gates as they closed. Savino's estate was surrounded by a wall and though everything was shrouded in shadows, she thought she could make out spikes on top of the fence. The mansion itself was big, dark and gloomy. From her vantage point, pulling up to the front of the mansion, she couldn't see a single light on inside.

Think logically, she thought to herself.

If they were going to kill her, they would take her out to

the middle of nowhere and put a bullet in her head. Not bring her back to the fancy mansion where bloodstains on the Oriental rugs would probably not come out.

The car halted and her door was opened for her. A hand reached inside. Raina hesitated for a few seconds before taking it and allowing the person to help her out. She gripped her side as it twinged in pain. Her back was on fire. But there was nothing she could do about that at the moment, not until she a bed and got some rest.

She was escorted up to the mansion doors by no less than three very large men. Apparently, it took this kind of muscle to escort one small helpless injured twenty-one-year-old woman. For some reason, Savino really didn't want to lose her, which was a frightening thought.

Her intent in going to the Italian Godfather was to brazen her way out of Italy. She had planned to use her stepfather's name to get herself safe passage through checkpoints. Instead, she somehow managed to intrigue Savino enough to gain herself entry into his private sanctum. On the upside, her stepfather likely didn't know about this yet. Possibly she could still wiggle her way out of the situation.

The door swung open and she stepped inside the mansion. It was the fanciest house she'd ever seen. Sotza's Venezuelan home was incredible too; a beautiful mix of rustic and modern coming together in an almost old English style. For the brief time that she lived there, she had enjoyed exploring the many rooms and the gorgeous gardens beyond the house.

Savino's home was different. It was bigger than Sotza's. Raina couldn't begin to guess how many rooms would be in this building. But it had a cold feel to it, an unused feel. The entryway was dark. No one greeted them and no lights were turned on. It was spooky.

"This way." Her escort waved her down the hallway on the right.

Raina nodded and trailed after him, squinting into the different nooks and crannies to try to get an idea of what the place looked like. It was really quite dark in the hallway and she might have actually lost her footing if it weren't for the vague shape of the man in front of her. He led her past several doors before opening one on the end and waving her inside. As she stepped through the door, she heaved a sigh of relief. Now this room she could work with.

It was big and cozy, lined with bookshelves, dominated by a huge masculine desk and leather chair. French balcony doors led outside, but she couldn't see anything in the darkness beyond. If she had to guess, there was probably a well-manicured lawn and garden out there. A roaring fire in the fireplace beckoned to her and she turned towards it holding her hands out. The door closed softly behind her and she looked over her shoulder in time to hear a click.

Raina checked the door, rattling the handle. Locked. She thought about getting angry; she thought about beating on the door and screaming for help. Like the damsel in distress from the movies.

Perhaps it was the gunshot wound, but she didn't have it in her to throw a fuss. All she could muster at the moment was mild curiosity. Why had she been brought to Savino's home? And why was she locked inside what was probably his office?

Though she was fairly certain that the answers to those questions couldn't be anything good, she also didn't believe she was in any immediate danger. Savino's response to her at the club would have been much different if he'd intended her harm. If he'd hated her on sight, or worse, been indifferent, she'd probably be floating face-down in a canal.

Drawn to the warmth of the fire, she sat in one of two

giant leather chairs. She kicked off her shoes, pulled her knees up and tucked her feet underneath her. Her back gave a painful twinge, but she was so relaxed and comfy that she didn't want to move. It seemed strange to feel this at ease in the home of someone she should probably consider an enemy. But she didn't. There was something about the dark cold mansion with the one warm and friendly room. The house projected a kind of loneliness. She couldn't hate lonely.

Raina considered herself an extroverted introvert. She loved being at home alone, reading her books, and working on her graphic art. But she also loved going out. She loved dancing, dating and talking to people. Her work in forgery gave her the opportunity to meet all kinds of people. She got a small peek into the illicit lives of others as she worked on their fake documents. She loved those glimpses and held each interaction close to her heart. She would never betray a customer. Unless that customer was Antonio Savino and he'd had her shot.

Raina's eyes grew heavy as she sat in the chair waiting. What exactly she was waiting for, she didn't know, but she may as well have a snooze while she waited. She pulled a pillow out from behind her back and curled it into her stomach, wiggling in the chair until she found a comfortable position. She fell asleep like that and didn't wake until the door rattled.

By the time Raina came fully awake Savino was already in the office and striding toward her. She shoved a handful of blonde hair out of her face and blinked sleepily up at him smothering a yawn with her hand.

"Signore Savino," she said softly. "Thank you for bringing me to your home. It's quite lovely."

"Call me Giovanni, please." He sat in the chair opposite her, crossing one leg over the other and watching her with interest. "My apologies for not warning you about this mausoleum. It's hardly the proper place to bring a young woman such as yourself, but there was no other safe haven that I could think of. My son has as much access to the city as I do, it wouldn't take him long to find you. In fact, he will find you here."

Raina shivered at that thought. Her fight or flight instinct was telling her to get up and start running, to burst through those French doors, race across the lawn and scale what she suspected was a razor-sharp fence. Of course, she couldn't do that.

"Am I going to be alright here?" she asked unsteadily.

Giovanni ignored her question, instead calling loudly toward the hallway, "Doctor, please come in." A thin and wiry man wearing a sweater over a pair of dark brown pants drew Raina's attention. "Dr. Danilo will examine your injury."

Raina thought about denying them, but Giovanni hadn't exactly given her an option. And it probably wouldn't hurt to get her wound looked at by a real doctor.

Raina attempted to stand, but the doctor put his hand on her shoulder. "No need to get up. I understand the wound is on your back. Lean forward in the chair and point at where it is."

Raina did as he asked, clutching the arm of the chair and leaning against it. She turned her face into the side and rubbed the softness of the chair against her cheek. She pointed at the spot on her back where the bullet hole was.

"It's already been sutured," she told him as he used medical scissors to slice through the gauze wrapped around her middle. She winced as he peeled the wad of gauze from her skin. It hurt like a bitch.

The doctor was quick to reassure her. "The wound is bad enough but seems to have missed everything important. You're a lucky woman. Whoever sewed you up did an excellent job. The stitches are even, and you'll only have a slight pucker of the scar."

"There goes bikini season," she said dryly. Raina didn't really give a shit about bikinis or any other kind of beachwear.

At the age of twelve, Raina had kidney transplant, a surgery that cut her wide open at the back. The ensuing scar was big and ugly. She didn't really care about it anymore, but at that young and tender age she'd been horrified by it. She had made sure it was covered at all times. Teenage years were awkward enough without adding to it a major illness and surgery. Raina tried to bury those memories as best she could.

The doctor finished treating and dressing her wound. He smoothed her shirt down her back with clinical economic movements. She respected his cool professional presence; it was like a balm to her after all that had happened that day.

The doctor gave her instructions on how to care for her wound, when the bandages could come off and when the sutures could come out. She listened to him intently, though she had to fight to keep her eyes open. She caught a glimpse of Giovanni watching her thoughtfully. She could almost see the gears in his brain working.

When the doctor excused himself and left the office, closing the door softly behind him, Raina decided it was time to speak plainly. "Why am I here, Giovanni? Not that I don't appreciate your hospitality, but when I came to you for help, this wasn't exactly what I had mind."

He studied her, not saying anything for several long minutes. She didn't interrupt the silence as she suspected he was gathering his thoughts. He seemed like a man that didn't often speak without thinking, a quality that she could appreciate. She had never really been one to speak out of turn, unless she was fired up about something.

"You are an interesting young woman. Your boldness is both infuriating and refreshing, but there is a fine line between the two. I fear your youth could lead to an impetuosity that could get you killed in this world... the underground I mean. And that would be a shame." He seemed to debate with himself on what to say next, perhaps on whether or not to speak his mind. Finally, he nodded to himself and continued, "If anyone else came to me with your demands, your blackmail —"

"Information, not blackmail," she hurried to assure him.

"Do not interrupt me again." His voice rang with steel. She shivered and sealed her lips. "At best I would have given you a few dollars and had you shown back onto the street to deal with the fallout of my son. At worst I would have had you killed myself."

He sat staring at her and when a long enough period of time passed, Raina felt it was safe to speak without being accused of interrupting. "And what made you change your mind? Made you decide to take me on as a charity case?"

He tilted his head, his strong hawk-like features cast in flickering shadows from the fireplace. "The most truthful answer is your stepfather. Sotza carries a lot of weight in the circles we share; he could make my life extremely difficult if I was involved in the disappearance of his daughter."

Raina narrowed her eyes at him. Though Giovanni respected Sotza, he also seemed to have a lot of power in his own right. Having gotten to know him a little, she suspected he wouldn't normally help someone in her position, despite her relation to Sotza. "Is that the only reason you brought me here?"

His sharp gaze roved over her face as he contemplated his answer. "I wish for you to marry my son."

Luckily, she was too stunned for her face to match her inner thoughts. There was not a snowball's chance in hell that she was going to marry Giovanni's son. She'd kill him herself first.

Giovanni continued to speak. "You seem cool and collected, but I will know better as I get to know you. Must be reasonably intelligent to carry on your business as a forger. You would be a good wife for my son. You're beautiful and frankly, it would help forge a relationship with your stepfather. I am getting older, but I need my son settled before I can hand my empire to him. You are just the woman to do it."

The word "no" wanted to burst forth from Raina so badly that she had to bite down on her soft lower lip to stop it from flying out. Giovanni didn't like being interrupted when he was speaking. She also suspected he didn't like hearing the word no. As far as he was concerned the future bride of his son had walked up to him in his club with a gunshot wound and begged for his help.

Before Raina could say much of anything, Giovanni stood and held his hand out to her. She slid her hand into his and allowed him to help her stand. "I will have someone show you to your room."

Raina had no doubt that there was a lock on that door too. She was definitely rethinking her decision to enlist Signore Savino's help. Her recklessness could lead to an all out mob war if things didn't end well.

Mateo would want revenge if anything happened to her. There was something about his attachment to her, their mutual attraction. Raina didn't believe in soulmates, but she didn't know how else to explain Mateo. It was part of the reason why she ran from him; to protect herself. His passion, his obsession, everything about him, it was too much. She couldn't handle that kind of love.

No, she didn't have any choice but to trust Giovanni. For now.

CHAPTER SIX

Finding Raina was the easy part, figuring out how to get her back was an entirely different matter. Mateo had been on his feet for nearly seventy-two hours. No sleep, little food – a shit ton of aggravation. As much as he wanted to go after Raina without delay, he knew he needed sleep first. He wasn't getting her back if he couldn't use his brain.

Mateo was sitting in a booth in the restaurant located in the lobby of his hotel. It wasn't exactly an upscale hotel. He needed to try and blend while in Italy. He couldn't toss his money and weight around, raising questions about who he was and where he came from. As a result, the restaurant was low-quality, overpriced, and dingy.

Sitting with him in the booth were two of his people, Thomas and Angela. Angela acted as Mateo's second when he left Sotza's sphere of influence and went to work on his own. Mateo had Sotza's blessing when it came to working outside of Venezuela, trusting Mateo to make decisions based on Sotza's best interest. Despite being raised in an underworld filled with men, Angela was as bloodthirsty and skilled as any of them. She was the shadow in the dark that no one saw coming. A cute, innocent looking young woman who could take a man out as easily as smile at him. In fact, Mateo dared any man to tell Angela to smile. It would be the last thing he did.

Thomas was another who Mateo trusted implicitly. He'd been with the Sotza cartel for a decade, living on the compound and working his way up through the ranks. He often chose to work with Mateo so he could travel the world.

"Thomas, I want you and the rest of our men to sit on the house. Make sure you track any and all of Raina's movements if she leaves the grounds. Try not to be seen by Savino's men, but if you are, tell them the truth. I have a hunch that Raina told Savino the truth about who she is and that's why she's being kept at his estate." Mateo downed the rest of the water in his cup and threw a few french fries into his mouth. He turned Angela. "I want you to go and talk to Savino at his club, arrange a meeting."

She snorted. "He won't talk to a woman. Venezuela is bad enough when it comes to getting men to treat me like an equal, but Italy? The Sicilian Cosa Nostra? Not a chance."

"Watch your tongue with me," Mateo snapped, his voice hard. "You don't get to argue with my orders."

Angela had a chip on her shoulder a mile wide and she wasn't afraid to mouth off her opinion. They were of a similar age and had worked together from their teen years on. Mateo was willing to take more lip from her than he did most people. But not in this instance, not in Italy. He needed a tight crew here.

"A beautiful woman is more likely to get close to Savino, maybe convince him to drop his guard."

Despite his order that she shut up and do as he says, Angela couldn't help but voice one more opinion. "That's easy for you to say. We don't know what Raina said to him to get him to adopt her. What if it was something else about her that drew him, besides her beauty?" Her lip curled in disgust as she said the last word.

"Then I guess we'll find out when he sends your body back to me in pieces. Now get out of here and go deliver my message. I want a meeting with Savino at his earliest convenience. Use Sotza's name if you have to."

Mateo didn't give her another opportunity to argue. He pulled out his wallet, opened it and tossed a few bills on the table, then shoved his chair back and stood. The room swam for second. Fuck, he needed to get some sleep.

He strode away from the pair and out of the restaurant into the hotel lobby. He bypassed the elevator and took the stairs up three flights. He strode down the hallway to room 407 and used his key card to open it. He didn't care about the shabbiness of the room; he'd slept in worse places. Swamps, jungles, Siberia. He was dead on his feet. At this point he would sleep just about anywhere.

But as he lay down on the bed and closed his eyes, Raina's face emerged. It was pale and pinched. No less lovely than usual, but worried. Terrified even. Though she had been brought into the world of the mafia via her mother and stepfather, she had never experienced the kind of violence she'd seen earlier that day. She'd been shocked into the reality of the lifestyle in a brutal way. Mateo couldn't blame her for running from the clinic. She probably saw him as another gun-toting mobster, like Antonio Savino and his posse.

Before falling asleep, Mateo vowed to hunt down the fucker that had made her world a little bit darker. He didn't give a shit if the man who had Raina shot was also the son of the most powerful man in Italy. If Mateo had to, he would slaughter them all.

With that thought he allowed sleep to overtake him. He dreamed of Raina. Her soft skin, shining hair, deep blue eyes that a man could get lost in for days and a grin that spelled all kinds of trouble for the man in her life. For Mateo.

CHAPTER SEVEN

Raina woke suddenly from a sharp stabbing pain in her back. She gasped and bolted upright, then immediately regretted the action as she cried out in pain.

"Ow, shit!" she yelped reaching around to touch her back. She must've rolled over onto the wound or stretched funny in her sleep and the pain woke her up.

That was a hell of a way to greet the day. She took several deep breaths trying to regain her composure. Tears burned behind her eyelids, but she quickly dried her eyes. There was nothing to cry about. It was just a little pain, nothing she hadn't dealt with before.

When she managed to pull herself together, she inched her way to the edge of the bed and gingerly placed her feet on the floor. She decided to take a short rest rather than stand up immediately and risk falling over if she happened to receive another jolt of intense pain or a wave of dizziness.

She hated that she was in such weak condition while sheltering in the home of someone who might be an enemy. It made her vulnerable and Raina didn't like feeling vulnerable.

She was pretty sure she got that personality trait from her tough as nails mother. Vee also hated feeling vulnerable.

But Diane, Raina's adoptive mom, always wore her feelings on her sleeve. Everyone knew where they stood with Diane. She was the kindest hearted person Raina knew. Sometimes Raina wished she was more like her adoptive mom than her birth mother. Yet, she was also able to recognize that each woman had given Raina unique characteristics that made up her whole person. She couldn't regret something like that.

She gripped the edge of the nightstand and slowly pulled herself up onto her feet. Motherfucker, her back was on fire. It hurt much worse than it had the night before. Was it infected? Had she somehow managed to tear the stitches in her sleep?

She thought about it and decided the wound was probably sore from being slept on. After she'd had her kidney transplant, she'd had good days and bad days, depending on what her body decided to throw at her. There were definitely times where the incision site hurt much worse than other times.

Raina wasn't one to seek drugs, but if anything was going to drive her out of that bedroom and in search of civilization within Giovanni's great mausoleum of a house it was her need for painkillers. She tugged at the T-shirt that she'd been given to sleep in. She thought it might belong to one of the Italian men guarding the estate. It was a plain black T-shirt that covered her up for the most part, though it bared her legs more than she was comfortable with.

She gave her pile of clothes on the floor a disparaging look. She hated the thought of putting them back on. They were dirty, they were bloody, and they represented her trauma of the day before. She wanted nothing more than to bury them in a deep hole and never look at them again. Which sucked, because those had been her favourite jeans and the leather jacket had been specially made for her in France.

Another thing Antonio owed her.

She made her way carefully down the hall toward the bathroom that she'd been shown the night before. She relieved herself, washed her hands and attempted to put her hair into some semblance of order. The fine blonde strands were not usually difficult to arrange. A quick finger comb and some fluffing and she no longer had a wicked case of bedhead.

She went through all the drawers and the medicine cabinet searching for ibuprofen or Tylenol but came up empty. Dammit, she was actually going to have to go look for someone.

Raina wandered down the staircase to the lower level, looking this way and that at the house furnishings. She hoped they would be less gloomy than they had the night before, but her impression of an unloved and unlived in home was spot on. Dust covered pretty much everything and what the dust wasn't covering, drop cloths were.

It looked as though this place had been abandoned some time ago, but she knew otherwise. The library she'd been shown to the night before had been well used. The guest room she'd used hadn't sported even a speck of dust.

She bypassed Giovanni's office in favour of searching for a maid or a guard instead. Though she felt relatively certain that Giovanni wasn't going to have her killed, at least not yet, she wasn't quite up for a conversation with the man. She had yet to truly absorb the fact that he wanted her to marry his son, the man who'd had her shot.

She shook her head at the strange logic and continued through the lower level of the home. Nothing she was seeing was convincing her that the home was used for more than sleep and time spent in that one office. A formal dining room boasted a gorgeous chandelier that was covered in filth and a massive table with ten chairs draped in cloths. Such a creepy old house. She was about to move on to the kitchen when a voice from behind her stopped her.

"No doubt you think my home is strange," Giovanni said. He waited until she turned to face him before continuing. "My wife died eleven years ago. She loved this home, decorated it, made it completely her own. Since her death I have been unable to love it the way she loved it."

And yet he hadn't been able to move on and move out, Raina finished his thought silently. He must have been very much in love with his wife, she decided. It must've been completely heart-wrenching for Giovanni to have lost her.

Raina's heart went out to him. But not his asshole of a son. She was still going to stab that loser the moment she laid eyes on him.

"I'm so sorry for your loss," she murmured, meaning it.

He nodded his thanks. "This is a big home, with much potential. It should be filled with love, light and laughter once more. The voices of children. The way it was always meant to be."

Raina said nothing to this; she didn't want to encourage his delusion that she marry his son.

"In the city, in my business, I must be the Godfather. The big shot. Mafioso. But in my home, I have a heart."

And he was choosing to share that heart with Raina. It scared her that he was opening himself up to her, showing his vulnerabilities. She believed that this meant she would either have to die or become part of the family. The little she knew about these types of men, they had a code. Opening up, giving information to another person, was unheard of except with close family members. It frightened her that he was already considering her family. She wanted to disabuse him of the idea, but she also wanted to continue breathing.

She elected not to speak.

He seemed to realize that his nostalgia was somewhat out of place and a shutter dropped over his expression, pushing Raina out. "You were looking for something?" His voice was cool and steady once more.

"Yes, thank you. I was searching for some painkillers. My back is in rough shape this morning."

"My apologies for not getting them to you sooner. You are such a tough little creature that I'd forgotten you will feel pain like anyone else. Follow me." He turned and walked back in the other direction, toward his office.

Raina trailed after him thinking about the strange things he'd said. Why wouldn't she feel pain like anyone else? No matter how tough a person is, pretty much everyone felt pain. Had he been testing her? Testing her resilience?

Raina gave herself a mental shake. She was overthinking this. He'd already stated his intentions and she didn't think it mattered whether or not she was fainting or gritting her teeth and bearing the pain, he still wanted her for a daughter-in-law.

Strangely though, she was starting to soften towards the older man. He seemed lonely and somewhat out of touch. Brutal probably, though she hadn't seen any first-hand evidence. She wondered how she would be feeling right about now if he'd told her she would marry him rather than his son. Neither was a great option, but the older gentleman was far more palpable then his weasel spawn.

After showing her into his office, he went to his desk and picked up a pill bottle. He shook a couple pills out into his hand and gave them to her. She looked at his hand with narrowed eyes. It probably wasn't smart to take drugs from someone she didn't trust. And right now, Savino was on the far end of her spectrum of trust.

He caught on to her hesitation. "The doctor left these for you last night. I forgot to send them up to your room. I assure you they are simply a strong dose of ibuprofen, for your pain. He says he can bring more if you need them."

Raina shook off her skepticism, reminding herself he had plenty of other opportunities to drug or kill her. She took the pills and swallowed them dry, a skill she'd picked up in her early years of kidney failure when she had to swallow many pills and got impatient with waiting for water. "I don't think I'll need any more." She gave him a smirk. "I'm a tough little creature."

He flashed her a quick smile and then arranged his face back into business mode. "I will have some proper clothes sent to your room. I'd intended to do that before you got up, but you were out of bed earlier than expected. I'll show you our pantry while we wait for the clothing to arrive. After, we will attend a meeting."

"With your son?" she asked hesitantly, trying to keep the worry from her voice.

Giovanni shook his head. "No, Mateo Gutierrez. We will meet with him and discuss your future."

For a few seconds it felt as though all of the air was sucked out of the room. Elation crashed into terror and sizzled right through her body making her hair stand on end. Mateo was coming for her, exactly as she knew he would. Once more her flight instinct kicked in and it was everything she could do not to run. She didn't think she would make it far with both Mateo and Giovanni hot on her heels. How the hell was she supposed to get out of this?

CHAPTER EIGHT

"Who are you?" Raina demanded, as an elderly woman dressed head to foot in black invaded her room without knocking.

The woman's hair was twisted into an intricate and severe knot on top of her head. It was steel grey, a colour that seemed to go with her sour expression. Though the woman hadn't said a word yet, Raina guessed that this was about the least fun person she was going to meet in Italy.

The woman dumped a pile of clothes on the bed and muttered, "Dress."

Though she'd only said one word, she had a thick accent. "English?" Raina asked curiously.

The woman shook her head and pointed at the pile in the bed. "Dress."

"Convenient," Raina muttered darkly.

Her host spoke perfect English with only a hint of an accent. As did his son and all of the men that Raina had met so far associated with either of the two mafiosos. It seemed strange that this old woman was affiliated but didn't speak English.

Raina picked at the pile of clothes on the bed, curious as to what might have been chosen for her. She held up a dress. It was pretty, flirty and short, nothing Raina would ever wear if she had a choice. The neckline appeared to be plunging, but she wouldn't know for sure until it was on and she saw how it fit. The fabric was soft and clingy. It would hug her body and likely give her curves that she didn't actually have.

Along with the dress was a pair of silk lace panties, garters, and silk stockings. There was also a pair of three-inch black stiletto heels with tiny straps around the ankles. She flipped them over to look at the brand. Valentino. Italian. She smirked.

Next, she picked up a short fluffy jacket. She wrinkled her nose as her fingers sank into the luxurious fur. She glanced over at the silently disapproving woman and asked, "Is this real?"

The woman stared at Raina without so much as a blink.

"You have a smudge of dirt on your nose," Raina said casually, pretending to turn away as she said it. Out of the corner of her eye she saw the woman lift her hand to touch her nose, look at her fingers and then drop her arm. Raina turned around, her eyes narrowed. "I knew you knew English. Why do you want me to think we can't communicate?"

The woman narrowed her eyes at Raina in return, but still refused to speak. Raina felt her temper rise, but held on to it, trying to rationalize. There could be any number of reasons why this woman refused to speak to her, but Raina despised being toyed with. She preferred people be plain with her, speak what they thought.

"Did Signore Savino tell you not to speak to me?" Raina demanded. Still the woman refused to speak. Raina picked up the furred jacket and tossed it aside. "I won't wear it as long as there's a chance it might be real. I don't believe in the slaughter of animals for fashion."

The woman betrayed her feelings for Raina's statement with a wrinkled nose and a slight role of her eyes. Oh, now it was on. Raina rounded on her. "What, you think animals should be destroyed for our pleasure?"

Still nothing, though the woman crossed her arms tightly in front of her and stared a hole in the wall opposite. Raina felt as though she badly had something to say but was afraid to speak her mind. "Well if you won't speak to me, then I'm going to have to guess your thoughts. You think since I eat meat that I'm a hypocrite. Well I'm not. I don't like meat either, I only eat it because I have to have a very well-balanced diet on account of my kidneys. I had kidney failure when I was a child and I had to have a kidney transplant. Since then, I've had to watch my diet extremely carefully, which includes a small amount of meat. But I won't have you thinking I'm a hypocrite – "

"It's not a real fur, idiota! It's a fake. Oi, young people speak too freely these days! The car will arrive for you in fifteen minutes." The woman turned on her heel and stomped away.

"Knew she could speak English," Raina muttered, picking up the fake fur jacket.

It was really amazing what design houses could come up with these days using synthetics. The jacket was as luxurious and soft as real fur, to the point that Raina hesitated to wear it anyway. She didn't want to be accused of animal murder, and who knew what PETA representatives she might run into while she was out and about in Venice.

Raina decided to skip a shower, since she didn't want to get her bandage wet, choosing to have a quick bird bath instead. Then she pulled on the panties and the dress. She picked up the garter and stockings. Raina had never worn anything like it before and she didn't think the few minutes she had left were enough to try and figure it out. She dropped them and reached for the heels.

The shoes fit like they were made for her feet. Someone had paid attention, either to her feet, or her shoes while she was sleeping. The thought probably should've freaked her out, but she was getting use to Giovanni's ways. He was a strange one, but she didn't think he meant her any real harm.

She checked herself in the floor length mirror next to the dresser. She looked good. Really good. Raina rarely wore dresses. She'd grown up as a farm girl and was happiest when she was wearing jeans, a T-shirt and running shoes, but since meeting her mother and seeing far more of the world, she'd come to gain an appreciation for fashion. Not necessarily high-fashion or brand labels, but more a desire to look good when she left the house. Raina smiled at the mirror. She thought maybe she looked a bit like a period dame, the side candy of a 1920's gangster.

Reluctantly she picked up the fake fur jacket and tugged it on. It was pure white, a beautiful contrast to the royal blue of the dress. Okay, she was willing to admit, the jacket made the outfit.

She descended the stairs quickly, aware that she was two minutes past the allotted fifteen minutes. When she arrived by the front door, Giovanni was waiting for her, glancing at the watch that he pulled out of his pocket. A smile tugged at her lips. It suited him; the pocket watch attached to a gold chain. She rather thought he'd be dashing with a monocle as well, but she wasn't going to tell him that. She didn't think that their relationship had progressed to that point yet.

"Ah, there you are, bella," he said, a chiding note in his voice as he tucked his watch away. Then he looked her over with admiration, all chiding aside. "You are stunning. Shall we, Ms. Sotza?" He gave her his arm.

She didn't bother to correct him on the Sotza. Her name

was Raina Duncan, after her adoptive parents. Her last name mattered to her, because the Duncans had raised her. They had been good to her. Not only did she feel she owed them her allegiance, but using their last name was also a sign of respect.

Raina loved her birth mother and she adored her stepfather, but she would not erase her past by taking on Sotza's name. However, she wasn't going to argue with the Italian Godfather. The name of Sotza was what was keeping her safe at the moment.

She grinned at Giovanni and took the arm that he offered her. "Thank you, signore."

He led her out the door toward an idling limousine with tinted windows. He opened the door and helped her slide onto the seat. He closed the door carefully and strode around to the other side.

Giovanni was smooth and she appreciated it. He was a gentleman, much like her stepfather. She had no doubt Giovanni could be as brutal as Sotza, but he managed to keep a veneer of civilization at the same time. She hoped he was living on this side of sociopathic, the side where he could actually appreciate her plight, rather than treat her like another piece on his chessboard.

They chatted easily as they drove. Raina wasn't surprised, Giovanni was an easy person for her to get along with. She asked him about life in Italy, what he loved best about the country and what he thought she should see as a tourist. He was happy to answer her questions, even sometimes becoming animated as he spoke. He was passionate about Italy; a man who clearly loved his birth country.

They arrived at a parking lot where they left the vehicle and stepped into a waiting boat. The wind slapped her in the face as they made their way through the canals. Normally the sights and smells of Venice would capture her completely, but she was preoccupied with her upcoming meeting with Mateo. Her stomach was filled with butterflies.

Before long they were at the club, Banditos. Giovanni stepped out onto the dock and held his hand out to her, helping her until she was standing next to him smoothing her dress over her thighs. She released a long breath as she looked at the door of the club with apprehension. In the light of day, it looked like a regular building. Not nearly as exciting, or sophisticated, as it had the night before. She supposed it was probably this way with all nightclubs. They would never look as awesome in the cold light of day as they did at night.

"You have nothing to be nervous about, I will make sure that you're protected at all times and that you are not harmed by this man."

"It's not me I'm worried about."

Giovanni gave her an unconcerned smile. "I will also be fine, bella."

Raina let out a short laugh. "Clearly, you have never seen Mateo angry before."

Giovanni squeezed her hand again and led her toward the door, which a bouncer opened for them. "Clearly *you* have never seen Mateo Gutierrez angry before or you would not be standing here talking to me." Giovanni threw her own words back at her, but in a much more sinister way. A shiver slid down her spine as she stepped into the darkness of the club.

CHAPTER NINE

A good night's sleep put Mateo in a better mood. At least a less-likely-to-murder-on-sight mood. His first thought was Raina; the deep and abiding gnawing feeling of concern that wouldn't go away until he set eyes on her, had her back in his care.

He sat up and swung his legs over the side of the bed, placing his feet on the floor. He ran a hand over his hair and face and then stretched his back and neck, cracking his shoulders.

He glanced at the cheap clock. He'd slept for nearly eight hours. Mateo was usually a strict six hours per night guy.

He snatched up his phone which was plugged into the charger next to the clock. A message blinked at him. It was from Angela.

Meeting with Savino. Banditos. 11 AM.

It was now 10:15 AM. The message had come in late the night before. Angela had done good, arranging a meeting so quickly.

He pushed himself off the bed and opened the blinds, allowing weak sunlight to filter through the dirty window. He took a quick shower, washing his hair and running soap over his body. He dried off and looked through his bag for some clothes.

He hadn't brought much with him in the way of nicer clothes. He rarely wore a suit, preferring outfits that allowed for easier movement. But a meeting with a man of Savino's standing called for one. He hadn't anticipated needing a suit here, believing that he would grab Raina and get out of Italy. He should've known his future bride would throw a wrench into his plans.

Mateo growled his frustration and tossed aside the pair of jeans he'd been holding. If he had taken a room in a more upscale hotel, he could have called the concierge to get someone to shop for him. But with barely half an hour left before the meeting, he was on his own and running out of time. He was about to jerk the towel off his hips and dress in his worn jeans and a T-shirt when a knock sounded at the door.

He picked his gun up off the nightstand, checked to make sure that it was loaded and walked carefully toward the door. Standing to the side he said loudly, "Who is it?"

A female voice filtered through. He couldn't tell what she said, but she sounded like Angela. In one swift move he unlocked the door and jerked it open reaching out for her.

"Hey!" she yelled in annoyance as he dragged her inside. She tripped over her combat boots and let go of the garment bag she was holding, reaching out to grip the doorknob so she wouldn't fall over.

Mateo didn't give her time to right herself, he shoved her to the side, looked both ways down the hall and then slammed the door shut. He locked it and gave her a narrow look. "What are you doing here?"

She huffed out a breath and strode further into the room. "I figured since your ass was getting some beauty sleep this morning, I better get you some appropriate attire for your meeting with Savino. He surrounds himself with smartly dressed people, which tells me he isn't one to enjoy the presence of a roughneck."

Mateo grunted and walked away from her, leaving her to pick up the garment bag and toss it on the bed. He was being ungrateful, but he didn't care. He never cared. This was him. He didn't observe social niceties. They were a waste of time and likely to get a person killed.

"You spoke to him." Not a question. He wouldn't have a meeting with the man if Angela hadn't met with him first.

She nodded. "A strange man, but I don't think he'll have us all killed or anything. As long as you don't say the wrong thing."

They looked at each other, both knowing what the other was thinking. Of course Mateo was going to say the wrong thing. He was an enforcer, a second-in-command. He was rough, he was brutal, he was in no way diplomatic. The boss made the negotiations. Mateo's job was to keep the boss safe and make sure everyone abided by Sotza's rules.

Miami was going to be a test of Mateo's ability to change. If and when he finally got his hands on the city.

Neither of them said anything as Mateo unzipped the garment bag and examined the suit inside. He raised an eyebrow at it. "How much did you spend on this?"

It was easily one of the most expensive suits he would ever wear. Sotza, his employer, was always impeccably dressed in these things, but Mateo had never seen the point. He could work and fight much more easily wearing his own clothes.

"You don't want to know."

No, he didn't. Though Mateo was paid very well, with more money than he could possibly spend in a lifetime, he put most of it away. He sent half of it to his family in Caracas.

The rest he squirreled away. For what, he didn't know. But he was the type of guy that figured eventually a path would open up to him and he would know what to do.

He dropped his towel, uncaring of Angela's presence, and began dressing. She rolled her eyes, made a clucking sound and turned to face the wall. He smirked at her back. For such a bad ass, she sure got all uppity about seeing a naked man. There was nothing between them or he wouldn't have dropped the towel in front of her. Angela was like a sister. They had each other's backs. She was his employee. Sometimes they acted like friends. But no more than that.

As he dressed in the fancy suit, he said, "Tell me about Savino."

"He's extremely wealthy. He has enough influence in Italy to sway elections. To choose candidates that'll enable his business empire and then ensure their victories. Those that cross him have a tendency to disappear and the judicial system here doesn't seem to get involved. Obviously, he's bought the police, which I suspect is how the son was able to track Raina."

Mateo had been afraid of that when she'd run from him at the clinic. Afraid that in her panic she would rush to leave the country and end up in the hands of a man who wanted her dead. Though her presence in the home of the father did not bode well, at least she'd had the sense to pull weight on her stepfather's name. That alone would keep her safe. For now.

"Turn around," Mateo growled. Angela obeyed and when she was facing him, he handed her the tie.

She stepped up to him and dragged it around his neck using her fingertips to press it up under the collar. With quick efficient motions she tied it for him, keeping her face from betraying what he knew she was thinking. A badass murderous motherfucker like Mateo needed help with his tie.

He'd never been able to tie the fuckers, not even as a boy. Probably had something to do with his father passing away before he was five and then being raised by his mother and two sisters.

Mateo debated packing his things and preparing to check out of the hotel but decided to leave it for now. He didn't trust Raina not to throw another wrench into his plans. He wanted to leave Italy immediately, which likely meant that his contrary fiancé would want to stay for a while. Perhaps vacation in the home of one of the most dangerous men on the face of the planet. It would almost be amusing if it wasn't so terrifying.

CHAPTER TEN

Raina's leg jiggled under the table as she swept the club with nervous glances. She tapped her phone again and looked at the time. 10:58 AM. He would be here in a few minutes.

That thought alone sent her heart rate soaring and a ripple of apprehension through her muscles. She had to force herself to sit still and not flee the building. This was for two reasons. She was honest enough to admit that she was deeply and hopelessly attracted to Mateo. She tried to keep it on the down low, tried to bury it so that she didn't have to think about it. She feared what Mateo would do if he knew. He was already relentless and determined. How much scarier would he be if he knew she returned his feelings?

The second reason she was nervous was more obvious. Mateo was one of the most terrifying men in the world. He had such an air of unleashed violence about him that anyone standing in his vicinity would immediately sense the danger.

And for good reason. He moved fast, like lightening. Or a big cat stalking its prey. Mateo was also patient and intelligent. He thought through everything he did before executing his plans. But when he executed, it was with speed and precision. Probably one of the reasons he was still alive. Raina had no doubt that Mateo had made enemies in his days.

Giovanni, who had been off to the side speaking in low tones to one of his men, joined her at the table and sat. "I took the liberty of ordering you a drink."

A frosted glass of orange juice was placed in front of her. Raina smirked. "Nonalcoholic?"

"I have had the opportunity to learn some things about you. Among those things is the terrible disease and surgery that you had to go through as a child. I now regret forcing alcohol on you last night, knowing now why you choose not to drink."

Raina shrugged. "It won't kill me to have a drink once in a while, I just have to be careful. I was lucky enough to get a second chance at life and it would be a stupid thing to risk that."

Giovanni nodded thoughtfully, internalizing her statement. It was good, she wanted him to realize how much life and freedom meant to her. He seemed determined that they should be allies. Now if he would stop pushing his murderous son on her, she would be much more comfortable in his presence.

Before they could speak again, they heard a commotion in the hall leading to the front door of the club. Giovanni snapped his fingers at his man and pointed. He left to go check.

"Mateo," Raina guessed.

"Indeed." Giovanni picked up his drink and calmly took a sip, his dark eyes on the door where Mateo would soon emerge.

Giovanni's man came striding back to their table. His shoulders were rigid, his eyes were down, his hands were clasped. Interesting. Raina didn't have a ton of experience with mafia men, but she found it noteworthy that the minions of the big guys acted differently. Sotza's men feared and respected him, but the way they spoke around him, it was more relaxed, as though there was a certain kind of equality. Giovanni's men, on the other hand, took their deference to him to the extreme.

Giovanni's men made it clear that there was no equality. They didn't speak their minds around him, they didn't share thoughts that weren't in complete agreement with Giovanni and they were clearly meant to be seen instead of heard unless Giovanni needed something from them.

"Speak," Giovanni said to his man with a wave of his hand.

"They refuse to give up their weapons," the man grunted.

Giovanni thought about it for a couple of seconds, turning the problem over in his mind. He turned to Raina. "What do you think, my dear? Do you believe that Gutierrez and his people will shoot up my club?"

Raina blew out a breath and thought about it. This question, her answer, it was a big responsibility. Did she tell Giovanni that Mateo would mean him no harm? What if she was wrong? She had seen Mateo's reflexes, had fought with him physically, she knew at least some of what he was capable of and she suspected there was so much more. Or did she tell Giovanni that his men should disarm Mateo's?

A shudder rippled through her at that last thought. She imagined if Giovanni's men tried touching Mateo there would be a bloodbath. She turned her gaze up to Giovanni's waiting one and said, her voice slow and thoughtful, "As you know, Mateo is a very dangerous man. I have seen nothing to dispute this in the time that I've spent with him. However, it's my impression that he's also a thoughtful man. He doesn't pull his gun unless he means it and he doesn't attack people without a reason. I believe you have nothing to fear." She paused, tilted her head and narrowed her eyes. "I'm not entirely sure how these negotiations will go. I'm not sure what he'll do if you say something that he doesn't like."

Giovanni nodded. "You make some good points." He turned to his man. "Let the man in already, I've had enough waiting. They may keep their weapons, but make sure you and your men are close. Don't get jumpy, don't pull a weapon unless you have my go-ahead."

Raina felt a little sick at that. She didn't want anyone pulling any more weapons. She'd already been shot once. And that was the most violence she'd experienced in her short life so far. She was desperately hoping that they could have a nice sit-down brunch together and have a civilized chat about her future.

Mateo didn't wait for either his men or Giovanni's, he quickly strode toward their table. Ignoring Giovanni entirely, Mateo rounded the table to where Raina was sitting. He dropped to his knee next to her and took her hand in a hard grip.

"Tell me you're okay." His voice was an agitated growl. And though his appearance was immaculate, there was a wild look in his eyes that she'd never seen before.

At first, Raina was so surprised she couldn't speak. What was he doing? How could he put himself in such a vulnerable position right next to a potential enemy? All of Giovanni's men were at his back, their hands twitching towards their holsters as they tried to figure out what Mateo was doing with her. Did he actually care this much? That he might put himself in danger over her?

"I'm fine," she said quietly for his ears alone. He continued to have that wild look. She placed her hand on top of his where he gripped her and squeezed. "Really, Mateo, I feel fine. Giovanni has been treating me like a queen."

Mateo's shoulders stiffened at her use of Giovanni's name, but he didn't chastise her for it. "Your wound?" he persisted.

"Honestly, I'm fine," she said insistently, glancing around at the people surrounding them, embarrassment colouring her cheeks. She was just as tough as the rest of them, but Mateo was treating her as though she was a delicate doll.

"She is in near perfect health," Giovanni said, his voice jovial with an edge of curiosity. His dark eyes lingered on her lap where Mateo's hand clasped hers. "My personal physician saw to her and made sure that she will have no lasting ill effects from her wound."

Mateo stood slowly, his entire body tense. Raina held her breath. He stared down at her, his dark eyes piercing through flesh and bones and thoughts.

Whenever he did that, whenever he looked at her with such an intense gaze, she felt like she could divine his thoughts. Blood, sex and violence. She gave a slight shake of her head, silently telling him she truly was fine.

His shoulders seemed to relax a fraction. No one else around them would've seen the interaction, it had been so fast and intimate. No one would know that she had silently called off the bloodbath that he would've instigated on her behalf, had Giovanni hurt her in any way.

Mateo sat on Raina's other side, his body shifting in a way that very subtly blocked her from view of the club. A woman plopped herself down into the chair next to Mateo. At first, Raina thought the woman belonged to Giovanni. But body language and the way she was dressed told Raina otherwise. This one was Mateo's.

Raina studied her with the cool air of indifference on the outside and raging jealousy on the inside. The woman was beautiful, with dark serious eyes, hair falling in soft waves around her shoulders and a small compact body with more curves than Raina could ever hope to grow.

Raina knew that she was being unreasonable, that her jealousy was unwarranted. She had no real claim on Mateo, despite his obsession with her. She'd never given him any indication that she felt the same. The irrational side of Raina wanted to stamp her ownership all over the wild Venezuelan gangster.

"Thank you for agreeing to meet with me." Mateo's eyes were on Giovanni as he spoke.

Considering the smoldering cauldron of violent intentions buried beneath a fancy suit and bland expression, Raina was impressed that Mateo was keeping such a polite front.

Before Giovanni could answer, Raina's curiosity got the better of her. She stuck her hand out toward the woman. "Raina Duncan. And you?"

The other woman looked momentarily startled but then seemed to gather herself. She looked at Raina as though seeing her for the first time, and for all Raina knew maybe this was the first time. The woman shook her hand, a firm quick jerk before she let it go.

"Angela Santiago." She seemed to hesitate, then she added, "I work for Mateo and your father."

Raina pursed her lips and nodded thoughtfully. She was impressed. She hadn't realized that the Latino macho men who made up the Venezuelan underworld would allow a woman such a position. Perhaps Sotza, or Mateo, or both, were more forward-thinking than she'd given them credit for. While she certainly didn't approve of the way they procured wives, she liked the idea that they worked with women.

"Pleased to meet you," Raina said politely, some of her jealousy melting away.

Angela nodded, her eyes drifting away from the table to scan the club. Raina wondered if Angela was a bodyguard. She was small but she dressed badass in denim, leather and heavy boots.

A slight tension rippled through the occupants of the table as they all fell silent for a few seconds. The seriousness of this meeting was starting to set in. Dangerous people sharing a table in a club owned by one of the most powerful men in the world.

Raina wondered who held more power, Giovanni or Sotza? Mateo, acting in Sotza's stead, was just as powerful as his boss. Raina recalled a conversation that she had with him when she was living in the mountain compound in Venezuela for that brief month. His words still struck a chord of apprehension within her. He'd said to her, "No man is my master."

A person only had to spend a matter of minutes with Mateo to see the coiled strength within, the leashed violence, the intelligence and the terrifying determination. Mateo knew exactly who he was and where he was going in life. This is why the idea of spending the rest of her life with a man like that, a man who was already married to the mob, felt too frightening for her to contemplate.

She would admit to being attracted to him. Who wouldn't? On the surface, he was everything a woman could want; good-looking, wealthy, self-confident. But underneath, he was dark. And while Raina had come to terms with the fact that she would inevitably be drawn into the mafia life by who she was, who she was born to, she wasn't yet ready to accept an arranged marriage.

She glanced over at Giovanni who wanted her to marry his son. No, she wasn't interested in marriage with any of the options she was currently faced with.

"Business," Mateo said in a cool voice letting the occupants of the table note that he was impatient to get the upcoming negotiations over with.

"Drinks first," Giovanni insisted.

As if out of nowhere, a woman stepped up to the table with a tray. She lowered it with professionalism, not rattling the drinks. Though no one at the table had ordered, except for Giovanni prior to the Mateo's arrival, the waitress placed specific drinks in front of Mateo and Angela.

Mateo raised a brow and glanced down his drink. "Gin," he observed, a slight edge of sarcasm to his voice.

"With a twist of lime." Though the drink itself was innocuous, Giovanni wanted everyone at the table to know that he'd done his research. He was prepared for this conversation. And he was in control.

Angela shrugged her shoulders, rolled her eyes, picked up her drink and slammed it. She set the glass down on the table with a clunk and said, "Good drink."

Raina was starting to like this Angela chick. She had attitude and if anyone could appreciate a decent attitude it was Raina.

"Now, business." Giovanni's voice held no more warmth.

"Sotza wants his daughter back immediately, unharmed." Mateo's voice dripped with ice. "Thanks to your imbecile of a son, I'll be handing her over with a hole in her. How do you suggest we rectify this situation?"

Raina sucked in a breath at Mateo's aggression, but Giovanni did nothing except nod. "My son has certainly made a bad move with this young lady. I regret that she came to harm within my city. Had I known she was here, I would have made sure that her stay was more pleasant."

"I insist that you release Raina to me and allow us safe passage out of your territory." Mateo's voice held aggression. He wasn't here to negotiate; he was here to make demands.

Having spent some time with Giovanni, Raina didn't believe that threats were the way to go. She felt tension running through the older man and worried that he might try to set his bodyguards on Mateo. If it came down to a fight, she wasn't sure who she was more worried about, Giovanni's men or Mateo.

She placed a hand on Giovanni's arm and gave him a slight squeeze. She turned her gaze to Mateo. "Signore Savino has been nothing but kind to me. Please, as a personal favour, keep the conversation as pleasant as possible."

She held Mateo's gaze, and eventually saw a slight softening in the deep brown depths. She knew it was for her sake alone and her heart stuttered over the meaning of it. The power she could wield with this man... if only she would allow him into her life.

Mateo bowed his head toward her and looked at Giovanni. "I apologize if I come across as short. I'm eager to reunite Raina with her family. Her mother has been beside herself with concern when she found out about the shooting."

"My mother knows?" Raina gasped in dismay.

She hadn't spent a lot of time with Vee in Venezuela but in the short amount of time that they'd spent together Raina had learned how completely and unreservedly protective her mother was of her. It was a disaster, Vee knowing that Raina had been hurt. It threw the entire Italian episode into a more sinister light. If Vee felt that Mateo couldn't get Raina back, she wouldn't hesitate to call in favours. To ask her husband to come after the people that had hurt her daughter.

Raina turned to Giovanni. "If my mother knows about the shooting, then that means Sotza is involved. Your son is in grave danger."

Giovanni nodded and patted her hand where it lay on his arm. "I had guessed as much when you showed up in this club demanding to see me. My son is in a safe place, I'm not worried for his safety at the moment. I had hoped we could find a way through this mess that might preserve his life."

Raina finally realized exactly why Giovanni had decided that she should marry his son. He believed that in making her his daughter-in-law, he was providing his son with immunity from Sotza's wrath. Though Raina didn't know Sotza very well, she knew enough to understand that if someone hurt her, it didn't matter what their relation was. He would kill them as easily as he would kill a stranger, perhaps even easier.

"You're in luck," Mateo drawled, watching the mini drama from across the table. "Sotza is trusting me with these negotiations. He believes that I will find a way to return Raina to her family, punish those that hurt her and keep the peace between our organizations."

Raina rather thought that was an impossible list to reconcile, but she admired Mateo's self-confidence. He certainly believed himself capable.

"And how do you suggest punishing the perpetrator of Raina's injury without going to war?" Giovanni asked.

"You will be required to hand him over to us as a sign of good faith and justice." Mateo said it as though it was the most natural thing in the world.

Raina's gaze swiveled back to Giovanni. Giovanni brought his hand down on the table, not hard enough to knock over drinks, but with enough force to emphasize his point. "Of course, you know that I will never hand over my only child. This is a ridiculous suggestion and if you continue to insist on the impossible then these negotiations will end."

Mateo shifted his shoulders slightly, not quite a shrug, but enough to give the impression of carelessness. "You'll do as you think best. But once Raina is safely away, we will go to war with you and that war will not end until I have your son's head in the box and on its way back to Venezuela where her mother will gleefully receive it."

"No!" Giovanni snapped. "You will not come into my club, in my city and make such demands. You will show me respect or I will have you all killed and sent back to Venezuela in pieces."

Giovanni moved his arm away from Raina's touch,

showing her that he was including her in that last statement. Her mouth went dry and her heart sank.

What was Mateo doing? Why was he setting the older man off, unbalancing him? She had to believe that there was some rhyme or reason to this madness. The Mateo that she knew always had a strategy and she suspected this was no different. She just wished that she was in on it.

Mateo didn't speak again after Giovanni's threat. He let it hang there, as though showing everyone in the room that he was in control and Giovanni was being ruled by his emotions. Clever. Raina thought perhaps Mateo was trying to undermine Giovanni in front of his people. At least half a dozen men stood off to the side pretending not to listen.

As if coming to the same realization, Giovanni looked at Mateo speculatively. His voice was back to its normal tone as he said, "Perhaps we come to another agreement, one that will be mutually beneficial to both of our organizations."

Mateo shook his head. "You have nothing that we're interested in. Business is good in the Americas and the Butcher wants no more partners." Raina thought that he dropped Sotza's nickname on purpose, especially coming on the heels of Giovanni's chilling threat.

"I'm not suggesting a partnership, more of a merger. A marriage, between our two children, our two houses." Giovanni looked proud of himself for coming up with the solution. He didn't see Mateo stiffen in his seat, his hand twitching against his glass. "Our two organizations are extremely powerful on their own, if we merge then we could be unstoppable. We would have half the world at our fingertips. It is not a thing to be taken lightly."

"No." Mateo said the word with a simple finality. He didn't say anything else.

Giovanni ignored Mateo's denial. "Of course, you'll need

to take my proposal to your boss. I am confident that he will see the sense in it."

"I have no need to take your proposal anywhere. It won't leave this table. Raina is engaged to another and no amount of negotiating will change this."

Giovanni looked at Raina in surprise. "She told me nothing of this when we spoke last night." His voice was chiding.

Raina gritted her teeth. Was now a good time to speak, set the record straight? Was a woman actually engaged if she had no intention of marrying the man? Perhaps she should get up excuse herself, go to the washroom and slip out. It had worked in the animal clinic; it could work in the nightclub.

There is a slight lift to Mateo's lips. "The young lady is taking her time in reconciling herself to the idea of marriage."

Raina had no choice but to roll her eyes at that. "Sure, it's the marriage I object to," she said sarcastically.

"And who exactly is the lucky groom?" Giovanni asked thoughtfully.

"Me," Mateo said simply.

"Of course," Giovanni said. He shrugged his shoulders in a negligent manner. "A natural pairing that will tie up an empire nicely."

Giovanni echoed Raina's earlier thoughts. The trapped feeling that she got whenever she thought about being forced to live out her life as a mafia wife.

"I have become attached to this young lady. I will, of course, hand her over unharmed. But I must insist on one more night with her. The idea of a young person in the house again gives me comfort."

"Absolutely not," Mateo said quickly. "I'm not leaving here without her."

Raina looked from one man to the other. She didn't really want to stay with Giovanni for one more night in his creepy old mansion, but she also didn't want to deal with Mateo, who would put her on instant lockdown and have her every move watched. She'd have a better chance of slipping away from the high-security mansion then her would-be fiancé.

"You won't be leaving here at all if you don't allow this condition," Giovanni drawled coldly, his eyes chips of ice. "Do you really want your future wife drawn into a gun fight?"

Raina's heart pounded in her chest as every man and woman in the club tensed, awaiting Mateo's response.

Mateo stared back at Giovanni as though they were the only two people in the room. Finally, Mateo gave a short jerk of his head. Though he spoke to Giovanni, his intense gaze moved to Raina as if burning her features into his memory. "You will hand her over in the morning. If not, then I will consider us at war."

"Good, that's settled then," Giovanni said jovially pushing his chair back and standing. He reached a hand out to Raina, helping her from her seat. "I will have her delivered to you tomorrow morning in your hotel suite at 10 AM sharp."

Waves of tension flowed from Mateo as she and Giovanni turned away from the table and left the club. Raina shivered and wondered what would happen between them when she no longer had Giovanni as a buffer.

CHAPTER ELEVEN

Raina sat stiffly in the back of Giovanni's limo as they headed back to the mansion. She glared out the window ignoring the passing scenery.

"You seem agitated," Giovanni commented.

She turned her glare on him. "I get that way when people threaten to chop me up and send me back to my parents in pieces."

Giovanni chuckled and reached out to pat her hand. "Posturing, my dear. Your suitor back there would have respected me less had I simply given in to his demands. He was posturing as well. He knew damn well I wouldn't give my son up to him."

Raina thought that there was rather a lot of wiggle room between handing her over to Mateo or mailing her home in pieces. She didn't particularly like either option, but she knew which one she would choose if she had to.

"Would you have me killed if you believed it necessary? If you believed you had the upper hand with my stepfather and Mateo?"

To his credit, and though it chilled her to the bone,

Giovanni actually gave thought to her questions. Finally, he shook his head. "No, I don't believe I would. Perhaps it's my age, perhaps it's your age and the fact that you are a woman. But the idea of snuffing out your light is untenable to me. I feel invested in your future now, though you have brought this problem to me."

Raina blushed. Everything that had happened to her in the past few days had been a blur. She hadn't really stopped to think about the consequences of her actions. Giovanni was such a force of nature, head of the Italian mafia. How could she hurt him? But he was still human, still capable of emotion. It had to bother him knowing that his son's life was in danger.

"Did you decide to keep me with you tonight as insurance so that Mateo won't go after Antonio?"

"You are a smart one, aren't you?" Giovanni said with a laugh, patting her hand again. "Though I do enjoy your company, your presence will ensure Antonio's safety for another day until I can get him out of the country and hidden from Mateo. Your young man has quite a bloody reputation, one that rivals even his boss. Gutierrez is an unparalleled hunter and he doesn't quit. Two skills that I would love to have on my payroll but has also put me in a quandary. To be completely honest, if I thought I could get away with it, I would have Gutierrez taken out while he is here in my city. But that would put me at war with your stepfather, not something I'm sure I could win."

Raina was shocked with how candid Giovanni was being with her. She supposed he no longer needed to keep anything from her. They both knew the score now.

"Did you ever intend for me to marry your son, or were you trying to frighten me?" she asked curiously. The idea was clearly off the table now, but she wanted to know how serious Giovanni had been about it.

He shrugged. "It would have been a good merger. But no, I don't believe a marriage between you and my son is appropriate at this time. One or both of you would end up dead and I've become rather fond of you."

Raina let out a laugh. Giovanni had a gift for both overstatement and understatement that she was beginning to appreciate. She liked the Italian Godfather and thought she might miss him when she left. Perhaps he would allow her to come back to Italy for a visit sometime.

"So, for now, we get to enjoy each other's company for one more evening. You will indulge my desire for company, will you not?" he asked, attempting to look rather pathetic. An attempt that didn't work on Raina given his expensive clothes, jewelry and overall attitude of arrogance.

"Of course," Raina said warmly. Now that she was comfortable in the knowledge that he wouldn't try to have her killed or hand her over to his son in marriage, she was willing to relax and enjoy his company for an evening.

"Tomorrow," he said, giving her a wink, "we will work on extricating you from Italy and continuing your adventure."

Raina grinned at Giovanni. She suspected that she had made a lifelong friend and ally in one of the most powerful men in the world.

CHAPTER TWELVE

Sotza was not pleased that his second-in-command hadn't managed to retrieve his stepdaughter. Vee was even less pleased.

"There was absolutely no excuse to have left that club without my daughter." Vee's voice echoed sharply through the room.

Mateo's phone sat propped up on the nightstand on speakerphone. He was laying stretched out on the bed, his arms behind his head, his eyes closed. He was not relaxed though. He was thinking. He didn't trust Savino, didn't trust the man to hand Raina over. Mateo believed he had another plan.

"There were no less than a dozen of Savino's men inside and outside the club. Had I brought everyone on hand with me, they wouldn't have been enough to get us all out alive. Raina might have been shot during the standoff. I had no choice but to allow Savino to leave with her."

"I don't believe that. You're supposed to be a professional, Mateo, and you're telling me that you couldn't extricate one girl from Italy. Incompetent - " Mateo tuned Vee out as she continued on her angry tirade.

Mateo was steadily losing patience with Vee. Only two things kept him from going on the offensive with her; his employer would have him killed and Mateo loved her daughter. He refused to do anything to harm Raina, even indirectly. She would never forgive Mateo if he went after her mother. Which left Mateo to suffer the woman's disrespect.

"You made the correct choice." Sotza interrupted his Vee.

He was used to stepping in between his wife and his second-in-command. From the moment Vee helped her daughter leave the Venezuelan mountains, helped her leave Mateo, she'd made an enemy of him. Sotza cared for them both and tried to keep the peace, though it tested his already thin patience.

Focusing on his boss, Mateo said, "I have people near Savino's estate where the guards won't see them. Ready to storm the place if it seems like Raina might be in any danger, though I got the sense that Savino feels somewhat paternal toward her."

"Good enough for now," Sotza said.

"Not good enough!" Vee snarled into the phone. "I need to hear her voice, know that she's alive and well."

"My word is good enough," Mateo snarled back. There was only so much he was willing to take from the woman and insulting him at every turn was unacceptable. She acted as though he wasn't just as invested in keeping Raina alive.

There was some unintelligible mumbling from the other side of the phone, then the slam of the door, loud enough that even Mateo's phone jumped. He smirked. Señora Sotza had left the office.

"Between you and me, my wife will not be happy again until she sets eyes on her daughter. Get the girl and bring her home. Do not delay if you can help it." What he didn't say was that his marriage would not be a happy one until Vee got what she wanted.

Mateo didn't envy the other man his choice of wife, but he got it. Despite his better judgement, Mateo was hopelessly fucked up over the daughter. And the daughter was very like the mother. It was a mystery to him how he could love one and despise the other. But he wasn't the type of guy to look too deeply at himself and his motives. He lived his life the best way he knew how. And what he knew was that having Raina in his life would complete him.

"I'll bring her home, you have my word," Mateo told his boss.

"I have full confidence," Sotza said calmly, and they both knew it was true. Mateo would not be Sotza's second if Sotza didn't trust him completely and utterly.

A slight smirk curled the edge of Mateo's lip. "You can tell your wife to prepare for a wedding. A happy occasion should put her in a better mood, don't you think?"

"You enjoy testing my patience." There was humour in Sotza's voice. "My wife would gut me with her new dagger if I so much as suggested her daughter might be marrying into the organization."

Mateo opened his eyes to stare at the ceiling. "It's a fact. Best she prepare herself. I will be marrying Raina."

As soon as he could get his hands on her.

CHAPTER THIRTEEN

Once again Raina slept well in Giovanni's mansion. She was growing more comfortable around Giovanni and his home. It was almost a shame that she had to leave. She suspected that spending more time with the proud Italian would give her a real glimpse of Italy. With that in mind, she decided to try to convince him to let her visit sometime in the future.

She pulled herself from the bed, wincing as her back muscles pulled on her stitches. The healing process was going to be long and painful, but she was grateful that no permanent damage had been done. It could've been much, much worse.

There was a pile of clothing for her on one of the chairs. She pulled them on one at a time, grateful that a dress had been chosen for her because it was so much easier on her injury. She could pull it over her head and tug it down, she didn't have to deal with a waistband pressing against her bandage.

She brushed her teeth and ran a comb through her blonde hair. She eyed it critically in the mirror. It was getting long again and she preferred to keep it around shoulder length. Her hair was fine and there was a lot of it. It tended towards the curly side and would get hopelessly tangled if she wasn't brushing it often. She placed the comb on the counter, gave her appearance one more critical look, and left the bathroom.

She meandered down the stairs slowly, lightly touching her fingers against the banister and looking around her as she descended. The house was definitely much less gloomy during the day. The darker furnishings, the austere pictures on the wall, there was a certain charm to them. Though she wouldn't want them in her own home, they suited Giovanni.

She found him at the dining room table, which had been uncovered and dusted off. On his placemat was a plate with toast, a glass of orange juice and a cup of coffee next to his elbow. Spread out in front of him was a newspaper. He looked up and caught sight of her, a smile stretching his lips.

"I'm going to miss you when you're gone, bella." He folded the newspaper and set it aside. "You have brought life to my home. I've always been careful of who I allow inside, becoming guarded throughout the years. It was necessary, as I have many enemies, but still, you're like a breeze of fresh air in this place."

Raina sank into the chair beside him and smiled. They had only known each other for two days, yet they seemed to have forged an unlikely friendship. The Italian Godfather and the young daughter of American mafia royalty. The child of farmers. She felt an appreciation for Giovanni. Though he was somewhat old-fashioned, quite arrogant, and liked to have his own way, he wasn't completely unreasonable. He'd helped her when she needed him. She was grateful and always would be.

"I've been thinking about that," she said, reaching for the pile of toast and taking one off the top. It was still warm to the touch, butter making it soft. She placed it on a plate in front of her and spread jam on it. "Maybe we could see each other again sometime."

She felt as though there were a connection between her and Giovanni. Completely platonic, but kindred spirits. The thought of never seeing him again was depressing.

"I would like that very much," Giovanni reassured her. "You're welcome in my home anytime you want, my dear. Even if you bring a boatload of trouble with you."

Raina didn't bother to point out that it was Giovanni's own son that had started the boatload of trouble. She glanced down at the time on her phone. It was 9:28 AM. She was expected in Mateo's hotel suite soon. She would have to leave the house right away if she wanted to get there on time.

Giovanni seemed to sense her mood and reached out to squeeze her hand. He studied her thoughtfully. "I'm curious about your feelings towards the young man that professes himself your fiancé."

Raina's heart sped up as an image of Mateo flashed through her mind. As always, her feelings were conflicted. Part of her wanted him desperately, wanted the dark power that he possessed, that rock solid body, the devotion that he offered her. But the rest of her shied away from the idea of marriage to a man as entrenched in the mafia as Mateo was.

"I can tell by your expression that you're not sure of your feelings. Do you want to go to him? Do you want to leave Italy with him? Go back to your stepfather?" He studied her carefully as she thought about it.

"I don't know," she murmured. She spoke her thoughts out loud. "On the one hand I would love to see my mother again. But doing that means going back to Venezuela and facing a wedding that I'm not sure about, that I haven't agreed to."

"And this wedding, "Giovanni said. "It is something that you do not want?"

Raina shook her head. "I don't know. I... I feel like I'm too young to get married. I haven't seen enough of the world. I don't know what the future holds and I fear if I marry Mateo, I'll never get a say in my own future. I'm not afraid of my feelings for him and there are some very strong feelings. No, I'm terrified of what the future holds. I'm not quite ready to face it yet."

Giovanni nodded thoughtfully. He picked up the napkin that was across his lap and dabbed his lips then dropped it on the table. He leaned back in his chair and looked at Raina, but his gaze was in a different place, maybe thinking of a different person.

He confirmed her thoughts with his next words. "My wife, Antonia, was very young when we married. Nineteen years. She was so beautiful, so bright, so full of life. She was thirty-four when she died."

Raina could hear the longing and the love in his voice and it made her heart ache with sympathy. "I'm so sorry for your loss, Giovanni."

"It's been many years since I lost her and I still see her face in my head as clear as day. She might have left me, but I haven't lost her." Giovanni stopped for a few seconds, overcome by emotion. He gathered himself. Raina surreptitiously swiped at her eyes. "Ours was an arranged marriage but we were happy."

Raina believed that he was trying to tell her something. Perhaps it was that her and Mateo's passion might overcome the origin of their relationship. That their story could end as happily as Giovanni's and Antonia's.

Giovanni's eyes sharpened, away from the past as he looked toward the present again. "We married too young. There were too many things that we both should have done before we settled down. And though ours was a great love, I have many regrets. I didn't treat her as well as I should have.

I didn't have the patience for my family, didn't spend enough time with them. As evidenced by the way my son has treated you. My wife should've been given many more years of freedom before she was tied to the mob."

Giovanni reached into the breast pocket of his jacket and pulled something out. He placed it on the table in front of Raina. She recognized it instantly, because she had made many forgeries of these documents before.

"A passport." She reached for the document and flipped it open. It was a replica of her old passport photo, the one that would have been in her studio apartment when Antonio's men had shot it up. The passport looked completely legitimate, though she knew it was a skilled forgery.

"You will use this to go anywhere in the world that you want." Giovanni reached out to take her wrist in a tight hold. His hand was as tense as his voice when he spoke. "You must choose very carefully where you will go, because Mateo Gutierrez will be directly on your heels. He doesn't like to lose and he's world renowned for his tracking abilities."

Raina looked at Giovanni with a smile filled with relief and happiness. She wouldn't have to make a decision about Mateo. At least not right now.

"I've managed to elude him for two years, I've no doubt that I can get myself lost somewhere in this world."

Giovanni shook his head and waved his hand in the air. "I've known of Gutierrez's reputation for a long time now. Had I been able to employ him I would have. But your stepfather keeps him close at hand, utilizing his skills only for himself and the Sotza Empire. Mateo is the best tracker in the world. He's unparalleled. I have heard that his skill is like magic, the uncanny ability to know where his victims are hiding."

A chill slithered down Raina's spine. "Then that would mean that he always knew where I was. That he chose to allow me to travel the world for those two years. That he has now chosen to come and collect me."

Raina wanted Giovanni to deny her words, to tell her that wasn't Mateo's plan. That somehow he managed to find her in the nick of time to stop Antonio's men from killing her. She knew better. She'd been stupid to think otherwise. Naïve.

"He will find you wherever you choose to go next. That is why I implore you to choose carefully. Don't try to hide or evade him, because it won't work. He'll find you, he'll scoop you up and he'll take you home. If you wish to make the most of the few days you have left of freedom, choose a destination that truly means something to you."

Wise words, Raina thought to herself. Where should she go? If Mateo was going to follow her, then maybe she should give up and hand herself over. Because there was a part of her heart that was in Venezuela, that longed to go back.

Then it hit her. She knew exactly where she was going to go and it wasn't straight into Mateo's arms. Not yet. That was a future problem. She was going to run one more time, with Giovanni's help.

Then another thought occurred to her. She looked at Giovanni with concern. "Your son."

She didn't say more than that, she didn't need to. Giovanni had told them that his son was hidden away and Mateo wouldn't find him. But today he was telling her that Mateo could track anyone. And Giovanni was about to lose Raina as his leverage.

Giovanni seemed to slump in his seat, aging somewhat. He was about to lose his only child and there was nothing he could do but stand by and accept the loss, because his son had committed the grave error of attempting to kill Sotza's princess.

Raina's heart ached for him and for the decisions he'd had to make in the past few days. He was an intelligent man. He probably realized from the moment he intended to let Raina go that he was signing his own child's death warrant. She didn't understand why he didn't fight harder for the life of his son and it wasn't her place to ask him.

Giovanni leaned over and kissed her cheek before sitting back in his seat. "God speed on your journey, my young friend."

CHAPTER FOURTEEN

Mateo was lying on his hotel bed fully clothed, his legs stretched out, his arms over his head, his hands tucked under his biceps. It was a deceptively lazy pose. Deceptive because the coiled tension running through him meant he could be on his feet in a split second. He was not relaxed. He was annoyed, bordering on angry.

It was 10:05 AM and Raina had not been delivered to his hotel room as promised. Apparently, Giovanni was not afraid of playing him, a mistake that would cost the old man dearly. Mateo didn't deal well with hitches in his plans and so far, Italy had been a complete clusterfuck.

In fact, when Mateo really thought about it, he realized that the common denominator was Raina. If Mateo were to be honest with himself, he would've realized from the moment he set hands on her that she was going to throw a huge wrench into his life. That day, more than two years ago, when he had first seen her, his whole world had turned upside down. She was the most beautiful woman he'd ever seen, her energy and joy in life so fucking attractive, that he'd lost all sense. In reality he didn't know if she was the most beautiful woman in the world, but to him she was the gold standard.

And touching her, fucking touching that soft skin, it'd gone straight to his head. He'd forgotten who he was and what he was doing there, that he was supposed to be picking up the daughter of his boss's new love interest. It should have been a simple chore, almost beneath him. But that day Raina had shown him exactly how not beneath him she was.

She turned on him in an instant, like a wildcat, fighting for her freedom. He'd been so stunned by her he almost hadn't reacted quickly enough. Of course, she had been no match for him, but the struggle had been sweet. Her slim curves wiggling underneath him, her scent invading his nostrils. The only thing that had stopped him from fucking her into the ground right then and there was the campus security guard who stumbled upon them.

Reflecting back, Mateo was grateful for that interruption. That hadn't been the time, nor the place. But their time was coming soon, very soon.

If he could only find the damn woman. He was getting tired of losing her. He picked up his phone and commanded it to call Giovanni Savino's number.

Giovanni picked up on the first ring. "Gutierrez," Giovanni said jovially enough. "I've been expecting your call."

"It's after 10." Mateo didn't bother with pleasantries. There would be no point if he had to kill the other man. "Tell me where my woman is."

Since Mateo was being blunt, Giovanni decided to give him the same respect. "Your young Ms. Duncan is no longer in Italy."

Mateo quickly calculated the complexities of this new situation. If Raina was no longer in Italy, then Giovanni no longer had leverage over Mateo. He was essentially unleashing the younger man and inviting him to come and destroy his home. The only way that Giovanni would take such a risk is if he believed he might be able to gain the upper hand. Go on the offensive.

Mateo slid his hand from behind his head and underneath his pillow gripping his gun and pulling it out. "You've decided not to honour our agreement," Mateo stated.

"I have warned my son," Giovanni said, his voice betraying a hint of worry. "He is my blood."

Mateo stood and reached for his holster which was slung across his leather jacket on the back of the hotel chair. With quick efficient movements he pulled the holster on. He pulled his second gun from the holster. He placed each weapon on the table, strapped his knife to his belt and shoved his taser in his other pocket. Though Mateo was right-handed, he'd spent many years teaching himself to be equally as efficient with both hands. He was an excellent shot with both his right and his left hand. He could gut a man in seconds with either hand. And the taser was just for fun.

"I apologize for coming across as unprofessional," Giovanni said formally. "I don't usually play such games, nor do I condone them. But for the sake of both my son and the young lady I decided to renegotiate terms."

"You let her go." Mateo was relieved.

When Giovanni said that she was no longer in Italy, Mateo had been concerned that Giovanni had done something to her. Perhaps passed her along to his son. Mateo had seen Raina's and Giovanni's interactions and had come to the conclusion that the two had bonded. He was glad that that seemed to be the case.

"Raina reminds me of the daughter I never had but always wanted. Free-spirited, lovely inside and out, sharp as a tack and able to use her intelligence as a weapon. I've come to admire her. It seemed a shame to force her into a marriage that she doesn't want."

Mateo was surprised by the other man's assessment of Raina. He wasn't wrong. In fact, he had described her perfectly. But it took perception to see these things in another person. And in Mateo's experience most people weren't perceptive enough to pay attention to their environment, let alone the complexities of the people around them. Raina was young, and impetuous, it would be easy to write her personality off as youthful arrogance. But there was so much more to her than that.

While Giovanni spoke, Mateo prepared his things, packing his bag and making sure every weapon he had was on hand. He sent a quick text to his people letting them know that they were about to be attacked. He sent them coordinates for meeting and told them to scatter and re-converge in an hour. As per Mateo's long-standing rule, every member of his team texted back with a thumb's up, telling him they were all alive.

They didn't question his order. And though they were protective of him, treating him like the boss when they were with Mateo instead of Sotza, he was still head of the security team.

"Well you may have come to understand Raina's personality, I don't believe that you understand what she needs. The more she runs, the more likely she is to get herself into trouble. And next time, I may not be able to make it in time to save her from the Antonios of the world."

Mateo's words must've hit home, because the older man sucked in a deep breath, almost a gasp. He'd been part of the mafia long enough to read between the lines. Mateo blamed both Antonio and Giovanni for what happened to Raina. Raina's departure from Italy opened the door for Mateo to do what he needed to do to ensure that the entire underworld knew that a threat to his woman was a threat to him and Sotza's entire organization.

"My son did a very stupid thing by going after Raina. Regardless of who her family is, I would never condone his actions. He hired her to do a job and then he double-crossed her. I assure you I taught him better." Giovanni sounded exhausted all of a sudden. "He has grown too arrogant for his role as my successor."

"You're stalling." The older man was keeping Mateo on the phone and he was doing it for a reason. He was giving Antonio and his men time.

Mateo stood to the side of his door, his guns at the ready.

"As are you," Giovanni said coldly.

It was true. Mateo needed to ensure that everything was in place before he confronted Antonio's team, the one he would've mobilized when his father warned him that Mateo would be coming after him. They were either on their way or here already. Mateo hoped that his own team had managed to leave the hotel, that he'd gotten them the message in time.

Mateo dropped to one knee and reached up to unlock the door. The click of the latch was like the starting shot of a race; within seconds all hell broke loose.

The door smashed open banging into the wall. Two huge men came crashing through the door guns blazing. It pissed Matteo off that they didn't seem to care what the fuck they hit. What if housekeeping had been in the room?

He heard the lamp shatter, the TV explode, and bullets thunking into the furniture and the walls. Fucking unprofessional. If Mateo wasn't planning on killing them, he'd be having a long conversation with them about the etiquette of gunplay.

Mateo lunged to his feet behind them and put a bullet in each of their heads. They both died instantly, hitting the ground in unison. For Mateo, killing was poetry. It had a certain flow to it that appealed to him.

His phone was still on speaker and Giovanni's voice was

sharp and agitated. "Antonio, Antonio, mio bambino, are you there?"

Mateo held the phone up to his face as he glanced around the corner and into the hallway. There was no one out there, though he was certain there would men in the building, more for him to kill. "I'm still here," Mateo said, his lip lifting in a sneer. "You can tell your son I'm coming for him."

CHAPTER FIFTEEN

Twelve hours and one connection after her conversation with Giovanni and Raina was touching down in Pennsylvania, her home state. She thought coming back to Pennsylvania would give a sense of coming home. It had been over two years since she was kidnapped from her University campus and this was her first time back.

As she gazed out her window, she felt a sense of nostalgia, but not home. Maybe the home feelings would come back to her when she was back with her mom and dad, in their farmhouse. Or maybe she had outgrown her home. She grew up there, but she knew at a young age that she was adopted. It wasn't something that her mom and dad told her, because they would never want to hurt her, but more a deep-seated knowledge that she wasn't blood-related to them.

And while blood shouldn't matter, unfortunately, as Raina grew from a small child into her teens it came to matter to the Duncan family. At age nine, Raina was diagnosed with kidney failure. She went on dialysis for three years, and when she turned twelve, she was deemed old enough, or desperate enough, to receive a lifesaving transplant.

It wasn't until she had met Elvira, her birth mother, that she realized who the kidney donor had been. She'd seen the scar on her mother's back; a scar that matched Raina's.

If Joe and Diane have been able to donate a kidney to Raina, she was positive that they would've handed over every single kidney they had between the two of them. That was how much her adoptive parents loved her. And she loved them back. Wholeheartedly, unreservedly and without question. Even when Raina found out that they were also mob-affiliated, it hadn't changed the way she felt about them. They were her parents and that would never change.

Sometimes Raina felt a slight sense of guilt that she couldn't give them exactly what they wanted in a child. Not that they ever told her otherwise, but she knew, deep down, that they'd wanted a daughter a little more like them. One with both feet and a brain planted in reality. A child that didn't long to explore the world and everything in it. A child that wouldn't use her intelligence for illegal gain.

From the moment Raina learned that forging documents was a thing, she'd been in whole hog. Something about the fine detail, the subterfuge and outsmarting the authorities called to her when she worked. It was something she didn't want to lose and tried to work on as often as she could. Something that she tried to keep from Joe and Diane, but she suspected she failed.

Raina was deep in thought when the plane finally taxied to a halt. She snapped back to attention when the people all around her began to stand, stretch and reach for the overhead bins. Raina waited until it was her turn to disembark before she stood, grabbed her purse from under the seat in front of her and her overnight bag from the bin above. Her back jolted in pain as she reached up, reminding her of her recent injury.

It felt so strange being back in the United States, back at

the airport where she'd taken her very first flight as a child. They'd flown to Philadelphia for her kidney consultations. Raina had loved going to the big city. She'd felt important and special.

Raina followed the lineup of people ahead of her off the airplane, into the airwalk and through the airport towards arrivals.

Raina hadn't told anyone that she was coming, just in case something happened to her plans. Like Mateo somehow finding and stopping her. So she was completely unprepared for the sight of her loved ones when she walked through the sliding frosted doors. When they caught sight of her, they made an unholy amount of noise, drawing attention from the people around them.

Raina grinned from ear to ear and threw herself at her parents. They enveloped her completely between the two of them. They were both taller and wider than her, so it wasn't a difficult thing to do. After a long family hug, then separate hugs for each of her parents, Raina turned to her two best friends, Cass and Noah.

Cass squealed and squeezed Raina so hard that she had to fight for air. Cass's long curly brown hair surrounded them in a cloud. The second Cass let go, Noah snatched Raina off her feet swung her around, crushing her in a bear hug. She yelped as her back twinged but didn't demand he put her down. It felt good getting a Noah hug. This was how Noah had always greeted her and Cass when he hadn't seen them in a while.

She squeezed him extra hard and then let go. She studied him for a second, admiring the way his features seem to be growing out of their youthful roundness. He was a man and a good-looking one at that.

"How did you know I was coming?" Raina asked happily, her arms around Cass and Noah as she turned back to her parents.

Joe took Raina's overnight bag while Diane answered her question. "Mateo told us," she said as if that explained everything.

Raina blinked and tried to make sense of what her mother had said. Since when were her parents on a first name basis with Sotza's second-in-command?

They made their way toward the baggage claim and as they walked, Diane answered her unspoken question. "The night that we left with you from Venezuela in the helicopter, he was following close behind. It was very shortly after we put you on a plane to Beijing that he... met with us."

Diane cast a glance toward Cass and Noah. Cass was watching Raina and her parents carefully, as though she sensed that she had missed something very important in Raina's life. Diane was being careful as she talked, making it sound as though Mateo was simply a family friend instead of the man who probably confronted and terrorized her parents. A shiver ran through her.

"But he didn't follow me to Beijing?" Raina asked thoughtfully.

"I think Mateo saw the wisdom in allowing you to follow your plan of travelling the world. You were too young for a boyfriend... of his age." Joe spoke this time, his voice less tearful than Diane's. Raina studied him carefully. Though he seemed happy to have her back, he also seemed different. Aged somehow.

Raina's heart broke as she realized the impact of the last few years on her family and friends. Cass and Noah had probably been given some kind of story about her travelling the world. It was a miracle they even still cared enough about her to show up at the airport given she hadn't been able to speak to them. She'd essentially been in hiding. She hadn't really spoken to anyone except her birth mother, who had assured her that she was passing on messages to Joe and Diane. While

Raina had been enjoying her time exploring city after city, country after country, her friends and family had been suffering.

She would have to find a way to make it up to them. But for now, she was exhausted and truly happy to be home.

They collected her bags and made their way out of the airport, driving back toward the farm, which was about forty-five minutes away. They dropped Cass and Noah off at their home in the town closest to the farm. The three of them agreed that they would see each other the next day. Then Raina watched with curiosity as the other two made their way inside the same apartment building. Was something going on between them? Maybe they were roommates? Maybe they had separate apartments in the same building? The apartment building wasn't a place that Raina had ever visited before. It made sense that Cass and Noah would move out from home. Both were the same age as her, twenty-one.

As Raina, Joe and Diane drove out toward the farm, Raina was able to speak freely. She spoke with enthusiasm of all the places she visited, all the things she'd done. They were an avid audience and some of Joe's heaviness seem to lift as she spoke, as he realized that Raina hadn't been suffering, that she had been safe and happy while away from them.

"It's so wonderful to hear you speak of your adventures. Of course, we always knew where you were. Mateo kept us updated every step of the way. In fact, he would call at least once a week. It helped, knowing that someone like him was keeping an eye on you," Diane said with a smile and an obvious soft spot for a hardened killer.

Raina was stunned. Not only had Mateo known about Beijing, but, as Giovanni had suggested, it was starting to sound like he'd known where she was the entire time she was gone. She'd had no reason to look over her shoulder constantly as she travelled because he'd been with her every step of the way. Maybe not physically, although she'd bet money that he had people on her.

While a part of her had suspected, actually knowing how close he was the entire time pissed her off. She'd never really been free. She'd only been given a couple more feet of leash. He could've picked her up at any time. And why the fuck was he talking to her parents once a week?

"He's not a good person, mom. He's dangerous and you should keep your distance from him," she snapped, glaring out the window as they pulled into the farmyard.

Diane seem taken aback by Raina's vehemence. Raina was usually pretty even-tempered. She would always stand up for herself if she thought there was a need, but she rarely snapped at anyone. Mateo brought the worst out in her.

"We know he's dangerous, dear," Diane said dryly, as though Raina was speaking the obvious. Diane and Joe knew exactly who Mateo was and the organization that he was affiliated with. They'd been involved in a similar scene in Miami before adopting Raina and moving to Pennsylvania. "But I won't pretend that I'm not grateful to him for ensuring your safety and for keeping us updated. If it weren't for that we would've been out of our minds with worry."

Raina's annoyance melted away and she reached out to take Diane's hand. "I'm sorry, mom. I should've called. But I thought I was being watched; I didn't think I could be in contact with anyone without them picking me up. Now I know it wasn't necessary."

Diane waved her hand in front of them as if the waving away Raina's words. "You have nothing to be sorry for. From the moment you were taken and reunited with your mother, things were out of your hands. We've always loved you and that will never change. You were doing what you thought was best."

Raina's eyes misted over. Her parents were the definition

of unconditional love. It didn't matter what she did, how badly she screwed up, they would never blame her. Which is why she felt so protective of them. People who could think, feel and act the way Joe and Diane did were rare in her opinion and she would do whatever it took to protect the love that the three of them had for each other.

They carried Raina's things into the farmhouse, dumping the suitcases by the door. Joe would carry them to Raina's old bedroom later, after the three of them had a good visit and maybe watched some TV. Now that Raina realized the extent of Mateo's relationship with her parents, she knew that he wouldn't be far behind.

She didn't know what he intended to do with her after that; whether he'd allow her to have her visit or drag her straight back to Venezuela. So, she would have to make the most of her time with her family and friends. She was done running. This was it. Her standoff on her home ground.

"What's for supper?" she asked happily following her mom through the front entrance and into the kitchen.

CHAPTER SIXTEEN

Raina examined herself in the mirror in her childhood bedroom at her parent's farm. She looked pretty damn hot, if she did say so herself. She had flat ironed her hair until it was straight as a stick and sitting about halfway down her back. It was normally a wavy curly, but sometimes she liked the look of another style. It made her feel chic and different. Like a woman about to have a night on the town, even if the town had a population of only 3000 people.

They were going to a country bar; the only real bar in the area.

Raina was wearing a pair of tight black skinny jeans with rips in the thighs and knees. The jeans were about three years old, left behind from when she went to college. They still fit perfectly and gave her some extra confidence. Raina was small boned, small featured, short, and well, pretty much small all over. Including her ass. But somehow, through magic unknown to her, the jeans gave her a real ass, lifted up, and stuck it right out there. She couldn't wait until some cowboy filled his hands with it.

She also wore an off-the-shoulder red peasant blouse and a

pair of genuine cowboy boots. She never really needed them, and to be completely honest, she had bought them for the country bar scene a few years ago. But they were gorgeous and she wasn't going to let their lack of authenticity stop them from shining. She loved them for their brown leather, heels, and rhinestones.

"You make that look good," Cass said, breezing into Raina's room and flopping down on the bed.

It was like old times and it made Raina smile with gratitude. It was like she never left. Everyone was treating her as though she'd only been gone on a vacation, not left for two years without a word.

"I know, right? Don't you love the boots?" Raina stuck her foot out for Cass to see.

"You've never touched a cow in your life, unless it came in burger form," Cass pointed out.

"Shush!" Raina laughed. "The boots don't know that."

Cass and Raina talked about what they were wearing, where they were going and who they might see there. Raina sat at her desk with a small mirror propped up against her lamp and applied her makeup. Raina rarely wore very much make up, though she liked the effect of making her features look more sophisticated. She put a bit more effort in for their evening out.

"I think Evan, Darcy and Dwayne are going to be out tonight. Darcy had a thing for you, didn't he?" Cass asked with fake innocence.

Raina didn't say anything. Yes, Darcy had had a thing for Raina and had never kept it much of the secret. At one point in her life, she'd indulged in a few fantasies about him. Of throwing his cowboy ass onto a hay bale and climbing on top of him. But she was smart enough to know that the reality probably wouldn't match the fantasy. That big cowboy was best left locked up in fantasyland.

Being involved in the underworld, the way she'd been dragged into it, changed her perspective on everything. Darcy, the town she grew up in, the farmhouse, it all seemed so innocent to her now. It was like all those things were now a part of her childhood, neatly packaged and set aside to examine when she felt nostalgic. This place was no longer her reality, and like Alice in Wonderland, she couldn't stay.

When Raina finished putting on her lip gloss, she pressed her lips together and turned to face Cass. "Time to go?" She stood up and twirled. She was truly very excited for a night on the town with old friends.

"Time to go." Cass stood and straightened her skirt. She wore a short black skirt with a black tank top emblazoned with a broken heart and the word 'heartbreaker' across it. On her feet were a pair of hot pink stilettos.

Heads turned when Cass and Raina entered the bar. It was so obvious that it was almost laughable. Raina looked at Cass and whispered, "Why are they staring at us?"

Raina had a healthy amount of self-confidence, something she'd built up over the years. She objectively knew she was a good-looking woman, but she'd never turned this many heads before by walking into a room.

Cass burst out laughing. "They're not looking at us, they're looking at you specifically. You disappeared straight off your university campus without a single word for two years, and suddenly you show back up again looking like a supermodel." Cass looked her up and down. "A really short supermodel."

Raina grinned and rolled her eyes. "Sure, thanks. Small town curiosity then."

They made their way to the back of the room, weaving around tables and heading past the bar to where Noah was waving at them from a table in the corner. Raina was grateful he thought to come out ahead of them and grab a table, because the room was crowded and she wasn't sure they'd have gotten a table otherwise. Noah already had a drink in front of him and next to his drink were two glasses of champagne.

Raina and Cass slid into their seats and thanked Noah for the drinks. They toasted and took a sip. Raina savoured the bubbles as they touched her tongue. This would be her only drink for the night. As always, she had to be very aware of everything she put in her body, but a glass of champagne with her two best friends was a necessity.

Cass picked up the conversation where they left off. "When you were taken away and no one knew where you were, we were frantic. Noah and I practically burned the university down searching for you. Your parents drove up and helped us. They were just as bewildered and frightened as we were, but for some reason they didn't want to go to the authorities."

Cass looked at Raina questioningly and Raina shifted in her chair. She knew why Joe and Diane wouldn't want to go to the police. They probably suspected the mafia connection was the reason for Raina's disappearance. They would have known that her life could've been even more in danger had they involved the police.

Curious, Raina asked, "And did they go to the police eventually?"

Noah gave her a strange look. "No, you contacted them two days after you went missing and told them where you were before they could make the decision to report you missing." At Raina's blank look he continued, as if trying to prompt her. "You told them you needed time to yourself to figure things out. That you wanted to travel, that you felt bad for dropping out of University, which is why you took off without a word."

Raina sat with her mouth hanging open. It was quite a

story and not a bit of it was true. But that wasn't what shocked her. Of course, her parents would have had to come up with something to appease her friends when Raina didn't come back. They would never understand why her parents wouldn't report her missing. What surprised Raina was the timeline. Two days after she'd gone missing. Who had contacted them and what had they said to her parents? Joe and Diane would've been frantic. Had someone taken that into consideration and attempted to reassure her parents?

Raina knew the answer to that. Mateo. He would have wanted to reassure her family; not only to keep them from going to the police, but because he would've known it would hurt Raina to know that her parents were upset. Raina knew this as well as she knew herself. Because she knew Mateo.

Unwilling to go down that path, Raina drained the rest of her champagne, giving herself a nice buzz. She grinned broadly at her two friends. "Who wants to dance?"

CHAPTER SEVENTEEN

"So, you and Cass," Raina said casually while she was dancing with Noah.

Raina was having an awesome night. She and her two best friends spent hours talking and dancing, talking and drinking, Raina mostly drinking pop and flirting with the local cowboys. Though Noah didn't join in, he was totally fine with the girls objectifying the boys. He knew it was all in good fun.

Raina's gunshot wound gave her the occasional bolt of pain, but it seemed to be healing quickly. As long as she didn't dance too energetically, she felt fine. Good enough for the occasional two-step.

Cass had gone to the bathroom. Before leaving Raina and Noah on the dance floor, she said she was going to order more drinks and have them waiting at the table. Raina decided to take this opportunity to grill Noah about his intentions toward her friend. Of course, he was equally Raina's friend, all three of them having grown up together, gone to high school together and then off to college together. They had been inseparable until the day Raina was kidnapped.

Now, dancing to the beat of Old Town Road, Raina confronted Noah about this new development in their trio.

To his credit, Noah didn't miss a beat, and he didn't pretend he didn't know what Raina was talking about. "I love her," he said simply, his gaze straying toward the table.

When he didn't immediately see Cass, he swept the bar with a hawk-like gaze until he spotted her ordering their drinks. He visibly relaxed when he set eyes on his girlfriend. She was leaning over the bar, her ass stuck out. It was clear exactly where his gaze had zeroed in on.

"Thank you, Captain Obvious," Raina said, rolling her eyes at him. "You've been in love with Cass since kindergarten. I think the whole town knows that's why you've been hanging out with a couple of girls through your entire educational career. What I'm asking is, when did she sit up and finally notice?"

Noah grinned, his pride in their relationship clear. "A few months after you disappeared. I started dating this girl, kind of a goth punk chick. She was pretty cool, into literature and art, but way too intense for me."

Raina wasn't surprised at this assessment. It's why she had never considered him romantically, not even in her fantasies. Dude was so laid-back he was practically in a coma. "Cass took it hard, me dating other girls. She got mean all of a sudden, picked apart everything about them, and about me. I couldn't figure out why she suddenly did this about-face. She was always such a sweet person, never had a bad word to say about anyone. And then all of a sudden, BAM! She wouldn't stop talking smack."

Raina giggled. Noah had a way with words. He always had; he was the clown in school.

"So she finally came around to your way of thinking. And now? Is it all rainbows and happily ever after?"

Noah shook his head. "It wasn't that easy. We sort of

stopped being friends while we were figuring ourselves out, but because you were missing, we still had to see each other. We had to organize searches and everything. It was this weird time in our lives, where we couldn't stop arguing, but we still wanted to be together."

Raina grinned and bounced an extra bounce to the beat of the music. "And then fighting turned into kissing... and kissing turned into fuck—"

"Yeah, yeah, yeah. That's pretty much exactly what happened. We're predictable."

"No." Raina poked him in the chest. "It's a classic relationship starter. You need to read a romance novel or watch a romcom. You'll see what I mean. Boy meets girl in some kind of meet-cute, boy and girl fight, fight, fight, then they kiss, kiss, kiss, then..."

"You're finding this way too amusing," Noah said dryly.

Raina laughed out loud, throwing her head back and enjoying the carefree moment. Yeah, she was amused. This was the most fun she'd had in years. She'd gone globetrotting, she'd gone to incredible places in the world, explored new cultures, new people, new countries. But it really came down to this. The people that she knew and that knew her. Their love for each other transcended all that. Places were cool, but they couldn't care about a person's well-being. Raina loved Noah and Cass and hoped the best for them. She knew that they felt the same about her.

"So, have you proposed to her?" Raina was dying of curiosity.

The song ended and they stopped dancing, though they continued to stand on the dance floor.

"No, I haven't asked her yet," he said quietly, his eyes on the woman now sitting across the room one leg crossed over the other, a dreamy expression on her face as she waited for her companions to come back. "I have the ring though. I'm just waiting for the right moment."

A lump formed in Raina's throat and she had to swallow it before she could speak. Thinking about her relationship, or non-relationship with Mateo, she put her hand on Noah's sleeve. "Every moment is the perfect moment. If you wait too long or try too hard to capture a certain moment, you'll waste time waiting for something intangible. My advice if you want it, is don't miss out on one minute of the joy in knowing you're going to spend the rest of your life with the person you love."

Noah nodded thoughtfully. "Maybe you're right. Every time I try to settle on a day and time, I change my mind. Nothing seems right. People keep telling me the right moment will present itself, but it hasn't and I'm starting to think it never will."

Raina smiled at him. "It's not about the perfect moment, it's about the perfect person. If you think you found her, then don't waste a single second, create the moment."

The way Mateo kept creating moments for them. He was patient, he was relentless, he never gave up. Raina didn't know if Mateo loved her, though she suspected he might. What she did know is that she could rely on him. He would come for her. He would always come for her. He was the master of making his moments.

Noah and Raina weaved through the tables making their way back to where Cass was sitting. Before they made it to the table though, they were intercepted by a couple of cowboys.

"Well aren't you looking fine tonight, little Miss Raina." One of them stepped up to Raina his arms outstretched.

"Darcy! I heard you might be out tonight." Raina opened her arms to him and allowed him to envelop her in a bear hug.

He stood close to her his arm slung over her shoulders, a section of her hair between his fingers where he played with it. Darcy was a good guy, but he loved to get into a woman's space. Raina didn't mind tonight though. Some light flirtation was good for her.

"Dance?" Darcy asked her.

Raina looked at Noah and then toward Cass who was watching them with curiosity, her lips tilted up in a grin because she knew that her friend was getting hit on. Noah nodded toward Darcy and his boys and then said to Raina, "Whatever you want to do, I'll be at the table with Cass."

After Raina agreed to dance, Noah left her in Darcy's care. A fast-paced country beat dictated their first dance. They two-stepped energetically, laughing and talking about nothing. It was noisy and Raina was starting to feel out of breath from dancing half the night. She relaxed and allowed Darcy to swing her around in his strong embrace.

When they finished the dance, she attempted to go back to her table, but Darcy grabbed her hand to stop her. "Hey, don't go leaving me yet. I don't want to lose you for another two years. Dance with me again."

He didn't really ask her, but assumed he had her consent. Raina didn't want to make a fuss since she was having a good time, so she melted into his arms for the next dance, a love ballad. They swayed together to Taylor Swift's Lover.

Mateo would have a fit if he saw another man touching her. Every time they saw each other, the atmosphere was fraught with emotion and he made it clear that he didn't want her near his men unless it was purely business. He'd been that way right from the start, right from the moment he took her from her University campus to Venezuela.

"So, where'd you go for those two years?" Darcy asked, demand in his tone.

Raina didn't like the way he asked the question, as though

he was entitled to an answer. It was really none of his business; they'd never been an item. He'd been too much of a playboy and Raina was two years behind him in school. Though he'd noticed her, neither had ever acted on any kind of romance. Story of Raina's life, all fun and fantasies, no action.

"Travelling." She didn't give him more. She didn't want him thinking that she owed him something.

He didn't take the hint. "Travelling where?"

Raina sighed. She would either have to potentially offend him and tell him to back off or find a way to answer his question that didn't include talking about her bullet wound, her family connections, or any other assorted information that might come up that he shouldn't know.

"I went to a lot of different places. I started in Venezuela." Though not willingly, she thought silently. "Then I flew overseas, into Amsterdam. I travelled around Europe, then London, Glasgow, Edinburgh. Then, Shanghai, Beijing, Seoul, Australia. And then I finished in Italy."

The look of supreme male confidence melted into something close to jealousy. "That's a lot of places. Did you have fun?"

Raina felt impatient at the questions. They were pointless. Did she have fun? Of course she had fun. She travelled the world, something that most people wanted to do but couldn't find either the time or the money. She was in a position where she'd been able to do something incredible with her time. She was lucky.

But something was stopping her from sharing her experiences with Darcy. Maybe because she knew he didn't actually care about the answers.

"Yeah, it was mostly fun." Except for getting shot and causing a great big mess in Italy.

Darcy hauled her closer until Raina's breasts pressed

against his chest. Though she was all good with a little light flirtation, she sensed that Darcy was in this for a one-night stand. Maybe more. She tried to ease back in his arms, but he tightened his hold and didn't let her go. She was about to demand that he stop dancing so close to her when he leaned down to whisper in her ear.

"I've missed you. I gotta be honest, I came out tonight because I heard you were back in town. Knew I'd see you out and about eventually. You're a girl that knows how to have a good time."

Raina wrinkled her nose. She didn't like the connotation behind that. Maybe he meant it innocently, but she suspected he was insulting her. Treating her like she might be easy, might give up the goods because he thought a woman who travelled the world was a woman with experience. Which was her business if she was. Of course, she never really had the opportunity to whore it up, but either way, it didn't mean he got to speak that way to her.

She was about to open her mouth and tell him so when he was forcibly torn away from her. One minute, Darcy was standing in front of her, leering and making inappropriate comments, and the next he was flying backwards so hard that he hit a table, which flew out from under him and smashed into another table.

Miraculously, no one seemed to be injured. Except for maybe Darcy, or at least his pride. He was picking his way out of broken glass and table and gradually climbing to his feet a look of dazed bewilderment on his face.

Raina looked around wondering how he'd managed to fling himself backward so hard, when she discovered the answer standing right next to her. A towering, rage-filled, or so he looked, Mateo was staring down at her like she was going to be his next victim. She took a quick step back before he could fling her into a table too, but he caught her arm and held her still.

"Got you," he said, sinister promise in his deep tone.

CHAPTER EIGHTEEN

Raina didn't know how they did it, but suddenly Cass and Noah were standing in front of her, their body language protective. Cass's arms were crossed tightly over her chest, her eyes were narrowed on Mateo.

"Who the fuck are you and why the fuck are you touching my friend?" she demanded without missing a beat.

Mateo didn't even look at her. He hadn't taken his eyes off Raina once since downing Darcy, who was still picking himself up off the floor, a dazed expression plastered on his face.

"You got here faster than I thought you would," Raina noted, her gaze on Mateo. She still didn't entirely trust him not to throw her into a table. He looked really pissed.

"I always know where you are, chica. Every step of the way. Everywhere you go. I'm never far away." His words could be taken as either comforting or as a threat. Raina didn't want to take them either way.

When Cass didn't immediately get an answer to her question, she got right in Mateo's face and growled, "Were you the reason she had to leave university so suddenly two years ago?"

Both Mateo's and Raina's eyes snapped to Cass. How on earth had she made that leap in logic? She was correct, but she shouldn't know.

"What exactly did my parents tell you?" Raina asked.

Cass looked guilty. "They told me some stuff."

At Raina's horrified expression, Cass quickly tried to reassure her, "After you disappeared, I wouldn't leave them alone. I couldn't accept the explanation that you ran off to go travelling. It wasn't like you to not contact your family or friends."

Raina realized that Cass had been hurt by the idea that her best friend had abandoned her. Over the past few years, Raina had struggled with her feelings over leaving her friends and family. She felt sad, angry, guilty. But ultimately, she had also realized that she had no choice. At the time, it was the only path she could've taken.

Raina leaned over and hugged Cass. She held her and said in her ear, "I'm so sorry that I had to leave you without an explanation and sorry that my parents told you. You shouldn't have been burdened with that."

Cass shook her head. "It doesn't matter. I was threatening to go to the FBI. I told your parents that I would tell the authorities that they'd kidnapped their own daughter and that they were keeping her locked up in the barn if they didn't tell me what really happened to you. I didn't give them much choice."

Raina burst out laughing. It was just like Cass to get overinvolved. But Raina felt good knowing that her best friend had her back. Raina would've done the same for Cass, had Cass suddenly disappeared off the face of the planet.

"We're going." Mateo grabbed Raina's arm and started pulling her away from her friends.

"Wait!" Cass leapt forward and grabbed Mateo's arm, trying to hold him in place. He glared down at her hand and then up into her face. Cass instantly let him go, as though reading her own death in his eyes. Raina didn't think that he would murder her friends, but he sure gave the impression that he could and would do it without batting an eye.

"It's okay," Raina said reaching out for her friend. When she saw Noah's concerned expression, she reached out to squeeze his arm as well. "Really, it's fine. I need to talk to Mateo anyway. You two go ahead and have a good time, I'll see you later. Maybe tomorrow."

Raina glanced at Mateo to see if she'd told the truth. His eyes told her that she absolutely would not be seeing her two friends the next day... maybe never. She had to fight back tears. Was this it? Was he going to drag her away from her family and friends once more? And the man wondered why she didn't want anything to do with him. He was an asshole. He might be an attractive asshole, but that was no excuse for assholiness.

Raina hugged Cass and Noah goodbye. Noah's hug was much shorter than Cass's as Mateo dragged her from the other man's arms with a hand on her neck. He didn't say a word to her friends, just pulled her away and strode through the bar toward the exit.

It was then that Raina finally noticed his backup. Though they were Latino mobsters and should've been out of place in a country bar, they somehow managed to blend into their environment. Raina supposed it was part of the job. Don't get noticed until it was time to get noticed.

The cool air slapped her in the face as they stepped outside and she paused to breathe deeply, taking it into her lungs and cleansing the tension of the past few minutes. Mateo pulled her down the wooden steps of the bar, dragging her toward a black SUV with tinted windows. There were two SUVs to accommodate all of his men. She guessed she should be flattered. It took a whole contingent of highly skilled gangsters to pick up one small woman.

As they reached the SUV, Raina finally managed to tug her hand away from his. She stood with her hands on her hips and her chin jutted out. "What the hell was that?"

Mateo didn't miss a beat. He stopped, turned, grabbed her around the waist, picked her up and hauled her into the side of the SUV. He had a hand at her back to stop her from slamming too hard into the metal, but there was enough force that she got his point. He wasn't happy with her. She probably should've kept her mouth shut. Still, what the hell?

"You didn't have to beat up Darcy like that," she snapped, his anger making her even angrier.

"Don't you ever say another man's name to me again," he snarled, pointing a finger in her face.

Raina's mouth dropped open. Mateo had his moments, had shown her before that he had a temper, but this was the first time he wasn't acting the picture of reason. He was demanding that she never say a man's name to him? How did a person do that? Was she supposed to avoid interacting with men forever? She figured that was about the only way that she would never speak another man's name.

"That's ridiculous," she said, somewhat unnecessarily since everyone in the vicinity knew that it was ridiculous.

"You let him touch you. You let them both touch you. You. Are. Mine." He emphasized each of the last three words by smacking his hand into the vehicle next to her head. She blinked up at him in surprise. Her heart was hammering in her chest. A combination of fear and lust sent her adrenaline soaring. "The only man that gets to touch you is me. Remember that. Because the next man that touches you does not get the allowances that these men did. The next man who touches you dies."

Before she could respond, before she could tell him that he was being ridiculous, he yanked her up the vehicle until her feet were dangling off the ground and he swooped in for a life altering kiss.

CHAPTER NINETEEN

Mateo broke the kiss and, in one smooth move, swung Raina away from the vehicle far enough that he could open the rear passenger door and lift her inside. Raina was so stunned by the kiss that she barely noticed as he pulled the seat belt around her and latched it, his shoulder brushing hers as he leaned across her body.

"Where are we...?" Raina started to ask, but Mateo slammed the door on her question and strode around to the other side of the vehicle.

She watched curiously as he had a conversation with two of his men before climbing in the back with her, slamming his door shut and buckling his own seatbelt. Two of his men got in the front while the rest made their way to the rear vehicle.

"Where are you taking me?" Raina tried to hide the fear in her voice.

Mateo always had a rhyme and reason for everything he did, but when she didn't know what that was, he came across as unpredictable. Raina didn't like unpredictable. And now she was completely at his mercy. She doubted he would give her another opportunity to run away.

"Home," he said shortly.

The vehicle began moving, taking a left out of the bar parking lot and onto the highway, away from the direction that would take her back to the farm.

"Not the farm, I'm guessing?"

"Not the farm," he confirmed.

"Can you please give me a little more?" she demanded, her voice rising. "Are we driving, are we taking an airplane, a train, a bus? And where exactly is this home that you're taking me to? Venezuela?"

Mateo turned to look at her, his deep chocolatey eyes gleaming in the darkness. "Not Venezuela."

Raina was bewildered. If they weren't going to Venezuela, then where were they going? For some reason Mateo was being even shorter with her than usual. Almost purposefully evasive.

She narrowed her eyes at him. "Are you hiding something from me?"

He looked at her for a while, as though really seeing inside her head. Some of the tension released from his body and he relaxed against his seat. He sighed deeply and ran a hand over his face. He looked tired. Like really, really tired. As though he hadn't slept in weeks.

A stab of guilt pierced her. He hadn't slept because he'd been following her around Italy and then following her back to America as she ran away from him, playing a silly game. Though she had a valid reason for not wanting to go with him, she still cared about his well-being.

"You need to get some sleep," she murmured.

He shrugged. "I'll sleep when I'm dead."

She smirked. "Warren Zevon. Now tell me what you're keeping from me."

"Warren who?" Mateo gave her a strange look.

"Singer songwriter. The first person to write the lyric, 'I'll sleep when I'm dead'."

Mateo's lips twitched in amusement. "And you know this because?"

Raina shrugged and tried not to return his semi-smile. She was trying to be mad at him, trying to grill him on their destination. "Because I spent two years of my childhood in hospitals and my dad distracted me with movie and music trivia."

"And you remember everything you hear?" He seemed genuinely curious, as if charmed by learning this new facet of Raina he hadn't known before.

"Only the random stuff," she countered.

Raina thought maybe Mateo was avoiding the previous topic. There was something up and it was making him edgy and evasive. Mateo was always on high alert, but this was different. He seemed distracted instead of his usual hyper focused.

She was surprised when he started speaking of his own volition without having to be prompted again. "Your stepfather is giving me Miami."

Raina thought she must not have heard him right. "Sotza is giving you a city? Like a whole city? Is that even possible?"

Mateo looked over at her, his lip still curled in a half smile. "Yeah, he's giving me a city."

"Are you being sarcastic?" Raina demanded.

"No, chica, I'm not. Sotza is handing over the reins to the Miami underworld. He's done with the chaos of the past several years. He wants someone in command who can be strong and decisive, someone who will put down any competitors or challenges. He wants me to take over."

Raina didn't know how to react. On the one hand she was shocked. Could a person just hand over his city to another person? That didn't seem right. But then again, she didn't know everything there was to know about the mafia and how they worked. Maybe they did hand cities over to each other like gifts. It sounded like they also stole cities from each other too.

On the other hand, Mateo was the perfect choice to bring order to a chaotic situation. He was ruthless, brutal and brilliant. He was methodical and patient when required. He knew how to play the long game.

"But doesn't Sotza want to keep you with him?" she asked, curious how it would work. Could Mateo still be second-in-command to Sotza while living and working in Miami? She didn't think so.

Mateo confirmed her last thought with his next sentence. "I believe that Sotza would keep me with him in Venezuela if he could, but Miami is a sensitive issue. It's the gateway for most product; the chaos will weaken trade where routes are already established. Sotza understands that there must be sacrifice in this business. I'm needed in Miami."

Mateo's quiet confidence in his ability to follow through on Sotza's command, to bring an entire city under control, sent a zing of attraction through her. Mateo knew what he wanted and he went after it.

"He must trust you a lot," she murmured thoughtfully. She never really thought about it, but of course Sotza would trust Mateo. Mateo would've had plenty of opportunity to betray Sotzao over the years if that had been his intention. He'd probably proven his loyalty over and over again.

When Mateo didn't respond to her last comment, Raina asked, "What about me? Where do I fit in?"

"You're with me," Mateo said with quiet finality.

"But what does that mean? Stop giving me such cryptic answers and tell me what the heck is going on."

Raina was beginning to feel frustrated. In romance novels, the heroines always adored the strong silent type. Raina was beginning to see exactly how frustrating strong and silent could be. She would much prefer if the man used his words.

He flashed her a quick smile, as though he found her annoyance cute. He would find it much less cute when she found something to bash him over the head with.

"What that means is you're with me; you will always be with me. Going forward you belong to me. If I'm in Pennsylvania, then you're in Pennsylvania. If I am in Venezuela, then you're in Venezuela. If I'm in Miami, then you are also in Miami." His voice was firm but with an edge.

"But... if you're going to be the new... what? The new boss of Miami? Like Sotza is in Venezuela?" At his nod she continued. "But then, what does that make me?"

"My wife," he said, his tone brooking no argument.

His wife.

She'd known that he wanted to marry her, but she'd been treating the idea like some distant dream that she might eventually have to face but wasn't in a hurry to reach. Something she could get out of or that she might have a choice in. But now, in the back of this vehicle, heading towards a future in Miami with this man, she realized that her destiny was about to be written for her.

"So you're going to be the new boss of Miami and I am going to be your wife." It was as though saying the words out loud helped to solidify the concept.

She wasn't exactly sure what she was looking for from Mateo. She supposed she wanted some kind of acknowledgement that this was a big deal. That marrying the boss of Miami was as terrifying a thing as she thought it was.

"You are as good as my wife already. We'll get the paper and have the ceremony, but you'll stand with me as I take over the city." He said it with quiet authority.

"I'm scared." Her heart was starting to hammer with anxiety.

She was a long way from that young and eager University freshman who'd worried about nothing more than an overdue English paper. She never aspired to be the wife of a mob boss, never imagined it was a thing, except maybe on TV and in movies.

He looked at her, his expression filled with something she couldn't quite pin down. Pity? Satisfaction? The two emotions were opposite, yet that's what she read on his face. As though everything were falling into place for him and he couldn't be happier, but he knew the sacrifices Raina would have to make to stand by his side.

He picked her hand up and kissed the knuckles, sending her heart soaring. "Nothing will touch you so long as I'm alive."

CHAPTER TWENTY

Raina wanted to ask about her parents, demand that Mateo take her back to say goodbye to them. But she knew he would refuse and since Mateo had been in touch with her parents for the past two years, she suspected he would update them on this new development. If not, then she would call them when she landed in Miami. She was relatively certain that Cass would call them and let them know what happened at the bar.

The vehicle started to slow and Raina looked around in confusion. It was close to midnight so she couldn't see anything out of the tinted windows, but it seemed as though they were going to stop on the highway.

And then they did stop on the highway. "Why are we stopping here?"

Mateo didn't answer. As soon as the SUV stopped, he opened the door and got out, walking around to her side. He opened the door and helped her out, though she was tempted to smack his hand when he unbuckled her seatbelt. Enough was enough, she was a grown woman. She slid out of the vehicle, but Mateo didn't back up so she was forced to stand flush against him. He slid his arm around her waist resting his broad hand on her hip. They stood that way for a few seconds then he escorted her to the front of the vehicle.

"Get the plane ready," he told one of his men.

Now Raina was really confused. Plane? But they weren't anywhere near the airport. Their small town supported a tiny airfield that could barely land a Cessna. And that was all the way on the other side of the town. There was no airport around here.

Raina was about to tell Mateo that he was somehow mistaken when she caught sight of an airplane rolling toward them up the highway. It was being driven off a side road that led into a farmer's field. Apparently, they had ditched the aircraft to come and collect her. Mateo never failed to surprise her.

"I was expecting something bigger," she said sarcastically.

She hadn't been expecting anything at all, let alone an airplane out in the middle of nowhere on the highway from which they clearly intended to take off.

"The luxury jet's in the shop." Mateo's voice was so deadpan that for a second Raina believed him, but then she caught sight of his smirk.

Playing along, Raina said tartly, "Well, this will have to do for now, but in the future, I fully expect the luxury jet to be ready and waiting for me."

As the plane stopped Mateo guided her toward it. "Your wish is my command, princess."

Raina noticed Mateo did that a lot, called her all sorts of endearments. Princess, chica, baby. Was he going to pick one, or continue to rotate them? She wasn't sure how she felt about all the endearments. Sometimes happy, sometimes not. She wondered if he called other women by these endearments. No, that seemed unlikely. She couldn't picture the super serious Mateo casually calling a woman princess. Not unless he meant it.

He helped her onto the airplane and this time when he reached over to buckle her seatbelt, she smacked his hand. "You do know that I've been buckling my own seatbelts for the last twenty years?"

"Your safety will always be my priority. If I do it for you, then I know it's done right."

He sounded so serious the smile fell from her lips as she stared at him sitting next to her.

"I will never stop wanting to protect you. This is something that you'll indulge me in without complaint. I'll accept a lot from you, but not this. If I tell you that something is for your safety, then you will listen, without argument, without hesitation."

Raina was generally an argumentative person. She questioned everything. The government, the police, the media, laws, lawyers, parents, both adoptive and birth, doctors; the list could go on forever. In her opinion, questioning was a sign of intelligence. Blind following was a sign of complacency or fear.

But when Mateo laid down this law, she was more inclined to listen. There was something about him. The tone of his voice, his expression, his earnestness. This was one area that she knew he wouldn't fuck around with.

"You've probably noticed by now, but I'm not very good at following orders." When it looked like Mateo was about to further lay down the law, she shook her head and interrupted, "This is the one time that I'll try harder. I believe you. I believe that you have my best interests at heart. So I'll try to listen if it's something that has to do with my safety."

Mateo studied her for second. "Don't try. Just do. If you can't then I'll make sure it gets done."

Raina tried to hold onto her temper. She didn't appreciate

it when she extended an olive branch toward her "future husband" and he rejected it.

"You know, for someone who professes that he desperately wants to marry me, you don't seem to give two shits about what I think. Or how I feel," she snapped furiously. The plane began to taxi down the highway. "You just tell me where to go and what to do. I don't appreciate being talked to like I'm five years old and don't know how to listen. When I tell you that I'll try to listen to you about things that concern my safety, I mean it."

"So far you haven't once gone where I wanted you to go or did what I wanted you to do," he said dryly.

"Exactly. And I never will if you keep talking to me this way. Give me a reason to listen to you and I might actually do it."

"I doubt that," he drawled, his gaze outside the window on the ground as the plane lifted off.

His hand tightened on his arm rest. It was so subtle that she might've missed it. Was he afraid of flying? She couldn't exactly ask him because two of his men were in the small airplane with them, one flying and the other... she guessed he was bodyguard.

"My point is, if you expect me to play house with you, then I'll need you to stop being the tough guy all the time. Always telling me what to do and scolding me about every little thing. Happy marriages don't work that way." She crossed her arms tightly over her chest and tried hard to not say anything else. She thought she'd ended on a poignant note. But then she couldn't help herself. "And another thing," she turned to glare at him. "What was that at the bar? You can't go around beating up anyone and everyone that touches me."

He didn't turn and look at her; his gaze was still firmly on the rapidly disappearing ground. "Yes, I can."

Well, he had a point. He probably literally could beat up any man that touched her. "Okay, maybe you can, but that doesn't mean you should."

"Yes, it does." Still he wouldn't look at her.

She didn't know if she should be amused or annoyed at this point. He was definitely the most stubborn man she'd ever met. There was no give in him. He claimed to want her, claimed to want to keep her safe and happy, but she didn't know yet if she could trust him to give her the tools she needed for that happiness.

As she was staring at him, he finally turned to look at her. He reached out and put his hand on her shoulder. It was big and warm and wrapped over her delicate bones. She didn't know why he did it. Was he trying to comfort her? She wasn't really in distress, she felt perfectly safe with him, if a little annoyed. No, it felt more like a claiming. Possession. He was telling her who she belonged to.

"What are you thinking when you look at me like that?" he asked her.

She was surprised that he asked her something like that in front of his men. Mafia guys had an image to project, but Mateo didn't seem to care what his people thought of him. At least not about anything connected to Raina. He said and did what he wanted where she was concerned.

She thought about giving him a flippant answer, but the moment didn't feel flip. She chewed on her lip for a second and then told him the truth. "I was thinking... that you'll do anything for me." Though her voice was quiet, only just above the noise of the airplane, it rang with conviction.

He nodded slowly, looking at her, studying her fierce features. "I would do anything for you," he agreed, tipping her chin with his fingers. "Even the things that you don't want me to do. You belong to me, it's my job to see to your safety and comfort."

"At the expense of everything else?" she replied with a frown. "Conflict is a part of life. You can't disappear all those things for me. Life doesn't work that way."

He leaned over capturing her face and pulling it towards him. They met in the middle, him pressing his lips against hers with a stinging kiss. He leaned back, his face inches from hers. "Watch me."

CHAPTER TWENTY-ONE

Raina was completely wiped out by the time they were entering the airspace outside of Miami. Her eyes were closing involuntarily and she was constantly smothering yawns. It had to be after 3 AM.

Mateo kept his hand on her for almost the whole flight, switching it from her shoulder to her arm and then her knee. At first his need to be constantly touching her was disconcerting, but she quickly got used to it. And now, as exhausted as she was, her mind barely able to process any thought, the hand on her knee was comforting. As if sensing her need for touch, he squeezed her.

Raina must've fallen asleep in the few minutes it took them to descend through the clouds and land on the small aircraft runway next to the Miami airport. The door was opened, and a rush of cool air slapped her in the face. She breathed deeply, inhaling the scent of ocean into her lungs. She loved that smell. Growing up on a farm she'd become used to dirt, cows, horses, man sweat, and various other scents. The smell of Pennsylvania was the smell of home. But the scent of the ocean? This was where her heart longed to be. When she travelled, she tried to always pick places near an ocean.

Mateo disembarked the airplane first and reached for her, wrapping his fingers around her waist and lowering her to the ground. His men were doing an airplane check before leaving. She stood waiting for them until Mateo tugged on her arm and nodded his head toward a waiting SUV, black with tinted windows, like the one's he'd picked her up in. What were these? Thug vans? She snickered at her own joke and then yawned widely.

Mateo led her over to the SUV, where Thomas, Angela and another man were waiting. The man she didn't recognize was taller than Raina, but shorter than Mateo. He was built like a boxer; stocky, big muscles, thick neck, closely shaved hair, and a fuck-off attitude that she could sense for miles. She liked him immediately.

Raina sensed that the man was something more than a regular thug. He wore his suit like he was born in it and his expression was pure professional. Raina stuck her hand out and said, "Raina Duncan."

His lips split into a grin that was so big and shiny that Raina was taken aback. She'd pegged him as a serious mafioso guy, but he was looking at her like she was his lost pet puppy come home. Weird, she'd never met the guy.

He grabbed hold of her hand and pumped with vigor for far too long considering they just met. He covered the back of her hand with his other hand and said enthusiastically, "Danny Russo. I've been wanting to meet you for years. You're the spitting image of your mama."

"You know Vee?" Raina asked, shaking off some of her exhaustion. She'd been dying to know more about the place where her mom grew up. Maybe this guy could give her the scoop.

Mateo took her arm and tugged her hand out of Danny's,

giving the other guy a hard stare. "Danny was Vee's second-in-command."

Raina grinned. This was perfect. She could get all the dirt on her famous underworld mobster mama. "And do you work for Mateo now?" she asked Danny.

Danny nodded. "More like work with. When your mom found out that he was heading to Miami to take over, she got in touch. Figures I can show him the ins and outs of the city."

"Enough talking," Mateo growled, tugging Raina away from Danny. "She's exhausted, needs a bed." He put his hand against the small of her back, careful to avoid her injury, and pushed her toward the open back door of the SUV. "Get inside. I'll be right back."

Raina climbed into the vehicle, hesitated, then slammed the door shut behind her. Though it wasn't exactly a cold night, she still felt chilled. Probably because she was so tired.

Danny slid into the driver's seat of the SUV and twisted around to look at her again, shaking his head. "Spitting image. It's amazing. You could be twins."

Raina blushed. Her birth mother was drop-dead gorgeous. Raina was okay with believing she looked like the other woman, though she didn't feel that gorgeous right now. Her glasses were drooping down her nose, her formerly flat hair was beginning to frizz in the humidity and her clothes felt like they fit too tightly. She longed to be in a set of loose pajamas and sleeping soundly between the cool sheets of a bed.

She leaned her head back against the seat and started to fall asleep, only waking up for a few seconds when Mateo climbed into the vehicle. He took one look at her and moved into the center seat, buckling her in, and then himself. He reached an arm around her neck and tugged her against his side until her head was pressed to his chest over his heart. At first, she lay stiff in his arms, but gradually the heat of his body seeped into her hers, encouraging her to melt against him, the steady beat of his heart pattering a soothing rhythm in her ear.

The next time she woke she was being lifted from the vehicle and hoisted up against Mateo's chest. She snuggled into him. She loved the way it felt being in his arms, being held by him, being protected by him. She might be confused about her emotions when it came to her mobster boyfriend, but her body knew it wanted Mateo one hundred percent of the time.

Mateo had a murmured conversation over her head with Danny. It was brief. She didn't really pay attention to the sentences but caught enough words to get the gist. Mateo wanted Danny to come by in the morning to help him outline some kind of plans. Maybe plans on how to take over the city? She didn't know, and at the moment, she didn't care. She was about two seconds away from falling asleep on Mateo and possibly drooling all over his nice shirt.

He strode into the house, his shoes tapping against the marble floor. Raina wanted to care about the house they were in; the house that was going to be her home. She got the impression it was big, beautiful, spacious, and utterly opulent. She'd have to check it out tomorrow. For now, she hoped there was a bed as luxurious as the rest of the house.

Mateo took the stairs to the second floor two at a time. Then it was more marble floor, followed by door after door. How many rooms did this place have?

Finally, Mateo stopped in front of a set of double doors at the end of the hall and pushed them open. He hoisted her up against his body to shove the door wider and strode inside. He deposited her on a bed, which was thankfully big and plush with lots of blankets and pillows.

Perfect.

Raina curled into a ball on her side and prepared to fall

asleep, but before she could do that, Mateo pulled her up into a sitting position. She tried to slump back over, but he grabbed her and forced her back up.

"Whyyyyy?" she whined groggily.

Instead of answering, he turned her until she was facing away from him and lifted the back of her shirt. It wasn't until his fingers touched the bandage that was taped to her back that she realized he was checking her wound. He gently pried the tape from her skin, hesitating slightly when she cried out in pain. Once the whole thing was off, he tossed it onto the nightstand and ran his hand over the wound. It didn't hurt, it felt more like heat against her skin as his knuckles brushed the affected area.

"The skin looks healthy," he murmured from behind her. "The stitches'll need to come out soon. I'll have to find a doctor for you tomorrow."

"You would know, snitches need stiches, right?" she giggled at her own joke and then yawned. "Are you done?"

"Almost." He slid to his knees in front of her and she blinked at him, wondering what he was doing. Was he proposing marriage to her? Seemed a little strange considering he as much as told her he was marrying her, with or without her permission.

Then she realized what he was doing when he reached for her shoes and pulled them off one at a time, digging his thumbs into the arch of each foot and massaging gently. She moaned and flopped back on the bed, a rush of happy tingles running through her body and swirling in her stomach. Okay, this was heaven. A beautiful luxurious bed and a man at her feet giving her the best foot massage of her life. Okay, the only foot massage of her life, but whatever, a kidnap victim had to take what she could get.

When he finished, he stood, towering over her. She thought now he would leave, but he didn't. He reached down, took her hands and tugged her to her feet. She made a complaining sound which turned into a yelp when he reached for her jeans and undid the button. She tried to slap his hand away, but he pushed them aside and finished unzipping her jeans.

"What are you doing?" she asked, covering her lower belly with her hands.

"I'm not going to hurt you," he said calmly. "I want you to be comfortable. And you won't be comfortable in these clothes."

"I can take them off myself," she said, her voice high. She didn't want him to see her naked. She wasn't ready for that.

He hesitated and gave her a long look, then nodded his head. "It's probably for the best if you do. I finally have my woman in my home base, I'm not sure how well my control will hold."

She didn't know how to respond to that. She wrapped her arms around her chest and said, "Good night, Mateo."

Mateo took her hands, unfolding her arms and leaning in, pressing his lips hard against hers. His breath was a whisper across her skin as he said, "Good night, Raina."

CHAPTER TWENTY-TWO

Raina slept like the dead and woke up feeling disoriented. She yawned and stretched underneath the heavy blanket, squinting her eyes toward the window. It was a bright and sunny morning. She slapped her hand around her night table until she found her glasses. Shoving them on, she looked groggily at the alarm clock. 11:30 AM; almost lunchtime.

Raina sat up, shoving hair out of her face. She looked around and then realized she didn't know where anything was. Had her purse been captured with her? Where was her phone? She was going to be pissed at Mateo if he lost her phone. It was less about the phone itself, though she had some valuable contacts in there. No, she wanted her phone case.

She had found the coolest iPhone place at a Disney store in Paris. It had a picture of Betty Boop on the front riding a motorcycle and Raina's name emblazoned across the bottom. It was silly, but for some reason, that cell phone case was a symbol of her independence. It was the first thing that she bought for herself when she'd been on the run. First time she stopped long enough to shop for something.

Raina climbed out of bed and stretched. She was wearing only her panties. A quick look around the room told her that there were no clothes there for her. She was forced to pull on the clothing that she'd worn the night before. Bar-star was not a good daytime look.

She found a packaged toothbrush and toothpaste in the bathroom, which she used. Feeling better, she made her way down the stairs, looking around. The house was insane. The furnishings were big, beautiful, opulent. Not really her style and a little tacky if she was being honest, but the place itself was incredibly luxurious.

There were so many rooms that she lost count as she went by them. She didn't stop to look inside any of them yet; she figured she could do that later, after breakfast.

Raina descended to the first floor of the mansion and found herself in the lobby by the front door. She glanced around and found an archway off to the side. She went through and, after a few minute's exploration, she found the dining room, which sported a ridiculously long table and at least a dozen chairs. Mateo was sitting at the head of the table, engrossed in a conversation with someone on his cell phone, a piece of toast held aloft in his hand.

He was wearing a suit instead of his usual jeans and T-shirt. He looked mouth-wateringly good. Even the scowl wrinkling his brows was sexy.

He caught sight of her and his serious expression shifted. He didn't smile, but there was a softening to his features as he watched her.

He waved at the chair on his right, indicating that she should sit down. Raina narrowed her eyes at him and headed around to the other side of the table, sitting in the chair on his immediate left. She may as well establish immediately that she was no dog to be ordered around.

Mateo continued to listen to whoever was talking on the other end of the phone, but Raina could tell he was also paying close attention to her. He reached down and pulled something from his pocket, setting it on her placemat. Raina immediately recognized the little blue bottle. Her pills. So he did have her purse somewhere.

Raina started piling food on her plate. In front of her was a spread of every kind of delicious breakfast food imaginable. There was a plate filled with toast, one with waffles, another with scrambled eggs, and yet another with bacon and sausage. There was also a big bowl filled with a variety of fruit. Raina was going to ignore that particular dish until she made her way through all the fatty stuff.

She didn't often allow herself to indulge this way, but she also didn't often have that many options spread out in front of her hungry gaze.

As she reached for another fistful of bacon Mateo grabbed her wrist. Without missing a beat in his conversation, he pushed her hand toward the fruit plate. Once again, she narrowed her eyes at him, laser beaming him with her displeasure. She pulled her hand away from his and once again reached for the bacon this time snatching it fast and shoving it into her mouth before he could stop her.

"Excuse me, I'm going to have to call you back. Give me half an hour." Mateo ended the call and set his phone on the table, then turned his gaze to Raina's face.

Raina grinned at him as she chewed her bacon. She was being childish, but she couldn't help it. She wasn't about to let some man tell her what to eat.

"I thought we established that your health is very important to me," Mateo said in a growly voice that did strange things to the pit of her stomach. "Stop eating the bacon and move on to the fruit. It's better for you and will promote better kidney health."

"If you don't want me to eat bacon then don't give me the option," she said tartly, picking up the cloth napkin next to her plate and wiping her fingers of bacon grease.

She actually did kind of want some of the strawberries and blackberries that she saw in the fruit bowl, but now it was a matter of principle; she couldn't touch that fruit.

Mateo reached out, swiped the fruit bowl and dumped half of it on her plate covering her toast and eggs in fruit.

"Hey!"

Mateo grabbed her hand before she could start throwing berries back into the bowl. "You need to have a better attitude when it comes to both me and your health. If you want our marriage to be a pleasant one, then you'll follow a few basic rules."

"Well that's an easy problem to solve," she said sarcastically. "We're not married yet, so I think I'll do as I please."

"Do not declare war with me, little girl. I've won every battle, skirmish, and war that I have partaken in. If you choose that path, you will not win."

Raina rather thought that his feelings for her gave her an edge in any war they might be about to embark on, but she didn't want to show her hand by telling him that. Instead, she pushed her plate away from her and crossed her arms over her chest. "I'm well aware of my needs. I've been living with the consequences of kidney failure since the age of nine. I rarely indulge in things that I know are bad for my body. I don't need a keeper to tell me to stay away from bacon."

"Apparently you do."

Raina could feel her temper soaring and had to take several deep breaths to stop herself from shouting at him. She was getting absolutely nowhere and now wasn't the time to throw a fit. The way things were going, she thought that there would be plenty of time for that in the future. She decided to change the subject instead.

"Who does this house belong to?" she asked. "I mean, besides you. It's obviously been here for a while and the furnishings don't exactly seem like your taste. Too gaudy."

He wiped his mouth with his napkin and dropped it next to his empty plate. "The mansion used to belong to the former Miami boss, Ignacio Hernandez. He was killed about four years ago. The mansion was then entrusted to Reyes through marriage."

Raina stared blankly at him, the gears of her mind working hard as she tried to piece together what she knew of the Miami underground scene. She only got bits and pieces from Mateo, Sotza, Vee and some of the men. Then it hit her, this was the mansion that Casey Reyes used to live in.

Mateo answered her unspoken question. "Señora Reyes lived here with her former husband prior to his death."

Though Raina had never met Casey Reyes, nor her formidable husband, she'd heard enough about the woman to feel a closeness to her.

Now, Raina was inhabiting her old home, the place where Casey's first husband had died in a brutal takeover. Raina wondered how Casey felt about the house now. If she would come visit some time or if she preferred the structure be burnt to the ground.

After breakfast, Raina went back to her bedroom and gathered a pen and a pad of paper. With new determination she wandered the halls, counting bedrooms, cataloguing furnishings and artwork and taking note of outdated styles. She wrote down several pages of notes.

She didn't know exactly why she was doing it. She never cared about interior decorating in the past. Maybe it was because she was bored, or maybe because her life had spun out of control and making what changes she could helped her feel like she was back in control. Whatever it was, she thoroughly enjoyed the work. It gave her a feeling of purpose.

She'd been exploring the second floor for nearly an hour and was on her seventh bedroom when she wandered into the room that Mateo had claimed. She knew right away, without anyone telling her. It smelled like him; like man, sunshine and ocean.

She backed up and nearly left, but then curiosity and a sense of purpose drove her inside. She was here for a reason. She needed to take inventory before she could start work on her redecorating plan. As far as she knew she hadn't been banned from any part of the house.

Raina wandered around the heavily masculine room, touching a large armoire, a desk, chair, bed. The bed would have dominated the room, since it was a California king plus, but the room itself was pretty damn big. The more she looked at it, the more she realized it must be the master bedroom. It was bigger than all the other rooms, including hers, and the furnishings looked slightly more used.

She wandered to the window and pulled the heavy wine-coloured curtains aside. They looked expensive, but oppressive. She made a note to get rid of them.

She sank down onto the bed, testing the mattress when the door opened and Mateo strode inside. He was distracted, a leather portfolio in one hand, his eyes distant. Then his gaze landed on her and a flash of surprise crossed his features before it was replaced with a cross between pleased and predator.

"Didn't think I'd see you in my bedroom this quickly," he drawled, walking slowly toward her.

She shrugged. "I was bored."

"And you found your way in here? I'm flattered." He raised a thick dark eyebrow.

She rolled her eyes at him. "No, gangster. I wanted to take

inventory of the mansion's furnishings so I can start redecorating."

"Redecorating?" He sounded surprised.

"Yes," she said firmly. "If I'm going to be forced to live here, then I want a say in what it looks like."

"No one's forcing you," he pointed out.

"Oh really?" She stepped closer to him, hands on her hips. "What do you call the choices you gave me? Can I leave? Continue on my path of self-discovery and independence?"

"Of course not. You can stay here or go home to Venezuela... for a while."

"That's not a choice!" Her voice was sharp with annoyance. "If I live on the side of a mountain in Venezuela I'm as trapped as if I was in prison."

He shrugged his indifference. "You exaggerate. You're being given a choice, you don't like it, therefore you choose Miami. You choose me."

She suspected he was toying with her since she was positive that he wouldn't allow her to leave, even if she chose Venezuela.

"Narrowing my choices down to one isn't a choice, Mateo. You need to go back to school."

"Never went to school," he said, crossing to set his leather portfolio on his desk.

She gaped at him. "How did you never go to school?"

"My family was too poor. I had to help bring in money so we could survive."

"But...." She was floored by this information. In a few succinct sentences she learned more about Mateo than she had in the two years prior. "You're so well spoken. You can read and write. You're smart!"

He gave her a dark stare. "Don't need school to be smart. I taught myself how to read and write; Sotza had a tutor available to any of his people that wanted more education. When

I wasn't too busy, I'd avail myself of the tutor's services. I also enjoy reading and do it as often as I can. Usually every night before bed."

Raina was seeing Mateo in a whole different light and she didn't know what to think. His determination to seek education after having been denied it as a child was an admirable trait.

"What do you like to read?" she asked tentatively.

He leaned his ass against the desk, studying her. Was she asking him too many personal questions? She had always been inquisitive, without a lot of personal boundaries. She wanted to know what made people tick. She was a student of human nature. And the more she knew about a person the easier it was to get what she wanted out of them. The easier it was to create masterpiece forgeries.

Finally, he answered her question. "I read the news, world events, human interest stories, that sort of things. I also enjoy novels." He walked straight toward her, so quickly that she took a step back bumping into the bed. He stopped next to her and bent to open the nightstand next to the bed. He pulled out several books and handed them to her. She glanced at the titles. Thrillers, mysteries, and a romance. She raised an eyebrow and held the last one up.

He shrugged carelessly. "It's like porn for the brain."

She gaped at him and then burst out laughing. He grinned and took back all the books except for the last one, the romance. "Take it, read it. I think you'll like it."

Her smile slowly faded as she stared up at him, her fingers tightening on the book, her heart pounding in response. The idea of reading the same words as him, of reading the same sex scenes he'd read, picturing them in his mind while they played out in hers. It was hot.

He reached out, touched her cheek, then pushed her hair back off her forehead. She became painfully aware of what she must look like. Her big glasses firmly in place, no makeup, the same rumpled clothes she'd worn the day before. He didn't seem to care. He looked at her like she was the most beautiful woman on the planet.

"Thank you," she whispered, in response to his giving her the book.

He winked at her. "Don't dog ear the pages, fucking hate when people do that."

She burst out laughing as she imagined this big thug who was capable of murdering people being annoyed at the bent pages in his romance novel. He was such a strange contradiction. Painfully domineering and egotistical, but he also had a wicked sense of humour. Five minutes in his company and she was running a gamut of emotions, from laughter, to anger, to fear. This thought sobered her. She didn't know the real Mateo. Not really. And she didn't know how to get to the heart of the man she was supposed to marry.

"I think I'll go back to my room."

He nodded, his eyes following her, his expression unreadable, as she slipped past him and headed for the door.

"Raina."

She turned to look at him.

"I'll have some clothes sent to your room until you're able to do your own shopping."

"Thank you," she murmured, clutching the book to her chest.

He continued to stare at her as though mapping out her every feature.

"I will see you at dinner, mi amor."

CHAPTER TWENTY-THREE

Raina called her mother the next day, to get Casey Reyes' number. She was eager to get started on the renovations but didn't want to move forward until she had Casey's blessing.

Vee was concerned that Raina was in Miami with Mateo and took up most of their phone conversation talking about it. She grilled Raina on everything from the moment she was shot in Italy until she arrived in Miami.

In response to Vee's question about Raina's wound, Raina assured her, "I'm feeling better now, but getting shot hurts like a motherfucker."

Vee chuckled her agreement. "Yes, it does."

Vee had been shot in the arm during Nico Garza's takeover attempt on the Venezuela mafia. Though the attempt had been unsuccessful, two men had died and Vee and another woman, Garza's second-in-command and lover, had been hurt.

"How is Miami?" Vee asked tentatively.

"It's good. I haven't been here long and so far I'm on

house arrest. Maybe Mateo anticipates trouble as he locks down Miami."

Vee paused before answering, "So, you know about that."

"That Mateo is being handed Miami on a silver platter, with a ready-order bride in the wings?" Raina tried and failed to keep the bitterness from her voice.

Vee's reply was swift. "You wish to be removed from the situation?"

"Is that an option?" Raina asked hopefully.

Her mother sighed deeply. "To be honest, not really. Sotza has given his blessing to a merger between you two, and though my wishes do hold some weight, he'll have the final say."

"Do my wishes mean nothing to him?" Raina asked sharply, her eyes narrowing.

Life was so much simpler with Diane and Joe, her adoptive parents. They only wanted her to be happy. Things in this organized crime world were so complicated, she felt like a piece on a chessboard.

"Of course your wishes matter to Isaac," Vee defended her husband. "Neither of us would allow you to be sacrificed if we thought you would be unhappy."

"You think I'll be happy with him?" Raina asked incredulously.

"Yes, I do," Elvira countered, her voice sharp and pointed. "I've seen you two together; there's definitely something there. Even though I'm not happy about your involvement in Miami's mob scene I can't object to the way Mateo feels about you."

"We'll end up killing each other," Raina protested. "We're both so stubborn."

Vee chuckled. "Mateo wants to do a lot of things with you, my dear, but he most certainly doesn't want to kill you."

"It was a figure of speech," Raina muttered.

"Do you think you can give him a chance?"

Raina thought about it, but every time her brain tried to settle on the idea of marrying Mateo, of sharing intimacy with him, she shied away from the thought. "What's the alternative?"

"You move to Venezuela and live on the compound with us, where your options in men are seriously limited. You've become more of a target now than you ever were before, which means you now require a lifetime of protection." Raina opened her mouth to defend her choices, but Vee interrupted her, "It doesn't matter, Raina. The fact is, you're mafia royalty whether you like it or not. Whether you're living on a farm in the middle of nowhere with Diane and Joe or if you're jet-setting across the world, forging documents and partying with K-pop bands in South Korea."

Raina's eyes widened in horror. "You heard about that?"

"So did Sotza and so did Mateo. If you hadn't decided to leave South Korea on your own, I guarantee Mateo would've come after you. He wasn't happy with some of the things you got up to. There are pictures, Raina."

Raina giggled and buried her face in a pillow as she imagined what those pictures contained. "I wanted to have some fun."

"I know, sweetie," Vee said comfortingly. "And so you should have as much fun as you want. You've had far too many things go wrong in your short life. To be honest, I was happy to hear about your exploits when the reports filtered in to Sotza. I had to talk him down a few times, beg him to not go after you himself, but I think he also understood your need to explore the world and establish some semblance of independence."

Raina was happy that her parents understood, but she was even more conflicted about her future. She was only twenty-one, not ready to settle down. Yet, that's essentially what they were all asking of her. She felt like a child again, in desperate need of a hug and advice from her mom. Both of them.

After she got off the phone with Vee, Raina immediately dialed the number for Casey Reyes. She had a long and satisfying phone conversation with the mafia queen of Bolivia. Casey had at first been understandably leery about Raina staying in the mansion, and in Miami, for that matter.

Casey was also mob royalty, having grown up the daughter of a man high up in the organization. After a terrible incident, where her entire family had been killed in a mob hit, she'd been married off to the man who had killed her family and forced to live in the home that Raina now inhabited.

"Are you sure this is what you want?" Casey asked, concerned for her best friend's only child. "Miami is a vicious place to live when you're involved in the underworld scene."

"I don't have much choice," Raina told her. "My... fiancé is taking over and he wants me here with him." Raina hesitated in calling Mateo her fiancé when he hadn't actually proposed to her and she hadn't actually agreed to marry him, but she didn't know what else to call him. Boyfriend seemed like a weak word for what Mateo wanted.

"Well, I suppose I can understand that. Love has a way of making us do stupid things."

Raina didn't correct Casey about the love thing. She sure as shit wasn't in love with Mateo, but she didn't want to argue the matter, or make Casey even more concerned about her well-being. Instead, they discussed the people Raina needed to see and places she needed to visit in order to make connections in the East Coast hub city. Raina was impressed with the plethora of information Casey gave her.

When Raina hesitantly brought up the house and her redecoration plans, Casey was enthusiastically on board, much to Raina's relief. If Casey had objected, then Raina wouldn't have touched the mansion.

"Please tell me you'll bulldoze the office. I fucking hated that place," Casey said, a dark tone lacing her voice.

Raina didn't know what happened to Casey in the office, but she was more than ready to agree. "I haven't been in there yet, but I promise to gut the place when I get my hands on it."

"Oh good!" Casey said happily, and Raina could hear her clap her hands. "Tell me everything you plan on doing. I always wanted to get my hands on the place, but Ignacio, my late husband, may he never rest in peace, wouldn't let me touch anything."

They swapped decorating notes and tips and Raina promised to start a Pinterest board so she could update Casey on all her ideas and Casey could remotely take part in the renovation.

By the time they hung up Raina was smiling and feeling more relaxed than she had in days. Maybe weeks, or even months. Though she didn't want to live pinned under the heavy thumb of her family, she felt safer and more secure than she had in a while.

CHAPTER TWENTY-FOUR

The following day Raina felt energetic and ready to get shit done in her new home. She researched designers in Miami and found one who came highly recommended, Daniela Velazquez. When Raina called, the woman was upbeat and intrigued by the project, asking a ton of questions, some that Raina had answers to and some she didn't.

They agreed to meet in person the next day, which left Raina to explore on her own for one more day.

Raina was eager to do the one thing she'd been dying to do since her phone conversation with Casey; explore the underground bunker. Casey had told her of her traumatic time in the bunker and though Raina was saddened for the other woman, she was also wildly curious. What was it like down there? Would there still be a body?

Casey's bodyguard had been killed in the bunker and as far as Casey knew, he was still down there. After the mob war, the mansion had been largely abandoned except for a cursory clean-up, which explained some of the outdated furnishings.

Raina wore a pair of sweatpants and a heavy sweatshirt. It was a bit much for the warm Florida day, but she was going underground. She wanted her skin protected from dust and sharp edges. She made her way down to the pool area, stopping to take inventory of the pool deck. She loved the pool itself and would enjoy it even more once she updated the furniture.

She made her way into the pool house, looking around in awe. Though she'd had a taste of how the wealthy lived when she was in Venezuela, she'd grown up on a farm where luxury meant there was enough hot water for everyone to shower. These past two years, when she'd gone on the run, exploring the world, she'd decided to live on less rather than more, though she had a healthy bank account balance thanks to her lucrative forging contracts. She hadn't wanted to draw attention to herself by throwing money around like it was water.

She touched a shelf piled high with fluffy grey towels, but when her fingers came away covered in dust, she realized the towels were supposed to be white. They hadn't been cleaned in years. She'd have to ask the housekeeper to assess the pool viability situation. It was becoming clear through her explorations that many things on the estate were suffering disrepair.

When she arrived where Casey had described the location for the entrance of the bunker, it took Raina a few minutes to find it. She had to shove one of the shelves out of the way and pull up a trap door. Her side twinged its unhappiness at the weight of the door, but she ignored it.

Raina peered through the darkness of the hole, trying to see into the bunker below, but it was pitch black. She couldn't even see the bottom. She chewed on her lip for a moment, thinking, deliberating on what to do. The smart thing would be to leave, tell Mateo about the secret bunker and beg him to let her come back here with the ladder.

Of course, Raina wasn't going to do that. There was almost no chance Mateo would let her go down into that hole until his men had secured it completely. But she wanted to be the one to explore it, to discover this facet of her new home. Casey had practically dared her by telling Raina about it.

She pulled her phone out of her pocket, tapped the flashlight app and shone if into the dark hole. She was relieved when it illuminated the bottom of the bunker, though she wasn't certain how far away it was.

After another moment of deliberation, she decided to go ahead with her original plan. She couldn't see a ladder or stairs to get down into the bunker and realized she would have to let herself drop. Before she could overthink it, she took hold of the ledge, turned around and slowly lowered herself into the hole.

Raina groaned as her stomach teetered on the edge with her legs in and her torso still on the outside. The pain from her gunshot wound flared and she grunted, pushing herself further back and allowing gravity to pull her body down.

She gripped the rough edge digging her fingers into the dirty concrete as she dangled above the floor that was somewhere below her at an unknown distance. She was going to have to let go. Because there was no chance of her being able to pull herself back up. Even if she wasn't injured, she still didn't have the upper body strength for it.

"This was a bad idea," she muttered to herself as she let go of the ledge and dropped into the dark hole with a yelp of fear.

It was somewhat anti-climactic as the ground wasn't really that far down. She hit the floor, her legs buckled and she fell over, banging her elbow on a wall.

"Ouch." She sat up and rubbed the offended area. She glared up at the hole above her, it was maybe six or seven feet high.

Raina fished her phone back out and held it up. The room flooded with light and she realized she was in a corridor. She got to her feet and dusted off her pants then moved cautiously through the tunnel. The floor was on a slant and getting steeper the further underground she went.

"This is the part where the serial killer, angry clown, Predator, alien stalks me into a dead end and murders me," she said, hoping that by saying it out loud she would be making the idea ironic thus negating the possibility of it actually happening.

Raina decided that she thought she was a lot braver than she actually was. Obviously she was brave or she never would have gotten into the underground bunker, but that was the extent of her bravery. She didn't want to go into the bowels of whatever it was she was following, but at this point she felt invested. It was either continue forward or admit she failed.

Luckily, the corridor ended shortly after that, leading into a big room with no other exits. Unluckily, there was indeed still a dead body in the room, as Casey predicted there might be.

Raina moved hesitantly forward, toward the skeleton on the floor. She crouched next to it, hovering her light over top. It seemed well preserved, with the clothing still intact and the bones all in one spot. That meant scavengers hadn't gotten into the underground bunker. There was no smell. She had been half expecting there to be the stench of death. She supposed that he probably did smell when he was decomposing, but now there were only bones.

This person had been Casey's bodyguard before Reyes had taken her from the house. This man had tried to kill Casey, having gone insane with psychotic love. He had died in the attempt and Casey had lived.

Ignoring the corpse, Raina explored the room, running her fingers down the walls, looking for an alternate escape route. There was none. It was becoming clear that this room was meant to be some kind of bolthole, not an actual way off the estate. Still, it might come in useful in the future.

Raina made her way back to the hole under the pool house, her shoulders slumping as she approached it. She'd really been hoping that there would be an alternate way out, because there was no chance she'd be able to reach the hole, let alone lift herself even if she was able to. She was going to have to call for help.

Mateo's phone rang twice before he picked up. "Raina?" he asked sharply. "Where are you? Are you safe?"

She chewed her lip. "Have you read Alice in Wonderland?"

"Yes," he growled. "Answer my question, are you alright?"

"I'm in the back yard," she said, stretching the truth. Technically she was under the back yard. "I could use some help getting back out of the rabbit hole."

"Did you hurt yourself?" he demanded. She could hear him moving, probably toward the back of the house.

"No," she was quick to assure him. "I'm just a little stuck."

"Where are you? I don't see you anywhere."

He must be looking for her on the estate lawns. "I'm in the pool house." Well, under the pool house.

Seconds later the door to the pool house opened and she could hear Mateo's heavy footfalls. She called out to him, drawing him towards the hole. He looked over the edge and down at her upturned face. His features conveyed a myriad of emotions. Bewilderment, annoyance, anger, concern. He shuttered his expression almost immediately. She wondered which emotion he decided to settle on.

"Did you fall in?" He knew better, though she supposed he was giving her the benefit of the doubt.

She sighed and thought about lying, but decided truth was

better. "No, I was out for a walk and thought I would explore."

"Do you always move shelves and lift trapdoors when you're exploring?" He crossed his arms over his broad chest and leaned against the shelf.

"Are you going to get me out of here, or what?" she demanded, frowning up at him.

He actually seemed to think about it, the bastard. Finally, he said, "I should leave you down there. It'd be a hell of a lot easier to keep an eye on you."

He moved away from the hole, his footfalls indicating that he was leaving the pool house.

"Hey! Where're you going?" she asked, worried he was actually abandoning her in the hole.

A few minutes later he returned with a ladder and a few minutes after that Raina was free of the bunker. She felt much better stepping out from the pool house and into the warm Florida sunlight. She ran her hands down her goose pimpled arms. As they walked toward the house, Raina glanced at Mateo.

"What are you going to do about the underground bunker?" she asked curiously.

"Leave it. It was put there for a reason, a good one."

Raina shivered. The hole was put there specifically for the inhabitants of the mansion to escape to if ever the need should arise. She felt uneasy at the thought that it had been used in the past and could still be used in the future. It was eye-opening to comprehend that now that she was firmly part of Mateo's life, she was also part of the mafia life, which could put her in danger. She kept having these moments of realization. Not like a gradual acclimatization to her new reality, but like these sledgehammer moments. It was disconcerting.

"Sure, do whatever you want with the hole in the ground. But you want might want to clear the body out first."

For a moment Mateo said nothing, then the import of her words sank in and he looked at her incredulously. "There's a dead person in there?"

She grinned at him, opened the glass sliding doors and went inside.

CHAPTER TWENTY-FIVE

The next day, Raina was pleased to see that, true to her word, Daniela Velazquez, interior designer, was making her way through the mansion with a tape measure and a notebook, Angela trailing after her with a bored expression. After she finished making notes, Daniela met with Raina in the dining room.

Raina loved everything Daniela came up with, despite there being a strange coolness to the designer. Raina still couldn't put her finger on it, but there was something almost hostile about the other woman. It was weird because she'd been pleasant and enthusiastic on the phone the day before.

Raina followed Daniela to the front door. Daniela shook Raina's hand and assured her that she would start lining up contractors and searching for design pieces. Raina watched Daniela walk toward her vehicle, a flashy red convertible. Maybe Daniela didn't like rich people? Or maybe she somehow knew her new clients were involved in organized crime and she didn't approve.

Raina shrugged and stepped back into the house, closing

the door and locking it. When she turned around, she nearly ran straight into Angela, who jumped back a step.

"I don't like her," Angela said bluntly.

Raina didn't think it would be particularly professional to agree. Instead she said, "She's a professional. It's not her job to make friends here."

Angela narrowed her eyes. "I don't trust her."

"Do you trust anyone?" Raina genuinely wanted to know. Angela's hard exterior seemed to cover a hard interior.

"No," Angela said with no inflection in her voice. "Except maybe Mateo."

Raina wondered why Angela was so untrusting. Oddly, Raina felt comfortable around Angela. She felt instinctually that Angela would make a solid ally if Raina could earn her trust.

"You've been with Mateo for a long time?"

"Since I was a teen," Angela said tersely. "If you'll excuse me. I need to get back to work."

Raina nodded and speculatively watched her walk away. There was a story there and Raina wanted to know what it was. She sensed that there was zero attraction between Mateo and Angela, yet they'd been together a long time. Had they ever considered hooking up? They would have made a good team. Deadly and beautiful.

Raina checked the time and realized she only had twenty minutes before she was expected at the dining table and she needed to shower. Mateo was a stickler for both punctuality and eating dinner together every evening.

Exactly twenty minutes later, Raina put the finishing touches on her makeup and admired herself in the mirror. When she took off her glasses, she could barely see herself in the mirror and had to lean in really close. She'd tried contact lenses when she was sixteen but had hated everything about them. It felt like putting sand in her eyes. The whole experience had made her appreciate her glasses even more.

Despite the annoyance of makeup application, she enjoyed the process of dressing up once in a while.

She chose a pair of black leggings with a soft shell-pink cashmere sweater. She wore a pair of cream-coloured spike heeled pumps on her feet. When she stood she wobbled, but after a few laps of her bedroom she got the hang of them. She'd found a limited supply of abandoned clothing in the closet and suspected that they belonged to Casey. After her conversation with the other woman she came to the conclusion that Mateo had put her in Casey's old bedroom.

There was only a handful of items. It was all good quality, but slightly large for Raina's petite frame. It became obvious that Casey was much taller than her and had longer feet. But Raina was able to make do. At least until she could get her own wardrobe.

Raina left the bedroom and made her way down to the dining room where she was five minutes late for the evening meal. As always, Mateo was waiting for her. He was a very punctual man and the sharp look that he gave her made it clear that he was taking note of her tardiness.

Raina smiled blithely and took her usual seat. She'd been at the mansion for four days now and was starting to settle into a routine. The only problem was that it was a routine she didn't particularly enjoy. She'd explored the mansion, taking notes and meeting with the interior decorator. Beyond that, she had nothing much to do and she was bored. She knew Mateo didn't want her leaving the mansion, but she had to convince him to lift the house arrest or she would go crazy.

The housekeeper, Lydia, came breezing into the dining room, her hands laden with dishes. Raina smiled up at her and helped take them out of Lydia's hands, placing them on the table. Raina liked Lydia. The older woman was cheerful, efficient, and always had a ready ear for Raina. Raina had spent more time in the kitchen since arriving than she'd spent in all of her kitchens combined when she was travelling.

Once Lydia left the dining room, Raina and Mateo began eating. The meal consisted of a roast chicken with rosemary seasoning, potatoes, vegetables, and dessert.

"Do we have any plans for tomorrow?" Raina hoped she sounded nonchalant.

Mateo glanced up from his meal with a raised eyebrow. "What do you want, Raina?" he asked, cutting through her small talk.

"I want to go out shopping for the day."

She expected an argument from him, the man who had to have eyes on her at all times, especially since the bunker debacle. Instead, he surprised her by saying, "Done. Let Danny know what time you want to leave and he'll put together a team for you."

Once Raina was over her shock of his quick capitulation, she protested, "Why do I need a team? I'm just going shopping."

Mateo continued to eat, only speaking once he swallowed. "You will have a team of men with you every time you leave the house," he said calmly. "This subject is not up for debate."

Raina badly wanted to debate the subject, but she wanted to leave the house more. She figured now was not the time to push Mateo on the ridiculous amount of security he insisted she have. She'd take that up with him next week, after she went shopping.

She gave him a tight smile. "Thank you. I'll speak to Danny and let him know when I'd like to leave and where I'd like to go."

They continued their meal in silence. It was a comfortable

silence though. They ate delicious food together, sipped wine, and watched the dying sunlight filtering through the window as it gradually gave way to dusk. The evening meal was becoming something that Raina looked forward to. A time for her to see Mateo with her own eyes, to assure herself that he still existed. She didn't know why she needed to do that. She suspected it had something to do with the feelings that she was developing for him, the feelings that she was still firmly in denial about.

As she finished her meal, she touched her napkin to her lips and placed it on the table. "I think I'll go back to my room now," she told him pushing herself away from the table.

Before she could stand, he reached out and took hold of her wrist. His dark eyes held the intensity that she was becoming used to whenever he said something important to her. She tensed under his grip.

"Your security team belongs to me, Raina. Which means they report to me." His eyes took on a hardness as she waited for his next words. "They report everything to me. Where you go, who you see, and what you do. Do not disappoint me."

She made a face and tugged her wrist away from his hand. He let her go. She preferred the Mateo that would joke around with her, whose banter, while dark, always held that edge of humour. This Mateo was far too serious. This Mateo was the boss and she didn't like it.

She debated on what she would say to him, epic retorts filtering through her mind. Finally, she settled on, "The only person who can disappoint you is you. If my actions disappoint you, then you've set me on too high of a pedestal."

He leaned back in his chair, sitting his elbow on the table as he contemplated her. "Perhaps I do set you on a pedestal. And perhaps you are correct, my expectations are too high."

She felt a moment of elation that he was agreeing with her, then he added, "But it's not my expectations that require adjusting. You will stay on top of any pedestal I set you on. I will make sure of it."

CHAPTER TWENTY-SIX

Raina told herself it was going to be okay, that she hadn't specified exactly what kind of shopping she wanted to do, and Mateo *had* agreed to let her go. She was in the process of wandering the isles of Office Depot with a frowning Danny. Angela was covering the main entrance while Thomas waited in the vehicle. Mateo had put all of his best people on her. Raina was starting to realize he meant it when he said she wouldn't be going anywhere without a security detail.

"What exactly are we shopping for?" Danny asked, skepticism clear in his voice.

It was possible that Danny was under the impression she would be shopping for things like clothes, shoes, and handbags. It wasn't her fault he was making assumptions, but she supposed she should come up with some kind of explanation to give him.

"Scrapbooking supplies," she said cheerfully, tossing another cartridge of ink into her shopping cart.

"You need a $2000 high-resolution printer, a precision

knife and paintbrushes for scrapbooking?" He pointed at the items piled in her shopping cart.

She turned to him with a disappointed expression, trying her hardest to look innocent. "Of course, I do. How else will I immortalize my memories?"

He snorted. "Seems to me you're collecting all of the necessary supplies for a printing press."

She attempted to look suitably shocked. "And what exactly would I need a printing press for?"

Danny crossed his arms over his chest and narrowed his eyes as he continued to trail after her. "You do know that your mother was keeping a close eye on you while you were in Pennsylvania? She was well aware of everything you got up to, including your little forgery business."

"Really?" She didn't know how to feel about that. She'd known that Vee had kept tabs on her to some extent, but Raina had done a good job of hiding her forging business. Not even Joe and Diane had known.

"Really," Danny confirmed. A brief smile lifted the edge of his lips. "Your mother is quite proud. She says you have a good head for business."

Raina beamed her pleasure. She couldn't help it. She was a good forger and it felt awesome to know that her mother, a badass mafia queen, thought Raina was a good businessperson.

"Are you going to tell Mateo?" she asked Danny.

He sighed heavily and rubbed at a spot between his brows. She wondered if she was giving him an irritation headache. Sometimes she did that the people.

"What exactly do you intend to do with this set up you're putting together?"

Raina excitedly told him her plan. "I still have a few commissions that I wasn't able to get to before I was shot in

Venice. I want to finish those and then ship the proofs to their owners. I had some really good clients; I can ask them for references. Then I'll put feelers out through the underworld, letting people know that I'm in town and my services are available."

"I don't want to dash your dreams here, missy. But the wife of Mateo Gutierrez, the newest boss in town, absolutely cannot be setting up her own side hustle. Especially one that her husband doesn't know about."

Raina frowned irritably. "We're not married."

She was pretty much over having people tell her what she could and couldn't do as Mateo's wife. As far she was concerned, they didn't even have a wedding date. She told Danny as much.

Danny took his phone out and started texting.

"Who are you texting?" she asked angrily, already knowing the answer.

"Mateo," he grunted, confirming her suspicions. But before she could start yelling at him for betraying her, he looked up with a smug expression. "Your wedding date is July 14th."

Raina's mouth fell open. July 14th was only a couple months away. "Did you just tell Mateo that I wanted a wedding date?"

"Yes." Danny calmly took hold of her cart and continued pushing it.

Well shit. That hadn't gone how she planned. Now she had a wedding date. She didn't want a wedding date. She had a fucking wedding to plan too! She had a business to set up and a wedding to plan. She decided then and there to never engage in a conversation like this with Danny again. That guy was too clever by half.

Raina continued shopping, spending the rest of the day doing exactly what Mateo had expected her to. She bought enough clothing, jewelry, shoes and handbags to fill her entire walk-in closet. She didn't particularly enjoy shopping, but there was something about using Mateo's credit card that gave her a vicious spark of glee every time she handed it to a salesclerk.

It was early evening when Raina decided she was finished. They headed back to the mansion, her sitting in the backseat with Angela. Danny and Thomas sat in the front seat. There were three more security men in the car behind them.

Less than an hour later, Raina made her way to the dining room where Mateo was waiting for her. Her heart gave a flutter when she looked at him. He looked good. He always looked good, but tonight, he was wearing a suit and tie. There was something about a man in a suit, his tattoos peeking out through the collar of his shirt and the ends of his sleeves, that made her feel all warm and tingly inside.

She sank down onto her chair and reached for her napkin. He intercepted her, placing his hand on her arm.

"Did you have a good day?" he asked, taking her napkin and smoothing it across her lap.

"Do you care?"

He frowned at her. "Don't play verbal games with me, Raina," he warned. "I will only tolerate so much of your lip. If I didn't care I wouldn't ask."

"I just mean that you already know what I've spent the day doing. Your men update you every single time I cough. I can't even go to the bathroom without one of them talking to you about my bowel health." She was being purposefully provocative to get her point across. It was one thing for him to send the security team with her and quite another to spy on her constantly.

Mateo didn't take the bait. "Having my men report on your movements is not the same thing as you telling me how you are. If I ask about your day, then you'll answer promptly and truthfully. I want to know your feelings, your desires, your frustrations, everything."

Raina stared at him completely tongue-tied. She didn't know what to say to that. He was so domineering, yet also sweet. What had she done to earn such devotion from him? She'd been nothing but contrary with him, yet he still spoke to her this way. He was endlessly patient while she pushed him at every opportunity. She didn't mean to punish him, not really. She saw a lot wrong in the world, especially the one she was being forced to inhabit, and she was taking it out on him.

She swallowed the snarky reply she'd originally planned on and told him the truth. "I had a good day. It was really nice to get away from the mansion for a bit and out into the city. Miami is beautiful."

"Yes, it is," he said, leaning back in his seat, his voice becoming more conversational. "Have you been here before?"

Raina shook her head. "We didn't have a lot of money when I was growing up and didn't have the opportunity to travel much. It was pretty exciting when we could go camping in a neighbouring county." Raina smiled fondly as she thought of camping with her parents. "A far cry from the places I visited in the past few years."

"Yet I sense that you wouldn't trade any of those camping trips for a trip to Paris. Am I right?" He asked, his eyes roving over her features, memorizing her expressions as she made them.

Raina nodded her head in agreement. "My parents are really amazing people. We didn't have much when I was growing up, but we had each other. No matter what was going on, I always knew that I was loved beyond measure."

The food arrived and their conversation fell off for a few minutes as Lydia placed the various platters on the table. She was serving Mediterranean themed dishes, including souvlaki chicken with tzatziki, Caesar salad and rice. There was a small plate of baklava for after their meal. Raina thanked Lydia for the food.

As they started to eat, the conversation continued. "I grew up quite poor as well," Mateo told her.

Raina looked up in surprise. Mateo rarely talked about his childhood, even when she had pushed him in Venezuela. "I lived with my mother, two siblings and my grandfather. Mi Madre was single and unable to support us, so me and my sisters had to get jobs."

"Is that how you met Sotza?" Raina asked curiously.

"Sort of. At first all of my jobs were legitimate. I did food deliveries on my bike, I delivered messages, but as I grew, I realized the more lucrative jobs were not legal. I gradually became mixed up in the local street gangs. That was where Sotza found me. I was supposed to rip him off, intercept an arms shipment along with a couple of other boys."

Raina sucked in a breath. "From everything I've heard of Sotza, that was a very dangerous thing to do. You could've been killed."

Mateo nodded and looked at her seriously. "That was why my boss at the time had his underlings do the dirty work. Rather than get his hands dirty he sacrificed us instead. Luckily for us, Sotza saw us as the young ignorant pups we were. He let us go and paid a visit to the boss. That was the last time I saw the guy. Shortly after, Sotza came to me with a job. Something low-level. But over the years I proved my loyalty and he promoted me up the ranks."

Raina was discovering a new admiration for Mateo. He'd not had an easy life, but he jumped on the opportunities that presented themselves, worked hard and earned everything he achieved. Though he worked on the wrong side of the law, he still held all the qualities she admired. He was honest, hard-working, loyal and protective.

"What about your family now?"

"I send them as much money as I can," he told her. "I'm in the advantageous position of making enough that I can make their lives far more comfortable. They don't know exactly what I do to earn my living, but they're grateful and supportive."

Raina could hear the fondness in his voice as he spoke of his family. "Do you visit them?"

He lifted his shoulders in a half shrug. "As often as I can, maybe once every few years. But I don't want to drag them into this business. If they're seen in my presence, they could become targets."

Targets.

That was what Raina had become. It was a vulnerable position to be in, especially considering she'd recently been shot by Italy's version of Mateo and his gangster thugs. Despite this disturbing thought, Raina vowed silently to find a way to reconnect Mateo with his family. It didn't seem fair that they all cared about each other, that Mateo sent them money, but they were unable to visit.

They finished their meal in companionable silence. After, Mateo took Raina's arm and walked her back to her room. This was a first, but not unwelcome. Throughout their evening meals she was beginning to feel closer to this quiet, thoughtful man. She wanted to know more about him, wanted to spend more time with him. Especially with their upcoming nuptials.

When they reached Raina's door, Mateo put a hand on her arm and turned her to face him. He wrapped his hand around her arm, holding her in place, but not tightly. If she stepped back, she could remove herself from his embrace. She didn't step away though. They stood silently looking at each other.

"I want to kiss you." His words were husky, his dark eyes

smouldering with what Raina suspected was lust. An answering arrow of heat shot through her.

"I want to kiss you too," Raina said breathlessly.

It was such a strange moment. Them standing together in a mansion where they were attempting to make a home. He'd forced her there, as he'd forced many parts of her life. She should hate him, yet he was impossible to hate. The moment felt almost like they were normal couple, falling in love, getting to know each other. She didn't want it to end. She didn't want to go back to the endless strife that seemed to be the mafia.

"May I?" he asked, a husky timber to his voice.

"Yes," she whispered, surprised he was bothering to ask. Mateo never asked for anything. Yet, this moment felt different. Separate from reality. They were just a man and a woman, experiencing an insane amount of chemistry.

He didn't waste any more time. He lowered his head to hers, curving his arm around her neck to hold her in place. Raina tilted her head back against his arm and waited for his lips touched hers. The kiss was beautiful, it was electric. It sent heat spiraling through her body, from her nipples to her pussy. Everything flooded with desire. And that from only the barest touch of his lips to hers. She wanted more.

She lifted her arms to wrap them around him, to pull him closer, to deepen the kiss, but he pushed her back, held her arms, his expression regretful. "Not yet," he said, almost to himself.

"When?" Raina demanded, then could've smacked herself. Seriously? When? She may as well get it over with and beg him for sex.

He chuckled. "Soon, mi amor. Trust me, I will not be able to wait much longer."

Raina didn't know why he was waiting at all, but she wasn't about to say anything that would make her sound even more desperate. She stepped away from him, murmured good night and reached for her door handle.

Before she could open it, his voice stopped her.

"Make sure that your scrapbooking project doesn't get you into trouble," he growled, well aware of what she was up to.

Raina threw a grin over her shoulder, winked at him and slipped into her room, closing the door behind her.

CHAPTER TWENTY-SEVEN

It took two days for Raina to properly set up her forging equipment. She chose an office on the ground floor facing the sprawling back yard. It had double French doors and softer, more feminine decor. She suspected it was meant to be a woman's office, but she didn't think it had ever been used.

She set up all of her equipment, her perfectionism at the forefront as she made sure everything was flawless. As per her usual, she printed a couple of fake passports and driver's licenses for herself, making sure that everything looked absolutely perfect. She beamed at the miniature picture of herself, pushed her glasses up her nose and set about finishing some of the contracts she had to leave behind in Italy.

Forging spoke to her. It was her art. It required precision, skill and a great deal of knowledge on world identifications. Passports were different from country to country. Many countries, including the US, used biographical microchips. They implanted the passports with chips that contained information on the holder. She also had to be sure that the picture used inside the passport contained the necessary biometrics; meaning they had to pass face recognition software.

She set out the tools she would need: glue, metallic stickers, ink pads and stamps. She picked up the first passport and carefully peeled away the binding thread. She used the intaglio printing process to create fine individual lines for the decorative border. As she worked, a sort of meditative state captured her. She lost track of time as she concentrated.

This passport would go to a Saudi princess intent on leaving her husband and her country. She had contacted Raina after learning that Raina was one of the top forgers in the world. The job was important to Raina, not only because the Princess was paying an exorbitant amount of money, but because Raina had learned bits and pieces of the princess's current existence and it wasn't pretty. Raina was determined to do her best to help get the princess out of her situation by creating a document that would be undetectable as a forgery.

She leaned back in her seat, completely satisfied with her work. She closed the passport and pushed it inside an envelope, sealing the envelope. On the front was an address the princess had provided. The document would go to one of her loyal followers, a servant inside her Dubai penthouse.

"I think we need to set up some ground rules for you. It took me twenty minutes to locate you in this mausoleum," Mateo's voice drawled from behind her.

Raina jumped, not having heard the door open. She twisted around in her seat to look at him.

"Maybe we should set up some ground rules for you," Raina countered. "You seem to come and go at will. Maybe a bell around your neck so I know when you're sneaking up on me?"

Mateo's lips twitched in amusement. "You want to know where I am at all times, mi amor?"

"Not really," she countered. "How about your ground rules include you knocking on doors?"

He took a few steps toward her, his dark eyes sweeping her from top to bottom. Raina felt self-conscious and quickly ran one hand over her thighs, smoothing her jeans and the other over her hair, tucking a lock behind her ear.

"If I were to knock on the door before entering, you would have time to gather yourself. I prefer to see you uninhibited, without the time for that sharp brain to come up with some kind of challenge for me."

Raina blushed as she imagined what he might see when walking into a room unexpectedly. Particularly, her bedroom.

She was about to say something tart in return when he stopped her, raising his hand and speaking. "I would like you to come outside with me."

Raina raised an eyebrow, then shrugged and stood. It wasn't like she had anything else to do. She had finished her last commission and was waiting for more to come in.

They left through the French doors of her office, which led straight out onto the pool patio. "This way," Mateo said, taking her arm.

Near the pool was an outdoor gym with weights, benches and mats. Raina had seen this area before while exploring the mansion, but she avoided it. She'd never really been a weightlifting girl. Her arms resembled sticks more than anything that might have real muscle.

Mateo escorted her onto one of the mats and then let go of her arm, standing opposite her.

"Fight me," he commanded her.

Raina frowned at him. "You want me to do what?"

"I want you to fight me."

Raina was beginning to believe that he was serious. She spent enough time with Mateo now to understand his various moods, not that there were many. He tended to be either neutral, serious or annoyed. Sometimes funny, in a dark sort of way.

She crossed her arms over her chest and glared at him. "If you recall, the last time I fought you, I lost."

Not only had she lost, but she'd ended up drugged and in Venezuela for a month, then two years on the run after that. If she learned anything from that experience, it was that she should avoid fighting Mateo.

He shook his head, frustrated. She sort of felt sorry for him. Mateo was a man of action, not words. He also held a great deal of power, which meant he didn't have to explain himself to many people. However, she fully intended to set the precedent that he would be 100% accountable to his future wife. Which meant explaining himself, if need be.

"Why do you want me to fight you?" she demanded. "We both know you can kick my ass. If you need an ego boost, go talk to Danny. He looks like he'll present more of a challenge."

Mateo was nearly a foot taller than her and weighed 100 pounds more. It was never going to be a fair fight between the two of them.

"When I picked you up on your university campus, you fought me," he said insistently, as if encouraging her to do it again.

She rolled her eyes at him. "Yeah and look how that ended."

"What I'm saying is, you had training. You challenged me, if only for a few seconds. That doesn't happen. Very few people, especially women of your size, are able to challenge me." He ran a hand through his hair ruffling it, obviously frustrated with the direction of this conversation.

Raina waved her hand dismissively in the air. "I caught you by surprise. You didn't know I'd taken any self-defense training. You probably thought you had an easy mark."

He nodded, pointing at her. "Exactly. I thought you would be an easy pick up, and you did take me by surprise. No one takes me by surprise."

She was beginning to get where he was going with this. Cautiously, she asked, "Are you asking for a rematch? Because I haven't exactly been honing my skills in case you hadn't noticed when I got shot in Italy."

"I'm not asking for a rematch, little girl," he said, with some amusement. "I'm looking to teach you a few things. In case anyone else ever tries to grab you. You take them by surprise, the way you did me. Only, if you're attacked again, you take them by surprise, you take them down, and you kill them."

She stared at him in consternation. She hadn't considered that he might want to teach her how to fight better. It shifted the way she viewed him. It was like he didn't care if she used her skills to fight him as long as she survived any other potential attack. That knowledge was something she didn't want to examine too closely. It fit with the apparent devotion he was showing toward her. She didn't know how to deal with it.

"You spend half the time watching what I eat in case it tips the delicate balance of my kidney health, yet now you're proposing to teach me how to fight. You don't make any sense to me," she challenged him, pointing out his contradiction.

Instead of defending himself, he said, "No, I don't imagine I do make sense to you. Not yet anyway."

"What does that mean?" she demanded, hands on her hips.

But before she could get an answer, he was lunging for her. She let out a shriek, flung herself to the side, gripped his elbow and tripped him. He didn't go down. He was too skilled to go down, but he stumbled and it took him a second to turn around and face her again. When he did, a grin was spread across his face, as if to say I told you so.

Raina clapped a hand over her mouth. She hadn't meant to do that; it had been automatic. Muscle memory from all those self-defense classes.

"Well done," he praised, striding back toward her. "Now, when I attack you again, this is what I want you to do – "

Raina had a surprisingly good time learning combat tactics with Mateo. He didn't just teach her self-defense, he taught her how to finish an opponent if she needed to. How to make sure the attacker stayed down so they couldn't grab hold of her again.

Over and over Mateo would attack and she was forced to go on the defensive. She learned different ways to throw her hands up, to lunge, to kick, to use dirty tactics to take an opponent down.

By the time they finished, she was laying on the ground, heaving for breath and grinning broadly. Mateo, who was standing over top of her, dropped to the ground beside her. She looked over at him. He had barely broken a sweat, whereas she was practically dripping. Still, he looked satisfied, pleased by her performance, which lit a small fire inside her. She didn't want to become his trained monkey and actively resisted his orders so that she could retain her independence, but deep down, she liked it when he looked at her like that, as though he felt pride in her.

"Again?" she asked, inviting him for another round.

He rolled over onto his hands and pushed himself up in a push-up, his biceps bulging against his T-shirt, threatening to tear the seams. He sat back on his heels and held a hand out to her. "Again."

CHAPTER TWENTY-EIGHT

Raina ached everywhere. It was the ache of using muscles she hadn't used in a long time. Throughout the week she'd been training with Mateo, Angela or Danny depending on who was available. The more she got out on the mat, the more she wanted to spar. All of her opponents were highly skilled, and she was learning fast.

Despite the fun she was having, Raina decided to take a day off to recover. She was curled up in her window seat, a plush blanket wrapped around her shoulders and a cup of herbal tea on the table beside her. At her feet was a battered romance novel that Mateo had sent to her room. The Hellion Bride by Catherine Coulter. Either Mateo had a thing for historical fiction, or he was making a joke at her expense.

She was in the process of painting her toenails bright pink. When she was finished, she was going to start the book.

Raina had to admit that her life at the mansion was starting to settle into a kind of pattern, an enjoyable one even. During the day she either worked or shopped. In the afternoons she usually sparred with whoever was available, and in the evenings, she had a leisurely dinner with Mateo.

So far he'd shown up for every single one, despite the pressure of taking over one of the biggest crime capitals in the world. Their meals had not only become a must, but something that she wanted to do. Sometimes, she and Mateo didn't speak at all, just sat and ate in companionable silence. Sometimes they chatted about their daily activities, like what Raina shopped for that day or how the renovations on the mansion were going. Other times, they fought like cats and dogs, but Raina loved every minute of it. For some reason, she felt safe using her sharp wit on Mateo. He never got angry with her and his counterarguments were intelligent. He filled her mind with things that she never thought about before.

Without warning, her bedroom door opened, startling her. She frowned at the presumption but let out a sigh when she saw Mateo.

"I thought we talked about the knocking thing," she grouched at him, carefully applying the next layer of polish to her toenails.

He didn't address her snarky comment, but walked closer to her, watching her carefully. He always did that. Watched her with a look in his eyes that he reserved especially for her. A kind of intense scrutiny, but not one that made her nervous. On the contrary, by the time his face smoothed into a blank expression she usually managed to catch a brief look of satisfaction. As though he was pleased with everything he saw when he looked at her. It started a small glow inside of her, one that grew brighter with every passing day, with every glance.

"May I sit?"

Raina shot him a skeptical look. "Since when do you ask?"

Mateo reached out for a chair and pulled it up next to the window seat, sitting beside her, close enough that his knee brushed against her thigh. At that single accidental touch, her entire body began to vibrate with tension. She didn't know how he did it so easily, but something about him made every particle of her being stand up and take notice. It was like the skin of her thigh had suddenly become hypersensitive.

"Pretty colour," he said, nodding toward her feet, his voice gruff.

Raina raised an eyebrow at him and stuck her toes out for him to admire. She replaced the top on the nail polish and set it aside, then shifted in the seat to give Mateo a piercing look.

"You didn't come in here to talk to me about my nails, did you?"

"Perhaps I like being with you, no matter what you're doing." His eyes held hers so that she could see the seriousness, though the banter was light.

She snorted and pushed her glasses back up her nose. "Next you'll tell me that you watch me while I'm sleeping."

He gave her a wolfish grin, one that stole the breath from her chest. He rarely looked at her like that and when he did, he captivated her. "You do this adorable snore when you sleep on your back. And you sigh like a woman having secret dreams when you roll over onto your side."

Raina stared at him in horror. Was he serious? Or was he just pulling her leg? She couldn't tell. But if she was being honest with herself, she would admit that he absolutely had the capacity, ability and arrogance to watch her sleep.

Sometimes he seemed like such a normal guy and then other times... she didn't have a clue what he was thinking.

"Are you going to tell me why you're here?" she pushed. "I doubt it's to watch me sleep since it's only 4 o'clock."

He nodded, his face growing serious. "Our wedding is less than two months away."

Raina made a hissing sound as she sucked air in through her teeth. "Thanks for the reminder."

"You do need the reminder," he countered, his voice

growing harder. "As far as I can tell you haven't made a single wedding plan."

"You expect me to plan this wedding? A wedding that, I should remind you, I want nothing to do with." A jolt went through her as she said the words. Something inside her brain whispered *liar*. "Why don't you plan the wedding?"

Mateo studied her, his face shuttered, not giving anything away. She wondered if she'd hurt him by telling him to his face that she didn't want to marry him. She shrugged it off. It was his own fault for forcing her into the situation. What did he expect? That she would be all sunshine and roses when it came to the idea of planning her own shotgun wedding.

"If you leave the wedding planning to me," he drawled. "Then we'll be getting married tomorrow in my office and you'll be moving into my bedroom directly after. Is this something you want? Would you like to expedite our wedding?"

He spoke with such a quiet intensity that Raina knew immediately he was serious. If he had the choice, he would marry her tomorrow. Her heart sped up at the idea and her mouth went dry. Though she suspected his question was rhetorical, meant to scare her, she actually gave it some thought. What if she did take the plunge? Marry Mateo tomorrow, move into his bedroom, become his wife for real.

A warm glow slowly spread through her body at the thought of marrying Mateo and sharing his bed in less than twenty-four hours. But that warm glow was followed closely by a wave of fear. She couldn't do it. She wasn't ready. The whole situation was too much. Mateo was too much. She was still learning how to navigate her new reality.

She shook her head. "I'd rather wait."

"Then you'll need some help. I don't think you're capable of planning a wedding in two months by yourself, and I don't want you stressing yourself out trying." He held up his hand when she opened her mouth to defend herself.

"You have some wonderful qualities, but I suspect event planning isn't one of them. You're a loner. And there's nothing wrong with that, but I believe some help will make this easier on you."

Okay, he wasn't wrong about the loner thing. Raina was one of those people that gained energy from being alone. She liked that Mateo didn't seem to mind that she wasn't a social creature. That she felt shy and awkward around too many people and tended to avoid crowds. Purposefully planning a wedding that would include a crowd did seem a little beyond her.

"Who are you suggesting help me?" she asked tentatively.

"Your mother." He said, tapping her phone, which was on the bench beside her, Betty Boop case on full display.

"Which mother do you think should help me?"

Her mothers were so different that Raina could only imagine what they would come up with for the wedding. Diane would definitely want more of a simple rustic theme; she'd be all about making the guests comfortable. Vee... well... Raina wasn't entirely sure what Vee would want. She didn't know her birth mother well enough yet, but she suspected Vee would be all about the expensive dresses, flowers and catering.

"Talk to both of them," he said as he stood up.

"Okay."

Mateo set the chair aside and stepped up to Raina's side, towering over her. She tilted her head to look at him, her heart pounding in anticipation. He reached for her, his hand going to her chin to tip her face up. She suspected he wanted a kiss, but as his hand touched her face, out of the corner of her eye she saw deep scrapes. She grabbed hold of his hand and brought it up to eye level. His knuckles were red and raw, and covered in scrapes.

She looked up at him, her fingers still holding his hand.

"You hit someone." It wasn't a question. She knew they were offensive wounds.

He didn't bother to deny it and he didn't try to joke it off by saying she should see the other guy. Instead he held her gaze and moved his hand so that he was cupping her chin. He was traced his thumb over the smooth skin and said, "So fucking beautiful. I don't know how I'll wait until our wedding."

His eyes narrowed as he scanned her. She squirmed in the window seat, suddenly wishing that she was wearing more than a brief pair of shorts and a cami top. She felt vulnerable and his words sounded like a warning.

"I don't know if I can wait until our wedding either," she admitted.

He released her chin and turned to walk away. At the door he paused and glanced back at her. "You may invite your mother for a visit, if you wish." He thought about it for second and seemed to gird himself for the next sentence. "Both of them."

Raina snickered as she pictured Mateo and Vee inhabiting the same house while the wedding planning was going on. She suddenly realized that was exactly the sort of drama she needed in her life.

CHAPTER TWENTY-NINE

The next day, at precisely 1 PM sharp, Angela escorted Daniela into Raina's office. Daniela inclined her head gracefully and gave Raina a tight smile before sitting primly on one of the leather seats. She was sophisticated, efficient, elegant, utterly beautiful and kind of terrifying.

Raina stood and came out from behind her desk, dropping onto the sofa across from Daniela. She narrowed her eyes at Daniela and watched as the other woman opened her leather portfolio and started spreading out samples on the small table in between them.

Despite Raina's every attempt, Daniela refused to warm up to her. Raina couldn't put her finger on why. There was usually a reason if someone didn't like her, but with Daniela, Raina sensed that whatever it was it wasn't personal. At least not personal to her. Perhaps, Daniela had a grudge against her mother.

"Did you happen to know an Elvira Montana?" Raina asked as casually as she could. "She would have lived here about five years ago. Perhaps used your services?"

Daniela looked up sharply, a frown marring her perfect

Latina features. "No, I haven't heard of her, but if she requires interior decorating then please give her my card." Daniela's voice was cool and professional. "Now if I could bring your attention to..."

Raina pushed her feelings aside. If Daniela chose not to like her, then that was Daniela's problem, not Raina's. Maybe Daniela was one of those women that didn't particularly like being around other women. Saw them as competition.

Raina buckled down and worked with Daniela for the rest of the afternoon, pouring over paint, tile, and texture samples. Raina wanted to enjoy the process; she really did, but the reality was, she really didn't care at all about matching anything. She was not a domestic goddess.

However, she did appreciate being surrounded by beauty, so she attempted to put some real effort into the project. Frequently, Daniela would give her head a small shake and redirect Raina if she believed Raina was going off the rails when it came to choosing samples.

It didn't take long before Raina realized that her home was going to be mostly fashioned by the elegant interior decorator. She decided not to care. If the outcome was beautiful, then Raina was more than happy to accept it. What she wanted out of this whole project was to erase any trace of Ignacio Hernandez from the home. So far, so good.

She was in the process of turning the man's office into a library. This was the one room that she was taking a heavy hand in decorating; it was to be a gift for Mateo. Knowing his love of the written word, Raina poured over hundreds of library designs on Pinterest and had chosen a few to combine.

The room was dark, but the windows and French doors leading out into the gardens would keep it from feeling oppressive. The bookshelves and the desk were made from cherry oak and she'd commissioned a couple of original paintings. When it was finished, the room would have a gothic romantic theme without crossing over into feminine. She thought that Mateo would appreciate his new library.

After she finished with the interior decorator, Raina settled back behind her desk to make a few phone calls. She decided to take Mateo's advice and speak to her mothers. Both of them. At the same time. She needed advice. It helped that they loved each other as well and made it clear that they had Raina's best interests at heart.

Raina set up the three-way call and waited breathlessly for the two women to connect. Vee was first.

"Raina?" Her voice was clipped but eager.

"I'm here," Raina said happily, smiling at hearing her mother's voice.

"I'm here too!" Diane's voice chirped. "So good to hear both of you. This was such a wonderful idea, Raina. I wasn't sure if I'd be able to figure out the mechanics of it, but Joe helped."

Raina smiled at the image of her mother struggling to understand a new technology. Diane was an extremely capable woman in many ways, but she had no appreciation for modern technology. Every time smart phones received a new upgrade, Diane was the first to shake her head. It had taken a lot of convincing for Raina to get her mom to give up her BlackBerry and buy a smart phone.

"Talk to me about this wedding," Vee demanded. "I want to know everything."

"Yes, everything!" Diane gushed.

It was funny that both of her mothers had the same reaction, but for very different reasons. Vee didn't want Raina marrying into the mob and had spent many hours over the past few weeks grilling Raina on her future plans. Vee made it clear that she didn't entirely approve of the wedding, but she didn't have a choice in the matter. If she had been able to help Raina escape again, she would've done it. Diane, on the other hand, loved Mateo and was extremely excited for the upcoming nuptials.

"To be honest, that's why I'm calling. I need help," Raina said. "According to Mateo, our wedding is supposed to be in a few months, but I don't have a clue what I'm doing. I don't know anything about flowers, dresses, wedding invitations. The whole thing feels like a nightmare, but he insists that it has to happen."

Vee snorted. "I've been in that boat and it wasn't particularly fun."

Vee had been completely against marrying Sotza, but he hadn't given her a choice. He had essentially locked her up until the moment she was forced to take her vows with him. Despite that, the marriage was a happy one.

"It'll be fine, honey," Diane said reassuringly. "Once we finish seeding the fields, I should be free to fly down to Miami and help you with some of this. I don't know if my tastes are any good for the fancy people that'll probably be coming to the wedding, but I'll help where I can."

"Thank you, mom, that's exactly what I needed to hear."

"If Diane is heading your way, then so am I." Vee's voice had more of a menacing quality than Diane's had. Raina bit her lip to keep from laughing out loud.

"I prefer if my fiancé stays alive until the wedding," Raina said dryly, pointing out the dislike between Mateo and Vee.

"I won't kill him," Vee assured her. "Not unless he tries to kill me first."

"Well that makes me feel better," Raina said sarcastically.

"Oh, you two," Diane said with gentle chiding. "So much alike."

Raina felt a rush of love for both women. It was beautiful to her that they were both able to love Raina and be part of her life while maintaining a friendship themselves. There was no jealousy and no fighting over Raina. They wanted her to be happy. It was hard not to feel loved when she was surrounded by such difference, but strong and independent women.

They made plans for both Vee and Diane to fly out the following week. They would stay for several days and help with the wedding plans, then they would be back in a couple of months for the actual wedding.

Raina hung up feeling content.

CHAPTER THIRTY

Later that night, Raina was sound asleep in her bedroom when the door was flung open. She blinked rapidly and shielded her eyes from the sudden glare of light coming in from the hallway. She pushed herself up in bed and stared toward the door squinting at the blurry person who interrupted her beauty sleep.

"Mateo?" she asked sleepily, covering a yawn.

"It's me," he confirmed, striding toward her bed, taking hold of the edge of her comforter and dragging it off her. "Get up, you're coming with me."

His voice was serious, his demeanor foreboding and closed off. What was going on? It must be something awful for him to wake her up this way.

As she climbed out of bed, Mateo strode to her closet, jerked the door open and disappeared inside.

"Hey!" she yelped, wobbling to her feet and taking a couple of steps after him.

She didn't want him rifling through her stuff, particularly the lingerie and other delicates. They hadn't established that kind of relationship yet and until they did, she didn't want him looking at the things she wore beneath her clothes.

Before she could follow him into the closet and scold him, he came back out and tossed a bundle at her. "Put these on, meet me downstairs."

"Are you going tell me what's going on?" she yelled after him as he quickly exited the room. She could hear his shoes tapping against the marble as he made his way rapidly down the hall toward the stairway.

She made a face, shoved her glasses on and began dressing in a pair of baggy sweatpants, a stretchy tank top and an oversized hoodie that zipped up the front. She pulled on a pair of sweat socks and running shoes and then took off after Mateo, curiosity driving her steps down to the main floor.

She was positive that if they were in a life or death situation that Mateo wouldn't have left her alone. He would've stayed with her while she changed, and he would've protected her as they left the mansion. No, this was something else, and she was dying to know what.

She nearly crashed into him as she hurtled down the marble steps to the main floor, leaping off the last two steps and landing flat on her feet. She gasped as a hand gripped her arm to steady her. She looked up into Mateo's deadly serious face. His eyes were shuttered, cold as the grave. His face was devoid of all expression. This was scary Mateo.

She took a step back and got another good look at him. Holy shit, was that blood on his clothes? She wanted to ask him, but he took hold of her wrist and walked her toward the back of the house. He was so fast that if she didn't keep up, she was positive he would drag her.

What the hell was going on?

He walked straight through the back door and into the yard, toward the outdoor gym. Once they were on the workout mats Mateo dropped her wrist, kicked off his shoes and reached for his shirt, dragging it over his head. He stood in front of her wearing only a pair of pants and a leather belt. His chiseled chest was only somewhat visible in the dim lighting of the backyard, but she squinted, trying to trace every detail.

"Do you want to tell me what's going on?" she asked him, hands on her hips.

He ignored her question and growled, "Take your shoes off, get into position."

Raina thought about it. The rebel in her wanted to argue, to demand what he was thinking, waking her up in the middle of the night and forcing her into the back yard for a fighting session. But the other part of her, the woman who was gradually becoming attached to the man standing across from her, urged her to do as he said.

For one thing, the faster she took off her shoes and got into position, the faster she could get her hands on that bare chest, even if it was a quick feel as he dropped her to the mat. But the other reason she was more inclined to obey, was the look on his face. Though it was completely blank, she sensed an underlying turmoil. Something was hurting him, something that he didn't know how to process. He was dealing by dragging her into the yard in the middle of the night.

She kicked off her running shoes, tossing them to the side of the mat and then reached for the zip on her hoodie. Though the night was somewhat cool, she would warm up quickly once they got started.

Mateo was merciless. He attacked, he punched, he kicked, he threw her across the open space. As she hit the mat for the third time and rolled until she hit the grass, Mateo strode over loomed over her. He wasn't even breathing hard, but he wore a thunderous expression. He was angry that she couldn't fight back the way he wanted her to.

He reached down and gripped both of her arms, lifting

her up so high that her feet left the ground before he set her back down. "Again," he demanded, taking a few steps back and lifting his arms in an aggressive position.

She shook her head, rubbing her shoulder where it had been jarred by her last fall. "I need a break, Mateo," she begged him. "I need some water."

There was a catch in her voice. She felt like she was going to cry. The Mateo that she'd been sparring with all week had been gentle, fun, patient. He'd been teaching her different defensive techniques, but he'd made it clear that sparring was also an excuse to get his hands on her. He hadn't hurt her. Now, he wasn't playing around. He hit her hard and yelled at her when she didn't properly defend herself.

She turned away so he wouldn't see the tears in her eyes and reached for the mini fridge that sat out next to the workout area. She pulled a bottle of water out and uncapped it.

Mateo came up alongside her and after she'd finished gulping down half the water, he took it from her hands, drained it and tossed the empty bottle over his shoulder. He took her arm and pulled her back onto the mat.

"Again," he said firmly.

Once more, Raina was forced to defend herself as Mateo came at her, taking hold of her arms, her hair, her waist and throwing her. He would aim punches and kicks at her while she was down, forcing her to roll away or kick up at him. She used every technique that he, Danny and Angela had taught her, every technique she learned in self-defense classes at university. It still wasn't enough. He countered every move she made almost before she made it and then he showed her why she needed to defend herself.

She knew that Mateo was stronger and more skilled than her, but she'd never imagined that he could be this brutal. And she knew, that even though he was hitting her hard, he was still pulling his punches. She suspected that if he really hit her full force that he would be shattering her bones. The thought that he had that kind of power made her shudder in fear. It was one thing suspecting that someone you cared about could do something horrible to you, it was quite another to see it firsthand.

Finally, after they'd been sparring for hours and Raina hit the mat for probably the dozenth time, she threw her arms up as he came at her and yelled, "Stop!"

Mateo ignored her scream, took hold of her wrist, flipped her onto her stomach and kneeled on her back, twisting her wrist up behind her until she felt as though her arm would break. This was the third time he'd done this to her and so far, she hadn't been able to break the hold.

It was at this point that an exhausted Raina burst into tears. She lay helpless beneath Mateo's bulk, sobbing her heart out. He moved quickly off her and fell to his knees beside her. He reached for her. She didn't trust him to be nice to her, if his intent was to comfort, so she shoved his arms away. She huddled on the mat, dropping her head to her knees, and allowing the tears to fall unchecked.

Mateo tried to touch her again and she jerked back violently, yelling at him, "Leave me alone, don't touch me!"

Mateo didn't touch her. He watched as she continued to cry, wiping the tears on the hem of her shirt. Finally, as the tears slowed and her hiccupping gasps stopped, he attempted to offer an explanation.

"You must learn, mi amor," he said urgently.

"I'm not your love," she lashed out, her voice wobbly with tears. "If you loved me, you wouldn't have done that to me. I'm going to be covered in bruises from head to foot. This isn't you teaching me self-defense, this is abuse."

He flinched when she said the word abuse, the look on his face suggesting she'd gutted him. Through their sparring session he had lost the emotionlessness that he'd been exhibiting before; he'd released some of the violent tension from within. Unfortunately, he'd chosen her as his punching bag.

"You have to understand, Raina, I – " he began, but she interrupted him.

"You're right, I don't understand!" she shouted at him, rubbing her shoulder. "You're impossible to understand. Sometimes, you're so sweet to me, I can't imagine a life without you. But then you do things like this. I watched you kill men in cold blood in my apartment. I could justify it because you were saving my life, but I'm coming to realize, there are two sides to you. And I don't feel like I can deal with that. I can't deal with *this* again."

Raina tried to stand up, intent on storming back to the house and locking herself inside. She'd go find a guestroom to sleep in so he wouldn't know where to find her and pick her up again, but Mateo stopped her with a hand on her arm. He gripped her and forced her to sit back down. She landed on her butt with a thump and glared at him, sniffling back more tears. Was he going to force her to fight again? If that was his plan, then he may as well beat her up, because she was done pretending to defend herself.

"Listen to me, Raina," he began, his voice hard, taking on that tone that she knew meant she wouldn't have a choice. She bit her lips to keep herself from screaming at him again. Maybe if she let him get whatever this was out of his system, he let her go back inside. "I will admit, I shouldn't have come straight to you tonight after what I'd seen, but I had to make sure you were okay. I had to set eyes on you myself."

"I was perfectly okay, sound asleep in my own bed before you dragged me out and beat me up," she snapped scathingly.

Mateo grunted his annoyance but didn't contradict her. He continued, "As you know, I've had my work cut out for me during this takeover. I knew it wouldn't go smooth, though things have been going better than I expected. Sotza is well respected in this area, and as his right-hand man, that respect seems to extend to me. However, there is some resistance coming out of Mexico."

Raina knew that Mexico had been the point of contention for her mother when Vee was boss in Miami. Mexico was the reason that Sotza had come to Miami to end her reign and install his own regime in the area. Miami had gone through many bosses over the past several years, Mateo was meant to become a permanent fixture.

"I had a liaison here, a Mexican-American who acted as go-between for me and several of the cartels. For the most part, the cartels have fallen in line. They're pleased that we intend to keep our trade routes intact, to allow the flow of goods to continue through our ports. But there is one, the cartel that Casey and Reyes were supposed to have crushed. Somehow, this cartel continues to have power, though the figurehead and his progeny are dead. They went after my middleman and his family. I knew the threat was coming, but I arrived too late to his house. It was a slaughter."

Raina's heart pounded in her chest. Sympathy, horror, terror. This was the shadowy mob life she feared, that she wanted no part of. "Who did they kill?" she asked tentatively.

He confirmed her fears. "My man was killed, his wife, his mother, their three kids. It was brutal. It was a message."

Raina felt sick. "My god, Mateo. I'm so sorry." She understood what he was not saying. This family wasn't just executed. If there was a cartel attempting to send a message, then they would have done it in the most gruesome way possible to ensure that the message was received.

Raina took a deep breath and reached out to touch Mateo. "You want me to be able to protect myself." Now she understood why he dragged her from her bed and out into the yard where he could repeatedly beat her. "You know this isn't the way to do it. This past week, the patience you showed me, I've learned so much. Tonight, I learned nothing, except that my boyfriend doesn't know how to properly deal with grief."

He lifted his head, guilt bright in his eyes. "I should've realized this was going to happen. I should've protected him and his family better."

She shook her head and rubbed her hand on his arm. "My understanding is that the mob rarely goes after family, right? You couldn't have known that they would target everyone under his roof. There's only so much protection you can offer a person."

Though her words were meant to be comforting, Mateo's gaze became sharp and fierce. He brought his hand down on top of hers and gripped it so tightly that she had to bite her lip to keep from crying out.

"Nothing can happen to you. I will wrap you in so many layers of protection, that this will not even be a possibility."

She reached up to touch his cheek, running her fingers down the rough whiskers. Two years ago, when she learned who her mother was, Raina had reconciled herself to the idea that she was essentially married to the mob. Maybe not literally, but through her family connections. And though she'd only had a vague idea of the dangers involved, she was a realist, she never once deluded herself into thinking she would be safe forever.

Instead of telling Mateo that he couldn't possibly protect her the way he wanted to, she agreed with him, she told him what he wanted to hear. "I trust you. I know that you'll never let anything touch me."

The moment was so intense, so fraught with emotion, that what happened next seemed inevitable. They reached for each other, his hands on her face, her hands on his face and they kissed. Raina didn't know who started the kiss and she didn't care. All she cared about was erasing the events of that evening, for both Mateo and herself.

The kiss was instantly explosive, igniting the smouldering chemistry that they'd been trying so hard to suppress. She didn't know why Mateo was waiting for the wedding. Perhaps he was giving her time to get used to him, or maybe he was a traditionalist.

For Raina's part, she had absolutely no problem with consummation. She had a normal libido and a healthy sex drive, but there was something about sex with Mateo that made her pause. He was so serious, so intense, even when he was trying to protect and love her. The idea of sex with Mateo scared her. Both physically, because he was a big muscular guy who kept himself in peak condition at all times, as well as mentally. She knew, without a doubt, that once they had sex there would be no going back.

But right then, their bodies dripping in sweat from the exertion of their workout, their emotions high, neither of them cared. They kissed each other with such intensity that Mateo's tooth sank into her bottom lip, cutting it open. Neither stopped as the taste of blood filled their mouths. It should have been gross, but Raina felt turned on by it. His love, his possession, was so fierce that it was like he couldn't contain it, even when he wanted to. It was a heady thought, the idea that she had this much power over him.

He pushed her back onto the mat and they rolled onto the grass together, their mouths still fused. Mateo's hands began tugging at her clothes, pushing her shirt up over her breasts. She cried out into his mouth as soon as his calloused hand covered her breast, squeezing, lifting, testing. His thumb brushed roughly over her nipple, drawing another cry from her. It was pure ecstasy. She arched up into his hand, silently begging him for more.

And he gave her so much more. His other hand shoved impatiently between their bodies, beneath the band of her sweatpants and into her panties. She gasped breathlessly as his fingers attacked her clit, then down to her opening where he gathered the wetness from her, dragging it back to her clit, rubbing furiously.

She shrieked at the intensity, but he caught the sound in his mouth as he smothered her with another kiss. She thrashed underneath him as he touched her in a way that he hadn't done before. It was too rough, too hard. When she masturbated, she touched herself lightly, drawing her orgasm out and tipping over the edge into a sweet ecstasy. This was so much different. She had no control over this. He drove her higher, higher, higher, until she was crying, begging, screaming for release. She wanted the orgasm, but it almost hurt.

He continued to hold her down, his fingers rubbing her, inside, out, all over her pussy. It was like he was attacking her with his brand of ownership. He was claiming her pussy for himself and she was helpless to stop him. With a piercing scream, her head flung back into the grass, her hair a halo, she came so hard that she felt the spurt of fluid into her panties soaking his fingers.

Tears trickled from her eyes, down her cheeks and dripped onto the ground. Mateo kissed her softly, his lips now caressing hers, no teeth or tongue. Though she could feel the imprint of his steel hard cock against her thigh, he didn't do anything about it. He wasn't going to fuck her right there in the grass as she thought he would. As she'd been half hoping.

He'd wanted to touch her, to make her come, to show her who her body belonged to. And after the way he touched her, she couldn't deny it. She belonged to Mateo Gutierrez.

CHAPTER THIRTY-ONE

Raina woke late in the morning, her body protesting the aches from her late-night sparring session. She rolled out of bed with a groan and stood unmoving for a few seconds, taking stock.

It had been a strange night. She wasn't sure what freaked her out more, the one-sided sparring session or the massive orgasm that Mateo had given her. She blushed thinking about it. It was the first orgasm given to her by another person. She didn't know how to feel about it. Part of her wanted to hunt Mateo down and demand that he finish the job and fuck her already, but the rest of her wanted to hide from him and never have to look him in the face again.

She felt unequipped for these feelings. In some ways, she'd been forced to grow up rather quickly, her kidney disease destroying some of her carefree childhood. But that also meant she'd been extremely sheltered. Her experience with the opposite sex was limited.

As a teenager, she'd been interested in boys, but several years behind her classmates when it came to sex and relationships. As a result, she now felt like she was on shifting ground. She didn't know where to step, how to step, if she should take any steps or let Mateo do the work.

A subdued Raina showered and got dressed, readying herself for the day. She chose a white summery top with a pattern of red roses splashed across it and a pair of capri jeans. She slid her feet into a pair of red flats, brushed her hair and pinned it back behind her ears with clips. On the inside she might feel uncertain but on the outside she looked fabulous. She snatched up her glasses from the nightstand and headed down to grab some breakfast from the kitchen.

She wasn't expecting to find Mateo still in the house. He was usually gone by that time of morning on whatever business he had to do while taking over Miami. But when she arrived in the kitchen, he was sitting at the breakfast table, leaning back in his chair, a steaming cup of coffee in front of him. His expression was dark and brooding and his frown only deepened when he caught sight of her.

Raina stopped in the doorway and stared at him. He was wearing a tailored suit, the dress shirt open at his tanned throat. He looked good.

She felt awkward. What did one say to the man who had essentially beat her up the night before and then gave her the best orgasm of her life? She blushed at the thought. Then she got angry. Fuck him for making her feel awkward.

"What are you doing here?" She didn't bother to take the edge out of her tone, she wanted him to know that she was still pissed. "Thought you'd be out breaking kneecaps or whatever it is gangsters do."

Mateo stared at her, not responding to her rudeness. Raina strode to the fridge and jerked it open taking the milk out and slamming it on the cupboard. She grabbed a bowl, a spoon and some cereal then poured herself a breakfast of Lucky Charms. She needed the sugary pick-me-up.

She eyed to the chair opposite Mateo then turned on her

heel and prepared to leave the kitchen. She would rather eat her breakfast in the big formal dining room than sit at the same table as Mateo right now.

"Sit your ass down." The growl came from right behind her and she jumped, spilling a couple drops of her milk. Mateo took her by the arm and pulled her toward the table, pulling a chair out and pushing her into it.

Raina's temper soared. "Excuse me? You are not the injured party here. I didn't drag you out of bed in the middle of the night and into a cold yard, then force you to fight for your life. I get to be angry, not you."

Mateo raised an eyebrow, giving her a look that suggested she had better stop speaking. "You do not get to be angry," he said calmly, with underlying steel to his voice. "Knowing how to defend yourself could save your life in the future."

"But that's not what you did last night." She picked up her spoon and attacked her cereal with a vengeance. "You took your own frustrations out on me. And that kind of behaviour isn't acceptable, Mateo. Not unless you want me to disappear again."

Mateo slammed his fist down on the table hard enough to make her cereal bowl jump and a wave of milk come splashing out. She flicked her hand in annoyance where the cereal had spilled over, sending milk droplets flying in every direction.

"If you so much as even think about leaving this property without the proper permission and protection, then I will lock your ass up so tight that you'll never see sunlight again."

She opened her mouth to argue with him, but the look on his face was so fierce that she decided to back down. For now.

"You will watch what you say to me. You will watch your step. And you will listen and obey every word I say. Do you understand?"

Raina's mouth fell open. She was used to Mateo being

demanding, overbearing and controlling. But those behaviours were usually mitigated at least by a slight sense of humour, combined with his desire and care for her. She didn't know what to do with this Mateo. He was too serious and frightening.

He slammed his fist down again and repeated himself, his voice taking on a terrifying tone. "Do you understand?"

Tears filled Raina's eyes. Not tears of sadness or grief, but tears of anger. She wanted to fight back, to defend herself. She'd been raised to believe that she was equal to any other person around her, man, woman, alien, whatever. But in this situation, in this household, she was not equal. And the knowledge stung her to the core.

"I understand." Her voice dripped with ice and she stared at him, unwilling to drop her eyes. There was so much more she was tempted to say to him, but she held it in. This was not the time. He was too volatile.

Mateo stood and she thought he was going to leave the kitchen, to go about his day. But he came around to her side of the table and knelt in front of her. He was tall enough that even kneeling his head reached the same height as hers. He touched her face, running his thumb down her cheek and then dropping his hand to her shoulder where he squeezed gently. He ran his hand down her arm, then her leg down to her ankle. He did the same on the other side and she realized that he was checking her for injuries.

"Does anything hurt?" The gentleness of his hands and his question were incongruous with their previous conversation.

She wanted to shout at him, tell him that everything hurt, especially her heart. But again, she didn't. She held it in. Something was going on with Mateo, something separate from their relationship, but something that affected their relationship.

She shook her head. "Just a few bruises, nothing worse than what I've experienced in the past week of sparring."

Mateo nodded and stood. He put his hand on the top of her head and then ran his fingers down her hair, rubbing the fine strands between his fingertips. Then, without another word, he left the kitchen. She suspected he was going to leave the house for the day, as per his usual.

Raina finished what was left of her cereal and wiped the rest of it off the table with a damp cloth.

When she was done cleaning up, she left the kitchen to survey the different areas of the house that were under construction. To avoid disrupting the household too much, Daniela and Raina agreed to section the renovations. At the moment, Daniela and her team of carpenters, painters, electricians and plumbers were working on the second floor, making their way through the guest rooms.

Raina wasn't planning to do much to the guestrooms, just update some of the styles and colours and add a few modern touches here and there. Nothing major. As she surveyed each room, she was impressed to see how far the team had come. She was pleased with the progress.

A frown marred her features as she made her way down the long marble hallway. Where was Daniela? The other woman had said that she would be here today, matching paint samples and upholstery samples in the various rooms. Raina wanted to meet with her, see if they could come up with a few ideas for the master bedroom. Raina had pretty much given the other woman run of the house, except a few rooms.

Finally, Raina pushed open the last door that she had left to check on the second floor, Mateo's bedroom.

"What are you doing in here?" Raina asked sharply, finding Daniela crouched next to the desk in Mateo's room, one of the drawers open.

Ever the picture of sophisticated coolness, Daniela didn't

jump at the sound of Raina's voice. She gracefully stood from her crouch and turned to face Raina. As always, her smile was professional, polite and distant. There was no warmth to this woman.

"I needed to get measurements in here, it's the only room we didn't discuss," Daniela said in her husky voice. She waved a hand behind her indicating the desk. "A vintage piece, very nice. Do you know where it came from?"

"No, I don't." Raina stood next to the open door and looked pointedly out to the hallway. "I believe I mentioned that I would need to speak to Mateo before we proceeded with renovations in this room."

Daniela walked gracefully toward Raina, an expression of self-condemnation and guilt on her face. Raina called bullshit. Every expression this woman had was carefully arranged.

As Daniela went to slip by Raina, she said, "Forgive me. I was so eager to continue with the work that I completely forgot what you told me about this particular room. I'll try harder to remember your instructions in the future."

Clever.

Daniela was placing herself firmly in the inferior position, the employee. She was doing and saying all the right things. Except for rifling through Mateo's room. And Raina didn't believe the woman's excuse for one moment. Daniela had been in there looking for something.

As the two women walked down the hall side by side, Daniela casually asked, "Where did you meet your fiancé? You're American, correct? And he's from somewhere else?"

Raina glanced at Daniela, trying to determine if the other woman was attempting to get information from her or if she was genuinely curious. Raina told herself to stop looking for a conspiracy where there was none. Daniela's probably met a lot of different people in her job, and Raina had to admit that she and Mateo made an interesting couple.

"My parents introduced us." Raina attempted to keep the bitchiness she was feeling from her tone. "Mateo did some work with my stepfather. We met two years ago and then reconnected recently."

"Oh, what a lovely story!" Daniela exclaimed. "I adore hearing about second chance love."

Now Raina knew for sure something fishy was going on with the other woman. Daniela looked and acted as though she was carved from an iceberg and now she was gushing about second chance love stories? Raina wasn't buying it.

"Sure," Raina said sarcastically. "We're a match made in heaven. If you'll excuse me, I have some work to do in my office. When you get those samples ready for me, bring them down and I'll have a look."

Raina walked away from Daniela without another word. She didn't know what was going on, but she was going to get to the bottom of it.

CHAPTER THIRTY-TWO

Raina couldn't sleep that night. Was she being paranoid? Seeing conspiracies where there were none?

She couldn't put her finger on it, but there was something off about Daniela. Right from the beginning Raina hadn't been able to warm up to the woman. Not that Raina had to be friends with every single person she met, but she had hoped to forge some kind of relationship with her interior designer.

Considering what a large job the mansion was and the huge potential for future work, she would have thought that Daniela would unbend enough to attempt being pleasant. Yet she wasn't. She was standoffish and frequently rude. If she hadn't been doing such a good job, Raina probably would've fired her by now.

She tossed and turned for well over an hour before finally giving up on sleep. She shoved the hair off her face and sat up with a deep sigh. Swinging her legs over the side of the bed she squinted at the alarm clock but couldn't quite make out the fuzzy numbers. She grabbed her glasses and shoved them onto her nose, then looked at the clock again. 1:36 AM.

She chewed on her bottom lip trying to decide what to do. There was no help for it. She needed to talk to Mateo. She was relatively certain that he would want to hear this, given his obsession with Raina and security.

She pulled on a pair of fuzzy pink slippers and grabbed a short cotton robe to cover her pajama pants and cami top. She made her way into the lit hallway, squinting at the bright light and walked to the master bedroom.

She hesitated for a couple of seconds, lost her nerve, headed back to her room, changed her mind, and headed back to Mateo's room. She lifted her hand to knock, then dropped it. Then she got annoyed at herself, huffed, and banged on the door so loud that the sound reverberated down the corridor. She cringed at the noise.

She heard movement from the other side of the door and stood back waiting. Mateo jerked it open, surprising her as much as she surprised him. He was disheveled from head to foot. His hair looked like a windswept mess and he wore nothing but a pair of unzipped jeans with the belt and buckle hanging open. Her eyes widened when she caught sight of the generous treasure trail heading straight down to his groin. She looked away quickly but thought she caught a glimpse of the base of his penis. Her heart thumped and every single thought in her head took flight.

"What's wrong?" he demanded, searching the hallway behind her. He braced his arms on either side of the doorway to look around. That's when she caught sight of the gun in his hand. Her mouth went dry. Maybe this was a mistake.

"I... I..." she stuttered and then shook her head.

It was unlike her to have to search for words, but the sight of him was disconcerting. What had she been thinking? Going to Mateo's bedroom in the middle of the night. This could've waited until the morning. She started to tell him she'd talk to him later, but he reached out and took hold of her arm, pulling her into his room.

He closed the door behind them and then dropped her arm, taking a couple of steps back.

"Tell me."

Raina started to pace, wringing her hands as she spoke. "I don't know, maybe I shouldn't have come. It's just..."

Mateo took her by the shoulders and turned her to face him. "Raina, I trust you. If you came to me at this time of night, then you have a good reason. Try to relax and tell me."

His calm voice and the warm caress of his long fingers curving over her shoulders did help to relax her. She took a deep breath and nodded, grateful that he was being so understanding, especially after their confrontation in the kitchen.

"It's Daniela, I don't trust her. There's something wrong, but I can't put my finger on what it is."

"The designer?" he asked with a frown. Raina remembered that he hadn't actually met Daniela yet. For some reason they were never in the mansion at the same time.

She nodded. "Yes, she's helping with the renovations. I don't know what it is about her, I don't even know if I have a legitimate complaint, but I don't trust her. I found her in your room yesterday, looking at your desk. I reminded her that she wasn't allowed in this room without permission, but she came up with a perfectly legitimate excuse. She said she forgot and she wanted to take measurements. If it had been any other room, I wouldn't have questioned her. But..."

"You don't trust her." Mateo crossed his arms over his chest, and dipped his head forward, as though thinking.

"I don't know why I don't trust her, it's not really anything she did, besides coming in your room when she shouldn't have. And anyone could've made that mistake. It was weeks ago that I told her to stay out of here. She could have genuinely forgotten."

Mateo lifted his head, his dark eyes piercing hers. "But you don't think she forgot."

"No, I don't believe it for a minute. She's sharp, pays attention to every detail. She's really good at her job and she's hypervigilant, almost to a fault. I don't think she'd be one to forget the house rules."

Mateo nodded. "Good enough for me."

He strode over to the night table beside the bed and grabbed his phone. He hit one of the contacts and then put the phone on speaker. Angela answered with a groggy, "Hello?"

Mateo skipped the pleasantries. "Angela. Raina doesn't trust the decorator, Daniela..." He looked up at Raina with a raised eyebrow.

"Velasquez," Raina supplied Daniela's last name.

"Thinks she's up to something," Mateo continued. "Check her out. I want to know everything. Family, friends, connections, clients. I want to know where she's from, where she's going and how long she's been here. Don't leave a single stone unturned. Satisfy me that this woman is on the up and up. If you flag anything as problematic, come to me immediately."

"Of course, boss," Angela said in a clipped voice.

They hung up and Mateo set his phone back down.

"Thank you," Raina said quietly, fidgeting. Now that the drama was over, she was back to feeling awkward. She really wished he would finish zipping up his pants. Her eyes kept straying to where she was positive she could see a hint of man stem. "Thank you for believing me and doing something about it."

Mateo inclined his dark hair head. "At best, you're wrong about this Velazquez woman and she's simply an interior designer. I would rather you come to me with your worries than ignore your instincts and get hurt. Thank you for trusting me enough to come to me with this."

Raina's heart ached at his words. He could be so wonderful sometimes. So heartfelt, that she wanted to grab hold of him and never let go. But it was the other times, the terrifying Mateo times that she didn't know how to deal with.

"I should go back to my room," she said in a near whisper, backing slowly away from Mateo's bed, toward the door.

"Stay with me." His words halted her in her tracks.

Why did he want her to stay? Did he want sex? Did he want to talk to her about Daniela? Her heart thumped in both anticipation and fear, though her good sense told her she needed to leave the room and leave quickly, because the heat was beginning to ratchet up.

He took a step toward her and she retreated a step. He didn't reach for her as she half feared, but he held her still with nothing more than his voice. "If you stay, I promise to be a perfect gentleman. I won't demand anything of you, but that you sleep next to me where I can see you."

It said a lot that Raina was beyond tempted. She was slowly trying to feel this new relationship out, and she sensed the thinning of Mateo's patience over their days and weeks together. He wanted her to warm up to him faster. She knew that it was only a matter of time before he lost patience completely. But when he asked her like this, telling her that he would respect her boundaries, her heart melted. She couldn't protect herself from this side of Mateo.

"Why?" she whispered.

What would he gain by having her in his bed when he couldn't touch her? Wouldn't that be torture for both of them? Because truthfully, Raina wanted him as badly as he seemed to want her. She was just more cautious, less experienced.

Mateo stepped up to her as though approaching a wild

animal. He tucked the hair behind her ear and then touched his finger to the edge of her glasses. There was a strange expression on his face. She realized it was tenderness, not something she'd seen from him before.

"I want to see what you look like when you sleep. I want to lay next to you, inhaling your scent. I want you to rest your head on my pillow, inhaling my scent in return. I want you to wake up in the morning knowing that you spent the night next to the man that will become your husband. I want you to get used to me."

Her mouth was dry and her hands were sweating. She didn't know what to do. Go to her own room and spend a restless night alone or give in to the undercurrents of dark desire that were permeating the air around them? Though he wasn't asking for sex, sexual tension vibrated through both of them.

"Will you stay?" His voice was husky and his eyes smouldering.

"Yes."

CHAPTER THIRTY-THREE

The next morning, Raina ran into Mateo as she was coming down the stairs and he was coming in the front door. They both stopped to look at each other. Once again, Raina felt self-conscious. The look Mateo was giving her told her she shouldn't.

Their night together had been just as he described; he hadn't touched her other than to pull the blanket up to her neck, kiss her cheek and tell her good night. Then he rolled over to his side of the bed and fell asleep so fast Raina realized he must be completely exhausted.

When she woke up in the morning, she was alone, sprawled out in the warm bed beneath the soft sheets. She stretched an arm out to Mateo's side of the bed, but it was cool. He'd left a while ago. She'd made her way back to her room for a shower and a change.

Even though she felt awkward about seeing him again, she was also happy. She tucked her hair behind her ear and gave him a shy smile.

"You slept well?" He eyed her outfit of skinny jeans with a short purple T-shirt that bared part of her stomach.

"Very well, thank you," she answered politely.

They stood a few feet apart. She watched him warily as he continued to look at her. Had he come back to see her? She wasn't used to seeing him at any other time of day except for mealtimes. She thought that he was probably out negotiating his takeover. He usually returned to the mansion tired, but generally pleased about his success. He rarely spoke about the specifics of the takeover, except for the night he took her out into the yard to spar, but she sensed that things were going well for him. Which meant, she supposed, that things were going well for her too.

"I have news about your interior decorator. Come, let's go outside to talk." He jerked his head toward the back door and turned to walk away, expecting her to follow.

This was probably the reason he came back to the house, to update her on her hunch about Daniela Velazquez. Raina was dying to know what he'd found out, so she rushed after him as he strode toward the back of the house.

He called out to Lydia as they passed the kitchen, "Grab us a couple of lemonades and bring them out to the pool patio, will you?"

"Please and thank you," Raina was quick to add.

That was one of the differences between Raina and Mateo. Though he'd spent his childhood in poor conditions, he'd spent most of his adult years surrounded by servants. And though he was still an employee on Sotza's estate, he was high-ranking enough that he'd gotten used to the presence of paid staff. Raina, on the other hand, had grown up on a farm. She learned how to fend for herself; how to pour her own lemonade and use her manners if she had to ask for something. If she hadn't, her mother would've smacked her on the butt with a wooden spoon.

"Have a seat." Mateo waved his hand toward the patio table.

She sank into the seat and looked at him expectantly.

Mateo didn't leave her in suspense. "We found the body of Daniela Velasquez."

"What?" Raina's mouth fell open in shock. Had she somehow managed to kill the interior decorator through her suspicions? Had Mateo murdered her, rather than looking into her background?

Before Raina could start demanding answers, Mateo continued, "The woman that you've been meeting with is not Daniela Velasquez. She's an imposter. From what Angela has managed to discover, Velasquez was killed weeks ago, after we moved in and started putting out feelers for an interior decorator. Whoever this mysterious woman is, she moved quickly. She knew exactly who we were. She found out what we needed and set herself up to be in a position to provide it."

Raina was stunned. She honestly didn't even know where to begin with this information. "But she was a really good interior decorator," Raina said, bewildered. "How does a person learn to become an interior decorator so quickly?"

She could tell by the look on Mateo's face that she'd amused him with her comment. She supposed it wasn't very badass of her to dwell on how good the imposter was at decorating. So she asked the next most important question. "If the woman I've been meeting with isn't the real Daniela Velasquez, then who is she?"

"And that's the million-dollar question." Mateo shoved his hands in the pockets of his pants, a serious look wrinkling his brow. "It's not an easy process, getting into my inner circle. Whoever she is, she did her research, she worked quickly, and she disappeared just as quickly."

"Disappeared?" Raina asked.

Mateo nodded. "She must've realized that you were suspicious yesterday after you found her in my room. We haven't been able to track her down. I have a couple of men out trying to follow her movements, but if she's a professional, I doubt she'll be back. Not until she's ready to show her hand."

A shiver ran through Raina. Ready for what? The possibilities were chilling. "What do you think she wants?"

Mateo accepted a frosted glass of lemonade from Lydia who walked out to them with a tray. Raina murmured her thanks, accepting a glass. She smiled her amusement when Lydia placed a bowl of grapes next to the drink. Lydia was forever trying to feed her healthy snacks, probably on Mateo's orders.

When Lydia left, Mateo continued, "I don't want to speculate on the imposter's intentions. First, we need to establish her identity before we find a motive behind her deception." Mateo walked over to Raina and put a comforting hand on her shoulder, squeezing and then running his hand through the loose hair at her ear. "The important thing is that you recognized her for what she was. She won't be bothering you again."

Mateo's words made her feel safer. She was comforted by his solid presence and his promise to protect her. She reached up, took hold of his hand and kissed the knuckles before letting go. She blushed at her own actions, though they were heartfelt.

"Thank you," she said, smiling at him. "Thank you for taking me seriously on this and for acting so quickly. It means a lot to me."

His shrewd eyes stayed on her for a moment. "You know I would do anything for you."

"Even the things I don't want you to do." She quietly echoed the words he'd spoken to her weeks ago.

Mateo leaned over and kissed the top of her head. "Exactly." He left his empty glass on the table and strode back to the house.

Mateo and Raina spent the next week settling into a new normal. Raina hired a new interior decorator who came with a plethora of recommendations and awards. He also passed an extremely thorough background check and interrogation style interview with Danny, Angela and Mateo. Once Mateo was satisfied the new designer was on the up and up, Raina was back to renovation planning.

The biggest change in routine the past week had brought was Mateo's presence at her door every night at around 11 PM, asking her to join him in bed. He was always polite, almost distant, and he never touched Raina without her permission. She was lulled into a sense of security to the point that she willingly took his hand and followed him to his room, spending each night in bed beside him. The routine had become such a pleasant one that she would've been disappointed if he hadn't come for her.

Raina felt happy and ready to start planning her wedding. She was excited for the arrival of both of her mothers within the next few days. They would know what she should do and how she should act when it came to both the mafia and a big wedding.

Diane Duncan arrived first. She brought with her a giant ray of sunshine, homemade baking, Raina's favourite stuffed unicorn and a warm heartfelt hug. She gathered Raina in her arms and held her close. Raina melted into her mother, wrapping her arms around Diane's ample waist.

"You look so beautiful, Raina." Diane tipped Raina's chin up to look at her face. She clucked her tongue and ruffled Raina's hair. "You'll need a haircut before the wedding."

They toured the mansion arm in arm, Raina showing off her new home to her mother. Raina was particularly proud of the renovations and lingered in the rooms that had been under construction. She was proud to show her mother to a bedroom that Raina had a personal hand in decorating.

The two women spent most of the day talking and discussing wedding particulars. Diane was especially interested in the food and had ideas about catering. Diane was generally easy-going; she wasn't one to shove her ideas down another person's throat. That is, except when it came to the wedding; Raina had never seen her mother so pushy. It was almost amusing to watch Diane lay out all of her catering plans and show Raina a plethora of menus she gathered online from local Miami caterers.

Mateo joined the two women for supper and received a warm hug and kiss from his future mother-in-law. Raina was reminded that the two had been in cahoots together for the past few years. She wanted to be pissed off about the subterfuge, but she was happy to see that her mother and Mateo getting along. It was like they skipped the awkward in-law phase and jumped right into years long friendship. They had a pleasant meal together, one of the easiest that Raina'd had since arriving in the house. The tension that always simmered between Raina and Mateo eased off with the arrival of her mother.

Unfortunately, a different kind of tension vibrated through the mansion with the arrival of Elvira Sotza the next morning. Vee was the epitome of calm cool sophistication. She gathered her daughter against her and held her close. Both women were the same height and build and could have been sisters. Once Vee assured herself that Raina was being well taken care of, she turned to greet Diane, accepting a warm hug.

"Oh, it does my heart such good to see you two together," Diane said of Vee and Raina, brushing a tear from her cheek.

Raina felt truly blessed with having two such mothers. The two women were complete opposites, yet respectful and loving of each other. There was no jealousy, no competition for Raina's attention.

To Raina's disappointment, Vee wanted little to do with the wedding. She shrugged it off as not her thing but listened carefully to whatever plans the other two made. Occasionally she would drop a comment, but mostly kept her thoughts to herself on Raina's upcoming nuptials. The only time she offered her two cents was when it came to Miami's local businesses. Vee knew where to find the best of everything and wasn't afraid to interrupt and tell Raina and Diane.

The one thing that Vee did want to discuss at length was Raina's contact with the imposter interior designer. She seemed deeply concerned by Raina's description of events.

"How old would you say she is?"

Raina shrugged. "Hard to tell. Definitely older than me, maybe around your age? But not older."

"Hmmm, interesting." Vee lapsed into thoughtful silence, then asked, "You say she's Latina?"

Again, Raina shrugged. "I assume so. She was definitely posing as Latina when she stole Daniela Velasquez's identity. But who knows if she actually is."

Diane shook her head. "It gives me the shivers to think that you were in such close contact with that woman. She could've done anything to you and no one would've stopped her."

Raina's smiled affectionately. "I can take care of myself, mom. And there are usually bodyguards close by, even in the house. It would've taken real effort for her to harm me here."

"Well, that's a relief," Diana said, hand over her heart.

"I don't like it." Vee frowned and reached for her water, taking a long drink. "This isn't over, whatever it is."

CHAPTER THIRTY-FOUR

"You," Vee snapped, striding purposefully towards her prey, one of the mansion security personnel.

Vee was pleasantly surprised when Angela turned around to face her. A wide grin split Angela's face as she was quick to greet her former employer. "Señora Sotza, awesome to see you again!"

The two women hugged. "I suppose I should've realized that you would be here with Mateo."

Angela nodded. "He prefers to have his own team around him during the takeover."

"I was sad to see you and Thomas leave, but you're right. Mateo works best when he's with his team. That is one thing I'll give him; he values those that are loyal to him. And you, my dear Angela, have always been loyal, whether he deserves it or not."

Angela shrugged. "Mateo is an easy person to give loyalty to. He's loyal to a fault himself."

"Yes," Vee drawled. "Loyal to a fault. It's difficult to earn that man's loyalty, but I see that those of you that have it will have it forever. It's why I haven't objected more stringently to this marriage between him and my daughter. I know that he'll protect her with his life."

Angela reached out to touch Vee's arm. "He's loyal to you as well," she said earnestly.

Vee smiled and waved a hand dismissively. "He's loyal to my husband, which means his loyalty automatically extends to me. He's never warmed up to me as a person."

Angela watched her with a shrewd expression. "I don't know why it bothers you, it's not like you've ever attempted to win him over."

Vee laughed. "You've never been one to sugarcoat things."

Angela shrugged. "What's the point in sugarcoating. The truth will come out anyway."

"Regardless, I don't think Mateo and I will become besties any time soon. Friendly maybe, but not more."

Vee had earned Mateo's ire by helping her daughter leave Venezuela after he made his intentions clear. He believed that Vee's actions constituted a betrayal to the Sotza cartel. Luckily, Sotza had seen it otherwise and hadn't punished his wife. Vee didn't think that she and Mateo would ever be close, but she respected him and for her daughter's sake she would try to be civil.

"Were you looking for something?" Angela asked, prodding Vee on her reason for seeking out the mansion security.

"Yes, I'd like to look at some security footage if you have it handy." Vee's voice was clipped and cool, back to business.

Angela hesitated and then nodded. "I don't think it should be a problem."

Vee understood Angela's dilemma. Angela and Vee had always gotten along well, two powerful women in a male-dominated cartel. Both had attitude in spades and could take care of themselves. Over the years of Vee's marriage, the two women had developed a friendship. They were stronger and more powerful together than apart.

Vee followed Angela down the hallway, her 4-inch black Louis Vuitton heels tapping against the marble as she walked. Angela showed her to a back room that had been turned into a security office. She ushered Vee inside and waved her toward a chair then took the other chair behind the desk, sinking down and tapping the keyboard to wake up the monitor.

Vee looked at Angela shrewdly. "I think Miami suits you."

Angela's eyes narrowed in thought. "I've always enjoyed America. There's a certain kind of... freedom... that I don't necessarily experience in Venezuela. More opportunity maybe." She finished with a shrug.

"I know what you mean," Vee assured her. "Misogyny runs aplenty in the world of organized crime. Here, you're far more likely to rise up the ranks than you would in a place like Venezuela. Though Sotza appreciates hard work, whether that work is coming from a man or a woman, his organization isn't that far out of the dark ages. Regardless, enjoy your time here. I'm sure you can make it permanent if that's what you want."

Angela treated Vee to a half smile and then focused her attention on the computer in front of her. She turned the monitor so that they could both see it. "What are we looking for?"

"The interior designer. I want to know what she looks like."

Angela nodded sharply and said, her voice hard, "I never trusted her. Worst customer service I've ever seen. She was rude to everyone, including your daughter. It was a miracle Raina didn't fire her."

Vee chuckled. "Raina sees the best in everyone."

"Okay, so the moment Mateo realized Daniela wasn't on the up and up, he had us pouring through this footage. I can tell you now, she's clever. Never once showed her face."

Angela quickly found the file on the desktop, opened it and played the first video.

Vee watched as a tall slender dark-haired woman wearing a wide-brimmed hat walked past the front entrance camera at a fast clip. She brought her hand up to her face as though to brush hair out of her eyes. The move obscured her features.

"Clever indeed," Vee said darkly.

"She does that every single time she walks past a camera, whether it's the camera at the front entrance, the back entrance, or the offices, where we also had cameras installed. She knows exactly what she's doing."

Vee frowned thoughtfully. "But what exactly was she doing? And did she accomplish what she set out to do? I assume she's been in the wind since suspicions were raised?"

"Si, yes," Angela nodded, using both English and Spanish as she spoke rapidly. "Raina was careful when speaking to Daniela, but it was clear that she was suspicious. And the woman is skittish. Probably from the moment she was caught in Mateo's bedroom, she decided her time here was done. As for her intentions? We don't know. We need to determine her identity first."

"Replay the footage for me, different angles please." Vee leaned in closer to the monitor and watched as Daniela walked past the camera over and over and over.

There was a familiarity about her. The way she walked, elegant but purposeful. The way she looked over her shoulder and surveyed her surroundings. The woman's posture. Her clothes, her shoes, her jewelry. Everything seemed to be carefully coordinated. The woman was almost militaristic with a side of elegance. Raina would bet the Venezuelan compound that she knew this woman personally. But how? And when?

"Thank you for showing me this. If you get in trouble with Mateo, let me know. I'll set him straight."

Angela shook her head and gave Vee a reassuring smile.

"You were kind to me in Venezuela. You showed me how powerful a woman could become. You showed me that a woman could embrace her femininity and still be a total badass. I've always looked up to you and I don't agree with the way Mateo treats you. But that's between you and him. As far as I'm concerned, you and I are friends."

Vee smiled a heartfelt genuine smile. "Thank you. I will treasure our friendship. If you're ever in need of help, you come to me."

CHAPTER THIRTY-FIVE

It was the night before Vee's and Diane's departure. They had been in Miami for four days helping Raina with her wedding plans. Diane was eager to get back to Joe and the farm. She talked about helping with the seeding and doing some gardening before summer arrived.

Vee, on the other hand, didn't seem eager to leave at all. "I'm not comfortable leaving Miami before you hunt down the imposter." She directed her comment to Mateo who was sitting at the head of the table, presiding over their dinner meal.

"Daniela Velasquez is not your problem," he said dismissively, forking a bite of roasted chicken and vegetables into his mouth.

"She preyed on Raina and anything that has to do with my daughter is, in fact, my problem," Vee said sharply, narrowing her eyes at Mateo in a glare.

"Can we not do this?" Raina huffed from her seat on Mateo's right-hand side. She was sitting across from Vee, with Diane on her left side.

Vee and Mateo had been arguing all week and it was

getting on Raina's last nerve. She understood their hostility, but she didn't condone it. Both of them were grown-ups, both of them had been bosses in the Miami underground, and both loved Sotza and Raina. That should be plenty enough in common for them to bury the hatchet. But rather than burying it, that they'd spent the entire week swinging it at each other, making nasty comments and undermining the others authority.

Raina turned her ire on her mother. "While I appreciate your concern, I am capable of taking care of myself." When Vee open her mouth to speak, Raina interrupted, "And I trust my future husband to keep me safe. He cared for your husband for over two decades; he's proved himself. You need to let this go and trust us to take care of it." Then Raina turned her gaze toward Mateo. "And you need to start getting along with my mother. I intend to have her here as often as I can get her. Deal with whatever grudge you have against her and then let it go. For my sake."

The mighty Mateo actually flinched at her last sentence, more than likely because he would do anything for Raina's sake, including treating her mother with respect. He set his fork and knife down on his plate and lifted his napkin to his lips before setting it on the table.

He turned to face Vee, his expression one of stiff resignation. "Forgive me, you will always be welcome in our home."

It became clear that Vee was struggling with what she would say next. Diane hid a smirk in her napkin and winked at Raina, while Raina covered a laugh with a cough. Vee was not one to let old grudges go. If a person was going to hate Vee, she was going to hate them back ten times worse. But ultimately, she knew that it was in her daughter's best interest to have Vee get along with her future son-in-law.

Finally, after enough time had passed that even Mateo was amused, Vee managed to say stiffly, "You're forgiven. And, of course, you must forgive me for any harm I may have caused you." She seemed to chew on the inside of her cheek before bursting out with, "Except for helping Raina escape. I don't regret that."

Before Mateo could get angry, both Raina and Diane burst out laughing. Diane put her hand on top of Raina's and squeezed, then directed her comment to Mateo, "I think that that's as good as it's going to get. Consider yourselves no longer at war."

"Indeed," Mateo drawled, his dark eyes still lingering on Vee with speculation. He directed his next comment toward her. "I hope that you know we're doing everything we can to track down the imposter. You'll receive any and all information regarding this matter. However, Sotza wants you back in Venezuela, and it's my duty to obey his wishes."

Vee grumbled something about how Mateo was no longer working for Sotza therefore he didn't owe the man anything, but no one paid much attention to her. It was obvious that it was going to take her longer to let go of their little war.

Later, in Mateo's bedroom, as Raina and Mateo were getting ready for bed, Raina turned to him. "Thank you for what you said to my mother at the dinner table."

"Diane is extremely easy to get along with. It will always be my pleasure to host her." He turned his back on Raina and pulled his shirt over his head, dropping it on a nearby chair. She held her breath as muscles rippled across his back, looking extra fine in the lamplight.

"You know that's not the mother I'm talking about," she said dryly. While his back was turned, she quickly stripped out of her clothing and pulled on a pair of sleep shorts and a cami top.

She continued to watch him as he unbuckled his belt and pulled his pants down his legs, bearing the nicest male ass she'd ever seen. Granted, she hadn't come in contact with very many male asses, but she was positive that those perfectly curved globes were highly unusual. Over the course of the past week, they had gradually gotten used to each other's presence in the bedroom. It had been more of a learning curve for Raina who had never shared her space before. Even in university, she'd used some of her forgery money to upgrade to a single bed suite.

Mateo eased into their new living situation as though nothing had changed. As though there had always been a space for Raina right next to him, waiting for her to fill it.

"You were right." He turned to Raina, giving her a piercing look that melted her heart and her panties. His serious mob boss look, but also sexy as hell. "Allies are stronger when united. Our marriage will create an even stronger alliance between the east coast hub and South America. It would be stupid of me to continue arguing with someone in Vee's position."

Raina tried desperately not to drop her eyes. She didn't need to glance at his penis. She really didn't. She dropped her eyes. Every thought in her head fled. For the most part Mateo's body was enveloped in shadows, but she could see enough to see a very large, very erect, very veined cock. He flipped back the covers on the bed, and slid underneath.

"I... I..." Raina stammered and blinked and then shook her head. Finally, she remembered what she wanted to yell at him about. "Our marriage is not about an alliance. If that's all you want from me, you can go find yourself another mob princess sacrifice."

Mateo flipped the blankets back, slid out of bed with the ease of a jungle cat and strode toward her. Raina's eyes flared wide and she took a couple of quick steps back, but she wasn't fast enough, he was on top of her in seconds. He stopped her, his hands on her arms, his dark angry eyes glaring down at her. The heat from his big body enveloped her in a warm hug.

"Our marriage will forge a strong alliance. This is a fact." His voice was hard, matching his stance and the angry energy coming from him. He meant every word. He wanted her to know exactly where she stood with him. "But you are much more to me than an alliance. If you had been born in a back alley on a distant continent, I still would have found you, and I still would have loved you. You are my queen, nothing less and nothing more."

Raina stared up at him, her heart hammering so hard that it felt like it would burst from her chest. Her skin felt prickly, like it belonged to someone else. The moment, the man, everything about the two of them was so significant that it felt like fate. Just as Mateo suggested. Maybe they were destined to be together, no matter who they were or where they came from.

Mateo slid his hand down her arm until he was clasping her hand. He tugged her toward the bed. "Come lay down with me, I want to read."

They snuggled under the covers together, Mateo's arm around Raina, her head on his chest. Together, they read his newest paperback romance, Rosemary Rogers' Sweet Savage Love, each waiting for the other to finish before Mateo turned the pages.

CHAPTER THIRTY-SIX

The next day, after spending most of the morning working on a new commission for papers for an American diplomat whose lover was a foreign national spy, Raina decided to go for a relaxing swim. Between hosting both of her mothers and engaging in a weird mating dance with Mateo, Raina was ready for some down time.

She loved Vee and Diane, but both women, each in their own way, were exhausting. All Diane had wanted to do was talk wedding, wedding, wedding. Raina was not a wedding person. Though her own wedding engaged her more than other people's, she still wasn't willing to put in a lot of effort. Raina was a hardcore introvert, she had little desire to be around crowds of people that she barely knew, especially as the center of attention.

Vee had been exhausting in a different way. Vee was born and bred to the mafia, which created a kind of edge. She expected the worst and she was cynical, almost to a fault. She was always looking for conspiracies and angles.

Raina admired her birth mother, and in some ways, they were very much alike. Both mother and daughter were shrewd, sharp and intelligent. They also had big hearts. It was a strange combination that was likely what got both women into trouble time and time again. They were sneaky, worked on the wrong side of the law, but they were also loyal and compassionate.

That's where the similarities ended. Vee's experiences had made her cynical and distrusting. She was suspicious of most everyone, especially men and she didn't keep her thoughts to herself. Sometimes Raina thought that when Vee looked at Mateo, she was seeing her first husband, Tony Montana. The man who had beaten, degraded, and nearly killed her.

Raina decided she wanted a swim and headed to her room to change. Ten minutes later, she emerged wearing a white bathing suit with a gold clasp between the breasts and one on each hip, a light blue bathing suit robe and flip-flops. She made her way back through the mansion, admiring some of the changes along the way. It was starting to feel like home.

After finding out about Daniela, Raina had re-renovated many of the styles that Daniela had chosen. Raina's new interior designer was on board with this, even if he found it strange that they were repainting freshly painted rooms. He favoured a bolder style over the modern whites and creams that Daniela had been choosing for Raina. Raina found that she enjoyed some of the brighter accents more than she would have thought.

At the pool, she dropped her robe and tossed it carelessly across a lounge chair. She kicked off her sandals, stepped up to the edge of the pool and dove into the clear blue water. The pool was heated so the water temperature was perfect; not too hot, not too cold. Raina powered through twenty laps, counting them in her head as she touched the edge of the pool. Each lap helped to ease some of the tension from her body. Her mothers were gone and the imposter interior designer was no longer in the mansion. Her forgery work was taking off and things with Mateo were going well. Raina had nothing to worry about.

After finishing her laps, Raina rolled over onto her back and floated, staring up at the clear blue sky dotted with fluffy, cotton ball clouds.

Because her ears were half underwater, she didn't hear Mateo approach and didn't know how long he'd been standing watching her before she spotted him. She rolled her head to the side and saw his big body blotting out the sun. She swam lazily over to him a happy smile on her face. He watched her, the gleam of a predator in his eyes.

"You're home early," she said huskily as she approached the edge of the pool where he was standing. "Break your quota of kneecaps for the day, gangster?"

He flashed her a quick grin, unable to help himself. Raina noticed that Mateo and most of the criminal type guys she'd been around rarely smiled. As though their go-to expression was deadly, serious, frozen in stone. Although Mateo seemed to have nailed the expression, he still showed his softer side once in a while.

"Something like that," he said, crouching next to the edge of the pool.

Raina had an immature impulse to yank him into the water, expensive suit and all. She was relatively certain he wouldn't get overly angry with her and might even find humour in the situation. But she reined in the urge. Maybe one day she'd give it a try.

He ran his finger down her cheek and tilted her chin. He lazily scanned her features and then dipped his gaze to her small breasts where they were tightly encased in the low-cut bathing suit. "Wanted to see you."

Raina grinned up at him. "Yeah? Why?"

"Want to show you something." He reached down for her,

making it obvious that he was going to pull her out of the pool.

Raina clutched the sleeves of his suit jacket as he gripped her underneath her arms and pulled her straight up from the pool, going from his crouch to standing position and setting her on her feet in front of him. Water poured off her, wetting the front of his suit and shoes. Maybe she should've pulled him into the pool; apparently he didn't mind getting wet.

"What do you want to show me?" she asked with a lift of her brow. "New puppy? Diamonds? The head of imposter Daniela on a platter?"

She almost regretted her last sentence when darkness replaced his pleasant expression. He shook his head. "We haven't been able to locate her yet."

The 'yet' in that sentence was significant. Raina had no doubt that he meant it. It wasn't a matter of *if* they found Daniela, it was a matter of when. Raina hoped the other woman had a damn good excuse for her subterfuge, because if she didn't, her head really would go on a platter.

"Follow me," he said, taking her hand. He allowed her to pull on her robe and flip-flops before leading her away from the pool.

"Where are we going?" she asked curiously, shivering when he ran his thumb down the inside of her hand, subconsciously rubbing her as they walked. She loved the feel of his hands on her.

"To the bunker." His tone was strange; dark but excited.

Of all the places he might want to take her, she definitely wasn't expecting him to say the bunker. "Why do you want to take me down there? You demanded I never set foot in there again without your permission."

"Consider this my permission."

Raina frowned as they rounded the pool house, walking

away from where she knew the entrance to the bunker lay. "This isn't the right way."

He inclined his head toward her and said mysteriously, "You aren't the only one who's been renovating this place."

Raina halted in her tracks and gasped in surprise as she was confronted with a concrete wall with a door in it in the middle of her lawn. Where had this come from?

Mateo answered her silent question. "It was built last week, while you were touring bakeries and decoration shops with your mothers."

"Yeah, but you think I would've noticed it back here anyway," she said faintly as he pulled her toward a door with a panel in the side.

He punched in a ten-digit long code that Raina immediately memorized. He didn't bother to hide it from her, so she figured he either didn't think she had the capacity to remember a code that long or he wasn't concerned that she could now enter this space.

"I had the building created to certain specifications. The way the land back here is graded, sloping away from the house, made for a perfect location for an underground building. The door is the only partly visible; the rest is under the estate."

As they made their way into the building, which was noticeably much cooler than the air outside, Raina wrapped her robe tighter around herself. Mateo walked at a fast clip, his hand tight enough on her arm that she didn't have a chance to stop and look around. Odd, considering he wanted to show her this building.

As they passed door after door, it started to become clear to Raina what the building might be used for. In Venezuela, on Sotza's estate, similar buildings existed. Raina hadn't been allowed inside them, but the staff gossiped enough that it hadn't taken her long to figure out what they were for.

"A prison." She looked at Mateo as if asking him to negate her words. He remained silent.

"You built a prison in our home?" she demanded incredulously.

She was too surprised to feel angry yet. But she knew the rage would come once the full implications of this building sank in. What it would be used for while she lived in the house only a few yards away.

"This is our backyard, not our home." Mateo's voice took on a growly quality.

Raina didn't know why he was getting annoyed, he had to know that she wouldn't approve of this addition to the mansion.

"Don't you use semantics with me," she snapped. "This is completely unacceptable. You didn't even talk to me about it."

Mateo stopped in front of another door with another panel. He punched another, separate, ten-digit code. Raina filed this one away too. This door would face the house, and when Mateo opened it Raina was able to see a set of stairs the extended into an even deeper subbasement.

Mateo slid his hand up her arm to grip her bicep. He pulled her down the stairs with him, as though he thought she might try to get away. As angry as she was, Raina was also curious. If he'd managed to build an entire warehouse on their back lawn, what had he done to the original bunker?

Mateo didn't say another word until they completed their descent where the air in the bunker became cooler again. Raina shivered in the darkness. Mateo flipped on a light switch without breaking stride and continued down the path that Raina was now familiar with. She glanced up, as if expecting to see the hole in the floor of the pool house, but the ceiling was smooth and the surrounding area smelled like paint.

She held her breath as they entered the bunker room that had once contained the corpse of Casey's bodyguard.

Raina was surprised to find the room completely renovated. There was now a wall blocking off the room. In the wall was a door with a barred window.

Mateo moved to the door and punched in a third code. Raina heard the click of a lock unlatching.

"Oh my God," she murmured.

It was a bedroom. A woman's bedroom. Well, maybe not, but definitely feminine touches, as though a woman were supposed to find the room comfortable. Which of course, any sane woman wouldn't.

There was a large queen-size bed dominating the middle. A wooden dresser, a mirror, a bookshelf, two nightstands and a mini fridge. On the floor was a huge Oriental rug, a bright splash of colour meant to make the room look homey. There was a door off to the side that Raina would bet led to a bathroom. Whoever was meant to stay in here wasn't meant to stay in discomfort.

Raina turned on Mateo, her eyes narrowed, her fists on her hips. "Who the fuck is this room for?"

Mateo studied her expression. "For you."

A wave of despair swept over Raina as she realized she was going to have to go on the run again. "Not a fucking chance."

CHAPTER THIRTY-SEVEN

"You're mistaken, Raina," he said calmly, watching her expression carefully trying to determine her thoughts.

Raina was nearly vibrating with fury. "I'm wrong in thinking that you intend this room for me?"

He shoved a frustrated hand through his hair. "Yes, of course this room is for you. But it's not a prison."

Raina pointed at the bars on the window, her hand shaking. "Prison."

He narrowed his eyes at her. "If it becomes a prison then it's a prison of your own making."

"What exactly is that supposed to mean?" she snapped, hands on her hips.

He took a step toward her, close enough that she could smell the subtle hint of his spicy aftershave. He was so breathtakingly handsome it fucked with her nerves. Her libido wanted to stand up and take notice of him even when the logical part of her brain wanted to stab him in the eye with the nearest pointy object.

"It means," he said, his tone dripping with ice as his eyes became glacial, "that if you ever try to leave here, leave me, this will become your prison. When I had it built, its intended use was as a bolthole in case anything happens at the mansion. But if you insist on taking this attitude, it can become a more permanent cage."

"Don't you threaten me, asshole!" she snarled. "I'm going back to the house to think long and hard about this marriage."

She whirled around and headed for the door, but she barely managed two steps before he was gripping her and swinging her back around to face him. Her heart thundered as she realized she must've gone too far. The look on his face was utterly terrifying, as though he was rapidly losing control. His eyes had gone from ice to fire, their dark depths snapping with emotion.

"Don't ever threaten me, Raina."

His head descended to hers in an angry kiss. Raina tried to break away but his grip became punishing. In contrast to his brutal hold, his lips took her on a familiar dance, teasing, coaxing, looking for a response. She tried to resist, but her body was so in tune with his that her response came automatically. Her lips softened and she opened her mouth, giving him access. Then she was kissing him back, her anger meeting his in a heated exchange.

After a minute, he lifted his head, angrily staring down at her. They were both breathless from the intensity of their angry kiss.

"It's time you understand a few things about our relationship." His voice was a husky growl and she could feel his cock, steel-like within his pants, pressing against her bare stomach. "I've given you more leeway than I have given anyone in my life. You are under the mistaken impression that we are equals and I am no longer willing to allow you to live under that delusion. We are not equal. We will never be equal. I am the boss here. I rule over this city, this house and the people within it. I rule over you. If I tell you to get your ass in this room, you will do it without hesitation."

Pain shattered her hopes as his words sank in. For months, he allowed her to believe that she would have the freedom she craved if she stayed with him. Now, he was essentially telling her that she had no autonomy whatsoever.

The realization cut deep.

Raina blinked back tears and tilted her chin. "You'll have to keep me locked in here until the end of time if you intend to stop me from leaving. Because as of right now, there's no chance I'm going to stay here and marry someone like you."

His hands tightened until she cried out in pain and jerked in his hold. Instead of releasing her though he slammed her up against his chest and lifted her until her feet left the ground. Raina was barely 5'2" and Mateo was easily a foot taller than her. She clutched at his suit for support.

"We are as good as married already. You will never be allowed to leave." He reiterated, his voice taking on a mean tone.

She snapped her hand up between them and slammed her cupped hand into his ear, boxing him. He dropped her but didn't let go of her arm. He reached up to rub his ear but didn't react otherwise.

"Fuck that, we aren't married, and at this rate, we never will be."

"As far as I'm concerned, little girl, the only thing left to do is consummate this relationship."

Raina's eyes flicked to the bed. She didn't know if he planned this, but she knew exactly where things were heading, and she didn't think it was a good idea.

"Don't you dare touch me," she hissed.

He swung her toward the bed until her knees hit the edge of the mattress.

Mateo bent over her, his broad form blotting out the light

above his head. "You belong to me. I negotiated for you and in my world, the promise of marriage is as good as the marriage itself. I can do whatever I want to you."

With every word he spoke he damaged their bond, slowly built up over weeks of getting to know each other. A few hours ago, she might have admitted to actually falling for this man. But now? Now, she couldn't imagine spending another minute with him let alone a lifetime.

"If you touch me, right here, right now, I will never stop trying to leave."

His hand swung around so sharply that she didn't have time to get out of the way. She closed her eyes and flinched, but the blow didn't land. She opened her eyes to stare at him and realized that he stopped himself. The fact that he'd intended to hit her was enough to shatter the last of her feelings for him. He didn't care. If he actually loved her, he would do anything to protect her, even from himself.

"You've made a big mistake." Her words were bitter, spoken from a broken heart.

"Then I have nothing to lose," he said coldly.

Before she could attempt another run on the door, he shoved her backwards onto the bed. She landed on her elbows and bounced on the mattress. She tried to roll away, but he dropped down on top of her, gripping her face and kissing her again, another brutal kiss. She automatically reached up to shove him away, but he slapped her hands. As she was drawn further into the kiss, she groaned and grabbed his head, opening her mouth and kissing him back.

Sensations flooded through her mixing with her anger. Her body screamed for his while her mind screamed at her to run. The combination was heady, driving her to arch her body up against him, smashing her breasts into his chest. He deepened the kiss, his teeth catching her lips, his tongue shoving into the back of her throat, choking her. She gripped the back of his neck to keep him from going anywhere.

His hands were hard and punishing as he tore at her robe, yanking it from her body and tossing it away. He didn't bother with her bikini top but yanked the bottoms down her body. Panic beat at her mind as she realized this was really happening. Mateo was going to have sex with her. No one had ever seen her like this, naked and exposed. She broke the kiss and tried to cover herself, placing both hands over top of her pussy.

"We have to stop." Her voice was breathless, but high with worry.

Mateo shoved her hands away and pinned her to the bed, his knee between her legs. He was allowing rage and lust to cloud his judgement. This violence was the product of Mateo's upbringing and lifestyle. This was the fundamental difference between the two of them. Mateo could control the rage if he wanted, but it was always simmering below the surface, he needed it to stay alive. But Raina had been brought up with love and compassion. Sure she got angry, but her base emotion was one of happiness.

Though hormones raged through her, begging her to pull him down for another kiss, she tried one last time to use logic. "You don't want to do this, Mateo."

His eyes held hers with a dark promise. "I have wanted to do this from the day I met you. Should've done it the day I met you. You would've had a ring on your finger and no reason to put your life at risk in Italy."

"It's always about my safety!" she yelled at him. "You need to get a life and stop controlling mine."

"Not going to happen," he growled, yanking his jacket off and throwing it to the floor.

While his hands were busy, she reared up and tried to roll off the other side of the bed. He yanked her back and attempted to grab both of her wrists in one hand. She wiggled one out and hit him on the side of his head, her nails raking down his cheek.

"Fuck!" he snarled and gripped both of her wrists so hard she thought they might break.

"Fuck you too!" she screamed up at him.

He dropped his head again and she flinched, believing he was about to take her mouth in another bruising kiss. He didn't, he dropped his mouth to her breast instead, sucking it into his mouth through the fabric of her bikini top. Without lifting his head, he tugged her top beneath her breasts and teased her nipples with his tongue and teeth. Sensations flooded through her until she was gasping and dizzy.

He released her hands to tear at his clothes. She heard the sound of cloth ripping as he wrenched his shirt off. She clutched his shoulders, her body shaking beneath his. He reached between them and she heard the distinctive sound of a zipper. Seconds later he was fumbling between her legs, thrusting them wider and guiding his cock toward her entrance.

"I'm not ready!" she gasped, fear zinging through her.

He either didn't hear or he ignored her. He gripped her bare leg and dragged it up the outside of his thigh. Time seemed to stand still as she heard and felt everything in slow motion. Her leg against the roughness of his pants, his lips buried in her neck, biting and sucking at her pulse beat. The steel of his cock against her soft inner thigh.

It felt like all the air was being sucked out of the room as he pushed inside her. She tried to gasp but the air strangled in her throat and she choked instead, lifting her head off the bed and then slamming it back down. Pain sliced through her. A pain she'd never experienced before, as unused muscles stretched and tore to accommodate him.

"So fucking tight," he growled dipping his head toward her.

Raina turned her head to the side and sank her teeth into his ear, biting down until he grunted in pain. He gripped her jaw between his thumb and forefinger, applying pressure until she was forced to open her mouth. He wasn't even remotely gentle and by the time she let go of him her jaw felt bruised. Using one hand he pushed her face to the side and held her head down with his fingers spread over top of her. She couldn't move her head; she couldn't bite him. She could only grit her teeth and take the pain of his body slamming into hers.

She assumed he would finish quickly, within a few minutes at the most. But he didn't. He kept moving inside her, kept holding her down with his brutal strength. Even while something inside her died at his ruthless possession, a spark came to life. A flare of pleasure that swept over her, despite the pain.

They still had weeks, months and years of history. History where she'd always been attracted to him, always wanted him. And though she didn't want to want him now, her body was crying out for his.

Wetness was gathering between her thighs as he established a rhythm that her body couldn't resist. Her heart hammered in her chest as instinct took over, reaching for the pleasure he was offering.

Tears leaked from her eyes, touching his fingertips where his hand was spread across the side of her face. They trickled down her cheeks, off her nose and onto the mattress. She closed her eyes and took a couple of deep breaths, then allowed her body to relax.

As if sensing her capitulation, Mateo relaxed his grip on her and began to touch her softly, running his fingers down her cheek, her neck and the swell of her breasts. Raina kept her eyes closed, but she concentrated on the places that he touched, reaching mentally for every bit of pleasure he was giving her. She could hate him after, but for now, she was going to take this moment and hold it close. Her first time with a man.

Raina's breathing sped up and her face became flushed with excitement. She bit her lip to hold in a moan, but he must've heard anyway. He took her jaw his hand and she flinched, but all he did was gently roll her head up until she was facing him.

He leaned down and took her lips with his, leading her into a familiar exploration. She wrapped her arms around his shoulders and returned his kiss, thrusting her tongue aggressively against his, the sparks igniting into a full frenzy as she was overwhelmed by the pleasure in her mouth and her pussy. Butterflies sang through her entire body. She couldn't resist Mateo; she didn't want to anymore.

"I need you to come for me,"

"Fuck... you." Her words were breathless and angry, at odds with the thrust of her hips against his and her arms wrapped tightly around his neck. Her body wanted what he wanted, it wanted to come.

"I will fuck you," he growled, using her words against her. "I will fuck you every day from here until one of us dies. That is the only way that you will ever escape me."

She glared up at him, her eyes an inch from his, his nose pressed against hers, her breath bursting from her lips in gasps as they stared at each other while her body reached for the heights of orgasm. This orgasm was different, nothing like the orgasms she'd given herself in the darkness of her own bedroom or the one Mateo had given her on the lawn behind the house.

This one was so much more intense, so much more out of her control. She was hurtling toward a gaping unknown and before she could stop herself, he shoved her over the edge. She cried out and sank her nails into his arms while flinging her head back into the mattress, her body as taut a bowstring as an orgasm ripped through her.

As she came, Mateo's cock seemed to grow bigger inside her and she gasped at the discomfort. His thrusts became more frantic, more painful. And then he was finished, sperm shooting inside her unprotected body.

Mateo froze, staring down at her with his dark shuttered eyes. She stared back at him, shock freezing her as well. They had gone from having a decent friendship, to a shaky relationship status, to this.

"Get off me." Her voice was quiet but firm.

She was surprised when Mateo actually did climb off her and then off the bed. He stood up, his broad shoulders back, his head up. She saw turmoil in him, but she didn't see regret. She saw pride, determination, ruthlessness. This was the man who would become her husband. Not the gentle lover that she been gradually getting to know over the past few weeks.

She crawled off the bed and bent over to pick up her bikini bottoms, trying desperately not to feel the shame that was slowly washing over her like a wave. Tears pricked her eyes. She wasn't sure if they were tears of anger or tears of hurt. Either way he had done this to her and she hated him for it.

She pulled on the bottoms and then reached for her robe, shoving her arms through the holes and belting it tightly. Without a word, without a backwards glance, she left, walking out of the bunker and leaving him behind.

Mateo didn't stop her.

CHAPTER THIRTY-EIGHT

Raina studied herself in the mirror of her make up table. To her eyes she looked different. Drawn. More serious. Even if her body didn't reflect it, she was altered. She felt as though she'd grown up overnight.

Raina had always thought herself more mature than her classmates growing up. She'd reined in Cass's impetuosity and helped organize Noah. She helped her parents on the farm. She was a responsible person. Yet she clung to her youth and some of her immaturity. She was only twenty-one, she shouldn't have to grow up so fast.

Mateo, he was older... she didn't know how much. She'd never asked him. She figured late thirties. There was something about him, something that didn't make the age gap such a big deal. But now, she felt as though the years were impossible to breach. His life experience, who he was as a person, had stomped all over her, showing her exactly how young she was. How not ready for this world she was.

She had to leave. She had no choice. She couldn't allow a repeat of what they'd done and she could no longer consent to marriage with a person like him. One day, she would piss him off again and they would find themselves back there in the bunker, in the same place. He would hurt her again, and again, and again, until she couldn't take it anymore. She would become Casey under Ignacio Hernandez's regime. She would become Elvira under Tony Montana's ownership. Raina would not allow that to happen.

She didn't feel the tears until she looked up at herself in the mirror. She touched her face as they dripped down her cheeks. She would allow herself to mourn this one night only, then she needed to get back to herself so that she could find a way out.

She pushed away from the makeup table and strode towards the bathroom stripping her clothes off as she went.

Raina took a hot shower that lasted nearly forty minutes. She scrubbed herself clean, washed her hair twice and shaved every inch of her body. Just because she was traumatized didn't mean she couldn't take care of yourself.

She pulled on her cami top and a pair of pajama bottoms and slid beneath her sheets. Though she wasn't afraid of the dark she decided to sleep with the light on; being able to see when she woke up would be comforting. She wouldn't have to worry about monsters in the dark.

Raina didn't come to Mateo's room, not that he expected her to, but he'd hoped. He should've known better though. What he'd done to her, anywhere else in the world it would be unforgivable. Even to him and his moral code it was unforgivable. Yet, he made no apologies.

It had been necessary to wake her up to the realities of their world. Raina was reckless. He'd allowed her those two years to establish her independence, but she got herself hurt. Here at the estate, she was attempting to control their home, to control him. She was taking more frequent trips out and chafing under the required security measures. He needed her to understand that he was the boss. He would always be the boss.

He needed to frighten her into listening to him without hesitation, without exception. She couldn't be her usual argumentative self if they ever came under fire. If they were attacked, she would need to react without thought, which meant obeying her master. Her husband. Mateo.

Yet, he hadn't thought he had it in him to actually hurt her. And it destroyed a piece of him, a piece he'd been holding onto for her sake. It was the part of Mateo that wanted a normal relationship, a normal civilized love. He was obsessed with this woman, but her safety had to come first. Even if that meant her safety came above her human rights.

With that last thought he left his room and strode down the hall toward hers. When he opened the door, he found her sound asleep in her bed, curled on her side with the light on. A shock of pain pierced him as he realized she was probably sleeping with the light on because she was scared of him. He'd become her monster in the dark.

The thought gutted him, and he continued to stand in her doorway looking at her as he brought his emotions under control.

He couldn't allow this to fester though. If he did, it would change the direction of his actions and he knew he was in the right. They didn't inhabit the regular world of rules and laws, they lived in the underworld. Where people died, they disappeared and loved ones mourned. He would not allow that to happen to Raina.

He scooped her off the bed and turned on his heel, striding back to his bedroom. She woke up as they were halfway down the hall and began to struggle in his arms. Her eyes were half open, her focus bleary.

"Wh - what are you doing?" she protested groggily.

Before she could begin fighting in earnest, he set her on the bed and turned to close and lock the door. She scrambled off the bed and flung herself to the opposite side of the room, her chest heaving in fear, her pupils dilated as she stared at him.

He realized immediately what she thought was going to happen. He lifted his hands and approached her slowly. "I'm not going to hurt you."

She angrily swiped at a tear that dripped from her eye. "I don't believe you."

"When have I ever lied to you, Raina?" he asked quietly.

"You said you would protect me, but you didn't, you hurt me."

"I know you can't understand right now, but by hurting you I am protecting you." He tried to approach her, but she jumped away and hit the wall behind her so hard she winced. He stopped moving so she wouldn't accidentally hurt herself. "I told you that I would make decisions in your best interest; even the ones you don't want me to make."

"Fuck you!" she snarled. "You don't get to tell me you know what's best for me after doing something like that. You... you... disgusting excuse for a man."

He gritted his teeth against her accusation, reminding himself that anger was not the way to go. He had allowed his anger to rein free in the bunker and now he would have to deal with the fallout.

"You need to calm down, Raina. This is your reality. You are my wife and you will sleep in my bedroom. I give you my word, I won't touch you. It'll be like our first night together."

"I'm not your wife." Raina eyed him, then the door.

"I won't let you leave this room. We can stand here all night if that's what you want, but you're not walking out that door before morning."

His words were spoken calmly though he was a raging inferno of emotion on the inside. Only Raina could do this to him, pull these kind of feelings from him. He was good at his job because he was a born killer. He enjoyed the hunt. But with Raina, he wanted to be a better person.

Finally, after several long minutes of motionless stand-off she said, "Okay, but you stay on your side of the bed. If any part of you touches any part of me it's getting bitten off."

He had to fight the unexpected urge to chuckle. He could definitely picture Raina taking a chunk out of his skin if he accidentally rolled over against her.

He stepped to the side and waved her toward the bed. She cautiously sidled past him and then slid beneath the sheets, settling her head on her pillow. Mateo decided to keep his pants on for now. He didn't want to frighten her again.

He slid into the bed beside her and pulled the blanket over top of them. She hissed in anger and wiggled further away from him before closing her eyes and tucking her hands in the prayer position underneath her head.

Mateo reached over and turned the lamp off, plunging the room into darkness. He didn't think he would sleep, so he lay staring at nothing and thinking about the future weeks and the problems they would hold now that he'd made an enemy out of his wife.

He thought that Raina had drifted to sleep, her breathing having evened out. But then her voice penetrated the darkness as she said so quietly he almost didn't hear, "I was a virgin."

CHAPTER THIRTY-NINE

Vee shifted uncomfortably, rolling over and trying to find a new position. Then she rolled back, shoved her pillow underneath her head and closed her eyes, trying to sleep again. The bright light pouring through the pointless filmy purple curtains penetrated her eyelids like tiny burning needles.

It was impossible, she couldn't get comfortable.

Vee rolled to the side of the bed and sat up, swinging her feet to the floor and sliding them into the slippers provided. She pushed her hair off her face and stretched, yawning. Then she stood, reached for her bathrobe, also provided by her generous host, and headed out to the kitchen for her cup of morning tea.

"Morning," Danny said, entirely too chipper.

Vee mumbled something incoherent, took the herbal tea he handed her and plunked herself down at the table. She stared blearily at nothing until the hot liquid started to take wake her up.

"Where're Christine and Sadie?" she asked after a few minutes.

Danny turned from the counter where he was making himself a sandwich. "Christine took Sadie to her daycare and then she's going to work. She works in accounting at UPS."

Danny's wife's job was so mundane the Vee almost couldn't wrap her head around it. Especially considering the dark and exciting world the Danny inhabited. "She's not mafia?"

It wasn't exactly a polite question to ask, but she was curious. How had Danny managed to meet a normal girl-next-door type, and then convince her to date him long enough for him to put a ring on it? Danny was as rough-and-tumble as they came, had fought his way up the food chain to become second-in-command to Vee and now Mateo.

"She's connected, but distantly. Has a cousin working for the Alvarez family." Danny named a local mob family that engaged in gunrunning. Technically they would be Mateo's competition.

"She seems sweet," Vee said noncommittally.

Christine did seem like a sweet woman. She had welcomed Vee into her home, knowing that Vee had a dark past and an even darker husband. She allowed Vee to spend the night under her roof without complaint. She'd offered up their daughter's room since they only had the two bedrooms and an office in the lovely seaside cottage. This was more than Vee would have done.

"Yes," Danny said firmly. "She's about as nice as they come. I don't deserve her, but I'll do anything to keep her."

Vee nodded. "Good man."

Danny sank onto a chair at the table taking a huge bite out of his sandwich before dropping it on a plate and opening his laptop. He turned it so that both of them could see the screen. He pulled up a file entitled Daniela Velasquez. Together, Vee and Danny went through each item in an attempt to track down the now deceased Daniela's connection with the mystery woman who took her identity.

So far, the only connection they could find was Mateo's and Raina's desire for an interior designer and the fact that the designer they chose came highly recommended and was Latina.

Vee rubbed her forehead and growled, "I don't know how to keep my daughter safe if I don't know what the danger is or where it's coming from."

Danny gave her a long look. "The danger is going to come from your husband once he realizes that you didn't board that plane to Venezuela. Which, at my estimation, was around midnight last night. Am I correct?"

"Are you lecturing me?" Vee demanded, glaring at him. "My daughter's safety is more important than Isaac's commands."

He grinned and held his hand up. "You're not my boss anymore, lady. I'm doing you a favour by letting you stay here, but you're not doing me one by setting the Butcher on my ass."

Vee felt a bolt of guilt. She hadn't thought about the fallout to the people who were sheltering her when Sotza discovered that instead of going home she decided to stay in Miami to hunt down any leads on the woman who deceived her daughter.

"I'm sorry, Danny. I didn't think about that. And you have a wife and daughter now. I should leave." Vee started to stand, but Danny reached out and grabbed her wrist.

"You're not going anywhere." He held her arm until she was forced to sit. "For one thing, I'm the only ally you have in this town who's capable of helping you with this. Your husband is going to come banging down my door anytime now and I'd rather you be under my roof than anywhere else.

I figure I have more of a chance of survival if I can hand you right over than if he has to wait to get his hands on you."

Vee let out a laugh. "You're not wrong about that."

They continued to research their prey until they came up with a lead. They were going to question the carpenters that had been working on the house alongside Daniela Velasquez. Mateo had tried talking to them but had gotten nowhere. The head contractor had seemed clueless about their employer. They knew she belonged to an interior design company, but they hadn't set eyes on her prior to construction at the mansion. This in itself was unusual, since most interior decorators had teams that they preferred to work with.

Danny and Vee found them at their new job, building offices in a warehouse near the docks. Vee felt a rush of nostalgia as she passed the dockyard. This had been part of her territory when she'd reined over Miami. She had fought valiantly for it when she'd gone to war with Sotza. Now, it belonged to Mateo.

Vee's heels tapped against the concrete floor as she made her way through the warehouse, searching for any sign of a carpenter. She found them at the back of the building, joking with each other and discussing which bar they wanted to hit up after their workday finished. It was Friday afternoon so they were probably going to knock off early and head out for drinks.

"Can I help you?" A bearded man looked up from his position where he was crouched on the ground next to a wall.

"I'm looking for the foreman," she said coolly.

Danny stood behind Vee, silent and mean-looking. They fell into their old roles, Vee as the boss and Danny her hired muscle. But he was more than a thug, he was her protection and she knew without a doubt he wouldn't fail her.

"You're talking to him," the man said, straightening up

from the floor and dusting off the front of his jeans. "Name's Lincoln Frye."

"Good to meet you, Lincoln," Vee said, her voice cool and professional. "I want to talk about a recent job you and your team did for Daniela Velasquez."

The guy frowned. "I'm beginning to think there's something shady going on with that job. First that tough guy that owned the house grilled us, then his woman bodyguard, now you. What's up with that place?"

"It's not the place we're concerned about so much as the woman who infiltrated it. The woman who hired you was an imposter. She was not Daniela Velasquez."

Lincoln's eyebrows raised and he looked genuinely surprised. Vee realized that she'd given him a piece of information no one else had. When Mateo and Angela had interrogated him, they hadn't given him all the information, which meant he wouldn't have known how to form his responses accordingly. He would've answered their questions, but not through the filter of knowing there was something off about the woman who hired him.

"Yes, the real Daniela was found murdered in her home. We think the imposter killed her and took her place. What we don't know is why." Vee didn't feel a single moment's hesitation about giving up all the information. She was confident she was doing the right thing, though Mateo likely wouldn't agree.

"Holy fuck," Lincoln drawled, his amazement building. He shook his head. "She was so fucking hot, hard to believe she could kill a person."

Vee closed her eyes for a moment and then opened them and exhaled. She hoped for his sake that this man never again met a woman who was both beautiful and deadly, because they were far more common that he apparently thought. Vee could kill him in an instant right where he stood, and he wouldn't even know he was dead before he hit the ground. She had a knife in her purse, and a gun in her holster at her back. Aside from that, she was also very good at hand-to-hand combat.

"We want to know what she was doing there. Did she ask you any questions about the place while you were renovating? Did she say anything to you that seems strange in hindsight?"

He thought about it, then shook his head. "Not really. Nothing set off any red flags. To be honest, she was a stone-cold bitch, none of us had much to do with her besides taking her direction on the renovations."

Vee felt deflated. This was the only lead she and Danny could come up with and it was going to be a bust. She was about to thank Lincoln for talking to her, when he spoke again.

"Though there was this one time that she loosened up enough to talk to me for more than two seconds. I asked her where she came from since she had a slight accent. I was surprised when she actually answered. I got the feeling she was proud of her hometown. Like she felt disgusted at having to be here. At the time it didn't really blip on my radar, but now, it does seem weird that a woman with a well-established interior design business in Florida would rather be in Mexico."

Excitement jolted through Vee and her hands shook when she clasped them together. "Where was she from? Where was her hometown?"

He didn't even pause, as though he remembered every detail of the conversation with the fake Daniela. "She was from the Durango region in Mexico, outside the city, up in the Sierra Madres."

Vee felt both elation and terror as she realized exactly who had come in close contact with her daughter. Desi. The woman who came to Sotza's Venezuelan island with her lover,

Nicolás Garza, to kill them both and take over the Venezuelan cartel. Mateo had hunted down the man behind the attack, but he hadn't been able to find Desi.

And if she was being honest, Vee had to admit that none of them had put a whole lot of effort into finding Desi. As far as they had been concerned, Desi was Nico's second-in-command, she'd been forced to follow his orders, then she'd run away when things got hot.

Well, Desi had just become a priority. Vee was going to hunt her down and play with her insides.

Vee thanked Lincoln for his help, handed him a roll of bills and told him to buy his team a round of beer, then she turned on her heel and walked away with Danny at her side.

"Do you know who Desi is?" Vee asked Danny.

"Yes."

That one simple word held a grim finality to it. If Desi was still after Raina, then Raina was in very big trouble.

They drove back to Danny's house in silence. They would have to come up with a plan, but for now Vee needed to decide what she was going to do with this information. Did she keep it to herself or did she discuss it with Mateo?

Mateo would be furious if he found out that she'd interfered, but he would be less furious if Vee shared the information. Vee didn't need to make an enemy out of Mateo. Still... What if he didn't take this seriously, what if he didn't take the proper steps to protect Raina?

Vee was still contemplating what action she would take when they arrived at the house. She got out of the car and started walking toward the house, so lost in thought that she didn't see the car with tinted windows until a door opened and a man got out.

He was tall, distinguished-looking, handsome and controlled. He wore his suit to perfection. Her heart stuttered when she caught sight of him. He strode angrily toward her, his face darkening into a thunderous frown.

"Elvira."

Dammit, he only ever called her that when he was furious. Well, two could play this game.

"Sotza," she said, using his last name, something she only did when he was being a dick.

CHAPTER FORTY

"We need to talk." Sotza's voice was cold and hard.

Vee was in very big trouble. Then again, she'd known she would be in trouble the moment she decided not to get on the airplane back to Venezuela. This was her reckoning.

Sotza eyed Danny who was standing slightly beside and behind Vee. His posture was somewhat protective but both men knew that Danny wouldn't make a move against the Butcher.

"Someplace private," Sotza said, jerking his head toward the house.

Sotza took Vee's arm in a tight grip as Danny unlocked the door, pushed it open and ushered the other two inside. Vee continued down the hall, showing Sotza to the bedroom she'd used the night before.

As soon as the door closed behind them, Vee began defending herself. "I had to stay, Isaac. Raina is my daughter, nothing else is more important."

Sotza took a step toward her, forcing her to back up until she hit the door. As he approached, she lifted her chin in defiance. He towered over her, placing a hand on the door next to her head. Though he wasn't being overtly threatening, his body language hinted at it.

"Agreed," he said quietly.

Vee was shocked. She hadn't expected such an easy capitulation from her husband. He was king of the underground in many South American regions and had to maintain a hard exterior in order to preserve his role. Even with Vee, he was often dictator-like. He frequently curtailed her decision-making powers. She was to go where he told her to go, stay where he told her to stay and do what he told her to do. Despite that, Sotza did respect his wife and held her to a high standard. She worked, lived and loved at his side.

"You agree?" she asked, off-balance.

"I do." His voice was deep velvet, though she heard the underlying steel. He was still angry with her. "But you do not have my permission to go off on your own. You knew when you made this choice that I wouldn't approve. There will be consequences."

"What kind of consequences?" she asked quietly.

Sotza could be breathtakingly brutal, even with his wife. She'd seen him working in his dungeon, experienced his anger firsthand. She wasn't eager for the consequences that he spoke of.

"You don't need to worry about that now. For the moment, we will concentrate on the safety of our daughter." He paced away from Vee, though he didn't go far given the limited space in the bedroom. "Unlike you, Mateo has been updating me with information on this potential threat against Raina. First, you will tell me what you've learned and then we will talk to Mateo. We'll find this Daniela bitch and we will remove the threat to our family."

Tears rushed to Vee's eyes. She felt guilty that she'd underestimated Sotza and his care for her daughter. She had acted impulsively, a character trait that some might call a flaw. A trait she had in common with her daughter. Vee threw herself at her husband and hugged him tightly around the waist pressing her ear to his heart.

"Thank you."

He stood stiff for a few seconds and then she felt the gradual loosening of his muscles. He lifted his arms and wrapped them around her, his hand cupping the back of her head as he held her to his chest. He dropped his head and pressed a kiss against the fine blonde hair.

"Raina is well loved, none of us will allow anything to happen to her. Mateo will hunt her enemies to the ends of the earth and beyond. He'll sacrifice himself for your daughter. You must trust him and trust me."

"I do," she insisted, sniffling back tears. She tipped her head up so her chin rested on his chest. He looked down at her. "I'm sorry I didn't give you the respect you deserve. You should've heard about this from me, not Mateo. I should've trusted you to help me. I just..."

"I'm not your ex-husband, Elvira. I will always take care of you and yours. Raina is my daughter as well and I will move heaven and earth to ensure her safety."

"I know," she whispered.

She was deeply moved by his words. There was a time, a few years ago when they had to fight hard for their love. Vee had denied him her daughter. She had told him to his face that he was not Raina's father. Now she knew better. Raina had two fathers; Joe Duncan and Isaac Sotza. Either one would die for her.

"Will we be staying in Miami?" she asked hesitantly.

This was a large part of the reason why she hadn't told Sotza that she was planning on staying behind. She feared he would order her to get on a plane, and if she didn't comply, he would've sent Mateo after her. Now, she feared something different. She worried that he would send her home to Venezuela and stay himself. A result of her own screwup.

He nodded. "Yes, we'll stay in Miami for now. But if you put one hair out of line, you'll find yourself back on the compound in Venezuela so fast your head will spin. You will be locked in your room until I can arrive to lay down your new law."

She wanted to argue with him, as she often did when he went all patriarchal on her, but she was so grateful to have him here and to have his support that she nodded. "I understand."

He stepped away from her, though he kept a hand on her back. He looked around the room, his eyes narrowing. "Grab your things, we'll be staying somewhere else. I don't think we'll both fit in the bed."

Vee giggled as she glanced at the tiny princess bed that she'd slept in the night before. A perfectly wonderful bed for a five-year-old girl, a complete nightmare for an adult.

CHAPTER FORTY-ONE

Raina watched dismally as her things were moved from her old room into Mateo's room. She was sitting on her soon-to-be old bed with her arms crossed and her eyes narrowed as the men moved everything out. They attempted to get her to come to Mateo's room and tell them where to put it all.

She bit her lip so that she wouldn't reply with, "Up your ass". It wasn't their fault that she and Mateo were fighting.

Fighting felt like such a weak word for what was happening between them. More like a catastrophic shift in their relationship. Raina was more confused than ever about what she felt for Mateo. True to his word, he hadn't touched her during the night. They had lain side by side, neither of them sleeping for a long time. She hadn't been afraid of him, not exactly. Even though he hurt her, she still trusted him when he told her that he wouldn't touch her.

But the fact that he had hurt her at all, deliberately and mercilessly, told her that he could do it again. And that was where most of her confusion came from. She wasn't going to delude or lie to herself; she was in love with Mateo, had been in love with him for years. He was a hard man to resist. He was devoted to her health, safety and comfort.

But the problem was the order of his priorities. Mateo would always put her health and safety above her comfort. Yet, Raina would argue that a person needed happiness for survival as much as they needed the basics.

That morning, she had woken up tucked against his side, her back to him, her butt pressed against his hip. Her hands had been underneath her head as though she had curled up against him in her sleep, seeking warmth. She didn't move; didn't want to move. In fact, she wanted to roll over against him and watch him as he slept, but she didn't. She still couldn't deal with her emotions over what happened.

They had sex. No, not sex. Sex was consensual. Mateo had attacked her, and she'd been forced to take it. And much to her shame, her body had betrayed her during the ordeal. Realistically, she knew that women were capable of orgasming under extreme circumstances but knowing that and feeling it were two different things.

Mateo had demonstrated to her, with his actions, how different their worlds were. Raina wanted love, respect and a marriage built on a foundation of equality and mutual caring. She didn't want a husband who would lay down the law, force her compliance and treat her like a prisoner if she dared to voice her dissent.

But Mateo inhabited the world of organized crime. A place where the rules were different. Raina would be naïve not to pay attention to that world; to assume that she wasn't a part of it because she didn't want to be.

The fact was, Raina was born to the mafia. She didn't have a choice. She'd never had a choice. That was why Sotza had ordered Mateo to pick her up two years ago, to bring her to Venezuela to meet her birth mother.

Now, like it or not, Raina was firmly entrenched in

Mateo's world. It was a depressing thought; one she didn't want to linger on. She pushed herself off the bed and stood, then headed for the door. She nearly ran into one of the bodyguards coming in for another load.

"Excuse me," he said politely and then went around her. He lifted Raina's makeup table in one arm as though it weighed nothing.

Mateo had told her that morning that he wanted her permanently moved into his room. He didn't want her thinking that she could escape back into her old room, pushing him out. He had informed her that her things would be moved over and that she didn't have a choice.

She had informed him that he could go fuck himself. She'd had the pleasure of watching his body tighten in annoyance, but he left without saying a word, denying her the fight she so richly wanted. The scratches visible on his face from their fight in the bunker would have to suffice her thirst for vengeance.

Raina went in search of Danny, hoping he would agree to take her shopping. She didn't really need to go shopping, nor did she have a strong desire for it, but she wanted to get out of the house. She couldn't sit there and watch as all her things were moved into Mateo's room.

Raina knocked on the door of the security office. A feminine voice told her to come in.

"Hey Angela." Raina tried to sound more upbeat than she felt. "Danny around?"

Angela shook her head and leaned back in her chair. "Nope. Mateo asked Danny to join him for the day. Mateo wants to reach out to some of Vee's old connections and thought Danny would be able to help."

"Oh." With all the turmoil of the past few days, Raina had forgotten that Mateo had a big job to do in Miami.

A tiny part of her forgave him for his actions of the day

before. Not only was he trying to establish the boundaries of their relationship, but he was under a great deal of stress. He was taking over one of the most important underground international hub cities in the world. The job was dangerous, though she had no doubt he would succeed. She couldn't imagine a world where Mateo didn't get exactly what he wanted. He wouldn't allow it.

"Did they take any bodyguards with them?" Raina asked, worried for Mateo's safety.

Angela smirked at her, as though she thought Raina's concern was cute. "You do know that both Mateo and Danny acted as bodyguards in a professional capacity, right? Danny was Vee's bodyguard for years, even before she became a boss, and Mateo has been Sotza's protection for more than two decades. They can take care of themselves."

Raina huffed. "I know, I know. I guess I just worry more now. Especially since I'm more informed about the inner workings here."

It was true. No one was attempting to sugarcoat Raina's new existence. She wondered if it was a group effort to keep her informed for her own safety. If she knew how bad things could get, then she might be less likely to place herself in harmful situations. Angela more than the others gave Raina the bald truth every time. Raina was grateful for that.

Angela seemed to take pity on her. "You don't have to worry about them. Not only are they capable of taking care of themselves, but they also took several men with them. I don't think they were doing anything particularly dangerous, but these days they seem to be taking back-up everywhere. They're protected and the house is like Fort Knox. We're all in good shape."

Raina smiled. "Thanks for the reassurance."

"No problem, chica," Angela said, putting a foot up on the

desk. "What can I help you with? You came in here looking for Danny. What did you need him for?"

Raina shrugged. "Nothing much, I wanted to get out of the house for a few hours. I was hoping he would take me shopping. But it's not a big deal, I can go another time."

Angela pushed herself away from the desk and got to her feet. "I'll take you. I can use a timeout from the desk. Who knew house security would involve so much paperwork? We'll grab a couple of the guys, eat some lunch and hit up the South Beach shopping. You haven't had a chance to check it out yet, have you? I've been dying to get over there myself, but Mateo's been keeping me busy."

Raina was surprised to hear Angela talking about wanting to shop. Angela was a no-nonsense kind of girl. She never wore makeup that Raina could tell, she kept her long dark hair knotted tightly at the base of her neck and she always wore militaristic clothes. Cargo pants, basic T-shirt and combat boots. She also tended to wear a utility belt with a variety of weapons.

Raina would be massively intimidated by Angela if they hadn't spent several weeks getting to know each other. Raina had discovered a total softy in Angela; a woman who had to put on a tough exterior to live in a man's world, while still managing to maintain her compassion. She cared about others. She checked on Raina often and Raina knew that Angela had conversations with Mateo, making sure that he was being safe and that he knew he had an ear if he needed to talk over any of his plans. Angela was well suited for house duty, organizing protection details and security. Raina was pleased that Mateo seemed to be grooming her for that particular job.

Twenty minutes later they were on their way to South Beach, Angela in the driver's seat, Raina in the passenger and the bodyguards in the back.

"Do you miss Venezuela?" Raina asked casually. "Do you think you'll go back there?"

Angela didn't take her eyes off the road, but she shrugged. "I don't have any family in Venezuela, but I do love the country. I'll definitely go visit. For now though, I prefer to remain at Mateo's side, whether that's here or somewhere else."

Raina nodded thoughtfully. She had felt a strong connection to her parent's farm. Her upbringing had been happy, and she wouldn't trade it for the world, but when she'd been kidnapped by Mateo and taken to Venezuela, her eyes had been opened to the wider world. After, when she'd gone on the run for two years, she had discovered in herself a deep desire to explore other places.

Though Miami was starting to grow on her, Raina still wanted to explore the world. Another unknown in her relationship with Mateo. Would he allow her to travel further abroad, or would he try to keep her in Miami? She didn't know, and not knowing was one of the fundamental issues with her relationship. Mateo would lay down the law and she would be expected to follow. How much autonomy she had in those decisions was yet to be established.

Raina had a surprisingly good time shopping with Angela. She discovered a hidden Barbie in the other woman. Angela loved colours in a way that Raina would not have suspected based on her tendency to wear only dark clothes when she worked. Angela chose several feminine items, including a pink dress, a red leather mini skirt that she paired with a bustier, a new pair of heels and a few items of jewelry.

Raina didn't buy much since she already had more than she needed at the mansion, but being out and about, breathing the fresh air with a hint of ocean and spending time with another woman helped to reorient her. She felt more like herself and more able to put the events of the past twenty-four hours into perspective.

She was still angry with Mateo, very angry, but she was seeing things more clearly now. Not much had changed besides her status as a virgin. She would still become wife to the mob boss of Miami. She was still the daughter of one of the most powerful families in the world.

But despite all that, she stayed true to herself. She still loved all the things that she had loved before, she still desired a relationship with Mateo and she still wanted to work. Forging was her art, an outlet, not one that she would willingly give up.

In fact, she purchased a few supplies while they were out. Angela had given her a long look but hadn't said anything. They were on their way back to the SUV when Angela slowed down, barring Raina with her arm. Raina's heart sped up. Angela was not a jumpy person; if she thought she had cause for concern, Raina believed her.

"Stay behind me at all times, don't leave, don't try to help me if we're attacked." Angela spoke quickly, turning completely professional on a dime. "I don't see the bodyguards."

Angela was right. Raina looked right and then left, searching the sidewalk for the two men who'd been trailing them all day. Neither of the men had gotten more than ten feet away from Raina at any point during the shopping excursion. Where had they gone?

"What do we do?" Raina asked, her heart thundering so loud she could barely hear. Did they stay on the crowded sidewalk and hope that whatever happened to the bodyguards didn't happen to them? Or did they try to run and hide?

"There's a door right behind you, go into the shop and head for the rear exit. Don't look back, I'll be right behind you."

Together they rushed into the shop, Raina hurtling

towards the back door. She could hear Angela behind her. She continued running toward the change rooms.

"Where's your exit?" Angela shouted at the shop person.

Raina was already in the back hallway so she didn't hear the answer, but Angela came sprinting after her, only a few feet behind. Raina was so concentrated on getting to the rear exit as fast as she could that she didn't hear Angela's words in time.

"Let me go first!" Angela shouted just as Raina hit the bar across the back door, shoving it open and slamming into the alley.

Everything happened so quickly that Raina didn't have a chance to defend herself or Angela who was right behind her. Something slammed into Raina so hard that she hit the door then rebounded and hit the wall. She crumpled to the ground, dropping her bags as she fell. She landed on her side and remained that way, stunned and hurt.

Seconds later, she heard a pop pop sound. It was like the sounds from her apartment when she'd been shot. She flinched, then curled into herself expecting to feel the hot tearing sensation of bullets ripping through her.

When nothing happened, she looked up hoping to find Angela. But the person crouching next to her wasn't Angela, it was Daniela Velasquez. Not Daniela Velasquez; the person who killed her.

"Get up." Her voice was cold and emotionless.

When Raina didn't immediately move, Daniela reached out and gripped her by the hair, yanking her to her feet. Raina let out a pained yelp and tried to defend herself, sending an elbow flying towards Daniela's face. Daniela ducked and punched Raina in the side. Raina screamed as she slammed back into the side of the building, pain radiating through her side and back.

Again, Raina tried to defend herself. She whipped around,

sending a fist flying towards Daniela's face, but Daniela grabbed her arm and punched Raina in the chest. Raina crumpled to the ground once more, the world spinning around her, the breath knocked from her chest and a burning sensation climbing up her throat. She rolled over onto her hands and knees and threw up.

The woman grabbed her by the hair again and dragged her off the cement. Raina caught a glimpse of Angela. She was lying motionless on her stomach, her head turned to the side and her eyes closed. She was so pale Raina feared she was dead. That explained the popping sounds. Daniela had shot her.

Raina was so dizzy and nauseous that when she tried to lift her arms to defend herself Daniela was able to easily knock them to the side. Daniela gripped her by the throat, lifted her off the ground and slammed her into the wall, smacking the back of Raina's head.

Daniela pulled her gun and pushed it underneath Raina's chin. Raina's eyes filled with tears as she saw her own demise rushing towards her. She was about to die, and she didn't even know what she'd done to deserve it.

"Why?" she whispered.

The cold eyes narrowed on her as Daniela debated whether or not to speak to Raina. It was clear that she intended to do the job she came to do, which was kill Raina.

Finally, Daniela answered, her words clipped. "It's not personal. Your fiancé killed Nico, and now I must kill him before he can kill me."

Raina didn't think that cleared anything up. "How will killing me also kill Mateo?"

"You're his distraction, my tool to getting to him. I need you dead so that he will become reckless with grief, so that he will begin hunting me once more."

Raina didn't think the logic added up, but she wasn't

going to argue with the woman who had a gun. "I don't think you want to kill me," Raina tried to reason with her.

Daniela laughed bitterly. "Your death means nothing to me. Another day, another job. Now close your eyes, sweetheart, and you will sleep. I'll make it quick."

Hysteria began to rise up in Raina as Daniela moved the gun to her temple. There was nothing left to do. Raina closed her eyes and waited for death.

CHAPTER FORTY-TWO

When the shot came it wasn't Raina who was hit. Her eyes flew open. Daniela screamed in pain, released her grip on Raina's neck, jumped back and slammed a hand over her hip which was now pouring blood.

Raina looked around in confusion and saw Angela who had rolled to her side, pulled her gun and shot Daniela. Angela was about to shoot again when Daniela took off down the alley. Rather than shooting at her though, Angela dropped her gun and collapsed onto the pavement.

Raina peeled herself off the side of the building and lunged for the gun. It took her two tries to pick it up because her hands were shaking so bad and her head was still spinning. She covered Angela with her own body and turned to watch as Daniela disappeared around the corner of the building.

Thank god she didn't have to make the decision of whether or not to shoot the other woman. Raina had never killed anyone before and she didn't want to start now. Not that Raina would've actually been able to hit her at that distance, having never used a gun before.

As soon as Raina thought they were relatively safe, she turned back to Angela and assessed her. Angela was out cold. Somehow she'd managed to wake up long enough to stop Daniela from killing Raina. Now it was Raina's turn to protect Angela.

Hands still shaking, she picked up her purse, dumped it on the ground and rummaged until she found her phone. She called Mateo as she was running her hands over Angela's body searching for gunshot wounds. There was a hole in Angela's T-shirt over her heart, but there was no blood. Raina lifted her shirt and felt around. Angela was wearing a heavy vest, most likely bulletproof. Hopefully her vigilance would save her life.

"Raina."

Raina's heart soared as soon as she heard Mateo's voice. Hearing his deep voice reassured her like nothing else could.

"Angela's been shot," she said, her voice high-pitched and panicked. "What do I do?"

"Are you safe?" he demanded.

"Yes, I'm safe enough for now. Angela saved my life. But please, Mateo, help me. What do I do?"

"Where was she shot?"

"In the chest, over her heart, but I think she's wearing something bulletproof underneath."

"Yes, good, it's part of her uniform." His voice was calm and cool, but she could hear the growing rage. Heads would roll over this incident. "Has she been shot anywhere else?"

Raina searched again and found another hole, this one on the left side of Angela's torso. This one had hit the bulletproof vest as well. "Yes, but in the vest again. I don't think she was shot anywhere else; I don't see any blood. Why is she knocked out?"

Raina's heart felt like it was going to burst from her chest. Her movements seemed slow and sluggish. She felt like an idiot, like she couldn't help Angela and she desperately wanted to.

Mateo's voice was calm and soothing. "Even though the bullets didn't penetrate her skin, there's still trauma in getting shot through a bulletproof vest. The one that struck her over her heart likely put a vast amount of pressure on her chest. Danny is on his way. He'll help. Trust him and do everything he says."

Tears trickled down Raina's face and she nodded even though he couldn't see it. "Okay, I'll wait for him." A sob escaped her throat. "Mateo... I don't know where the other bodyguards are... what if..."

"Raina, mi amor, you cannot worry about that now." His voice was gruff with concern, his accent thicker.

She swiped at an escaping tear and nodded. "Okay. I'll take care of Angela; you can trust me."

"Good girl. I'll meet you at the house." Raina garbled something in return and was about to hang up, but then she caught his last words. "I love you, Raina."

He hung up before she could return the words. She didn't know if she could yet anyway. With the events of the last few days, she felt burnt out, emotionally and physically. She wanted to lay down and turn the world off; no longer be responsible for anything, let alone her own feelings.

By the time Danny arrived she was a sobbing mess on the ground, one hand clutching her phone while the other tightly gripped Angela's hand. Angela still hadn't woken up and Raina was terribly worried. One of the shop employees had found her in the alley a couple minutes earlier and was sitting with her while they waited for Danny to arrive.

The shopkeeper had wanted to call an ambulance, but Raina had assured her that once her friend arrived, they would go straight to the hospital. She didn't know if it was true, but she figured it was the best thing she could say in the moment.

Two other men were with Danny. They covered the entrances to the alley while Danny checked Angela over, carefully picked her up off the ground, thanked the shopkeeper and strode to the SUV. After tucking Angela into the vehicle, Danny turned around and gave Raina a quick hug. "I've got you now, sweetheart. I won't let anyone hurt you."

Raina cried into his shoulder for a few seconds before pushing away. She insisted on climbing in the back seat with Angela and gripping her hand again.

CHAPTER FORTY-THREE

Mateo paced impatiently near the front doors of the mansion as he waited for Danny's black SUV to traverse the driveway. Minutes later he caught a glimpse of the vehicle hurtling toward him. Before it could come to a complete stop, Raina was launching herself out one of the back doors and towards Mateo.

He caught her, absorbing the impact against his solid body, as she flung herself into his arms. It felt good having her sleight weight smashing into him. She wrapped her arms around his waist and clung to him, pressing her face into his chest.

"I'm so sorry, I had no idea this would happen. I should've stayed home. I tried my hardest to fight Daniela off, but she was stronger and more skilled. What if something happens to Angela?" Raina's words came out in a garbled mess. Mateo was only able to decipher every other word, but he got the gist.

He ran his hand over her head and frowned as she winced when his fingers touched a spot on the back. "You did nothing wrong. This is not on you. If anyone should bear responsibility, it's me. I didn't treat Daniela as enough of a serious threat."

He shuffled Raina to the side as Danny emerged from the vehicle with Angela in his arms. He paused in front of Mateo. "Thomas found our missing men. Both dead. One shot to the head each while they were still in the car."

Raina collapsed against Mateo's side, using him for support as she learned the fate of her bodyguards. She was indirectly responsible for their deaths, for Angela being shot.

Mateo nodded toward Angela and said in a clipped tone, "Take her to her bedroom. The doctor is on his way."

"Doesn't she need a hospital?" Raina asked tearfully, tilting her head up to look at him.

Mateo shook his head. "We only use hospitals as a last resort. And the doctor isn't for Angela, he's for you. He'll check Angela over, but since there are no discernible injuries, she should be fine once she wakes up."

"But Angela is the one who got hurt!" Raina burst out, jerking back in his arms and frowning. "Daniela barely had time to touch me before Angela shot her."

Mateo hadn't known that Angela had shot Daniela. There was much he needed to find out. He spoke rapidly to his men, giving them instructions on how to organize security and instructing them to let the doctor through. They were about to go into full lockdown, no one in and no one out.

"Come." Mateo wrapped his arm around Raina's waist and walked with her into the mansion. She balked and tried to trail after Danny, but Mateo forced her up the stairs and into their bedroom.

"I'm fine!" she burst out once they were in the bedroom. "Nothing happened to me. I'm worried about Angela, and you should be too." There was accusation in her voice as she told him that he should be more concerned for his subordinate.

"Angela is part of my security team, which means there are certain risks that come with the job. You are our number one priority, and you will continue to be priority until I'm assured that you're not hurt." When it looked as though she intended to argue with him, he held a hand up. "I care about Angela too. I've known her since she was a teenager. But it's a fact, she would want you to be secure before anyone concerns themselves with her well-being."

Raina's jaw tightened and she narrowed her eyes at him. "Fine, I'm secure. But I want an update on Angela's health as soon as possible."

Mateo rolled his shoulders back, cracking his neck and easing some of the tension. He really hadn't intended to argue with Raina. He wanted some of their easy friendship back and he seemed to be pushing that farther and farther away.

"As soon as the doctor is able to look you over, both of you, then I'll allow you to see Angela. For now, I need you to sit down and rest." Her face softened and she allowed him to take her arm and help her into a sitting position on the bed. He sat next to her and ran a hand down her spine then massaged the base of her back. "You may not have been physically hurt, though I suspect at least a bump to the head. Regardless, the terror and adrenaline spike alone can cause complications. I need to be sure that you're okay. Will you do this, will you allow a doctor to look you over? For me?"

They stared at each other, her deep blue eyes big and uncertain. It tore at his heart knowing that he was forcing her into a lifestyle where things like this were possible. He made enemies, he was a target, which made her a target too. He loved her too much to be okay with this, yet his love wasn't unselfish enough that he was willing to let her go.

"Okay, I'll talk to the doctor." She reached out and took his hand, as though she knew he needed reassuring. "Really though, I'm okay. The back of my head hit a wall and she punched my chest, but that's all she had time to do."

"She shouldn't have even been able to do that much." Mateo growled, fury rushing through him, igniting his desire for revenge. He stood, releasing her hand. "I need to go downstairs to confer with security and check on Angela. I'll be up in a few minutes with the doctor and an update."

Raina nodded, but as he was walking away, she stopped him. "The woman, Daniela, or whoever she is... she said you killed someone she knew." She looked at him expectantly.

"Don't worry about it for now. We'll talk later."

As Mateo left the room, Raina was crawling up the bed to lay down in her favourite position, on her side with her hands in the prayer position under her face. He wondered if she would take a nap or wait for the doctor. All he wanted to do was curl up next to her, hold her against his body and reassure himself that she was both real and alive.

Mateo strode down the hallway and took the stairs two at a time as he descended to the lower level. He snapped his fingers at Thomas and jerked his head towards his office. "Get Danny and meet me in here."

Mateo shoved the door open and strode inside. A half smile lifted his lips as he looked around. The place was in complete chaos, protective plastic sheets over his desk and chair, construction equipment everywhere and sawdust hanging in the air. The sight of such renewal gave him hope. Raina was renovating his office to erase the memories of its past occupant. A sentiment he wholeheartedly agreed with.

Danny and Thomas shuffled into his office, closing the door behind them.

Danny nodded his head toward Mateo and started speaking. "Boss. Angela is awake, she doesn't remember much of the incident, but she seems to be okay. Says when she was shot, she was flung backward into a doorframe and hit her head. I think that's why she was unconscious for so long. Might have a concussion."

Mateo was relieved. He was worried something more had happened to her than they hadn't been able to see. He cared about Angela. He considered her a sister and had watched over her from the moment she became part of Sotza's organization. She had trained under Mateo and worked for several years as his protégé.

"Make sure the doctor is aware of all her injuries," Mateo said to Danny. "I'm putting you on house security while she's recovering. Consider us in full lockdown until the Velasquez situation is ended. I want a full-time guard on my wife. The only time he doesn't need to have eyes on her is when she's in my bedroom or in the bathroom. Otherwise, he is to be two feet away from her at all times."

"Consider it done." Danny turned to leave the office but glanced back at Mateo. "Have you talked to Sotza?"

Mateo gave Danny a hard stare. "Si, I have, but I should have heard about it from you first. You're my man now, not theirs. Do not mix your allegiances again."

There was a moment of tense waiting as the two men stared at each other while Thomas pretended he wasn't part of the conversation.

Danny nodded stiffly. "Of course. It won't happen again."

Just like that Danny swore his allegiance to the new Miami boss. He left the office without another word.

Mateo turned his focus to Thomas. "I need you to go back to the store where the attack happened. Find out who in the area has security cameras and if there are any CCTV cameras in the vicinity. Get as much footage as you can. Take it to Sotza, he and Vee can look it over. It's time to put this bitch in the ground."

Thomas seemed to hesitate as if he wanted to say something. Mateo waited, but Thomas shook his head and left the office. Mateo frowned. Thomas had been acting strange lately, inconsistent and indecisive; two things that could easily get a man in security killed. Mateo would have to talk to him. Perhaps America didn't suit the native Venezuelan. He might need to be transferred back to Sotza.

Mateo called his former employer. Sotza picked up on the first ring. "Mateo, what can I do for you?"

Mateo launched straight into an explanation of the day's event, bringing Sotza up to date on everything that Mateo knew so far. "Thomas will come straight to you once he has the video footage."

"Good. We'll look it over, let you know if we find anything. For now, stay home, take care of the girls."

He hung up and minutes later the doctor arrived. Mateo escorted him upstairs to see Raina first. She sat up with a frown when they entered the room.

"Have you seen Angela yet? How is she?" Raina asked hurriedly.

"The doctor will see you first, then Angela." Mateo used a stern voice so she understood there would be no argument. He turned to the doctor, Shane Wilson. "You've been filled in on her condition?"

Dr. Wilson nodded as he approached the bed. "I was told that Ms. Duncan had kidney failure as a child and was given a transplant. That she now has one functioning kidney. May I?" He asked Raina, indicating her head. "I was informed that you sustained a bump to the head. Can you tell me where it is?"

As he looked her over, Raina said, "I've been doing great since the transplant. I don't have any problems as long as I take my medications on time."

"You're on the antirejection meds? Are you on any other medications?"

She shook her head and he continued the examination. "I

understand you were shot recently." His words were said with professionalism, as though there was nothing unusual about treating a gunshot victim. She wondered if he worked for the mob.

"Yes, I was shot." She twisted on the bed and lifted the bottom of her shirt, showing him the puckered red wound on her lower back.

Dr. Wilson continued to look her over until he was satisfied. He spoke mostly to Raina, though he occasionally directed his words toward Mateo. "You had a nasty shock today. You'll want to rest and take it easy. Have some Tylenol if your head hurts, otherwise you're in perfect health."

Raina smiled at him. "Thank you. Are you going to go check on Angela now?"

The doctor smiled indulgently and nodded. "She's next on my list."

"Take good care of her."

Mateo walked the doctor out. Once the door to the bedroom closed, he spoke. "When is the soonest you can run tests on her."

"Tests?" The doctor asked.

"For her kidney," Mateo said, a hard edge to his voice. "Make sure she's as healthy as she can be. I want to make sure that her body is strong and that it remains that way. I am in need of a full-time on-call physician. I want Raina checked regularly. I want to know the second anything is wrong."

The doctor looked at him thoughtfully and nodded. "I run a private clinic with two other doctors. It's definitely within my capabilities of doing this service for you. There will be a retainer fee and it won't be cheap."

"Send me the bill."

CHAPTER FORTY-FOUR

Later that night, Raina was getting ready for bed when Mateo entered the room. She held her night shirt up against her chest, but it didn't cover much. She felt shy around him. Awkward.

"I want you to hear this." Mateo didn't seem to notice her nudity. He sat down on the edge of the bed and held his phone out, tapping the speakerphone icon.

"Tell Raina what you told me earlier." Mateo's voice was grim and Raina's heart sped up in reaction. She sank down on the bed next to him, her near nakedness forgotten.

"Raina, how are you?" Raina was surprised to hear her stepfather's voice. She didn't converse with him often, but she liked him. He was a stern and serious man, but he made it clear that he would always have a soft spot for Raina.

"I'm doing okay, a little shaken up. How are you?"

"Perfectly fine. So is your mother, she's here with me."

Vee spoke next. "Raina, honey, I'm close by if you need me. I can be there in a few minutes. Say the word."

Mateo stiffened next to Raina and she gave him a sidelong glance. Obviously, he didn't approve of Vee's plan to come riding in on a white horse. Raina hadn't realized her mother was still in town and that Sotza had joined her, but she felt better having allies nearby. Not just for herself but for Mateo too.

"Sotza, tell Raina what you told me." Mateo interrupted their small family reunion to get the conversation back on track. That was his style though, no nonsense, no extras, business as usual.

Sotza switched gears, his voice becoming more serious. "We were finally able to get our hands on some video footage that showed Daniela's face. We know who she is. Her name is Desiree Navarro, companion and second-in-command to the late Nicolás Garza."

Raina frowned as she felt the air grow noticeably more chill. A heavy silence descended, and she dared a glance at Mateo. His brows were knitted in concentration, his face frozen in anger.

"This is on me," he finally said, his voice a low growl. "I decided she didn't constitute enough of a threat to occupy my time, even after I killed her lover. It was a mistake, one that has put Raina's life at risk. Desi's motive is revenge toward me."

"I would imagine that you are correct," Sotza said in a drawl. "But don't be hard on yourself. You were given the task of retrieving Raina and keeping her safe as well as bringing Miami back under control. This is a monumental undertaking, one that has required your entire focus. Though, collectively we should have thought to put someone on her trail. She is strong and intelligent, we underestimated her."

Raina heard some kind of muttered comment on the other end of the phone and assumed her mother was trying to speak, but it was clear Sotza didn't want her to. Raina smirked. She could guess what Vee was saying about the woman who had targeted her daughter.

"I have Danny on home security until Angela is well enough to take over. For now, I'll put twice the manpower on the mansion and a personal bodyguard on Raina." Raina shuddered at the reason for the extra security. She had come within seconds of death today. Mateo slid his hand up to the nape of her neck beneath her hair and squeezed, the gentle touch comforting. "Thomas will join me as I search for Desiree. We'll leave no stone unturned this time. We won't stop until she's been found."

"We can pool resources on our end," Sotza assured him. "You're not alone in this. Keep our daughter safe and we'll have your back."

They hung up and Mateo tossed his phone onto the side table. He leaned an elbow against his knee and rubbed a hand over his face, his exhaustion beating at him. Raina's heart melted. He was such a tough guy all the time, her gangster, but he was also vulnerable. As vulnerable as her in some ways.

She put a hand on his arm and squeezed. He looked at her over top of his fingertips.

She smiled tentatively. "I'm not afraid, you know. You'll make sure I'm safe. I have no doubt. But please, let me know if there's anything I can do to help you."

His eyes took on a strange gleam, one that she couldn't decipher. They seemed to convey a lot, at the same time as shutting her out. His body language was closed off, but she sensed he needed her, needed to reach out to her. She wished she knew more about relationships, and men, so she could give him what he clearly needed.

Finally, he spoke. "You are truly a treasure, mi amor. I have harmed you in a grievous way. Taking your dignity and using my lifestyle as an excuse. I have consistently put you in positions where you were vulnerable to attack. Yet still, you worry more about me than you do yourself."

Raina didn't know what to say. He wasn't wrong. If anyone

else had done to her what he'd done, she would hate them. She would be actively trying to find a way out and pulling in every connection she had to make sure he was wiped off the planet. But he wasn't just anyone. He was Mateo. And no matter what he'd done to her, he still belonged to her, like she belonged to him.

Maybe theirs was a twisted relationship. Maybe she should run as far and as fast as she could get, but for now, she was going to follow her heart, which was running full tilt toward the man sitting next to her.

"Will you kiss me?" she whispered, her words shaky. She was so used to him taking what he wanted that it felt weird for her to ask for something intimate.

His entire demeanor seemed to change, to relax and loosen. At the same time, a predatory gleam entered his eyes as he turned to her, his big body hovering slightly over hers since they were sitting so close together.

He took her chin between his fingers and tilted it up. "Always," he said, his lips descending to hers.

The moment was sweet, a greeting of their souls after a long and hard day. A reconnection. She hesitantly lifted her arms and wrapped them around his neck. He shuffled closer on the bed and pulled her body against his, deepening the kiss. They explored each other at a leisurely pace, gradually igniting the sparks that always hovered in the air around them.

Mateo lifted her off the bed and turned her until she was sitting on top of him, her knees on either side of his hips. He buried his hand at the back of her hair, clutching the strands. It hurt, but the pain felt good. It felt like the reaffirmation of life.

He broke the kiss and buried his face in her neck, inhaling deeply. "You smell so fucking good all the time. How do you smell so good?"

Raina giggled and buried her fingers in his soft hair, then ran her hand down the back of his neck. "I shower regularly, using soap and body wash. Then lotion after. Most of it's non-scented."

"Mmmm, then it must be your natural scent."

Raina knew exactly what he was talking about since he also had a scent, one that she would recognize anywhere. The first time she smelled him, she'd been flat on her back on the university campus after attempting to fight him. The first time that he kidnapped her. She'd been breathing heavily and had inhaled his scent of leather, man and aftershave. It had immediately gone to her head, though she desperately fought the attraction. Who had a thing for their kidnapper? Stockholm wasn't supposed to happen that fast.

Raina was beyond trying to understand her attraction to Mateo. He was a gangster and he did gangster things. He'd done terrible things to her since she'd met him, but the way he loved her, the way he held and protected her. It was more than she could resist. Besides, she wasn't exactly innocent herself. She produced high-end forgeries, and though she was discerning in choosing her clientele, she often worked for criminals.

Mateo lifted her in his arms and twisted, dropping her on the bed on her back. He crouched over top of her, his muscular forearms on either side of her face. Raina reached up and clutched his wrist, her breath puffing out in a gasp. Her heart sped up in fear, a fear that he read in her eyes.

Mateo gently removed the strands of hair from her forehead. "I won't hurt you. I promise. Please, let me do this."

Raina lay beneath him staring up at the ceiling above. If she let him have sex with her, was she giving him blanket permission to have sex with her anytime he wanted? She wasn't sure that's what she wanted. After their first time... she'd been so hurt and confused. It would take time to get over that completely. In fact, if it hadn't been for the attack today, she wouldn't be remotely close to forgiving him.

Yet, her body cried out for his. Something primal was telling her that this man was her mate, her partner. Something was begging her not to reject him.

"Okay," she whispered. "But only this once. Because I need you. I'm not sure if this is what I want."

Mateo's eyes hardened for second as his alpha instincts told him not to allow her leeway. But she could see in his eyes that his humanity was winning out, his desire to have his future wife love him back as much as he loved her.

"Please," she begged.

"We'll talk about it later," he assured her. "For now, I want you to feel good. I want to take away all the fear and pain."

"I want that to," she whispered.

After that, they didn't speak again. They didn't need to. Their love language was touch and he touched her everywhere. Starting at her face, trailing his fingers over the delicate skin there; her forehead, her eyelids, nose, and lips. He followed the soft touches with his mouth, kissing everywhere he touched.

He tugged the camisole that Raina had been clutching to her chest away and tossed it on the floor. Then he buried his face in her neck and licked and sucked gently as he trailed kisses down to her breasts. Flutters of sensation were rippling through her body, stealing her breath and making her feel giddy with every touch. Mateo's attentions gradually turned from gentle to more urgent as he sucked one of her small breasts into his mouth, rolling her nipple.

Raina gasped and clutched his head to her, arching her back and pushing her breasts up. He lavished first one with attention, then the other. She could feel the wetness gathering at her thighs, soaking her panties beneath her sleep shorts.

Mateo worked his way downward but didn't forget to worship every inch of her skin. His hands were everywhere, in places that his lips had been, igniting small explosions of yearning within her. Raina moaned her pleasure out loud, telling him exactly what she loved.

He dipped his tongue momentarily into her navel, causing her to gasp and lurch up in an attempt to shove him away. He grabbed her wrists and pushed her back onto the bed.

"You will take my kisses, no matter where I decide to place them." His words were possessive, but his tone was one of love.

He continued his path down, hooking his fingers into her panties and sleep shorts and dragging them down her thighs, exposing her. Raina dropped a hand between her legs, but he gently took it, flipped it over and pressed a kiss to her palm. Then he placed her hand on the bed next to her.

"You don't need to be shy with me. Every part of you is my definition of beauty; from your nearsighted eyes, to the scars on your skin, to this pretty pink pussy, to these ridiculously small feet." He dropped his hand down her body as he spoke and finished by gripping her foot. She laughed and yanked her foot away. But her laughter fled as he pinned her with a look. "Every part of you is mine, every part of you is beautiful."

Raina blushed. He was so intense, it was difficult to know what to say or do. But he didn't leave her hanging, he took control.

Mateo kissed her knees and then worked his way up her thighs, biting down gently on her flesh. Her breath sped up as he approached her pussy. She had to fight the urge to cover herself or to push his head away. She'd never done this before, what if she wasn't good at it?

And then she no longer had time to worry, because his face was buried between her legs and his tongue was exploring her most intimate parts. From the first touch of his tongue against her clit, Raina came unglued. How had she not known how fucking good oral sex was? Her education had been woefully neglected and if this wasn't a very awkward conversation to bring up, she'd be discussing this with her parents.

Raina could do nothing but clutch at the blankets underneath her and try to force her body to remain on the bed as she virtually levitated into Mateo's face. He gripped her hips and used his shoulders to force her legs wider as he ate her out. He lashed her with his tongue, drawing her out like a bowstring and then forcing her back before she could reach the edge. She was a mess of wiggling, wet, sweaty and begging woman. If this was what sex felt like, then she would become his willing slave.

Finally, Mateo lifted his head to pin her with a look. She blushed when she saw the glistening wetness of her fluids on his chin. "Now you come for me, mi amor."

He dipped his head back down and ran his tongue through her folds before concentrating on her clit. As he sucked and swirled, drawing her higher and higher towards a precious peak, he slid a finger into her body, penetrating her. That finger, combined with his magical tongue, sent her spiraling over the ledge.

She thought at first that she was screaming out loud, then realized most of the noise was in her own brain. Her mouth was wide open, whimpers spilling from her lips, her hands knotted so tightly in the blankets that her knuckles would ache later.

Her heart pounded as she drifted down from the most intensely explosive orgasm she'd ever experienced. She rolled her head to watch Mateo as he climbed off the bed. She reached out, intending to call him back, but then realized he was undressing. His movements were hurried but precise.

Each item of clothing was tossed onto the chair until he stood completely, gloriously naked in front of her.

Mateo really was built using the marble of the gods. He was hard and muscular, but every proportion was perfect. Even his penis, which was erect and curving upward toward his belly from a nest of dark pubic hair.

As he climbed back on top of her, Raina clutched at his shoulders and dragged him down for a kiss, thrusting her tongue into his mouth. He kissed her back with equal passion, sliding an arm underneath her waist and lifting her up against his body. He entered her in one smooth thrust. It hurt more than Raina was expecting. After their first encounter, she didn't know what would happen, but had hoped it wouldn't hurt again.

She knew she was wet enough to take him and didn't understand why it hurt. She whimpered and wiggled her body, trying to adjust. Mateo smoothed her hair back and said, his lips inches above hers, "It will only hurt for a few seconds, your body isn't used to this and needs time to adjust. Lay still, soon you'll feel good."

The pain was already beginning to fade, so she nodded and tried to relax underneath him. She lifted her knees experimentally tucking them high up against his waist in a way that felt natural. He kissed her lips and reached around to run his hand from her thigh to her knee, squeezing lightly as if to reward her.

When it became clear that Raina was no longer in pain, Mateo began to move within her, his body undulating on top of her in a rhythm that was beautiful to watch but hard to emulate. At first Raina felt clumsy, trying to lift her body to match his, but then she caught on, gradually becoming smoother with each thrust. She felt proud of herself, then the ecstasy took over.

His possession sent a storm of electricity, emotion and

sensation rocketing through her. It was brutal, it was wonderful, and it was perfect. As they continued to rock together, Mateo's movements became more and more uneven, his thrusts harder as his hips slammed into hers. After a few minutes, Raina stopped trying to match his rhythm and clung to him, allowing him to slam her down into the bed over and over again. It felt incredible.

She flung her head back and dug her nails into his shoulders as another orgasm washed over her in a wave of pure pleasure. She rode the wave as he thrust into her one last time, shooting hot semen against the walls of her pussy. Even that felt incredible. The wetness, the heat, his mark.

CHAPTER FORTY-FIVE

It took a while before the mansion fell into a routine of new normal. Raina was not allowed to leave the premises without a full security detail, which now included her fiancé. At first, she balked at the restrictions, but then she'd seen the livid bruises on Angela's chest. Angela was the one to convince her to take the new security measures seriously.

"She killed your bodyguards and shot me as easily as if I was an annoying fly. She didn't pause. She didn't know me and she didn't care who I was. If she could do that to me, what will she do to you? Someone who she actually has a vendetta against. Don't underestimate her, and don't force Mateo to split his focus between a bratty wife, his Miami takeover and his hunt for Desi."

Though they stung, Angela's words sunk in. Raina still blamed herself for Angela's injuries, though Angela didn't look at it that way. Angela was doing her job, the job she was meant to do, and she was proud to be able to take bullets for Raina's sake.

To appease Angela, Raina would accept her near house arrest, learning to accept the new restrictions. Which, for her sanity, now included a more hands-on renovation of Mateo's office and taking on more forgery commissions. Raina busied buried herself in work so that she wouldn't have to think about what her fiancé and parents were doing in the city; ruthlessly bringing Miami under the control of Mateo and hunting for Desiree Navarro.

Vee and Sotza stopped by almost every day. They visited with Raina, updated Mateo and sometimes ate supper with them. Though Raina had a similar routine in Venezuela, she was now two years older and wiser. Life had changed even though the members dining at her table hadn't.

Eight days had passed since Raina and Angela had been attacked. Angela was back on her feet and engaging in her full duties, though she had grown even more protective of Raina and checked in on her often. Since the two women were rapidly becoming friends, Raina didn't mind. Angela gave her someone to vent to, someone who understood both sides of the equation; a person inside the mafia, but also a woman with wants and desires.

Angela understood and sympathized with many of Raina's frustrations, and Raina, in turn, attempted to give Angela an ear to bend if she needed one, though Angela was more tightlipped. Raina didn't know if it was her nature or her job, but she didn't often open up.

Raina and Angela were deep in the middle of one such conversation, when they were interrupted. "Okay, but have you ever actually tortured someone —?"

Angela was saved from answering Raina's gruesomely curious question when a sharp knock sounded at the door. Thomas stuck his head in. "There's someone at the gate, says he knows you."

Raina was surprised that Thomas hadn't turned away the visitor. The mansion was on lockdown and everyone relevant in the city knew it. The only people allowed to come and go were staff and family.

Angela jumped in. "Send him away; no visitors."

"He says he knows both Raina and Mateo and that they would want to see him immediately. He's insistent that he won't leave without an audience. His words, not mine. Mateo is in the city on business or I would bring this matter to him."

Angela frowned and Raina figured she was about to snap at Thomas, reiterating her earlier comment. Raina asked, "Did he give you a name?"

"Signore Giovanni Savino."

Raina leapt to her feet, her hand on her chest. Giovanni was there to see her! She grinned and exclaimed, "Let him in right away! I'll meet him in the main sitting room."

Thomas nodded and strode away. As Raina was leaving the room, Angela stopped her. "Mateo won't like this. No strangers in the mansion, no exceptions."

Raina waved her hand dismissively. "Giovanni isn't a stranger, he's practically like a godfather to me." Raina smirked at her inside joke. Giovanni *was* the Italian Godfather.

As she was leaving the office, out of the corner of her eye she saw Angela get on the phone. No doubt about it, Angela was calling the boss. As close as Angela and Raina had come, Angela's first loyalty would always be to Mateo.

Raina waited excitedly for Giovanni in the sitting room and grinned broadly as he was shown in by Thomas. "Giovanni!" Raina rushed to greet him, stepping into his embrace.

His arms tightened around her and squeezed for a moment before he set her away from him. He looked her over, his lips curving in a smile. "As beautiful as ever, bella. Domesticity suits you. I am now less sad that you were picked up and brought to this place against your will."

She shrugged, hooking her arm in his and escorting him

to the sofa. She sank down onto a chair across from him. "It wasn't exactly against my will. I've known for a while that I would be marrying Mateo, and I enjoyed two years of freedom before he picked me up."

He watched her, his expression musing. He was wearing an impeccably tailored suit, dark, but with flare. In his pocket was a crimson red handkerchief and a set of diamond studded cuff links adorned on each wrist.

"The answer of a dutiful mob wife." Though his words were mild, the meaning was not. Raina understood that this was an opportunity for her to leave if she wanted to. Giovanni was checking on her and if he didn't like what he heard, he was willing to help her get out of there. She knew it was a lot to read into one sentence, but she had connected with Giovanni in Italy. They were two vastly different but kindred spirits.

She reached out, indicating that she wanted his hand. He took hers and allowed her to squeeze him. "Thank you, from the bottom of my heart. You have no idea what it means to have an ally like you. You graciously accepted me into your home, you protected me and then you helped me escape. All this because I am the daughter of a business associate."

Giovanni nodded gravely and squeezed her back. "I did not only do these things because of who your father is, but because of who you are. You remind me very much of my deceased wife."

Raina beamed at him. "Thank you, Giovanni."

Giovanni nodded decisively, released her hand and settled himself back in the chair. He looked around the room. "A very nice place you have here. Perhaps I should take your lead and do something with my monstrosity."

Raina grinned. "I'm more than happy to give you the name and number of my interior decorator... the nice one.

I'm sure he would love a trip to Italy, especially if expenses are paid."

The two spoke on a variety of subjects including the mansion renovations and Raina's up-and-coming forgery business. They spoke as though they had been friends for many years, though they hadn't actually known each other very long. Their friendship traversed age, station, and an ocean.

They had been talking for about twenty minutes, sipping on cups of tea that Raina requested from Lydia, when Mateo and several armed men strode into the room. Mateo's face could have rivaled a thundercloud as he marched over to Raina, jerked her out of her chair, ignoring the clattering of her teacup and the splash of hot liquid as it hit the floor and shoved her behind him.

He pointed at Giovanni. "Start talking or I will have you questioned in my bunker and then removed from the grounds in pieces."

Raina tried to protest but Mateo grabbed her wrist and held tightly, a subtle threat. Raina bit her lip. She wanted to give him a shove right between the shoulder blades but decided to wait and see if the boys could work it out for themselves.

Giovanni stood and stretched lazily, arranging his suit jacket so that it sat perfectly on his tall lean frame. "I've come for a visit. The young lady standing behind you invited me when she was in Italy and I thought it would be rude not to accept. If I'm not welcome, then I will leave. I don't wish any harm upon your family."

"I don't believe you," Mateo growled.

Raina felt the tension thrumming through his body. She believed he really was ready to shoot Giovanni for arriving unannounced on their doorstep. Once again Raina wanted to intervene, explain that Giovanni was telling the truth and she invited the man for a visit. But Giovanni jumped in before she could speak.

"Of course, I can understand why you would think I mean you harm. You beat my son to within an inch of his life and threatened to kill him if he so much as sniffed near this continent. Any father might be upset by this. But I can assure you, I am not." Giovanni's voice was serious, as though he badly wanted them to believe him. "You did what I would have had to do, only you left him alive. Antonio betrayed me and that betrayal required a response. Though he is my only child, I would have had to beat him or worse, to send a message to the Cosa Nostra. Any challenges to my authority will not be tolerated. You saved me having to do something very painful."

"I took two of his fingers as a trophy. You condone this action against your own progeny?" Mateo's bald words were meant to prod the older man into an emotional response. It worked on Raina who flinched, but Giovanni continued to look bland.

"We both know that Antonio got off light." Giovanni's voice was hard with censure. "I love my son, but he deserved whatever you chose to do to him."

"You attempted to distract me while your son's men surrounded my hotel suite."

"Wouldn't you have done the same if your family was being threatened? As his boss, I condemned his actions and approved your presence in the city. As a father... I felt I had to do what I could to help him." There was no doubting Giovanni's earnestness.

Raina could feel the gradual loosening of Mateo's muscles as Giovanni spoke. Mateo believed the other man. Raina let out a sigh of relief, pulled her wrist from Mateo's grip, bent over and picked up the spilled teacup. She set it on a side table and then slipped around until she was standing at

Mateo's side. She would much prefer a united front than cowering behind her fiancé.

"I meant to kill your son; I won't lie. I beat him, I cut off his fingers in retaliation for harming my woman, then I shot him the way he had her shot." His words were cold and Raina felt his renewed anger as he spoke of her injury. "But as I pressed my pistol against his temple, I realized, I wanted him to remain alive. I wanted my threat hanging over his head every minute of every day. That was more satisfying than actually putting a bullet in his brain."

Giovanni looked grave and then nodded. "I appreciate your honesty. I thank you anyway for sparing his life. I can assure you he will not be a future problem. He's been banished from Venice, his assets stripped away and his connections severed. He has nothing left but a legacy of idiocy that will follow him and his mangled hand. I'm having him watched at all times. I do this so that none of us will have to watch our backs when it comes to him."

Mateo stared at Giovanni; his brow wrinkled in a frown. "Your generosity surprises me. I would think you'd want to kill the man who mutilated your only child, but I understand you. I would feel the same if I was betrayed in such a way, no matter who was the betrayer."

The two men seemed to settle on a temporary truce. Raina pushed for Giovanni to be allowed to take their evening meal with them. Mateo grudgingly agreed and the three of them set about having a pleasant evening together with good food and even better conversation. Raina suspected Giovanni was somewhat lonely, isolated over in Italy, with no family and few friends that weren't subordinates and business associates.

Raina begged Mateo to allow Giovanni to stay the night. At first, both men were hesitant, but Raina managed to win them over to the idea. She suspected Mateo was of the keep your-enemies-close camp while Giovanni was grateful not to have to search for accommodations in a tourist city.

Later, after Giovanni retired for the night, Mateo and Raina went upstairs to bed together. Mateo laid her down and set about telling her without words how much he worshipped her. She sighed happily and settled back on the bed, enjoying the embrace of her lover.

CHAPTER FORTY-SIX

Over the course of the following week Raina thoroughly enjoyed her time with Giovanni. Even Mateo seemed to loosen up around the older charismatic gentleman. There was a certain joy in Giovanni that was tempered by his profession, the loss of his wife and the betrayal of his son.

While he was still a badass old-school mobster, he knew how to appreciate the world around him.

"You've given me a fresh perspective on life, revived this old man." They were sitting together on the patio next to the pool enjoying a couple glasses of Long Island iced tea.

She wrinkled her nose at him. "Not that old."

He looked at her knowingly. "I have more than thirty years on you, bella."

"Okay, but I wouldn't call you an old man. You have more energy than most of us and you seemed pretty content hanging out at Banditos, lording it over all the peasants. All I did was bring a boatload of trouble to your doorstep, show you what a douchebag your son is and then bring Mateo down on you. It's a miracle you didn't decide I was more disposable." Raina took a long sip of her drink and then guiltily glanced around for Mateo.

He would be furious if he knew she was drinking alcohol. Of course, Raina knew exactly how much her body could take, but that didn't stop Mateo from worrying over every little thing.

Giovanni was sprawled out in a patio chair, his finger tapping against the edge of his own glass. "Had you been anyone else, you would have been far more disposable," he admitted.

Raina swallowed hard imagining how close to death she had come at this Italian mobster's fingertips. "Because of who my stepfather is."

He shook his head. "While Sotza is certainly capable of making my life uncomfortable, your affiliation with him would not have swayed me. No, you have only yourself to thank. You are a remarkable young lady. You fearlessly travel the world while building a client base among elite members of the underworld. Your activities are criminal, yet you have an impeccable moral compass. This is something I have always strived for myself; finding that balance between being a decent human being while fulfilling my duties as a kingpin."

"You were born to the mob?" she asked. "Like me, you didn't have a choice?"

"Yes, that is correct. My father ran the Savino family empire before me, and his father before him. We have a long and proud heritage. It's not always such a burden. There are many perks to being master of my universe." He looked at Raina shrewdly. "Do you not find the perks in such luxurious living?"

Raina wanted to deny that the money, prestige and open doors had anything to do with her ease in settling into the lifestyle, but truthfully, she couldn't. "Okay, you're not wrong. I like the clothes, the big house, the pool. But it still bothers me that the tradeoff can come at a high cost. There are certain things that Mateo has to do for work and I have no choice but to look the other way. Sometimes, it terrifies me how easily I've fallen for him. Do my morals mean nothing in the face of my feelings for him?"

Giovanni smiled knowingly and took a long sip of his drink. "My wife was much the same way. She despised what I did for work, but she loved me wholeheartedly and unconditionally. She had no choice but to settle into the life, she understood that there's only one way to leave the mafia. In a coffin."

"Did she find a way to live with it, to live with the things she knew you had to do?" Raina leaned forward against the table, completely invested in his answer.

Giovanni shrugged. "I don't think she ever quite reconciled herself to the life, and part of me believes that it may have led to an early death for her. But she supported me in most everything I did."

Raina smiled sadly and nodded. "Thank you for telling me, I feel better knowing that you were in a similar situation to ours. I love Mateo and I want to support him, but I don't always agree with his decisions."

Giovanni leaned across the table and clasped her hand in his. "You don't have to agree with him. My wife often disagreed with my actions, but I never lost an ounce of love for her. In fact, having her opinion helped ground me in the real world, kept me from being sucked into the vacuum of complete lawlessness that could too easily lead down a path of no redemption."

Raina spent the afternoon thinking over Giovanni's words and that night when Mateo came home, she walked up to him in the lobby of their mansion and hugged him. He was late, having missed their supper meal. She didn't comment though.

The tension vibrating through his body told her he probably had a long and tough day. She simply hugged him tight, pressing herself against his body and laying her head over his heart.

Mateo dropped the leather folder he was holding, ignoring it as it hit the floor and papers slipped out. He wrapped his arms around her and held her close against him, dropping his face to her head and inhaling the scent of her hair. It was such a private moment that gradually the men that had come in with Mateo drifted away, leaving the couple in a bubble of their own.

Mateo pulled back enough so that he could look down at her face. "What's this all about? Everything okay?"

She nodded and smiled up at him. "I... I guess I just wanted to say hello." She felt suddenly shy, like she didn't know what to say to him. But this is what Mateo did to her. He sent her libido into overdrive which erased every sane thought in her head.

"Well, you can say hi to me anytime you want."

This was one of the things that she adored about him. Mateo loved Raina without question, without exception. Though he had strict rules when it came to her health and safety, he was quick to give her anything else she desired, including access to him and his body. He was completely invested in their relationship and despite some of his more questionable actions, Raina's heart belonged to him. Right or wrong, she would follow him into hell. Just the same as he would follow her.

"Are you hungry?" she asked him, tilting her head up to see his face.

"Yes." His answer came out in an emphatic growl.

Raina started to turn away from him. "Your supper is warming in the oven. I had Lydia make a plate for you. Is that okay?"

He grabbed her arm and swung her back around into his chest. "No, it's not okay. It's not food I want right now."

"Oh." She blushed, but she didn't have time to respond. Mateo picked her up, holding her close against his chest as he strode up the stairs, taking them two at a time in a dizzying pace.

He shoved their bedroom door open and then booted it shut. He dropped Raina onto the mattress and then came down on top of her. They both laughed as his heavy weight landed on her, knocking the breath out of her.

She looped her arms around his neck and looked up at him. "You know I love you, right? Sometimes you make me crazy, but the loving never stops."

He framed her face with his hands and gazed down at her, his dark eyes melting to a deep chocolate. "I have waited years to hear these words from you. You are mi amor. Only you, always you." He lifted her hand and pressed her palm against his chest over his heart. "This organ beats for you alone. The day that I lose you is the same day that I leave this earth in the hope that I will find you in the hereafter."

Tears sparked in Raina's eyes as he spoke. She hadn't expected a declaration like this, but she believed him. She believed every word. Mateo didn't lie. He was the definition of intense brooding honesty.

She was saved from having to pull words from a brain gone silly with love and hope. His head descended to hers and he took her lips in a heated kiss.

They removed their clothes in an awkward twisting of limbs and fingers while trying to maintain their kiss. Raina grinned broadly and laughed into his mouth as he tried to tug her shirt over her head but got a button caught in her hair. Without breaking the kiss he tried to untangle the button without tugging too much at her scalp.

"For fuck's sakes, why do women's clothes have so many

buttons and zippers and stuff?" He broke the kiss so he could examine what was going on with her hair.

Raina laughed at him and slid her hands between their bodies to work on his belt buckle. He lifted his hips giving her some room, but the raging hard on pressing against his zipper made it more difficult to get everything undone.

Finally, Mateo made the adult decision that they should stand up and remove everything, then start over. They laughed like teenagers as they tugged clothes off and hopped around on one foot trying to drag socks off their feet. It was ridiculous and it was hilarious, but it was also sexy. Raina's breath shortened as his body was revealed to her.

Mateo had always had a hard body, rippling with lean slabs of muscle. But lately, he'd been amping up his workouts. The muscles in his arms and thighs popped out bigger than ever and his stomach was so tight she actually wanted to try bouncing a quarter off it. She believed the workouts helped him with the stress of his Miami takeover.

It felt good to see him grinning at her. It made him look younger, closer to her age than the fifteen years that separated them. When he grinned with happiness, he looked like a beautiful boyish charmer to her.

When they were finally naked, he reached for her. She flung herself into his arms and gave a hop. He caught her and lifted her against his body helping her wrap her legs around his waist. He fell backwards on the bed, Raina landing on top of him.

She pressed her hands against his pectoral muscles and leaned over to kiss him, her blond hair creating a soft halo around them, cutting the world off as their kiss deepened and they lost themselves in physical sensation.

Raina tried to roll off Mateo so he could climb on top of her, but he caught her by the hips and held her still. He broke their kiss and said, "I want you to stay on top. I want you to fuck me, to take your pleasure from my body."

She bit her lip and looked down at him, thinking about it. Her voice was breathless when she replied, "But I don't know what I'm doing. We've only done this a couple times. What if I screw up?"

He held her face above his, her hair still swirling around them. "You can't screw up. I will never let that happen. I was born to worship you, just as you were born to belong to me. Whatever comes our way, we will always deal with it together."

Raina's heart nearly burst from her chest. She knew he was talking about more than her being on top during sex. He was talking about the rest of their lives. His words were so beautiful, so romantic. She wanted to hold him close to her heart and never let go.

She nodded, comfortable now that Mateo wouldn't let her screw up a new sex position. He would guide her, and he would catch her if she fell.

"Lift yourself up on your knees." He wrapped his hands around her waist and helped her. "Now reach between us and place my cock at your entrance. Don't worry, you can do it."

Raina blushed at his instructions, but she reached down between their bodies and grasped him in her hand. Though he was hard as rock, his skin was softer than she thought he would be. This was her first time touching him there. She took an extra few seconds to ran run her hand up and down the shaft and then swirled her thumb over the tip.

It took some maneuvering but finally she was able to press the velvety tip of his cock against the entrance of her pussy. He held her above him until she was ready, then he said, "Now lower yourself slowly. I'll help you."

Inch by inch, Raina lowered herself onto his cock, impaling herself. At first, the sensations were wonderful, sparking pleasure throughout her pussy. But as she continued filling herself with his rigid penis, the pressure became uncomfortable.

It was a strain for Mateo to lay still, she could tell from the look on his face. But he was patient with her, allowing her to take him in her own time. And she did. It probably took her minutes before she was fully seated on top of him and several more minutes before the pain receded and she was ready to start moving.

At first, she had a difficult time finding a rhythm; she felt awkward wiggling her hips and moving around on top of him. After a while though, she realized that simply rocking back and forth sent incredible sparks of pleasure rushing through her. He groaned, indicating that he was also enjoying what she was doing. She loved that she could see his face, that she could control how much of him she took. She could control the rhythm, the speed, everything. She felt powerful.

"Touch yourself." She almost missed what he said, between the gruffness of his voice and being lost to her own pleasure. She stared down at him, not moving.

Mateo took her hand and curled her fingers until three of them were against her palm. Then he took her forefinger and her middle finger and pressed them to her pussy, over top of her clit. She gasped as he increased the pressure, helping her masturbate herself. The sensation stole her breath. It was more incredible than anything she'd experienced before. His hand on hers, her touching herself, her on top rocking back and forth. It was almost too much, but not enough.

Lost to the world around her, Raina flung her head back and arched her back, closing her eyes. She continued her rhythm, climbing higher and higher towards her favourite peak, the one just out of reach but so worth the pain of getting there. Finally, when she thought she could take no more, when she was positive that she was about to lose her rhythm, Mateo pressed her fingers hard against her, pressing her clit against her pubic bone.

"Come for me," he whispered up at her.

A kaleidoscope of colours shot past Raina's closed eyelids, sending fireworks through her head and frying every thinking brain cell she had left.

Raina was so lost in her own pleasure that she stopped moving on top of Mateo, which she guessed didn't work for him since he took hold of her hips and began moving her himself. He pushed her hips back and forth, forcing her down on his cock and then back up again, over and over until she could feel him flaring wide inside her.

She gasped, clinging to his shoulders. She was so much more full when she was on top of him that she didn't know if she could take it. She leaned forward against his chest, digging her fingernails into the flesh as he flung his head back, pressing it into the mattress and grunting his pleasure as he spurted his seed up inside her.

Raina collapsed on top of him, grateful that he was big enough to take her weight without complaint. They lay that way for several long minutes, completely spent, completely satiated.

Raina definitely wanted to try that position again. And again. And again. She didn't think she would ever get enough of being on top. Being in control.

As she had that thought, Mateo flipped her over onto her back and crawled on top of her, pressing kisses all over her face, neck, and chest until she was laughing hysterically and shoving him over onto his side of the bed.

CHAPTER FORTY-SEVEN

Mateo's and Raina's truce didn't last long. If Raina was being honest with herself, she would admit that they'd probably never have a completely contention free relationship. Although this time, their difference in opinion was monumental, one she didn't think she would be able to overcome. In the course of twenty-four hours she had discovered that she was more in love that she could ever imagine, then she was sent spiraling into despair with only a few words from her fiancé.

It happened the following morning, after a night filled with sex, laughter, and the occasional bout of sleep. Raina had woken up feeling completely satisfied, totally in love and ready to greet the world with her happiness. She stretched and reached over to Mateo's side of the bed, not really expecting him to be there.

She was surprised when her hand landed on hard hot flesh. Her eyes popped open and she rolled her head to the side, looking at him. Mateo was looking back at her, his beautiful eyes expressing love though his face had fallen into its familiar granite lines.

She understood. He would have to go back to work in a few minutes, remove himself from their bubble and face the underground world that he was challenging.

"Good morning." She smothered a yawn against his shoulder.

He smoothed the hair off her forehead and leaned over to kiss her. "Good morning, mi amor. You were sleeping soundly, and I didn't have the heart to either slip away or wake you."

"So you decided to watch me instead. That's creepy you know, watching a person sleep." She said it with a grin and pushed herself up, rolling toward the edge of the bed.

"It's not creepy if you're fucking the person."

Raina laughed as she made a beeline for the bathroom, shoving the door shut. She quickly relieved her screaming bladder, washed her hands and then ran back to the bed, hurtling herself on top of him. He caught her with a grunt and held her in place, her body sprawled out on top of his.

They lay that way for a few minutes, enjoying the warmth of a nice long hug. Finally, Mateo set her aside, tucked the blanket around her legs and got off the bed to get dressed. She realized he was staying home when he pulled on a pair of gym shorts, a T-shirt, socks and running shoes. He was going into the yard to work out.

Not wanting to end her time with him, Raina asked, "Want help with a sparring session?"

He shook his head. "I need to work out hard this morning. Got to keep my skills at peak levels in case anyone decides to challenge my takeover."

Raina was hurt by his words. Obviously, he wasn't feeling the desperate need to spend more time with her, the way she wanted to be with him. She mumbled defensively, "I can spar pretty hard. You don't have to go easy on me."

He looked down at her and when she refused to lift her eyes, he tilted her chin. He wanted her to see how serious he was. "You will never be required, nor will you be allowed, to ever spar as hard as me. Not even as hard as Angela. That isn't your role here. You are my wife, keeper of my heart and my home. Though I want you to have some defensive skills, I won't allow your fragile body to become exhausted by the work."

Raina wanted to argue that she wished he thought of that weeks ago on the night he woke her up from her bed and dragged her into the yard to torture her with a brutal sparring session. But she knew that would be petty. He'd been upset, out of his mind over worry for her. This was different.

However, despite her understanding the difference, she didn't agree. "I'm not some delicate flower, Mateo. I can take a solid beating if I need to. You don't have to go easy on me all the time. I'm not going to up and die on you."

The last traces of softness left his eyes, leaving behind the awful blankness. She hated it.

"You will not die because I won't let you. This is not up for discussion. You'll never be placed in a position where you're forced to give more than you can take. I won't allow it."

"So all I'm good for is setting up your home, organizing your meals and laundry and having your babies?" she demanded. As much as she enjoyed feeling protected by him, she also felt stifled by his overprotection.

"No babies." The two words were said without inflection. At first, Raina didn't understand.

"What do you mean 'no babies'." She let out a humourless laugh. "So far I haven't noticed us using any protection. And I'm guessing you would've mentioned it by now if you wanted us to be using it. I assumed you wanted babies."

Mateo stepped away from the bed, putting distance between them. "It's not about wanting babies, but about having them. We won't be having any."

Raina frowned, attempting to understand his words. She really hoped he wasn't thinking what she thought he was thinking. The man was unbelievable. He wanted to control every aspect of her life, especially her health. But she was going to go out of her mind if he suddenly decided that she couldn't have babies simply because she'd had a kidney transplant when she was twelve years old.

"Is this about me? You don't think that I can have a baby?" she asked incredulously. "Have you done any research? Plenty of women who've had transplants go on to have perfectly healthy babies."

"I've done my research and I have determined that your health is not worth the risk."

Raina's mouth fell open. This really was about her. And this was a really serious conversation. Perhaps one that they shouldn't be having while she was still in bed naked. Raina climbed off the bed and reached for her bathrobe dragging it over her nude body and belting it tightly. She turned to face him, giving him the full wrath of her glare.

"You do *not* get to make this decision alone," she said furiously pointing at him. "This is my body. I've always intended to become a mother and if you think you're going to stop me, then you're going to have one hell of a fight on your hands."

He continued to stare at her without expression though she wanted to believe that there was a hint of sadness in his eyes. "I was afraid you would think this way."

She threw her hands up in the air. "A lot of women want babies. Of course, it's natural for me to want one too. When I was a child, my parents made sure to ask all the right questions. We were told that I should be able to carry a baby to term without a problem."

"But there would be a strain on your body. You only have one kidney and you're still required to take immunosuppressants to make sure your body doesn't reject the kidney, which means your health is always at risk. Even the flu can become deadly for someone like you. I won't allow you to take that risk. It's too great. I won't allow your life to be shortened by even one day if I can do anything to help it."

Raina was too angry at him to absorb the sheer magnitude of what he was saying, what he was willing to do for her.

"That isn't your decision to make alone. We either make it together, our I will make it by myself."

"No, you won't." His voice was calm, but there was a thread of steel underlying it.

"And how exactly do you intend to stop nature?" she demanded sarcastically. "We haven't exactly been practicing safe sex. I could be pregnant already. What do you intend to do, have me abort the baby? I'll tell you right now, that's not going to happen. Or if you plan on forcing protection for the rest of my life, I'll go find the nearest fertility clinic."

Finally, he showed her a glimpse of anger, his eyes narrowing and his lips tightening. "You're not pregnant and I will not be getting you pregnant. Nor will you be seeking out any fertility clinics. You won't enjoy the consequences if I find you sniffing around one of those places, either now or in the future."

Raina huffed out a breath, rolled her eyes and crossed her arms over her chest. "I don't see how you intend to stop me from getting pregnant. We've had sex at least a dozen times now. In my estimation, given the time of month, I could easily be pregnant."

"No, you can't." His voice was so positive that it finally dawned on her that he knew something she didn't.

"Why do you sound so sure?"

He looked as though he didn't want to speak, as though he didn't want to devastate her with his words. Then he seemed to harden himself to her feelings and said, "Two years ago, after you left Venezuela and I realized that you were the only woman I would marry, I had a vasectomy. Even then I realized that it wouldn't be possible for you to carry my child."

Raina was so stunned that she took several steps back, groping behind her for the chair and then collapsing into it. A vasectomy. She hadn't seen that coming. She didn't know of many men that would choose to have one at Mateo's age. Especially a man that hadn't fathered any children. She'd assumed he would want children.

Then it hit her. He wanted her more than he wanted a child of his own flesh and blood. This thought hammered home exactly how obsessed with her he had become.

Yet, despite his sacrifice, Raina wasn't ready to process the heartbreak this meant for herself. Mateo would never let her go, would never allow her to seek out the opportunity of having a baby. He loved her too much. And if she was being honest with herself, she loved him too much to leave. But the truth that he just laid on her was shattering.

"I'll never have a baby." She looked up at him, tears shimmering in her eyes, catching a glimpse of his own grief before he shuttered the emotion.

Mateo kneeled at her feet, lifted her hand and kissed the palm. Wordlessly he stood, gave her a long look and then left the room.

CHAPTER FORTY-EIGHT

Raina wandered listlessly through the mansion unsure of what to do with herself. She wasn't sure if she was in a state of shock, acceptance, grief, or anger. She thought probably shock since she couldn't seem to process her feelings.

After Mateo left, Raina had stayed in the bedroom in an attempt to avoid him. She tried to busy herself with his latest romance novel, Christina Dodd's The Prince Kidnaps a Bride, but she couldn't seem to settle into it. After a few hours of pacing the room, taking the longest shower of her life, and spending extra time on her hair, makeup and clothes, Raina figured enough time had passed that she could leave the bedroom. She walked down to the kitchen and stood staring at their fully stocked refrigerator for nearly ten minutes before deciding that she wasn't hungry.

Raina wandered the house and the grounds and then she went in search of Giovanni. He wasn't the one she wanted to discuss her problem with, but he was a houseguest and someone deserving respect, it was her job to make sure he was comfortable and happy in her home.

But when she found Angela sitting in her office, Raina discovered that Giovanni had left for the day. Apparently, he and Sotza had set up a meet and were going to discuss some transatlantic trade. Raina stood looking at Angela for a few uncomfortable minutes. Though she didn't know who was uncomfortable with those minutes, Angela seemed unflappable and Raina was too much in shock to feel anything. She considered unburdening on Angela but decided that their friendship was still at a vulnerable stage, not the cry-all-over, trash-talk-the-bad-boyfriend and eat-a-bucket-of-ice-cream-together stage.

Raina closed the door to the office and left Angela to herself. She decided to try and work for a couple of hours. She sat down at her desk and pulled out the proofs for a set of fake passports under the name Kevin Glad. Of course, that wasn't the man's real name. "Kevin" needed fake passports for Australia, South Africa and the Senegal.

Raina had been curious when he commissioned her and had done some digging on the dark web. She discovered that her new client was wanted for trafficking women and children. Raina judged him. She judged him big time. She also made the decision to risk her reputation by giving him detectable papers. Meaning, he would be stopped the second he tried to enter a country with his fake passports. He would be extradited to his home country and put on trial.

Raina hoped there would be no damage to her reputation, but she knew in her heart that she would never be able to allow a man like "Kevin" free and easy movement throughout the world. She was going to put a stop to his activities, even if she had to do it single-handedly.

Working on the passports helped ease Raina's mind. She became so absorbed in her art that she didn't have the capacity left over to dwell on a future that had become suddenly more bleak. After a few hours she finished up the commission and set the freshly done passports aside.

"Now what?" she asked the empty room with a miserable sigh.

It was now two o'clock in the afternoon. She should be hungry, but she didn't think she could stomach food quite yet. Raina had always been an emotional eater. But she was also an emotional non-eater. When she felt anxious or depressed, she wanted all the food everywhere. But when she felt like this, like there was a gaping hole in her chest, she couldn't touch her meals.

Raina only felt this way twice before. Once, when she was a child and she found out that her kidney failure had become so acute that she'd have to have a transplant. The second time was when she was around fourteen and found information that confirmed she was adopted. At the time she had thought that her birth mother had abandoned her. She hadn't understood why Elvira had given her up and Raina fallen into a deep pit of angry despair.

Yeah, that was exactly how she felt. Angry despair. She was angry because her fiancé had made a monumental decision about their mutual future without consulting her. And she felt despair because she knew that despite the steps he took to ensure she would never have his child, she still loved him too deeply to contemplate leaving him. So, she was left with this deep aching hurt inside. A hurt that she didn't know how to get rid of.

Finally, Raina decided that she needed to do the healthy thing and contact someone who could talk her through the feelings. Someone who could give her the comfort she needed during these dark hours until she could reconcile herself to the idea of never having a baby.

Raina called Vee, but her birth mother had been

distracted and cool on the phone. Apparently, she had been part of the meeting with Sotza and Giovanni and was anxious to get back to it.

"You can adopt, sweetie," Vee said, somewhat impatiently. "I understand that this was a shock. But Mateo is not wrong. Your body is delicate and fragile, we don't know that it can take the stress of birth."

"That isn't the point!" Raina growled her frustration. "He should have at least talked to me. It's my body, I should be the one who decides. He can't make decisions like this for both of us."

Vee sighed deeply. "Raina, I sympathize, but you need to face reality. You're about to become a mob wife. Your duty is to your husband. As much as it galls me to say it, you will be expected to obey. You have a husband who adores you and will do anything for you. He'll lay down his life for you. That's not something common in our world. Don't make any rash decisions without considering this. Mateo won't let you leave, but he can make your life miserable if you don't cooperate."

Raina felt like her mother refused to understand her point of view. Vee was speaking from her own life experience. She'd had deep trauma after the abuse she suffered at the hands of her first husband, Tony Montana. She'd risen up to become a fierce queen, but it was obvious that her inner scars were not yet healed.

Raina murmured her thanks for Vee's advice, said goodbye and ended the call. She took several deep breaths, swiped at her eyes and reminded herself that Vee loved her deeply and would always be on her side.

Then Raina made the even bigger mistake of calling Diane. She poured her heart out to her adoptive mother, even telling her about Vee's unsatisfactory reaction. Unfortunately, Diane's emotions went in the complete opposite direction.

She was devastated by the news, possibly even more so than Raina. She cried and mourned the loss of grandchildren. Finally, Diane calmed down enough to offer her small bit of advice.

"You can adopt," Diane said with a sniffle, a glimmer of hope in her voice. "Why didn't I think of that right away! We adopted you and look how wonderful that turned out? There's no reason why you can't do the same."

Raina shook her head. "Would you have adopted if you were still deeply entrenched in the Miami crime scene? Or would you have felt terrible about keeping a child who could have gotten adopted by perfectly normal parents, living a perfectly normal and safe life. Would you take that chance away from a baby? Bring them into a life where they could be hurt, or expected to become something like an enforcer? I don't think I can do it."

"Oh dear, I see what you mean." Diane started crying again.

Raina listened to her mother, attempting to comfort her.

Raina supposed having a baby would have the same outcome as adoption. She would be purposely bringing a child into a life filled with danger. But somehow, giving birth was different. As though if she gambled with the possibility of pregnancy, it was out of her hands when it actually happened. But that wasn't taking responsibility. No matter what, the idea of children growing up around organized crime was a murky one. Perhaps Mateo was right, maybe not about the vasectomy, but about not bringing babies into their world.

Raina decided to call her best friend. That was who she needed. A good dose of someone who would agree with her no matter what. Who would be angry and sad on her behalf. She would be happy on Raina's behalf too.

Whatever Raina needed; Cassie would give.

Raina tapped her contact and waited for her to pick up. At first Cassie had been livid on Raina's behalf, calling Mateo every name in the book and threatening to march down to Miami to castrate him. Her wildly imaginative descriptions of what she would do to Mateo made Raina laugh out loud until she felt better. After a while Raina felt the need to defend Mateo. Then, Cassie switched gears into 'let's fix this' mode.

"I understand your reasons for not wanting to adopt, but what about having a surrogate baby? I'm sure it's not something you've thought of, but you should. Then you can have one of your own without putting strain on your body and leave the moral decisions behind." Cassie sounded proud of her ability to find a compromise.

Raina laughed. "And who exactly is the surrogate supposed to be? Do I post an ad on Facebook for one? How would that even work?"

There was silence on the other end of the line, stretched until it became awkward. Raina wondered if she'd missed something. Finally, Cassie said in a serious voice, "Me, of course. I would never allow you to accept a baby from anyone else. Not when I'm perfectly healthy and willing. It would be an honour to create such a precious gift for you."

Raina was floored by Cassie's suggestion. She'd known that her best friend was a wonderfully unselfish person, but Raina didn't think she'd ever given Cassie the real credit she deserved. This was beyond anything she could've imagined.

Raina wanted to argue, wanted to talk Cassie out of it, but in the face of such a heartfelt gift, even if it turned out to be a thought and not a reality, Raina could only say one thing. "Thank you. I wish I could hug you so tight right now. You are the best person I know."

Cassie was sniffling on the other end of the phone. "I feel the same about you. You're my person, Raina. No matter what happens, you will always be my person."

They remained silent for a minute and finally Raina took a deep breath and said, "This is way too heavy for a couple of twenty-one-year-old girls that should be enjoying spring break on a beach."

Cassie burst out laughing. "Spring break was a month ago. You're such a drop out."

CHAPTER FORTY-NINE

Mateo smiled tightly as Sotza strode toward him. Sotza clapped him on the back. "Good to see you, my boy."

It wasn't often that Sotza became even remotely effusive with his affection, but it had been months since the two men had seen each other. Sotza had recruited Mateo when he was a young teen. Until he went hunting for Garza and then over to Italy, Mateo had never spent more than a few weeks at a time away from the Sotza compound. Over the years, Sotza had become a father figure to him.

Since Sotza's arrival in Miami, he and his wife had been busy hunting the elusive Desi. Mateo had been otherwise occupied with his Miami takeover. The two men decided it was high time they meet.

They agreed on one of the clubs that Mateo was inheriting in his takeover. It was big, flashy, gaudy, everything Mateo despised. He was not a club man, nor would he ever be. Unless Sotza ordered him to hang onto the clubs, they would be the first thing he would sell off. He'd invest the money in a series of restaurants where it would be less of a headache to move illegitimate money.

"This place brings back memories." Sotza glanced around the cub as they made their way to a back booth, both sliding in to take a seat.

"Yeah? Been here before?" Mateo didn't really care, but his boss was one of the few people he was willing to put in lip service for.

Sotza gave him a shrewd look. Sotza knew of Mateo's antisocial tendencies but appreciated the effort. "This is where I first met my wife. She walked in that door," he pointed at the front entrance, flooded with Miami sunlight. "She had two bodyguards flanking her. She walked right up to me as though she owned the world and looked down her long nose like I was lower than the gum she might scrape off her high heel."

Mateo snorted his amusement. "Like mother, like daughter. Sounds like the look Raina gives me when she's pissed off."

"And have you managed to piss off my stepdaughter?" The question was casual, but Mateo could sense an underlying curiosity. Though Sotza was old school in many ways, he wouldn't force a merger if he didn't think the couple was happy.

Mateo appreciated the position that Sotza was in now. He was stepfather and protector to his wife's grown daughter. He also held a genuine affection for the girl. Yet, he had watched Mateo grow up and flourish under his regime. Though they never spoke the words, Mateo was aware that Sotza held great love for him. Mateo felt the same for his boss. He loved and respected Isaac Sotza. There wasn't much he wouldn't do for the man.

"I would guess that she gets mad at me about as often as

your wife gets mad at you," Mateo said with some amusement.

Sotza raised an eyebrow. "So it hasn't been a cakewalk then?"

"I wouldn't want her half as much if she acted any other way. That attitude is gold to a man like me. She's a fighter. If she didn't put up a fight once in a while, I'd wonder what was wrong. I'm not an easy man to deal with, and there are times I'm hell on her. She balks at the constant restrictions, but she understands the why of it."

Sotza nodded and waved over a server who hovered nearby. Both men ordered a drink and then lapsed into silence. Sotza was the first one to break it. "Sounds like I don't have anything to worry about. You'll take good care of her."

"Nothing else matters more to me than Raina." Though his words were meant to reassure Sotza, they were also the boiled-down truth. Nothing did matter to him more than Raina. She had become his entire world from the moment she confronted him on the campus when he kidnapped her. She had fought him like a wildcat, until he'd been forced to take her down to the ground and subdue her. The moment had been both illuminating and breathtaking. He had looked down at her face, screwed up in anger, her glasses askew. His lonely heart had found its mate and from that moment onward, beat for two.

"I believe this to be true." Sotza gave his blessing.

Two years ago, after Mateo kidnapped Raina and took her back to Venezuela to live with her parents, Mateo had gone to Sotza. He had asked his mentor to give Raina to him. Sotza had been taken aback by the question. Mateo didn't speak of his personal life, let alone ever mention wanting a woman. Sotza had even admitted to wondering about Mateo's sexuality. Mateo hadn't taken offence, as up to that point he had kept any liaisons both simple and brief. If he met a woman he wanted physically, he fucked her and then he walked away. He rarely went back twice.

But Raina had changed that. It was as though his body and soul had lain dormant until her arrival. The sight of her, her scent, her sass, everything about her had instantly locked him down. Until then, Mateo had scorned the idea of love at first sight. Now, he knew it to be true.

Sotza had agreed to Mateo's request, but on one condition. "You give her time. She's young, still a teenager. She isn't used to our world or used to men like you. She grew up in a loving household with good solid values. Her time here has been a shock. I believe, given more time, she will come around to appreciating our world; appreciating the opportunities the organization can provide. She was born for this. I have no doubt that when her day comes, she will shine."

While the rational part of Mateo agreed with Sotza, his heart screamed at him to take the woman and consequences be damned. It had taken every ounce of strength not to leave that office and hunt Raina down, take her back to his place and stake his claim. Instead, he had calmly asked, "How long?"

"As long as it takes." Sotza's words had been uncompromising and Mateo had made the decision to step back and give Raina the time that her stepfather requested. He reminded himself that he was doing it for her.

His gamble paid off. He now had Raina, they'd each declared their love and were planning their wedding. Even though she was pissed at him about the vasectomy, he had no doubt that once the storm passed, they would find their way back to each other. She was too generous and compassionate not to forgive him. Especially, since he'd done it with her in mind.

The thought of getting a vasectomy had not once crossed

Mateo's mind until he had researched Raina's condition. As soon as the realization hit him that giving birth could cause physical damage to his future wife, he made the decision without a second thought. He checked himself into the hospital and voluntarily elected to have a vasectomy. The doctor had frowned at him, asked him if he had children and tried to dissuade him, given Mateo's age at the time. He'd been thirty-four, healthy and virile.

But Mateo didn't give a shit about that. All he cared about was Raina and that she have a long and healthy life. If she had to do that without children, then so be it.

In an effort to divert the course of their conversation, Mateo said, "You met our guest, Giovanni Savino?"

Sotza took a long sip of his drink, then set it down on the table and looked at Mateo, an amused glint in his dark eyes. "An interesting man. He wants the world to believe he's an enthusiastic eccentric, but I believe he uses this flamboyance to lure people into a sense of complacency. I've heard rumours of his brutality. He's not the kind-hearted gentleman he makes himself out to be."

Mateo agreed with Sotza's assessment. "He wants us to think he's harmless, but his position suggests he's anything but harmless. Though I do think he feels genuine affection for Raina. You had a lucrative meeting?"

Sotza gave a short nod. "It was illuminating. We've become complacent over here in the Americas; we don't pay enough attention to what's happening across the ocean. Though Italy has an old and steeped tradition in the Cosa Nostra, I believe that Giovanni is interested in innovating some of their trade. He believes it's time to start looking to the west for business associates."

Mateo nodded his head, tossed back his own drink and commented, "After spending time with Savino I believe that he'll make a good ally."

Sotza lifted his drink in a toast. "To lucrative cross-border alliances. You, me, Reyes and now Savino. Between the four of us, we'll own a good chunk of this world."

Mateo lifted his glass and toasted to that.

They talked for most of the afternoon, Mateo updating Sotza on each of his Miami contacts and giving the older man a clear rundown on his activities. For his part, Sotza seemed impressed with Mateo's persistence and ingenuity. Miami was not an easy city to lock down, but it was too lucrative to allow it to fall into the wrong hands.

Sotza made a couple of suggestions that Mateo paid close attention to. Though Mateo had acted as Sotza's second-in-command for two decades, the other man was a born and bred leader. He slept, ate, and breathed organized crime. This was why he was Mateo's mentor.

Mateo left the club feeling good about things. He was now kingpin in one of the most lucrative organized crime cities in the world. He had connections all over the world and was in the process of cementing new ones. The woman of his dreams waited at home for him. She might be angry, but he would always want to see her, want to spend time with her. It didn't matter if she was screaming curse words at him, he would treasure every syllable.

When Mateo got back to the mansion, he decided to give Raina more time to herself and opened the door to his office, smiling, as he did each time he entered. Drop cloths and dust were his new normal when it came to this room. At first, he didn't see her standing among the plastic protectors covering the bookshelves. But then she turned when she heard him, her intense blue eyes piercing him as she tilted her head to the side, her blond hair spilling across her shoulder.

"You're back early," she said softly.

He was usually home around suppertime.

"Finished my meeting and decided I wanted to come

home. See how you're doing." His words were spoken with the careful deference of the man who knew he'd hurt his lover and didn't want to cause further damage.

She set the tape measure she'd been holding down on the edge of his desk and leaned her hip against the wood. She crossed her arms over her chest and shrugged. A protective gesture he'd come to recognize.

"I'm okay now."

Mateo stepped toward her, somewhat hesitantly. If she still needed space, he would give it to her. For a time. But she allowed his approach, not even a frown flickering her fine brows.

He didn't speak, sensing that she had something to tell him. After a few moments of gathering her thoughts she looked up at him. "Maybe you're right, maybe I shouldn't have babies. I feel strong, I feel tough and sometimes even invincible. When I'm not being shot at anyway." Her tone was wry, though he sensed the underlying seriousness. "But I want the chance to decide these things myself. I don't want to be told something as huge as that I won't be allowed to give birth to a child. It's unfair. You have to see how unfair it is, Mateo."

He closed his eyes and took a deep breath, wrestling with his words and thoughts. He truly thought about simply apologizing and nothing more. He wouldn't reverse his vasectomy; that option wasn't on the table. But Raina deserved more than that. She deserved his entire truth even if it made her angry again.

"Yes, it's not fair to have decisions made about your own body. And I am sorry that you were hurt by this decision. But I would make the same choice all over again. What's fair and what's not doesn't come into consideration when your health is on the line. Free will means nothing to me in the face of your continued survival. Do you understand?"

She nodded, still thoughtful. Not angry, which relaxed something inside him. He expected her fury, understood it even. Instead, she was attempting to see his side of things, though he refused to compromise.

"I do understand. And I think... I think that the way you love me is breathtaking." She stared at him, her eyes big blue pools of intelligence. "I may not agree with you. And I may actively take steps to defy you if we do have a similar disagreement in the future. But, for now, this isn't the thing that will break us."

Mateo's instincts screamed to life, telling him to lay down the law. He should deny her words, tell her that she will never be given the chance to defy him when it comes to her health. But he swallowed the words. He'd had enough truth for now, even though she would absolutely never be allowed to place herself in harm's way.

"What will break us?" he asked.

"I don't know." Her words were almost a whisper, they were wistful and hopeful at the same time.

Mateo closed the space between them, wrapping his hands around her waist and pulling her against his body for a hug. "The answer to that is nothing will break us. I won't let it happen."

She tipped her head back, her eyes shining and her lips stretching into a smile. He hadn't expected this from her, not today, maybe not for many days until she got over the shock of his earlier announcement.

"I won't let anything break us either." Her words were firm with conviction.

Mateo could do nothing other than kiss her. He lowered his head at the same time as lifting her up onto her toes, taking her lips in a kiss meant to convey all the feelings he couldn't express easily. Love, affection, awe, desire, admiration. This woman was the whole package and he was never going to let her go. They would grow old together, they would die together. He couldn't imagine a better life.

He deepened the kiss, his brain automatically searching for appropriate surfaces to lay her out on. He needed to seal this declaration with a solid fuck and he needed to do it now.

Unfortunately, he didn't get the chance. The whole world exploded around them in a deafening BOOM.

CHAPTER FIFTY

Mateo came to first, his ears ringing fiercely, his body vibrating with tension. Adrenaline shot through his body and his fight or flight instinct kicked in. He rolled onto his hands and knees and swung his head around searching for Raina. Dust hung in the air, stinging his eyes, but after a few seconds he spotted her. She was laying on her side facing him, eyes closed, arms curled into her body and knees pulled up to her chest. She wasn't moving.

"Raina!" He bellowed, lunging for her. His legs were wobbly and he fell to his knees next to her body.

He brought a hand down on her hip and rolled her onto her back. She groaned and one of her arms jerked up protectively over her chest.

"Mateo?" The word was faint, and he feared she was injured. Her eyes fluttered open and after a few seconds focused on him, a deep frown etching her features. "Wh- what happened?"

"Bomb."

The word barely left his lips when another explosion rocked the mansion. Everything shook and a deafening cracking sound told Mateo that a loadbearing wall was probably going down. He grabbed Raina, cradled her against his chest and hurled them both underneath the big sturdy desk. He curled himself around her thanking god that she was small. His big body barely fit into the space. He was able to protect his back and head, but his legs were still outside the desk.

He counted seconds in his head, waiting to hear another explosion. When none came, he crawled out from under the desk and stood, pulling his guns from their holsters.

He reached under the desk and took hold of her arm, pulling Raina out. He dragged her to her feet and held a hand over her arm as she steadied herself.

"I'm okay, do what you have to do." Her voice came out in her croak.

He badly wanted to check her thoroughly for injuries, but they didn't have time. He would have to get her to safety and for that he needed his hands free and Raina on her own two feet.

"Follow me, no more than a foot behind; keep your hand on my back so I know where you are. We're heading straight for the bunker. If you see anything questionable you hit the ground facedown and cover your head with your hands. You listen to everything I say. Got it?"

She nodded. "Let's go."

He leaned over and kissed her forehead. "I love you."

He unlatched the French doors that led out onto the pool patio and shoved them open. As though he was waiting for them to appear, a man came hurtling toward them, bullets spraying the side of the house. Mateo flung Raina back into the office and shot the man, one bullet to the head.

Whoever was targeting them weren't professional killers. The man had wasted at least a dozen bullets and hadn't hit anything important. Mateo felt marginally better once he realized this.

"Let's go." Mateo led Raina through the back doors. "Stay low."

Mateo spotted one of his men and shouted, "Cover us!"

"Got your back," he shouted back.

"Boss!" Angela's voice reached out to them as she rushed through a back door on the other side of the house.

"Meet us at the bunker," Mateo yelled at her.

As Mateo was glancing back to make sure Raina was following close behind him another explosion hit. He lifted his head in time to see the pool house go up in flames as it exploded out in all directions. A split second later the impact hit them.

A piercing pain stabbed Mateo in the chest, to the left of his heart, under his collarbone. He was flung back so hard that he took out the entire patio table set. The metal screeched and then crumpled under his weight as it collapsed into the concrete below. Mateo's head was ringing and his body didn't want to obey him as he shouted internally to get up and find Raina. All he could do was turn his head to the side, eyes narrowed against the smoke in the air and search for her body.

At first, he didn't see her, and panic began to set in. He forced himself to roll off the table, hitting a metal chair in the process and knocking it aside. He landed on his hands and knees on the concrete. The stabbing pain in his chest became nearly unbearable, but not as unbearable as not knowing what happened to Raina.

He swung his head to the side, searching for her as he struggled to regain his feet.

"I got her!" The shout came right before he heard a splash as a body hit the pool.

Mateo watched in agonized confusion as someone swam

toward an object floating in the pool. Mateo realized it was Raina as the man flipped her over onto her back and swam her to the edge of the pool towards Mateo.

Mateo dropped to his knees and reached for her, his heart thudding in his chest, each beat causing more and more pain as blood pumped out of his wound. But through the pain, relief shone like a weak ray of light as Raina's pale arm reached out from the pool towards him. She was alive and she was conscious.

He gritted his teeth against the pain as he wrapped his hands underneath her armpits and pulled her up next to him on the edge of the pool. Water poured off her as reached up to swipe at her glasses.

"Got to get to the bunker." His voice came out in a harsh rasp.

Mateo wasn't sure if he was reminding himself or telling Raina. Giovanni pulled himself out of the pool, kneeling next to Raina, his hand on her shoulder, his concerned gaze on Mateo.

"You're hurt."

Giovanni's observation woke Raina up and she craned her head around to stare at Mateo. Her eyes landed on his wound and she cried out as she reached for him.

Giovanni caught her wrist. "Don't touch it. We don't know if it's severed an artery. We have to leave it in there."

She made a pained whimpering sound but dropped her hand to Mateo's arm. Mateo looked down, only now realizing that there was shrapnel in his wound. A jagged piece of metal stuck out of his chest about four inches.

Raina slid her arm under his right shoulder and looked up at him. "I'll help you. Stand slowly. We'll go to the bunker together."

Mateo thought about telling her to let go of him so she could protect herself but realized quickly he was too weak to continue without her help. He nodded sharply and looked at Giovanni. "My guns... should be over by the table."

Giovanni lurched toward the table, searching for Mateo's guns as Raina helped Mateo stand. He was losing blood too quickly. If he didn't get help, he would die, and he couldn't die before he made sure Raina was safe. They had to get to the bunker. He had to get her into the bolthole.

"Got it." Giovanni came back towards them holding one of Mateo's guns. "I'll lead the way, you two stay behind me."

"Behind the pool house... what used to be the pool house."

"I know where we're going; I've wandered all over this property. I've seen your torture shed."

Of course he had. There was no chance a man of Giovanni's position wouldn't at least suspect that Mateo had a building on the property for security and interrogation.

As they shuffled towards the back of the property, they could hear a cacophony of noise coming from the house. It seemed like the people who were targeting them outside the house, were now scouting around inside. Good news for Mateo, Raina and Giovanni if the enemy didn't realize that they were no longer in the mansion.

As they lurched toward the outbuilding, Giovanni asked, "Do you know who's targeting you?"

Mateo thought about it. "Could be any number of people."

"It's Desi." Raina's voice held both conviction and a terrible kind of anger that Mateo had never heard from her before. It was a killing anger.

"Desi?" Giovanni asked as they approached the back door of the building.

Mateo gave Giovanni the code and heaved a sigh of relief as the three of them shuffled into the building, slamming the door shut behind them. All was quiet within the bunker. This building hadn't been penetrated yet. The walls were reinforced, built to withstand bomb blasts that were much bigger than the pipe bombs being blown up around the property.

Mateo knew exactly what his enemy was using as he had spent a few of his formative years under the tutorship of a hired bomber. Sotza had footed the bill for his education, believing that one day the knowledge would come in handy. Ironic that Mateo was now on the receiving end of that education. He didn't believe this had been Sotza's intention at all.

"Desi hates all of us," Raina explained to Giovanni as they made their way into the bowels of the building. "She was second-in-command to a Mexican cartel. Her boss attacked my mom and stepdad, trying to kill them so they could take the Venezuelan business. But Mateo stopped them and killed Garza. We think it's his girlfriend who's targeting us. She attacked me a few weeks ago."

Mateo hadn't realized that Raina knew he'd killed Garza. He certainly hadn't spoken to her about it. Had to be her mother. Fucking woman didn't know how to mind her own business. Mateo didn't need Raina getting to know the killer in him; might spook her.

"Nicolás Garza," Giovanni said musingly. "I've heard of him. My son attempted to do business with him shortly before he disappeared. I take it that was your handiwork?"

Mateo nodded grimly, unable to concentrate on almost anything besides the pain radiating through him. His body had been through a lot. Gunshot wounds, stab wounds, head wounds. Nothing he'd experienced in the past had made him doubt his ability to pull through. Until now. He feared that this piece of shrapnel was too close to his heart, that he might not survive.

"Through... there." Mateo lifted a bloody finger, pointing down the corridor that led to the bolthole he built for Raina.

He mumbled the code before they reached the door, fearful that he was about to pass out. He needed Raina inside that room. That room would protect her from everything, including a nuclear blast.

Giovanni punched the code into the panel and shoved the door open, looking back at Mateo and Raina as he did so. It was a mistake. A shot rang out, Giovanni's head burst into a spray of red, his body hit the doorframe and slid to the ground.

Raina's scream of terror was the last thing Mateo heard before he was shot. His body was flung backward and the world went black before he hit the floor.

He had failed.

CHAPTER FIFTY-ONE

Raina refused to allow shock to freeze her responses, taking away the precious second she needed to avenge the two men at her feet. She didn't know if they were alive or dead, but she was going to do her best to take down the threat for their sake.

She was going to fucking kill Desi with her bare hands.

Raina dropped to her knees, scooping up the gun that Giovanni had been holding. It was wet with blood. She didn't know whose and she didn't have time to care. She was facing a woman determined to kill her and everyone she loved. Raina rolled to the side of the door as bullets thumped into the wall behind and beside her. The second the shooting stopped, Raina swung her arm around the doorframe and shot at random.

A grunt of pain told her that she'd actually scored a hit. Impressive considering she'd never used a gun in her life. She wasn't about to waste a single second though. She flung herself into the room, crouching low and scanning as quickly as she could. Desi was bent over on the other side of the bed, clutching her thigh where blood was pouring freely. When

Desi caught the movement of Raina out of the corner of her eye, she lifted her gun.

Raina got her first, shooting as rapidly as she could until the chamber of her gun was empty and Desi was flung backwards as she took a bullet to the shoulder. Raina was starting to think she was a shooting prodigy, impressed with herself for managing to hit Desi twice.

Raina threw herself across the bed, rolling as she flung her gun at Desi's head, cracking her in the side of the skull with it. Raina smiled grimly as Desi cried out in pain and grabbed her head.

Desi staggered away from Raina, her hand moving to her belt where she pulled a knife, her movements slow and clumsy. Despite Desi having a good four or five inches on her, Raina was able to grab Desi by the throat and swing her into the concrete wall.

Desi's head hit with a sickening crack. She flinched and shook her head as if trying to clear it. Desi struck out blindly with her knife, finally scoring a hit on Raina. Raina cried out as fire slice through her upper bicep, but she was sure the wound wasn't that bad considering her grip on Desi's neck remained tight. Raina grasped Desi's knife hand, slamming her wrist into the wall next to her head.

The two women were in a standoff. Though wounded, Desi was bigger and far more skilled than Raina. But Raina had rage on her side. She wanted this woman to die and she wanted to do it herself. Every time Desi tried to hit out at her, Raina absorbed the hit and struck back. An elbow to Desi's chin, a fist to her chest and a knee to Desi's groin.

There was no doubt, Desi was taking the brunt of their fight. Blood loss was making her weak and clumsy.

"I'm going to enjoy slicing that pretty face off," Desi hissed, baring her teeth at Raina.

Raina punched her in the mouth, bloodying her teeth and

ending Desi's stream of vitriol. Raina leaned in close to Desi. "Right back at you, bitch."

Another minute of struggling and Desi was finally forced to release her hold on the knife, allowing it to drop to the floor with a clatter. Desi tried to drop to her knees, groping frantically for it. Raina brought her own knee up, hitting Desi in the side of the head and knocking her to the ground. Raina scooped the knife up and jumped on top of Desi, first dropping to her knees on Desi's chest, then straddling her.

Desi screamed in pain and flung her arms over her face, turning her head to the side as Raina lifted the knife, preparing it to plunge it into Desi's chest.

A hand gripped her wrist, stopping her. Raina threw her head back glaring up at the person who dared to stop her. Mateo stood swaying next to her, then dropped to his knees, his hand sliding away from Raina's. She twisted, still on top of Desi and pressed her hands to his cheeks, uncaring of the bloody knife she held in her hand.

"I thought you were dead!" she wailed, tears starting to flow.

"I... I would never... leave you." His voice was weak, and Raina realized how much effort it must've taken to pull himself up off the floor and come to her aid. "Don't kill her."

"But why?" Raina demanded swiping at her tears. "We need to finish this."

"Because you are not a killer and this woman deserves a slower death than what she'll find from a knife to the heart." This had not come for Mateo. He was already slipping away from her, his eyes drifting shut as his body slumped back against the bed.

It was Giovanni. He stood tall, proud and angry, blood pouring down his face and neck from his wound. This was the Italian Godfather. The man who ruled the underground of an entire nation. Not only was he alive, but he looked like the formidable kingpin he was, his cold gaze on the woman laid out on the floor.

He had a point. Desi didn't deserve an easy death. Not after everything she'd done to Raina's family.

Raina nodded at him. "Can you help me secure her so we can get help for Mateo?"

Giovanni dropped down beside Raina and set about making sure that the semi-conscious Desi would neither move or die anytime soon. When he finished, he helped Raina assess Mateo. They did their best to stanch the flow of blood from his wounds, pressing a towel that Raina found in the washroom around the shrapnel sticking out from his chest and another against a gunshot wound that went through the flesh in his side. They agreed that they didn't think any arteries had been severed, but he was still losing too much blood.

Moments later, the room filled with their people. Danny and Angela were the first ones in. Angela was quick to assure Raina that the house had been secured and anyone involved in the attack neutralized. They laid Mateo out on the bed and set to work saving the life of their leader. The boss of the Miami underworld.

CHAPTER FIFTY-TWO

Everything that happened after Desi was captured was a blur. Raina and Giovanni did their best to stabilize Mateo until the paramedics could arrive. They'd debated making the call, since the usual procedure would be to call a doctor they kept on standby for emergencies, but both agreed Mateo could be critical. It was better to make sure he survived first; they could deal with the fallout and potential city payoffs later.

Vee and Sotza arrived at the mansion at the same time as Mateo, Raina and Giovanni were being loaded into ambulances. Raina insisted on accompanying Mateo to the hospital, which the paramedic finally agreed to when she became nearly hysterical at the idea of leaving his side.

Desi had mostly missed when she'd aimed to kill Giovanni, clipping him in the side of the head. The wound looked much worse than it actually was. And after the paramedics had a look at him, they were told that Giovanni would likely only need a few stitches.

Mateo was another matter. Though the shrapnel in his shoulder had not hit a major artery, it had struck the bone and the paramedic who looked him over believed that there was damage to his collarbone. His gunshot wound was mostly superficial, though it would need stitching. He'd also lost a significant amount of blood and was covered in scrapes and bruises.

Raina hadn't realized that she'd been hurt until Vee grabbed hold of her and started shouting for a paramedic. Raina looked blearily at her mother. "Who needs a paramedic? Mateo and Giovanni are already being looked after." Raina looked surreptitiously around and added, "And anyone else involved is probably dead."

Vee grabbed hold of Raina's arm and held it up. There was a long gash on her upper arm. Blood was trickling slowly from her wound and down her hand, but she'd been so preoccupied with Mateo's injuries that she hadn't noticed. Now that she saw the blood, she felt woozy.

"Don't you dare!" Vee snapped, giving her a sharp two-fingered tap to the cheek. "We don't have time for fainters in this family. Pull yourself together, get in that ambulance and go for stitches."

Vee said this as she wrapped Raina's wound with a cloth napkin she snatched from the dining room. She stood next to the ambulance as Raina climbed inside. Raina looked at her mother and said calmly, "Someone let Desi in the bunker room. Only three of us had the code."

She didn't want to tell her mother exactly who betrayed them as too many people were standing around listening. She hoped Vee and Sotza would figure out who she meant.

"I'm on it." Vee answered, then she leaned up and kissed Raina on the cheek. "I love you."

"I love you too, mom."

Mateo tensed as consciousness rushed towards him. He expected a blast of pain to knock him on his ass but was instead greeted by a gentle fuzzy sensation. He'd been drugged. He hated that someone had administered what was likely morphine while he wasn't awake to give his consent. He needed his wits about him, needed to be able to think, to talk to Raina.

"I'm here." Her soft voice penetrated the mist that he was attempting to swim through to reach consciousness.

Finally, Mateo managed to pry his eyes open. He tried to speak but only a croak emerged. He let out a frustrated growl and tried to push himself up on the bed.

Alarm swept over Raina's features and she was quick to grab him, placing her hand carefully against his chest, away from his wound and giving him a gentle push back against the pillows. Mateo resisted for a few seconds, then gave in. Raina meant well, but he would have to get up and moving before long.

Maybe one day he would explain to her the extent of some of the injuries he'd suffered in the past. Every time he'd been shot, stabbed, or punched, he had no choice but to bounce back quickly. To force his body to accept and overcome whatever injury he'd sustained. He was a firm believer in mind over body because he had no choice. In his line of work, a bed ridden mobster was a dead mobster.

"Do you remember anything?" she asked him, reaching for a cup with a plastic lid and straw. She placed it against his lips.

Mateo gratefully took several sips, wetting his parched throat. He closed his eyes and tried to think of the events that had landed him... where was he? He opened his eyes and looked around the room. Fuck. They brought him to a hospital. Once he was recovered, he would have to have a long conversation with Raina about proper protocol when it came to injuries. He did not ever want to be checked into a hospital, nor did he want drugs administered.

"I remember the blast." His voice was stronger, though rough, as though he'd been coughing for days. "Going into the bunker. I remember Desi."

He could see her now, standing across the room from them, her gun raised. She'd sprayed them with bullets. Mateo had taken one in the side and fallen back. He didn't remember anything else.

"Where's Desi?"

Raina squeezed his arm and set his glass of water back on the table. "She's being held in the bunker. I tried to kill her, but Giovanni stopped me."

"He's alive?" Mateo was surprised that the other man had survived a shot to the head.

She nodded. "The bullet winged him, causing a gash on the side of his head. But that's the only injury he sustained during the entire standoff."

"You?"

She shook her head and played with the end of her sleeve. "I'm fine. Especially considering I survived a bomb blast, an impromptu dip in the pool and being shot at by a psychopath. All in the space of about ten minutes."

Mateo smiled wryly. It was just like his girl to make fun of a serious attack. She used humour to lighten the mood when darkness could easily emerge the victor. He appreciated her ability to look on the lighter side of things. She balanced him, balanced his serious nature and the darkness within him.

"My parents are at the mansion now, getting everything back in order. They've been texting with me while I waited for you to get out of surgery. It looks like there were three bombs. One in the lobby, another in the pool house and another in your bedroom." Raina filled him in on the details, giving him a thorough no-nonsense rundown. "Sotza is managing the contacts that've heard about the explosions and checked in. He's also organized all the house staff and security. We were lucky. We didn't lose anyone in the bombs. Desi attacked the mansion with two hired thugs, both are dead now. We think the bombs were planted while she still had access to the house and grounds and that she used a remote device to set them off. Sotza thinks she used the distraction of the bombs to get through our estate security and into the bunker."

"Makes sense." Though he trusted Sotza to take care of his holdings, he was concerned about the ripple effect this attack would have through the Miami underworld. Now was the time to make a show of strength. To show all of his contacts, new and old, that he would not be defeated so easily. "How long was I out? Help me up."

Mateo swung his legs over the side of the bed and reached for the IV in his arm. He suspected that he was getting a good dose of morphine along with his fluids. Before Raina could try and stop Mateo, he yanked the tubes from his arm. A trickle of blood welled up and ran down his hand from where he pulled the needle out.

"No, I won't help you!" Raina said, her voice going high with concern. "You need to stay in bed. You literally just had surgery, Mateo."

"Raina," Mateo took hold of her arms and gave her a shake. "How long was I out?"

Her eyes narrowed and she glared at him. "About four hours. They took you into surgery as soon as we arrived and you've been in recovery for about two hours."

Good. The sooner he got up and moving the less time his Miami contacts would have to wonder whether he was alive or dead, whether he had left a gaping opening for one of them to fill.

"My clothes?"

Raina's lips tightened and she continued to give him a death glare that made it clear how she felt about him being up so soon. Regardless, she pointed to a chair where there was a tidy stack of his clothes.

It hurt to get dressed, but Raina finally relented in her anger and helped him pull his clothes on, very gently pulling the zipper on his pants and buckling his belt. Despite the seriousness of the situation, she tilted her head up and gave him a half grin.

"Are you seriously getting hard right here, right now, after all we've been through?" she asked with an incredulous laugh.

He wrapped an arm around her neck pulling her in tight against his good shoulder. He dropped his head to kiss her. "Woman, I'd have to be on my deathbed to withstand your touch. And even then, pretty sure I'm going to be going to my grave with a permanent boner."

They laughed together, a much-needed moment. As they left the room, two bodyguards stood up from their positions outside Mateo's room and flanked them. Reinforcements that Sotza sent. A doctor tried to argue Mateo out of leaving, but Mateo was insistent. Finally, he was given a form to sign saying that he was leaving the hospital against medical advice.

Together, they stepped out into the balmy Miami night. Though Mateo badly wanted to go back to the mansion and put his house back in order, he had to make a few stops first. He had to go those damned clubs he despised so much, sit down, have a drink with his woman and show the world that there was not a thing wrong with the new Miami boss.

CHAPTER FIFTY-THREE

When they arrived back at the mansion, Mateo expected to be confronted with chaos. Instead, he found a well-organized household, busy putting everything back together. Even the front door, where a bomb had gone off inside the lobby, was almost completely fixed. New doors replaced the ones that had been blown off their hinges. Now, only some scarring on the paneling beside the doors indicated what had happened.

As they entered their home, they were confronted by Vee and Sotza. Raina broke away from Mateo and flung herself at her mother. Vee gripped her tightly and whispered something to her.

Sotza placed a hand on his stepdaughter's shoulder and squeezed, but his concerned gaze remained on Mateo. "You okay, son?"

Mateo jerked his head in a nod. "Fine," he said shortly. "Tell me what's been happening here."

Sotza gave him a wry look. "While you two were out barhopping, we were busy setting things in order." Mateo chuckled at Sotza's description. Far from barhopping, he and

Raina, along with their two bodyguards had spent time in two of Mateo's clubs. The entire experience had been agonizing, having to get in and out of the vehicle, which hurt like a bitch. Sitting in a booth, drinking a glass of water and talking to his fiancé as though everything were normal.

They had done it for the sake of appearances. Mateo could not afford to look weak now. Of course, Sotza knew that. "You're going to need to re-renovate your office and a couple of the rooms upstairs. A wall came down in the master suite. We moved your captive into a secure cell where she's being watched by a guard."

Mateo grunted his acknowledgement. "Angela?"

Vee answered, her eyes narrowing in anger. "We're holding her for you, though I'd dearly love to get my hands on that woman."

Mateo agreed. Angela's betrayal hurt the most. He could understand and even respect Desi's vendetta, but he didn't understand Angela. He'd known her since she was a child, mentored and cared for her. She befriended and then betrayed Raina. Mateo was beyond furious. It would take some real self-restraint to stop himself from killing her long enough to hear an explanation. He decided to tour the mansion first, giving himself time to calm down.

Once again, he was surprised to see how little damage the bombs actually did. They tore apart furniture, threw shrapnel into walls and doors, but otherwise left the mansion unscathed. They had clearly been relatively weak bombs, either built by an amateur or meant to cause little to no harm.

Finally, he was ready to face his enemies. Two women. In a way he wasn't entirely surprised. The mafia could be hostile towards women, unforgiving. A century ago, when organized crime rose up in the Americas, there had been an unwritten code that women and children were not touched.

Now, things were different. Gangs didn't always respect

the code. Too often women and children were killed during takeovers as one opponent would try to wipe out the entire family of another. Women also worked more and more in security, acting as bodyguards, or in Desi's case, second-in-command.

Still, Mateo was uncomfortable with the idea of killing women. So far, in his long and bloody career he'd managed to stay away from having to kill a woman. Though, after he finished Nicolás Garza, he had intended to hunt and kill the man's partner, Desi. Perhaps, it was his leniency toward women that stopped him from going after her right away. He regretted that now. His reticence could have caused the death of the only woman in the world who meant anything to him.

Mateo learned his lesson. He would not be going easy on Desi, Angela or any other woman who threatened his family. He strode across the backyard, skirting the pool, toward the bunker. Sotza was on one side of him and Giovanni on the other. Giovanni had made his way back to the mansion while Mateo was out at the clubs. Having been once more caught up in their family drama, the Italian Godfather was now invested in the outcome.

Though Raina wanted to come with him, Mateo had refused her. She had agreed to stay at the mansion with her mother, helping to put the pieces of the household back together. Mateo suspected Raina knew she wouldn't have the stomach for what was about to happen.

Mateo chose to see Desi first. He knew exactly what he wanted to do to her, and he wouldn't be nearly as heartbroken over it as he was with what was coming Angela's way. He entered the room, expecting to find a broken woman after the beating she'd taken at Raina's hands. Instead, he was confronted by a hissing, spitting, expletive screaming Desi.

Mateo, Sotza and Giovanni stopped in the doorway for a few seconds to admire the raging Latina beauty. Despite what

Raina had done to Desi's face, she was still a stunning woman. Her long black hair fell in a shiny wave around her shoulders and her tall body was encased in tight leather pants and a black zipped jacket.

"Desiree." He said her name coldly, drawing her attention.

"You!" she hissed, lunging at him. She was pulled back by the cuffs binding her wrists to the wall. "Just my fucking luck, you pulled through." Her gaze flited behind him to land on Sotza, her eyes narrowing first in recognition, then in hatred.

Mateo had to fight not to show his amusement. Even while facing a grisly death, she would still go down fighting, cursing his name and wishing every bad thing she could think of upon him and his family. Despite his anger that she put Raina in danger over and over, he could appreciate and sympathize with her.

They lived in a dangerous world, one where people like Desi and Mateo willingly threw themselves into some of the most dangerous situations imaginable. People they loved would die. It was a fact. But the loyalty and friendships they developed among members of their alliances forced them to avenge each other in a never-ending cycle of vendetta.

"You nearly took the life of my woman." Mateo stepped up to her, entering her space, unafraid as she lunged toward him, throwing her fists. He caught her wrist and slammed it back against the wall, scraping her knuckles on the concrete. "For that, your life is forfeit."

"I gladly give my life," she snarled. "You destroyed everything I had to live for."

She spat at him, intending to hit his face with the bloody saliva. But they were standing too close together, so it missed and hit his shirt collar. Mateo didn't flinch and he didn't move.

"So you decided to destroy the thing that I had to live for," Mateo drawled.

She stared at him, her dark eyes hot coals of hate. Her anger was so palpable that Mateo was surprised by her next words. "If I have any regrets in all this, it's that I targeted Raina instead of you. She's more innocent of this world then I originally thought."

Mateo raised an eyebrow. He hadn't expected Desi to unbend enough to admit such a thing. He thought some of her mixed feelings when it came to Raina probably came from the amount of time she spent one-on-one with Raina during the renovations. Raina was a difficult woman to hate.

Mateo switched gears, asking a question that had haunted him for weeks. "Were you in any way responsible for the death of my Mexican liaison and his family?"

Her face betrayed her before her words, her gaze dropping to the floor and her skin paling. As rage flooded his system, he had to check the urge not to punch her in the face and take her out right there.

"Yes," she admitted. "Since you decimated the Garza cartel, I didn't have the manpower I needed to come after you. I heard rumours of another family further east who despise the South American cartels. I teamed up with them and they went after your guy. It was a mistake. I don't kill children. I dropped them, which is why I had to hit the mansion with only a couple guys for backup. The plan was to bring an army to your doorstep."

Some of the rage left Mateo as she explained. He was surprised she was giving him the information so freely, but if she truly felt guilt over the incident, perhaps she was trying to cleanse her soul before death by confessing her part.

"If you think these words will move me to take it easy on you, then you're mistaken."

Her eyes flared in anger and she reared back, struggling in his grip, her moment of self-reflection over.

"I don't care what you think!" she screamed at him. "Get

it the fuck over with. I want the peace only my grave will provide."

Mateo gripped her chin. "Your death will be a long and agonizing one. Don't dream of that grave just yet, bitch. We're going to have some fun first."

"Do you think you can make me scream?" she challenged, her eyes dark empty voids staring back at him. Perhaps it wouldn't be so difficult to kill this woman.

"Count on it."

She gave him a bloody grin. "Good, then the underworld will know I'm coming."

Mateo didn't bother replying but turned and left the room reaching for the sanitary wipe his man handed him. He wiped the saliva off his collar and flicked the wipe into the garbage. He gave his man a penetrating look. "Prepare her for me."

Mateo had a method when he tortured his victims. He preferred them seated on a chair with their hands cuffed to the sides. There would be a strap around the neck keeping the head up so he could see the eyes as the life was slowly beaten from them.

Before they could move onto the next room, Giovanni cleared his throat, his thoughtful gaze on Desi's cell. "I have a rather large favour to ask. Before you deny my request, hear me out and take your time with the decision."

Mateo frowned at Giovanni. "You've been a friend to us. I'm willing to grant a request."

Sotza crossed his arms, his eyes narrowed in thought, as though he suspected he knew what Giovanni would say. "What are you asking?"

Giovanni smiled grimly. "I guarantee this is a request you will not want to grant, and I can give you my word now that I will abide by your judgement on this." Mateo waved his guards back so their conversation would be private. "I want you to give me that woman. Desi."

Mateo's frown turned thunderous and he opened his mouth to immediately deny the request. Giovanni interrupted him. "I can promise that whatever you do to her, while extremely painful, will be short-lived. Unless you intend to allow her to live longer than a few days, her suffering will eventually end. Give her to me and I can promise that her suffering will continue through a lifetime."

The two men stared at each other while Sotza remained silent. Mateo was tempted to take Giovanni up on his offer, but he was hesitant. Yes, he wanted Desi to suffer for more than a few days. But it disturbed him, the idea that this man who befriended Raina was eager to get his hands on the Latina assassin. There were some things that Mateo could not condone. Yet, for men like them, morality was murky, an ever-changing thing that couldn't be pinned down.

"Why do you want her?"

Giovanni's answer to the question would seal her fate.

"My wife... she died many years ago. Succumbing to a lifestyle that I forced her into. She was soft and sweet, not meant for mob living. I loved her too deeply to let her go. I am convinced, that it is my selfishness that eventually killed her." Giovanni gazed at the closed door to Desi's room. "That woman is fierce; she's strong and she won't die easily. Nor will her children. I want more than the one fuck-up offspring I managed to produce. I intend to leave a legacy behind in this world, children who are capable of taking over my holdings. She will make a fine mother." His light brown eyes landed back on Mateo, a hint of humour in their depths. "And I can promise you, she will suffer as I train her to become the perfect wife."

Mateo gave it a few minutes thought, but his mind had been made up almost immediately after Giovanni finished speaking. Though it was a difficult decision to leave Desi alive, Giovanni's proposal was the perfect solution. Mateo would not have to torture and kill her. Giovanni would do to her things that she hated, things that Mateo didn't have time for or the desire. Turning a woman like Desi into a Stepford wife was the perfect revenge. She would hate every moment.

First, he had to make sure his mentor was on board with the idea. Desi had personally attacked him in Venezuela while helping Garza. "What do you think?"

Sotza stood, his arms crossed over his chest, his eyes on the ground as he thought. He raised his head and pinned Giovanni with a serious look. "I will require your word that she doesn't leave your Italian property except in a body bag. You take responsibility for the woman. If she escapes, or you allow her off the property, we will come after you both."

"That is a fair demand," Giovanni agreed. He turned his attention to Mateo. "And you?"

"She's all yours but we'll have to discuss details. I don't like the idea of that woman breathing in the same world as Raina. I need to know how you intend to keep her properly secured."

"I'll get you a plan before I leave here with her. You have my word that this woman will remain in my keeping. She'll never be given the opportunity to become a threat again."

"Good enough."

The two men shook and Mateo re-entered Desi's room. She was now secured to a chair, her hands cuffed and her neck strapped. She glared daggers at the men, her malevolent gaze moving to each of them.

"What now?" she demanded.

Mateo knelt on the floor next to Desi, pulling his knife from the pocket of his jeans. He flicked the blade open, locking it in place.

She moved her head to stare down at him. Mateo put the blade against the pointer finger of her right hand; the most likely to be her trigger finger.

"Your life has been spared," he told her, then sliced the finger off in one clean cut.

To her credit, Desi didn't even whimper. Her face paled and her lips quivered. Involuntary tears shone in her eyes.

Mateo stood, tossed her finger on the table and strode to the door.

"Take care of your slave," he said to Giovanni, slipping past the other man and heading down the hall toward Angela's cell.

Sotza walked with Mateo, but waited outside the room, tacitly giving Mateo space to deal with a woman who had been his friend.

Mateo's conversation with Angela was surprisingly brief. She turned as he entered the door. Angela hadn't been secured. She was allowed loose in her cell. Her face was puffy from crying and her lip was bloody. Someone had punched her. If Mateo had to guess, he would say Vee.

"You betrayed me." The chill in his voice frosted the air in the room.

"It's not what you think." Tears filled her eyes.

Mateo grabbed her by the neck and shoved her into the nearest wall squeezing hard enough that she gasped for air. She didn't fight him though, her arms hung loose her sides. Her gaze was on his shoulder where a bandage was visible through the collar of his shirt. A throb of pain hit him reminding him that the bone had sustained a fracture.

"Then tell me exactly what happened. Speak quickly and don't leave out any details."

For good measure Mateo pulled his switchblade, still shiny with Desi's blood and set it against her throat over top of her pulse point. One wrong word and he was going to drain her.

She swallowed, closed her eyes and nodded as though gathering herself. Then, she opened her eyes and began speaking, swiftly and purposefully. "I didn't betray you. At least, not on purpose. You asked me to supervise the installation of the bolthole door and input the correct code once the panel was in. I did exactly as you asked, only there was a problem. Something electronic. I couldn't input the code. I had to call in a tech guy to help. And there's only one that I trusted."

"Thomas." Mateo's voice came out in a growl.

Angela's words rang true. He had requested that she input the code, making her, him and Raina the only three people on the grounds that had access to the bunker. But Angela had a weakness. Though she was a security expert, she was not a technology expert. Thomas had always been Mateo's man for IT stuff. He was a trusted member of their team, having worked with both of them for several years in Venezuela before moving with them to Miami. Hell, he'd even had Mateo's back in Italy. It was a shock to learn that he'd been the one to betray them.

"I tried to keep the code away from him, even knowing that you trusted him implicitly." Her voice rose with upset. "But he insisted that he had to enter the code himself. Something to do with whatever glitch the panel was experiencing. I don't know if he caused the tech problem on purpose in order to get his hands on the code, or if he took advantage of an opportunity."

Mateo didn't know either, but he would find out as soon as he got his hands on Thomas. It was a relief knowing Angela hadn't actually betrayed him. He dropped his hand from her throat and allowed her to move away from the wall.

"You should've told me he knew the code. This was a major fuck up that could've ended in both mine and Raina's deaths."

Angela nodded, tears spilling over and trailing down her cheeks. She sniffled and used the back of her hand to swipe at them. She didn't look like the badass mafioso woman he had become used to. Then again, Mateo probably didn't look all that fierce either after the beating his body had taken.

"I willingly accept your punishment, whether you take my life, my finger or whatever else will make this right. You've been so generous to me that I'm devastated I was part of this. I deserve whatever comes my way." She shuffled her feet and stared at the floor, her tears dripping onto the cement.

Mateo thought about it and then collapsed into one of the metal chairs behind him, elbow on his knee, his head in his hand. "Between you and me I haven't the desire or energy to hurt you. And I suspect Raina will set the mansion on fire if I try to send you away. When she finds out that you're innocent of betrayal, she'll advocate for you until I have no choice but to allow you to stay. There will be some changes though. I can no longer allow you to remain as head of security."

"I understand." Her voice was soft but hopeful. "I'll do anything you ask."

Mateo rubbed the back of his neck, thinking for a few minutes. "I'll have to check with Raina, but how does personal bodyguard to my wife sound? You'll have to take a step down in terms of security, but I think you'll both be happy with the solution."

Angela threw herself on her knees in front of Mateo and clasped his hand, not bothering to check the tears that were streaming down her face. "Thank you, thank you. I'll never again give you reason to doubt me."

Mateo placed a hand on her head, patting her gently. "I know."

CHAPTER FIFTY-FOUR

Thomas was located at the dockyard, attempting to use the getaway that Desi had originally arranged for them. Finding him there, actively attempting to leave to city hammered the final nail in his coffin. Unlike Angela, Thomas had guilt written all over him. Mateo had treated the guy like a brother. He'd allowed him into his home, entrusted him with his most valuable possession, Raina.

Sotza, Mateo and a half dozen of their people confronted Thomas at the dockyard. Thomas' reason for betraying the family had been greed. Money and position within Desi's cartel; the cartel she'd intended to resurrect from the ashes of her dead boyfriend. A motive that infuriated Mateo like nothing else. Though they were all mobsters, there was a code. A code that Thomas had broken. He betrayed his mob family for the sake of a better position.

Mateo didn't bother dragging the man home to his torture shed but allowed his fury free rein right there in the dockyard, next to the boat Thomas and Desi were going to use to escape. He painted the docks red until he was satisfied. Until Thomas was no longer recognizable.

Mateo and Sotza walked away from the dockyard, leaving the body behind for everyone to see. Thomas would be a statement to the Miami underworld; betrayal would not be tolerated.

Raina paced the bedroom, waiting for Mateo to come back. He'd been gone for hours and she was worried about him. What if his wound reopened and he bled out? He certainly wasn't taking very good care of himself.

He had a broken collarbone, yet he refused to put it in a sling before going to visit his captives. He told her that he couldn't look weak. Like when he forced her to go to the clubs with him, pretended that all was well and that they hadn't been beaten to hell and back.

Raina was on another lap around the room when the door was flung open, smacking against the wall. Mateo stood there for see few seconds staring at her, then his expression gradually went from worry to anger.

"I looked everywhere for you. I can't have you missing right now. You need to be where I can see you."

Raina frowned at him and then bit her lip to keep herself from pointing out that if he'd allowed her to go to the bunker with him as she wanted, he would've known exactly where she was.

Instead, she said calmly, "I've been right here in my bedroom all along. Yours was blown up, so I came back here."

"You should've had someone come tell me where you'd be."

Raina could understand why Mateo might be grumpy. He was probably exhausted; he was hurting, and he was dealing with the betrayal of a good friend. But still, she couldn't allow him to think that he could snap at her anytime he wanted.

"Exactly how many places did you have to search for me before coming here?"

His dark eyes narrowed on her and he took a menacing step forward. "I will beat the sass right out of you if you keep it up."

Raina bit back a grin. At the moment, he was about as capable of beating her up as she was of beating him. "Are you afraid to answer the question? How many rooms did you check before you came to this one?"

He gripped her by the back of the neck and dragged her into his chest, bending to place a hard, stinging kiss on her lips. He moved back far enough to give her a wry look. "I checked the family room, then I came here."

She laughed. "So basically, you searched the entire mansion for me. I definitely see why you're upset about this."

He released her and stepped back to sink wearily onto the bed. "Remind me to beat you as soon as I'm feeling better."

Raina dropped to her knees in front of him and reached up to unbutton his shirt, careful not to jar his injuries as she slid each button through the hole.

"When you're able to spar again, I'll be the first one lining up for you." Her eyes were shining with humour.

She felt a great deal of love for the man in front of her. She didn't know how it had come to this. How she'd gone from first hating him to tolerating him to now. She was so in love with him that she couldn't imagine her existence without him. It would be empty, meaningless. She needed him and he needed her.

Once the buttons were open, she reached up and gently slid the material off his broad shoulders. Mateo lifted each arm as she tugged the cuffs from his wrists. Then her hands dropped to his belt. His hand landed on top of hers.

"I'll do this part." His lip curled in a partial smile. "Remember, dead man with a boner?"

Raina lifted her hands up in surrender and backed off, laughing. While he worked on pulling his pants off Raina got herself ready for bed. She washed her face and hands, brushed her teeth and hair and pulled on a short night gown. Once he was settled, she crawled into the bed next to him, careful to snuggle against his good side. He held her close and dropped his head to hers, inhaling her scent and kissing the fine strands of hair.

"Thank you." His deep voice penetrated the darkness of the bedroom.

She tipped her head up to look at him, her eyes tracing the shadows on his face, visible in the dim light coming through the window. "Thank you for what?"

"For surviving; for giving me a reason to continue breathing."

Raina didn't know what to say to that, so she kissed his chin and whispered, "You're welcome."

CHAPTER FIFTY-FIVE

"How do I look?" Raina asked, turning to face her father.

Joe blinked rapidly and then ran a finger under one of his eyelids. "Like a queen." His voice was choked as he spoke.

He leaned down and kissed Raina's forehead before pulling the veil over top of the crown on her head and covering her face.

Raina's wedding day was an elaborate affair. Between Diane, Cassie and Vee, Raina barely had to lift a finger for it. Her gorgeous Marchesa gown had arrived two weeks earlier and fit her like a glove. It had a classic bell skirt with a sweetheart neckline and short sleeves. Diane had sewn the veil herself using a crown that Vee provided.

Cassie had harassed every flower shop in Miami until she finally settled on one that could supply her with everything she demanded. She wanted roses in every colour. There were blue, purple, red, pink, white and even black roses. The colourful combination was surprisingly stunning and elegant. There were two sections of chairs, one on either side of the aisle that Raina and Joe would walk down.

Moments earlier, Raina's bridesmaids had made their way down the aisle; Cassie, Angela and one of Mateo's sisters who flew in from Venezuela. On the other side stood Mateo, looking handsome and regal in his tuxedo. Beside him, standing tall, was his best man Sotza. Beside Sotza was Danny and Giovanni.

It was a beautiful summer day and everyone on their guest list seemed bright and happy. Many of them had already been through Raina's bedroom to wish her luck. Mateo's mother, Ana Victoria, had brought Raina a small spray of blue flowers which they pinned to Raina's skirt so she could wear something blue.

Raina hadn't had much time to spend with Mateo's family. They were polite but distant, a trait Mateo shared. It saddened Raina that Mateo wasn't close with his family. Circumstance had kept them separated over the years. He'd been busy working up in the Venezuelan mountains and flying around the world securing Sotza's investments. He also hadn't wanted his lifestyle to put their lives in danger or put them under the scrutiny of authorities.

Joe and Diane had flown in the week before, along with Cassie and Noah. They had all accepted Raina's and Mateo's invitation to stay at the mansion, which was large enough to hold many houseguests. Cassie and Diane had thrown themselves wholeheartedly into the wedding, supervising every detail, right down to the nail polish that Raina would wear. They chose a pink one with a light sparkle called Princesses Rule.

Vee and Sotza had flown in two days before the wedding. It was generally understood that Vee did not have a lot of time or patience for things like weddings, but she tried. She militantly kept everyone organized and in line when it looked like there might be an argument. Raina could definitely see how her mother had once been the boss of Miami.

"Are you ready?" Joe asked Raina.

Raina gazed up the aisle toward her future husband. Yes, she was ready. Finally, ready. She had feared this man, hated him, and loved him fiercely. Now, she couldn't imagine a life without him. She wanted to tie herself to him in every way possible so that going forward they would always be united.

"Yes, I'm ready." She gave her father a radiant smile and took the first step onto the aisle, a section of close-cut grass with flower petals strewn across.

Raina's train dragged behind her as she walked confidently toward Mateo. Her eyes were on him and he never once looked away. His expression did not change from his usual somber seriousness, which Raina appreciated. Perhaps Mateo was a man of few words. He wasn't particularly romantic and sometimes he said the wrong thing. But his heart was pure, and it beat for her alone. Only a fool wouldn't take hold of it with both hands and keep it safe.

As Raina approached the front, she turned to look at her father who lifted the veil from her face and set it over her head. Once again, he kissed her cheek. As Raina stepped toward Mateo, Sotza took a step toward her, waylaying her. He laid a hand on her shoulder and said, "I haven't had much of a chance to be a father to you, but I want you to know that you are the daughter of my heart. If you ever need anything you have only to call."

Raina had done so well at keeping her tears in check, but in a few words, Sotza summoned them to the forefront. The big, tough regal man who never unbent was allowing her space in his heart. A heart that belonged to Raina's mother.

"I know," she whispered, then smiled up at him. "Same to you. If you ever need me, I'll come to your rescue."

Sotza chuckled. "Just like your mother." He bent down and kissed Raina's other cheek then took his place next Mateo.

Their vows were simple and traditional, both agreeing that neither were poetic enough to write their own. Raina didn't mind, she loved hearing that he would hold her in sickness and in health, for richer or for poorer, for the rest of their lives.

The ceremony was short and when it was over everyone was ready to party. Their reception was a mixed group. Some of Raina's friends from her hometown and from her university. A bunch of Mateo's contacts. Even the formidable Bolivian boss, Reyes, and his wife, Casey, had made the trip down, along with Reyes second-in-command, Alejandro, and his wife, Gina, who was soft and sweet, her belly round with pregnancy. The look suited her.

Raina had been ecstatic to finally meet Casey in person and the women had chattered as though they were long-lost friends. Casey loved everything about the mansion renovations, which was a relief to Raina who worried coming back to the house would be traumatic.

Casey had admitted to some hesitation, but said she quickly got over it when faced with a home that looked nothing like the one she shared with Ignacio Hernandez. Though technically Casey was more Vee's friend than Raina's, Raina suspected that she and Casey had more in common, and that they would become even better friends in the future.

They ate and partied well into the night until Raina didn't think she could eat one more cocktail shrimp or dance one more dance. Of course, when Cassie dragged her back onto the dance floor for one last twirl, Raina had no choice but to concede gracefully. Mateo watched from the sidelines as his new wife imitated silly dance moves with her best friend. His eyes shone with happiness and Raina felt pride. She had put that look there and she would do whatever it took to ensure that it remained.

Raina was pretty much dead on her feet when Mateo

intercepted yet another person attempting to get her to dance again.

"Are you cutting in?" she asked, smothering a yawn against his shoulder.

He didn't answer. Instead he took her arm and beelined off the dance floor, away from their guests. Several tried to wave them down, but Mateo wasn't having it. He wanted his bride to himself. Raina trailed after him, her steps lagging with exhaustion. She'd had a long and very satisfying day and now she wanted nothing more than to kick off her heels and collapse into the nearest bed.

She was pleased to note that Mateo was dragging her through the mansion and up towards their bedroom. She was surprised when he stopped in front of the master suite. After the bombing, Mateo asked Raina to leave the renovation of the bedroom to him. She'd been curious but backed off, working on the other rooms instead. Mateo continued to share Raina's room, though he finished the master suite days ago.

She smothered another yawn, her eyes scrunching shut as Mateo pushed the door open and then bent to lift Raina off her feet. She giggled and clutched his neck, then gasped as she caught sight of the room.

"Oh my god, Mateo!" He set her on her feet so she could have a good look around the room.

"Did you knock down a wall?"

The room looked so much larger than it had before, as though it was two rooms in one.

He chuckled. "The bomb did that, I took advantage of an opportunity and made the room bigger."

A huge California king size bed occupied the middle of the room with a gorgeous canopy over top. The filmy material falling from the canopy definitely didn't suit Mateo. He had chosen it for her, and her heart ached with happiness as she looked around noting all the touches that he'd made for her comfort.

There was a brand-new make up table, a hope chest with a beautiful hand quilted blanket across the top. Raina touched the blanket with her fingertips as she recognized Diane's work. There were a series of three pictures gracing one of the walls and Raina's eyes filled with tears as she looked at them. They were all of her. A picture that Mateo had taken of her in a candid moment, with her head bent over a book and her hair swirling around her face, her glasses perched on the end of her nose. She had been in deep concentration when the picture was taken.

It had been taken in Venezuela two and a half years ago. She'd heard the click of his phone as he was taking the picture and she looked up sharply. She'd yelled at him for interrupting her, for always interrupting her. For following her around and harassing her, for insisting that she stay inside instead of sitting in the garden.

Now, she understood that he been worried over her safety. He was always worried for her safety. Raina knew that this would be a fight they continued for the duration of their marriage, between his desire to bubble wrap and put her on a shelf versus her need for freedom. But they would find a balance.

Each picture on the wall was the exact same. Except each one was done in a different colour tone. One was blue, one was pink, and one was purple. It was a beautiful homage to her, and it filled her heart with happiness to see it. She also noted that on her new make-up table was two photographs. One of Diane and Joe and the other Vee and Sotza. Raina was surrounded by the people that loved her.

She twirled on the spot and launched herself at Mateo, wrapping her arms around his neck and squeezing tightly. "I love it so much."

He held her tight, clutching her against his body before setting her away, taking her hand and leading her toward another door. "Come see the ensuite."

Raina was excited. What woman didn't love a brand-new bathroom?

The ensuite was a slightly different colour palette from the bedroom. She suspected Mateo had handed over the reins to her interior designer. She was so glad. Vito, the designer, had gotten to know her well over the past few months and had installed everything he knew Raina would want. A deep whirlpool tub, his and her sinks, and an environmentally friendly flush toilet. Lots of beautiful bright lights with the heat lamp above the tub. Next to the tub was a marble shower with a rainspout for a showerhead.

Raina grinned at Mateo and shook her head. "You've outdone yourself, gangster."

Mateo touched the back of her dress, his fingers lingering on the zipper. "May I?"

Her mouth went dry. It was strange, they'd had sex many times over the past few months becoming more and more adventurous with each encounter. Raina hadn't thought it possible, but her satisfaction with Mateo and sex was constantly increasing until she didn't think it could get any better. Yet he kept proving her wrong, sending her spiraling toward new heights.

Marriage though... that was different. She was about to become his wife not only in name, but physically as well.

Raina knew it made no difference to Mateo. He considered her his wife the moment he decided their union would happen. Today was just another day to him. Today was for her, the bride. Mateo wanted her to shine and gave everyone around them the leeway needed to create an incredible wedding.

"Yes," she whispered.

CHAPTER FIFTY-SIX

Mateo slid the zipper of her dress down until it reached the base of her spine, stopping just above her butt. His fingers lingered there, sliding through the zip and touching her skin. She breathed in deeply and let it out on a sigh.

It felt so damn good to have him touch her. The wedding excitement had been going on for weeks and they became gradually more and more separated through the entire ordeal. The culmination of everything had been a wonderful and beautiful occasion, but Raina was ready to have her husband to herself.

Mateo slid his hands over her shoulders and then down her front, sliding them into the top of her gown which was loose now. His hands lingered at her breasts, the rough fingertips barely grazing her aching nipples. That simple stroke over her sensitive skin sent arrows of pleasure shooting through her.

She moaned and turned in his arms, tipping her face up for a kiss. Mateo did not disappoint. He gripped her face with a hand on either cheek and pulled her up onto her toes where he plundered her lips with a heated, desperate need. He wrapped an arm around her waist and hauled her even further into his body, as though he couldn't get enough of her.

Raina clutched him, feeling the same. Having so many people in the house, interacting with them, being polite and always the gracious host had been a challenge. Mateo and Raina had been constantly on, every night falling into bed too tired to make love.

But this was their night, their time. Mateo reached out and turned the tap on in the shower. Then he helped Raina finish undressing. He touched and looked his fill with each part of her that was exposed to his hungry gaze. He dropped to his knees in front of her, and buried his face against her pussy, his hands clutching the backs of her thighs.

Raina gasped and grabbed his head, hanging on for the ride as he thrust his tongue against her slit, gathering the moisture that was rapidly growing there before attacking her clit. It was an incredible erotic moment, she standing over top of him in a position of power but also vulnerable in her nudity. Him, big, broad shouldered, kneeling at her feet, his face buried in her pussy. Her pale hand threaded through the strands of his black hair.

She continued to stare down as he used a finger to thrust up inside her driving her over the edge as his tongue continued to lash her wet and swollen clit. Raina threw her head back and moaned her pleasure as an orgasm washed over her, radiating from her center and hitting her in waves. Her knees buckled and Mateo clutched her close, holding her up. When she looked down, it was to find him looking up at her, her juices on his chin, deep possession in his eyes.

"Mi amor."

Her heart melted. Yes, she was his love. She would always be his love. She knew that because no one could love her the way Mateo loved her. He loved with his whole being, no part of him separate from her.

While he was still on his knees below her, he shoved his tuxedo jacket off his broad shoulders and let it pool on the floor. He undid the buttons of his shirt and yanked it off as well. Then he stood, towering over her, his hands going to his fly. Raina placed her hands on top of his.

"Let me." Her voice was quiet, barely above a whisper.

He nodded and allowed her to unbuckle his belt, undo his button and unzip his fly. She pushed his pants over his hips and down to his feet. As was his usual, Mateo wasn't wearing any underwear.

Raina attempted to drop to her knees, but Mateo stopped her, forcing her to stand straight again. "My woman does not kneel for anyone. You're my queen, never forget that."

She was awed by his words, the full meaning impacting her as she thought of their future together. Still, she was disappointed. "But what if this queen wants to suck your dick?"

Raina hadn't done that yet. She had never gone down on anyone before. Though they'd spent months exploring each other, this was one thing she hadn't done yet. Mateo hadn't encouraged it, believing that she would drive him over the edge faster than he wanted.

Of course, Raina had taken that as a challenge and had sought other ways to push him over the edge before he was ready. Mateo usually punished her with more orgasms than she thought her body could take. He was the king of multiple orgasms.

"You will not kneel." Mateo sounded firm and Raina continued to pout as they showered together.

Mateo's hands washed sensually over Raina's body, touching her everywhere, probably more than necessary to get her clean. She didn't mind though. His hands were incredible, and he knew how to use them.

When they finished, he used a new fluffy white towel to dry first her and then him. While he was drying himself, Raina walked back into the bedroom and over to the bed. She cast a look over her shoulder and then reached down to flip the big fluffy quilt over. She smiled as she saw the book on Mateo's side of the bed, sitting on his nightstand. It was a battered copy of Johanna Lindsay's Captive Bride.

Mateo walked up behind her, sliding an arm around her waist, and pulling her against his chest. He put his chin on her head and they stood that way for a few minutes. She could feel his cock between the cheeks of her ass, hard and ready to go, but they needed this moment together first. Breathing in sync, each contemplating their future together.

Finally, Mateo turned her in his arms and dropped his head for a kiss. As his lips held hers, he tried to gently push her down on the bed, but she resisted. He pushed harder; Raina resisted harder. Then, she maneuvered them so that his back was to the bed and she was facing him. She broke the kiss, looked up at him and grinned. Then she used both hands to shove his shoulders.

She should've known he wouldn't actually fall back on the bed as she intended. He frowned down at her as though wondering why the tiny fly was buzzing against his chest. She sighed deeply and rolled her eyes. "Can you please lay down on your back? We're going to pretend that I aggressively threw you down."

Mateo didn't move. "If you think that you'll be taking the dominant role on our wedding night, you need to think again."

Raina narrowed her eyes at him and stepped up, pressing her bare breasts against his chest. She tilted her chin to stare him in the eyes. "If you ever want a mouth on your dick again, you will lay down on your back, arms behind your head, eyes on the canopy."

To his credit he stood his ground for about twenty more seconds as he tried to determine the importance of blowjobs to his existence, then growled a stream of Spanish swear words, climbed onto the bed and lay down on his back. He followed her instructions to the letter, his hands behind his head, his biceps bulging and his eyes on the canopy.

Raina leapt onto the bed between his legs. She must have scared him because he flinched when she landed. She laughed out loud, then crawled up his legs toward his cock. She really did want to tease him more, but she was also dying to see what he tasted like. She took hold of the base and squeezed. Gently at first and then harder as she realized she could. She leaned over, the wisps of her blond hair having escaped from her intricate updo as she took the tip of his cock into her mouth.

She licked the hole in the top, gathering the moisture there onto her tongue and swallowing. It was salty, but not too salty and not gross as she half expected. She decided she liked it. Then, she sank down further, pushing his cock further into her mouth. She liked the feel. The stretch of her lips and cheek, the silky texture of his skin. She didn't know what to do with her teeth, was afraid she'd accidentally bite him.

Cassie had once told her she put shouldn't put teeth on a man's penis, so she tried to avoid it. Cassie had also told Raina that she should probably wrap her lips around her teeth, but when she tried to do that she pictured an old woman whose dentures fell out and then laughed out loud while still sucking Mateo's cock.

Raina ended up drooling on him and had to sit back, wipe her chin, and start again. Mateo continued to look up at the canopy an amused smile on his lips, though he did look strained.

Raina leaned over, took him in hand again and sank her mouth over top of him. This time she pushed a little further, toward the back of her throat, enjoying the feel of his steel threaded cock in her mouth. She pushed it against the top of her mouth then her cheeks, then toward the back again. At first, she had to consciously suppress her gag reflex, but the more she dipped up and down on him the further back she could go.

She was really enjoying herself, finding a nice rhythm and figuring out what to do with her hands. One running up over his chest while the other played with his balls. She liked the nice heavy feeling of them when he was excited. The weight in her palm. She thought that they were rather large although she hadn't seen that many penises or sets of balls in her life. Okay one, she'd seen exactly one. But she'd seen porn and knew for a fact that Mateo definitely stacked up to those other guys.

Mateo let out a grunt, which startled her into rearing back. Apparently, he didn't like that. He took hold of her head and pushed her back down to his cock. She happily took him back into her mouth and allowed him to take more control as he thrust up into her. This made it even harder to suppress her gag reflex, but she managed, only coughing on him a couple times.

"I'm gonna come." His words came out in a garbled grunt that she nearly missed.

Raina knew what it was like for him to come, but not in her mouth. She was curious so she stayed where she was, sucking him deep as he shot his load into her throat. She hadn't expected the warmth or the texture and gagged. She sat back on her heels and stared at him in shock.

Mateo was laying on his back, his legs spread around her

hips, one arm thrown over his head. Finally, he moved the arm and caught sight of the expression on her face. He laughed, a full-throated sound that Raina had never heard come from him before.

"You don't have to do that again, mi amor, if you don't like the taste." He sat up and reached for her, gathering her against his chest. He used his thumb to swipe at some leftover come on her lips. He went to wipe it on the quilt, but she caught his hand and pulled it up to her mouth, sucking his thumb and swallowing the rest of the come.

"I was surprised, that's all. I didn't know what to expect. But it wasn't bad, I want to do it again." She reassured him.

He tipped her over onto her back and kissed her all over her face and breasts. "You are perfect, my wife."

She clutched his head and wrapped her legs around his hips, holding him close against her. "We're perfect together, my gangster."

They made love throughout the night, alternately sleeping and then waking up to explore each other's bodies as though doing it for the first time. They whispered words of love and talked about their future together, finally falling into a deep sleep around dawn, their arms wrapped tightly around each other, Raina's head against Mateo's chest.

EPILOGUE

One year later

"Hurry up, we're going to be late."

Raina didn't look up from the delicate work she was doing at her desk. "How can we be late for a private jet?"

Mateo made a frustrated sound, one that she was used to. It never failed to make her smile. As much as she loved the man, he was far too serious and needed some contention in his life.

Enter Raina.

"Even private jets have take-off and landing times they need to follow. Now get your ass out of that chair and into the car. You were supposed to be ready hours ago. I don't even see a carry-on. What are you going to do on our flight over? Count clouds?" Though his words were annoyed, his tone of voice held affection.

This was their dance. A perpetual argument that would always end in Raina getting what she wanted so long as it didn't impact her health. Raina had wanted to go back to university. They had argued over that, but it had been the specifics, not the overall idea. Mateo loved that Raina wanted to expand her education. He'd been the one to suggest she take fine arts as her major, which was a program she'd never considered. It hadn't been practical back when she was the daughter of farmers.

Now, Raina was enrolled in one of the most prestigious art schools in the United States, learning new techniques from some of the most skilled teachers in the world. She had used some of her forgeries as part of her application portfolio. The school had been intrigued by her skill and ingenuity and sent her an invitation.

Mateo had been pleased by her acceptance and had treated her to the most amazing night on the town, which, in Miami, was something else. He'd taken her to one of his clubs, having decided not to sell, and up onto a deserted rooftop patio where he'd wined and dined her. Then they'd taken a small airplane to New York where they stayed in the penthouse suite of the Ritz-Carlton.

All this from a man who hadn't thought himself romantic. Raina thought his romance novels were rubbing off.

No, they hadn't argued about her intention to go back to school. They had argued about absolutely everything else. How many classes Raina would take per semester, how many hours per day she should study, what snacks she was allowed to eat, how often she took physical activity breaks. If she didn't love the man so much, she would scream at his overprotectiveness.

Raina decided to battle his extreme behaviour through gentle teasing. In the end, she usually got her way, all she had to do was wait out the beast. But the fights were fun and usually ended up in a bed or a closet somewhere.

Mateo also encouraged Raina to continue with her forgery business. They'd formed a partnership where she could provide documents for some of his contacts, as long as Mateo approved the work. It was a lucrative partnership that made Raina a modestly wealthy woman, independent of her husband's holdings.

Finally, Raina pushed away from her desk and stretched her neck, working out the kinks. Despite his current annoyance with her, Mateo massaged her neck and back, helping ease some of the tension of the day. Raina closed the project she'd been working on and set it aside for her assistant to mail. Another set of perfect passports finished.

"You're doing too much," Mateo said from above her. "I don't like it."

She tipped her head up and grinned at him. "You don't like anything except bubble wrap and Lysol spray."

Mateo grunted a noncommittal response because they both knew Raina wasn't wrong. If she allowed him, Mateo would take over her life completely and dictate every moment so she would be as safe as she could possibly be. He would keep her locked up and take her out only when he deemed it perfectly safe. But that was no way to live and Raina was convinced he would love her less if she didn't make his life hell. Just a little.

"Are you finally ready to leave, mi amor?" His voice became husky, telling Raina that the way he was touching her was turning him on. Her body warmed in response.

"Almost," she said huskily, standing and turning in his arms.

She stood on her toes and reached up to pull his head down for a kiss. All it took was the innocent touch of her lips to his and then the fire took over. Mateo gripped her by the neck and deepened the kiss, while reaching out and clearing a space on her desk with his other hand. Raina grinned against his lips.

Their delayed honeymoon to Italy would have to wait a few more hours. This was more important.

THE END

COMING SOON...

Book Four of the Queens: The Red Queen

SAVE THE DATE
TO CELEBRATE THE WEDDING OF

Desiree

&

Giovanni

2021 | VENICE, ITALY

ALSO BY NIKITA SLATER

If you enjoyed this book, check out some other works by #1 International Bestselling Author, Nikita Slater. More titles are always in progress, so check back often to see what's new!

ANGELS & ASSASSINS SERIES

Book One – The Assassin's Wife

THE QUEENS SERIES

Book One – Scarred Queen
Book Two - Queen's Move
Book Three - Born a Queen
Book Four - The Red Queen (Coming 2021)
Alejandro's Prey (a novella)

FIRE & VICE SERIES

Book One – Prisoner of Fortune
Book Two – Fight or Flight
Book Three – King's Command
Book Four – Savage Vendetta
Book Five – Fear in Her Eyes
Book Six – Bound by Blood
Book Seven – In His Sights

Book Eight - Burning Beauty
Book Nine - Chasing Ecstasy (Coming soon!)

THE DRIVEN HEARTS SERIES

Book One - Driven by Desire
Book Two - Thieving Hearts
Book Three - Capturing Victory
Novella - The Princess and Her Mercenary

THE SANCTUARY SERIES

Book One - Sanctuary's Warlord
Book Two - Sanctuary on Fire
Book Three - The Last Sanctuary
Book Four - The Road to Wolfe (Coming soon!)

STANDALONE BOOKS

Because You're Mine
Mine to Keep (a novella)
Luna & Andres
Loving Vincent
Stalked

AFTER DARK

In collaboration with Jasmin Quinn

Collared: A Dark Captive Romance

Safeword: A Dark Romance

Chained: A Mafia Marriage Romance

Good Girl: A Captive BDSM Romance

Hostile Takeover: An Enemies to Lovers Romance

Visit ***nikitaslater.com*** for more information and the latest updates!

STAY CONNECTED WITH NIKITA!

Don't miss one sexy moment. Keep in touch with Nikita for the latest news and updates about all of your favourite characters.

- Get more info and updates at **www.nikitaslater.com!**
- Keep up to date with **my blog!**
- Like and follow me on **Facebook**
- Follow me on **Twitter (@NikSlaterWrites)**
- Connect with me on **Goodreads**

Sign up for the newsletter today at receive exclusive updates and access to ***bonus content and chapters*** not available anywhere else!

www.nikitaslater.com
nik@nikitaslater.ca

ABOUT THE AUTHOR

Nikita Slater is the International Bestselling dark romance author of the Fire & Vice series, Angels & Assassins series, The Queens series and several standalone novels. Her favourite genre is mafia romance, the bloodier the better, though she loves to write about every subject under the sun. She lives on the beautiful Canadian prairies with her son and crazy awesome dog. She has an unholy affinity for books (especially erotic romance), wine, pets and anything chocolate. Despite some of the darker themes in her books (which are pure fun and fantasy), Nikita is a staunch feminist and advocate of equal rights for all races, genders and non-gender specific persons. When she isn't writing, dreaming about writing or talking about writing, she helps others discover a love of reading and writing through literacy and social work.

Made in the USA
Columbia, SC
14 June 2020